D1711430

The
Five Stages
of
Falling in Love

Rachel Higginson

Elizabeth Carlson is living in the pits of hell- also known as grief.

Her husband of eight years, the father of her four children and the love of her life, died from cancer. Grady's prognosis was grim, even from the start, but Liz never gave up hope he would survive. How could she, when he was everything to her?

Six months later, she is trying to pick up the pieces of her shattered life and get the kids to school on time. Both seem impossible. Everything seems impossible these days.

When Ben Tyler moves in next door, she is drowning in sorrow and pain, her children are acting out, and the house is falling apart. She has no time for curious new friends or unwanted help, but Ben gives her both. And he doesn't just want to help her with yard work or cleaning the gutters. Ben wants more from Liz. More than she's capable of ever giving again.

As Liz mourns her dead husband and works her way through the five stages of grief, she finds there's more of her heart to give than she thought possible. And as new love takes hold, she peels away the guilt and heartache, and discovers there's more to life than death.

Copyright@ Rachel Higginson 2015

This publication is protected under the US Copyright Act of 1976 and all other applicable international, federal, state and local laws, and all rights are reserved, including resale rights: you are not allowed to give, copy, scan, distribute or sell this book to anyone else.

Any trademarks, service marks, product names or named features are assumed to be the property of their respective owners, and are used only for reference. There is no implied endorsement if we use one of these terms.

Any people or places are strictly fictional and not based on anything else, fictional or non-fictional.

This ebook is licensed for your personal enjoyment only. This ebook may not be re-sold or given away to other people. If you would like to share this book with another person, please purchase an additional copy for each recipient. If you're reading this book and did not purchase it, or it was not purchased for your use only, then please return to Smashwords.com and purchase your own copy. Thank you for respecting the hard work of this author.

Copy Editing by Carolyn Moon
Cover Design by Caedus Design Co.

Other Books Now Available by Rachel Higginson

Love and Decay, Season One, Episodes One-Twelve
Love and Decay, Season Two, Episodes One-Twelve
Love and Decay, Volume One (Episodes One-Six, Season One)
Love and Decay, Volume Two (Episodes Seven-Twelve, Season One)
Love and Decay, Volume Three (Episodes One-Four, Season Two)
Love and Decay, Volume Four (Episodes Five-Eight, Season Two)
Love and Decay, Volume Five (Episodes Nine-Twelve, Season Two)
Love and Decay, Volume Six (Episodes One-Four, Season Three)

Reckless Magic (The Star-Crossed Series, Book 1)
Hopeless Magic (The Star-Crossed Series, Book 2)
Fearless Magic (The Star-Crossed Series, Book 3)
Endless Magic (The Star-Crossed Series, Book 4)
The Reluctant King (The Star-Crossed Series, Book 5)
The Relentless Warrior (The Star-Crossed Series, Book 6)
Breathless Magic (The Star-Crossed Series, Book 6.5)
Fateful Magic (The Star-Crossed Series, Book 6.75)
The Redeemable Prince (The Star-Crossed Series, Book 7)

Heir of Skies (The Starbright Series, Book 1)
Heir of Darkness (The Starbright Series, Book 2)
Heir of Secrets (The Starbright Series, Book 3)

The Rush (The Siren Series, Book 1)
The Fall (The Siren Series, Book 2)

Bet on Us (An NA Contemporary Romance)

Magic and Decay, a Rachel Higginson Mashup

Striking (The Forged in Fire Series) This is a co-authored Contemporary NA
Brazing (The Forged in Fire Series) This is a co-authored Contemporary NA

The references made to the five stages of grief were inspired by the Kubler-Ross Model on death and dying.

To Zach, please don't die.
Ever.

Prologue

"Hey, there she is," Grady looked up at me from his bed, his eyes smiling even while his mouth barely mimicked the emotion.

"Hey, you," I called back. The lights had been dimmed after the last nurse checked his vitals and the TV was on, but muted. "Where are the kiddos? I was only in the cafeteria for ten minutes."

Grady winked at me playfully, "My mother took them." I melted a little at his roguish expression. It was the same look that made me agree to a date with him our junior year of college, it was the same look that made me fall in love with him- the same one that made me agree to have our second baby boy when I would have been just fine to stop after Blake, Abby and Lucy.

"Oh, yeah?" I walked over to the hospital bed and sat down next to him. He immediately reached for me, pulling me against him with weak arms. I snuggled back into his chest, so that my head rested on his thin shoulder and our bodies fit side by side on the narrow bed. One of my legs didn't make it and hung off awkwardly. But I didn't mind. It was just perfect to lie next to the love of my life, my husband.

"Oh, yeah," he growled suggestively. "You know what that means?" He walked his free hand up my arm and gave my breast a wicked squeeze. "When the kids are away, the grownups get to play..."

"You are so bad," I swatted him- or at least made the motion of swatting at him, since I was too afraid to hurt him.

"God, I don't remember the last time I got laid," he groaned next to me and I felt the rumble of his words against my side.

"Tell me about it, sport," I sighed. "I could use a nice, hard-"

"Elizabeth Carlson," he cut in on a surprised laugh. "When did you get such a dirty mouth?"

"I think you've known about my dirty mouth for quite some time, Grady," I flirted back. We'd been serious for so long it was nice to flirt with him, to remember that we didn't just love each other, but we liked each other too.

He grunted in satisfaction. "That I have. I think your dirty mouth had something to do with Lucy's conception."

I blushed. Even after all these years, he knew exactly what to say to me. "Maybe," I conceded.

"Probably," he chuckled, his breath hot on my ear.

We lay there in silence for a while, enjoying the feel of each other, watching the silent TV screen flicker in front of our eyes. It was perfect- or as close to perfect as we had felt in a long time.

"Dance with me, Lizzy," Grady whispered after a while. I'd thought maybe he fell asleep; the drugs were so hard on his system that he was usually in and out of consciousness. This was actually the most coherent he'd been in a month.

"Okay," I agreed. "It's the first thing we'll do when you get out. We'll have your mom come over and babysit, you can take me to dinner at Pazio's and we'll go dancing after."

"Mmm, that sounds nice," he agreed. "You love Pazio's. That's a guaranteed get-lucky night for me."

"Baby," I crooned. "As soon as I get you back home, you're going to have guaranteed get-lucky nights for at least a month, maybe two."

"I don't want to wait. I'm tired of waiting. Dance with me now, Lizzy," Grady pressed, this time sounding serious.

"Babe, after your treatment this morning, you can barely stand up right now. Honestly, how are you going to put all those sweet moves on me?" I wondered where this sudden urge to dance, of all things, was coming from.

"Lizzy, I am a sick man. I haven't slept in my own bed in four months, I haven't seen my wife naked in just as long, and I am tired of lying in this bed. I want to dance with you. Will you please, pretty please, dance with me?"

I nodded at first because I was incapable of speech. He was right. I hated that he was right, but I hated that he was sick even more.

"Alright, Grady, I'll dance with you," I finally whispered.

"I knew I'd get my way," he croaked smugly.

I slipped off the bed and turned around to face my husband and help him to his feet. His once full head of auburn hair was now bald, reflecting the pallid color of his skin. His face was haggard showing dark black circles under his eyes, chapped lips and pale cheeks. He was still as tall as he'd ever been, but instead of the toned muscles and thick frame he once boasted, he was depressingly skinny and weak, his shoulders perpetually slumped.

The only thing that remained the same were his eyes; they were the same dark green eyes I'd fallen in love with ten years ago. They were still full of life, still full of mischief even when his body wasn't. They held life while the rest of him drowned in exhaustion from fighting this stupid sickness.

"You always get your way," I grumbled while I helped him up from the bed.

"Only with you," he shot back on a pant after successfully standing. "And only because you love me."

"That I do," I agreed. Grady's hands slipped around my waist and he clutched my sides in an effort to stay standing.

I wrapped my arms around his neck, but didn't allow any weight to press down on him. We maneuvered our bodies around his IV and monitors. It was awkward, but we managed.

"What should we listen to?" I asked, while I pulled out my cell phone and turned it to my iTunes app.

"You know what song. There is no other song when we're dancing," he reminded me on a faint smile.

"You must be horny," I laughed. "You're getting awfully romantic."

"Just trying to keep this fire alive, Babe," he pulled me closer and I held back the flood of tears that threatened to spill over.

I turned on *The Way You Look Tonight*- the Frank Sinatra version- and we swayed slowly back and forth. Frank sang the soft, beautiful lyrics with the help of a full band, while the music drifted around us over the constant beeping and whirring of medical machines. This was the song we thought of as ours, the first song we'd danced to at our wedding, the song he still made the band at Pazio's play on our anniversary each year.

"This fire is very much alive," I informed him sternly. I lay my forehead against his shoulder and inhaled him. He didn't smell like himself anymore, he was full of chemo drugs and smelled like hospital soap and detergent, but he was still Grady. And even though he barely resembled the man I had fallen so irrevocably in love with, he still *felt* like Grady.

He was still *my* Grady.

"It is, isn't it?" He whispered. I could feel how weak he was growing, how tired this was making him, but still he clung to me and held me close. When my favorite verse came on, he leaned his head down and whispered in a broken voice along with Frank, "There is nothing for me, but to love you. And the way you look tonight."

Silent tears streamed down my face with truths I wasn't ready to admit to myself and fears that were too horrifying to even think. This was the man I loved with every fiber of my being- the only man I'd ever loved. The only man I'd *ever love*.

He'd made me fall in love with him before I was old enough to drink legally, then he'd convinced me to marry him before I even graduated from college. He knocked me up a year later, and didn't stop until we had four wild rug rats that all had his red hair and his emerald green eyes. He'd encouraged me to finish my undergrad degree, and then to continue on to grad school while I was pregnant, nursing and then pregnant again. He went to bed every night with socks on and then took them off sometime in the middle of the night, leaving them obnoxiously tucked in between our sheets. He could never find his wallet, or his keys, and when there was hair to grow he always forgot to shave.

And he drove me crazy most of the time.

But he was mine.

He was my husband.

And now he was sick.

"I do love you, Lizzy," he murmured against my hair. "I'll always love you, even when I'm dead and gone."

"Which won't be for at least fifty more years," I reminded him on a sob.

He ignored me, "You love me back, don't you?"

"Yes, I love you back," I whispered with so much emotion the words stuck in my throat. "But you already knew that."

"Maybe," he conceded gently. "But I will never, ever get tired of hearing it."

I sniffled against him, staining his hospital gown with my mascara and eye liner. "That's a good thing, because you're going to be hearing it for a very long time."

He didn't respond, just kept swaying with me back and forth until the song ended. He asked me to play it again and I did, three more times. By the end of the fourth, he was too tired to stand. I laid him back in bed and helped him adjust the IV and monitor again so that it didn't bother him, then pulled the sheet over his cold toes.

His eyes were closed and I thought he'd fallen asleep, so I bent down to kiss his forehead. He stirred at my touch and reached out to cup my face with his un-needled arm. I looked down into his depthless green eyes and fell in love with him all over again.

It was as simple as that.

It had always been that simple for him to get me to fall in love with him.

"You are the most beautiful thing that ever happened to me, Lizzy." His voice was broken and scratchy and a tear slid out from the corner of each of his eyes.

My chin trembled at his words because I knew what he was doing and I hated it, I hated every part of it. I shook my head, trying to get him to stop but he held my gaze and just kept going.

"You are. And you have made my life good, and worth living. You have made me love more than any man has ever known how to love. I didn't know this kind of happiness existed in real life, Liz, and you're the one that gave it to me. I couldn't be more thankful for the life we've shared together. I couldn't be more thankful for you."

"Oh, Grady, please-"

"Lizzy," he said in his sternest voice that he only used when I'd maxed out a credit card. "Whatever happens, whatever happens to me, I want you to keep giving this gift to other people." I opened my mouth to vehemently object to everything he was saying but he silenced me with a cold finger on my lips. "I didn't say go marry the first man you find. Hell, I'm not even talking about another man. But I don't want this light to die with me. I don't want you to forget how happy you make other people just because you might not feel happy. Even if I don't, Lizzy, I want you to go on living. Promise me that."

But I shook my head, "No." I wasn't going to promise him that. I couldn't make myself. And it was unfair of him to ask me that.

"Please, Sweetheart, for me?" His deep, green eyes glossed over with emotion and I could physically feel how painful this was for him to ask me. He didn't want this anymore than I did.

I found myself nodding, while I sniffled back a stream of tears. "Okay," I whispered. "I promise."

He broke out into a genuine smile then, his thumb rubbing back and forth along my jaw. "Now tell me you love me, one more time."

"I love you, Grady," I murmured, leaning into his touch and savoring this moment with him.

"And I will always, always love you, Lizzy."

His eyes finally fluttered shut and his hand dropped from my face. His vitals remained the same, so I knew he was just sleeping. I crawled into bed with him, gently shifting him so that I could lie on my side, in the nook of his arm and lay my hand on his chest. I did this often; I liked to feel the beat of his heart underneath my hand. It had stopped too many times before, for me to trust its reliability. My husband was a very sick man, and had been for a while now.

Tonight was different though. Tonight, Grady was lucid and coherent, he'd found enough energy to stand up and dance with me, to tell me he loved me. Tonight could have been a turn for the better.

But it wasn't- because only a few hours later, Grady's heart stopped for the third time during his adult life, and this time it never restarted.

Stage One: Denial

Not every story has a happy ending. Some only hold a happy beginning.

This is my story. I'd already met my soul mate, fallen in love with him and lived our happily ever after.

This story is not about me falling in love.

This story is about me learning to live again after love left my life.

Research shows there are five stages of grief. I don't know what this means for me, as I was stuck, nice and hard, in step one.

Denial.

I knew, acutely, that I was still in stage one.

I knew this because every time I walked in the house, I wandered around aimlessly looking for Grady. I still picked up my phone to check if he texted or called throughout the day. I looked for him in a crowded room, got the urge to call him from the grocery store just to make sure I had everything he needed, and reached for him in the middle of the night.

Acceptance- the last stage of grief- was firmly and forever out of my reach, and I often looked forward to it with longing. Why? Because Denial was a *son of a bitch* and it hurt more than *anything* when I realized he wasn't in the house, wouldn't be calling me, wasn't where I wanted him to be, didn't need anything from the store and would never lie next to me in bed again. The grief, fresh and suffocating, would cascade over me and I was forced to suffer through the unbearable pain of losing my husband all over again.

Denial *sucked*.

But it was where I was right now. I was living in Denial.

Chapter One
Six Months after Grady died.

I snuggled back into the cradle of his body while his arms wrapped around me tightly. He buried his scruffy face against the nape of my neck and I sighed contentedly. We fit perfectly together, but then again we always had- his big spoon nestled up against my little spoon.

"It's your turn," he rumbled against my skin with that deep morning voice I would always drink in.

"No," I argued half-heartedly. "It's always my turn."

"But you're so good at it," he teased.

I giggled, "It's one of my many talents, pouring cereal into bowls, making juice cups. I might just take this show on the road."

He laughed behind me and his chest shook with the movement. I pushed back into him, loving the feel of his hard, firm chest against my back. He was so hot first thing in the morning, his whole body radiated warmth.

His hand splayed out across my belly possessively and he pressed a kiss just below my ear. I could feel his lips through my tangle of hair and the tickle of his breath which wasn't all that pleasant first thing in the morning, but it was Grady and it was familiar.

"It's probably time we had another one, don't you think?" His hand rubbed a circle around my stomach and I could feel him vibrating happily with the thought.

"Grady, we already have three," I reminded him on a laugh. "If we have another one, people are going to start thinking we're weird."

"No, they won't," he soothed. "They might get an idea of how fertile you are, but they won't think we're weird."

I snorted a laugh. "They already think we're weird."

"Then we don't want to disappoint them," he murmured. His hand slid up my chest and cupped my breast, giving it a gentle squeeze.

"You are obsessed with those things," I grinned.

"Definitely," he agreed quickly, while continuing to fondle me. "What do you think, Lizzy? Will you give me another baby?"

I was getting wrapped up in the way he was touching me, the way he was caressing me with so much love I thought I would burst. "I'll think about it," I finally conceded, knowing he would get his way- knowing I always let him have his way.

"While you're mulling it over, we should probably practice. I mean, we want to get this right when the time comes." Grady trailed kisses down the column of my throat and I moaned my consent.

I rolled over to kiss him on the mouth.

But he wasn't there.

My arm swung wide and hit cold, empty mattress.

I opened my eyes and stared at the slow moving ceiling fan over my head. The early morning light streamed in through cracks in my closed blinds and I let the silent tears fall.

I hated waking up like this; thinking he was there, next to me, still able to support me, love me and hold me. And unfortunately it happened more often than it didn't.

The fresh pain clawed and cut at my heart and I thought I would die just from sheer heartbreak. My chin quivered and I sniffled, trying desperately to wrestle my emotions under control. But the pain was too much, too consuming.

"Mom!" Blake called from the kitchen, ripping me away from my peaceful grief. "Moooooom!"

That was a distressed cry, and I was up out of my bed and racing downstairs immediately. I grabbed my silk robe on the way and threw it over my black cami and plaid pajama bottoms. When the kids were younger I wouldn't have bothered, but Blake was eight now and he'd been traumatized enough in life. I wasn't going to add to that by walking around bra-less first thing in the morning.

He continued to yell at me, while I barreled into the kitchen still wiping at the fresh tears. I found him at the bay windows, staring out in horror.

"Mom, Abby went swimming," he explained in a rush of words.

A sick feeling knotted my stomach and I looked around wild-eyed at what his words could possibly mean. "What do you mean, Abby *went swimming?*" I gasped, a little out of breath.

"There," he pointed to the neighbor's backyard with a shaky finger.

I followed the direction of his outstretched hand and from the elevated vantage point of our kitchen I could see that the neighbor's pool was filled with water, and my six-year-old daughter was swimming morning laps like she was on a regulated workout routine.

"What the f-" I started and then stopped, shooting a glance down at Blake who looked up at me with more exaggerated shock than he'd given his sister.

I watched her for point one more second and sprinted for the front door. "Keep an eye on the other ones," I shouted at Blake as I pushed open our heavy red door.

It was just early fall in rural Connecticut. The grass was still green; the mornings were foggy but mostly still warm. The house next to us had been empty for almost a year. The owner had been asking too much for it in this economy, but I understood why. It was beautiful, clean-lined and modern with cream stucco siding and black decorative shutters. Big oak trees offered shade and character in the sprawling front yard and in the back, an in-ground pool was the drool-worthy envy of my children.

I raced down my yard and into my new neighbor's. I hadn't noticed the house had sold, but that didn't surprise me. I wasn't the most observant person these days. Vaguely I noted a moving truck parked in the long drive.

The backyard gate must have been left open. Even though Abby had taught herself how to swim at the age of four- the end result gave me several gray hairs- there was no way she could reach the flip lock at the top of the tall, white fence.

I rounded the corner and hopped/ran to the edge of the pool, the gravel of the patio cutting into my bare feet. I took a steadying breath and focused my panic-flooded mind long enough to assess whether Abby was still breathing or not.

She was, and happily swimming in circles *in the deep end.*

Fear and dread quickly turned to blinding anger and I took a step closer to the edge of the pool while I threw my silk robe on the ground.

"Abigail Elizabeth, you get out of there right this minute!" I shouted loud enough to wake up the entire neighborhood.

She popped her head up out of the water, acknowledged me by sticking out her tongue, and promptly went back to swimming. *That little brat.*

"Abigail, I am *not* joking. Get out of the pool. *Now*!" I hollered again. And was ignored- again. "Abby, if I have to come in there and get you, you will rue the day you were born!"

She poked her head back up out of the water, shooting me a confused look. Her light brown eyebrows drew together, just like her father's used to, and her little freckled nose wrinkled at something I said. I was smart enough or experienced enough to know that she was not on the verge of obeying, just because I'd threatened her.

"Mommy?" she asked, somehow making her little body tread water in a red polka dot bikini my sister picked up from Gap last summer. It was too small, which for some reason infuriated me even more. "What does *rue* mean?"

"It means you're grounded from the iPad, your Leapster and the Wii for the next two years of your life," I threatened. "Now get out of that pool right now before I come in there and get you myself."

She giggled in reply, not believing me for one second, and resumed her play.

"Damn it, Abigail," I growled under my breath but was not surprised by her behavior. She was naturally an adventurous child. Since she could walk, she'd been climbing to the highest point of anything she could, swinging precariously from branches, light fixtures and tall displays at the grocery store. She was a daredevil and there were moments when I absolutely adored her "the world is my playground" attitude about life. But then there were moments like this, when every mom instinct in me screamed she was in danger and her little, rotten life flashed before my eyes.

Those moments happened more and more often. She tested me, pushing every limit and boundary I'd set. She had been reckless before Grady died, now she was just wild. And I didn't know what to do about it.

I didn't know how to tame my uncontrollable child or how to be both parents to a little girl who desperately missed her daddy.

I focused on my outrage, pushing those tragic thoughts down, into the abyss of my soul. I was pissed; I didn't have time for this first thing in the morning and no doubt we were going to be late for school- again.

I slipped off my pajama pants, hoping whomever had moved into the house, if they were watching, would be more concerned with the little girl on the verge of drowning than me flashing my black, bikini briefs at them over morning coffee. I said a few more choice curses and dove into the barely warm water after my second born.

I surfaced, sputtering water and shivering from the cool morning air pebbling my skin. "Abigail, when I get you out of this pool, you are going to be in *so* much trouble."

"Okay," she agreed happily. "But first you have to catch me."

She proceeded to swim around in circles while I reached out helplessly for her. First thing I would do when I got out of this pool was throw away every electronic device in our house just to teach her a lesson. Then I was going to sign her up for a swim team because the little hellion was too fast for her own good.

We struggled like this for a few more minutes. Well, I struggled. She splashed at me and laughed at my efforts to wrangle her.

I was aware of a presence hovering by the edge of the pool, but I was equally too embarrassed and too preoccupied to acknowledge it. Images of walking my children into school late *again*, kept looping through my head and I cringed at the dirty looks I was bound to get from teachers and other parents alike.

"You look hungry," a deep masculine voice announced from above me.

I whipped my head around to find an incredibly tall man standing by my discarded pajama pants holding two beach towels and a box of Pop-Tarts in one arm, while he munched casually on said Pop-Tarts with the other.

"I look hungry?" I screeched in hysterical anger.

His eyes flickered down at me for just a second, "No, you look mad." He pointed at Abby, who had come to a stop next to me, treading water again with her short child-sized limbs waving wildly in the water. "*She* looks hungry." With a mouth full of food he grinned at me, and looked back at Abby. "Want a Pop-Tart? They're brown sugar."

Abby nodded excitedly and swam to the edge of the pool. Not even using the ladder, she heaved herself out of the water and ran over to the stranger holding out his breakfast to her. He handed her a towel and she hastily draped it around her shoulders and took the offered Pop-Tart.

A million warnings about taking food from strangers ran through my head, but in the end I decided getting us out of his pool was probably more important to him than offering his brand new neighbors poisoned Pop-Tarts.

With a defeated sigh, I swam over to the ladder closest to my pants and robe, and pulled myself up. I was a dripping, limp mess and frozen to the bone after my body adjusted to the temperature of the water.

Abby took her Pop-Tart and plopped down on one of the loungers that were still stacked on top of two others and wrapped in plastic. She began munching on it happily, grinning at me like she'd just won the lottery.

She was in *so* much trouble.

I walked over to the stranger, eying him skeptically. He held out his remaining beach towel to me and after realizing I stood before him in only a soaking wet tank top and bikini briefs, I took it quickly and wrapped it around my body. I shivered violently with my dark blonde hair dripping down my face and back. But I didn't dare adjust the towel, afraid I'd give him more of a show than he'd paid for.

"Good morning," he laughed at me.

"Good morning," I replied slowly, carefully.

Up close, he wasn't the giant I'd originally thought. Now that we were both ground level, I could see that while he was tall, at least six inches taller than me, he wasn't freakishly tall, which relieved some of my concerns. He still wore his pajamas: blue cotton pants and a white t-shirt that had been stretched out from sleep. His almost black hair appeared still mussed and disheveled, but swept over to the side in what could be a trendy style if he brushed it. He seemed to be a few years older than me, if I had to guess thirty-five or thirty-six, and he had dark, intelligent eyes that crinkled in the corners with amusement. He was tanned, and muscular, and imposing. And I hated that he was laughing at me.

"Sorry about the gate," he shrugged. "I didn't realize there were kids around."

"You moved into a neighborhood," I pointed out dryly. "There're bound to be kids around."

His eyes narrowed at the insult, but he swallowed his Pop-Tart and agreed, "Fair enough. I'll keep it locked from now on."

I wasn't finished with berating him though. His pool caused all kinds of problems for me this morning and since I could only take out so much anger on my six-year-old, I had to vent the rest somewhere. "Who fills their pool the first week of September anyway? You've been to New England in the winter, haven't you?"

He cleared his throat and the last laugh lines around his eyes disappeared. "My real estate agent," he explained. "It was kind of like a 'thank you' present for buying the house. He thought he was doing something nice for me."

I snorted at that, thinking how my little girl could have... No, I couldn't go there; I was not emotionally capable of thinking that thought through.

"I really am sorry," he offered genuinely, his dark eyes flashing with true emotion. "I got in late last night, and passed out on the couch. I didn't even know the pool was full or the gate was open until I heard you screaming out here."

Guilt settled in my stomach like acid, and I regretted my harsh tone with him. This wasn't his fault. I just wanted to blame someone besides myself.

"Look, I'm sorry I was snappish about the pool. I just... I was just worried about Abby. I took it out on you," I relented, but wouldn't look him in the eye. I'd always been terrible at apologies. When Grady and I would fight, I could never bring myself to tell him I felt sorry. Eventually, he'd just look at me and say, "I forgive you, Lizzy. Now come here and make it up to me." With anyone else my pride would have refused to let me give in, but with Grady, the way he smoothed over my stubbornness and let me get away with keeping my dignity worked every single time.

"It's alright, I can understand that," my new neighbor agreed.

We stood there awkwardly for a few more moments, before I swooped down to pick up my plaid pants and discarded robe. "Alright, well I need to go get the kids ready for school. Thanks for convincing her to get out. Who knows how long we would have been stuck there playing *Finding Nemo*."

He chuckled but his eyes were confused. "Is that like Marco Polo?"

I shot him a questioning glance, wondering if he was serious or not. "No kids?" I asked.

He laughed again. "Nope, life-long bachelor." He waved the box of Pop-Tarts and realization dawned on me. He hadn't really seemed like a father before now, but in my world- my four kids, soccer mom, neighborhood watch secretary, active member of the PTO world- it was almost unfathomable to me that someone his age could not have kids.

I cleared my throat, "It's uh, a little kid movie. Disney," I explained and understanding lit his expression. "Um, thanks again." I turned to Abby who was finishing up her breakfast, "Let's go, Abs, you're making us late for school."

"I'm Ben by the way," he called out to my back. "Ben Tyler."

I snorted to myself at the two first names; it somehow seemed appropriate for the handsome life-long bachelor, but ridiculous all the same.

"Liz Carlson," I called over my shoulder. "Welcome to the neighborhood."

"Uh, the towels?" he shouted after me when we'd reached the gate.

I turned around with a dropped mouth, thinking a hundred different vile things about my new neighbor. "Can't we... I..." I glanced down helplessly at my bare legs poking out of the bottom of the towel he'd just lent me.

"Liz," he laughed familiarly, and I tried not to resent him. "I'm just teasing. Bring them back whenever."

I growled something unintelligible that I hope sounded like "thank you" and spun on my heel, shooing Abby onto the lawn between our houses.

"Nice to meet you, neighbor," he called out over the fence.

"You too," I mumbled, not even turning my head to look back at him.

Obviously he was single and unattached. He was way too smug for his own good. I just hoped he would keep his gate locked and loud parties few and far between. He seemed like the type to throw frat party-like keggers and hire strippers for the weekend. I had a family to raise, a family that was quickly falling apart while I floundered to hold us together with tired arms and a broken spirit. I didn't need a nosy neighbor handing out Pop-Tarts and sarcasm interfering with my life.

Chapter Two

"Hey-O!" Emma called from the open front door. "Where are you, Lizbeth?"

"In here," I called back over my second cup of coffee. This morning had been a dismal failure, and the kids were, as predicted, late for school. "Do you want a cup of coffee?"

My sister rounded the corner, flustered as usual. This was quite possibly a genetic trait, since I suffered from the same wild blonde hair and general air of confusion. She smiled at me, her full lips stretched tightly with unease. I recognized her assessing eye immediately. She was gauging my mood, deciding whether she would get emotionally-volatile-near-breakdown me or the somewhat holding-it-together me.

Today, I was in no way holding it together.

"I'd love one," she sighed a little out of breath. She dropped her oversized bright orange purse on my kitchen counter and slid onto a barstool next to Lucy. "Hey little girl, whatchya up to?"

"Coloring a picture," Lucy replied in her sweet four-year-old voice.

"Can I help?" Emma asked, already picking up a crayon.

"Just don't use green. We *hate* the color green," Lucy emphasized.

I cleared my throat and turned my back on them. That was my terrible influence and obsession with her daddy's eyes. It was unfair to take out my trauma on the kids, but I didn't know how to stop.

"For now," Emma agreed. "But I bet we learn to like it again."

"No psychobabble this morning, *please*!" I begged. I poured my sister her cup of coffee and handed it to her along with the creamer. She liked her coffee insanely sweet, and I wasn't even going to try to guess her creamer-to-coffee ratio.

"What happened?" she asked in her knowing, grownup voice that I still had a hard time taking seriously. She was my little sister, a good six years younger than me and a complete flake. But ever since Grady, she had actually stepped up to the plate and been a huge support system for me. I wouldn't be functioning today if it weren't for her.

"I didn't hug Abby when I dropped her off," I admitted and the tears were already falling. Hot mess did not begin to cover the train wreck I had become.

"Alright, start at the beginning." She pulled off her gauzy infinity scarf and settled in for the duration of my tale.

She was still getting her masters in counseling, so her schedule allowed her to stop by during the day and help me out. She was my saving grace in so many ways, but adult conversation was high on the list.

"Abby left the house this morning without telling me. I found her swimming laps in the new neighbor's pool." My anger still simmered under the surface, but more than that, the fear of almost losing her was choking me and I could barely breathe through the panic.

"Your sister is such a little fish," Emma looked down at Lucy and giggled.

"Don't make jokes, Em. She's only six. Anything could have happened to her and I didn't even know she left the house!" I stared into the black depths of my coffee and sniffled back more frustrated tears.

"Liz, you cannot keep blaming yourself for not being both parents. You *are* enough. You're everything these kids need." She smiled at me sympathetically and reached across to pat my hand. These were coping/comforting techniques she picked up from school and I found them mildly obnoxious.

I pulled my hand away from my sister's compassionate grip and looked at Lucy. She colored happily for the moment, but I knew this would be another picture added to the pile I was supposed to "keep for Daddy." The daddy she was convinced was just vacationing to heaven. The daddy she was positive wouldn't leave his family forever. The daddy that should be walking through the front door any moment.

I wasn't the only one struggling with denial.

The cold hard truth was that I wasn't enough. I *had never been* enough. My marriage was a partnership built on mutual love and shared responsibility. The house had run as smoothly as the chaos of four little ones would allow, but we ran it *together*.

Grady had always been a doting father. He would get up early with the kids, make holidays, important days at school and birthdays so unbelievably special for them, and most of all, he met me halfway with discipline. He wasn't a perfect man, and our marriage had been anything but.

I knew that. I told myself that often because it was too easy to idealize our relationship into utopic perfection. And imagining our life as perfect was a straight spiral into the dismal abyss of despair. But life had been good- really, *really* good, and easier and happy.

And now we were just barely surviving.

"So what happened with Abby?" Emma prompted.

"I couldn't get her out of the pool. She was being difficult like usual. Finally the guy next door found us and lured her out with a Pop-tart. By then, we were late for school. I had to walk all the children inside and stop in the office to sign them in. I was so mad at her. Mad because she left the house without telling me, mad because she went swimming by herself and I can't even think about the worst case scenario there, and mad because she made yet another morning difficult for me. I was so angry when I dropped her off in her classroom that I didn't even hug her or tell her I loved her." I was helpless to stop the tears that flowed freely down my flushed cheeks and dripped off my stubborn chin. "Now I have to wait until after school to see her. She has to go all day thinking I'm so mad at her that I don't love her anymore. And I'm making myself sick over it."

Emma's blue-gray gaze held mine, her own tears brimming at the corners. With equal parts conviction and concern, she promised, "Liz, you *will* see Abby again. You *will* get to hug her and tell her you love her. She's going to be alright. She knows you love her. There's not a doubt in her pretty red head."

I nodded, with my chin trembling and more tears falling. These were things I'd been trying to convince myself of all morning, but it helped when they came from someone else. Just because I lost one of the people I loved most in life, didn't mean I was going to lose them all.

At least I wanted to believe that. The hole in my chest argued differently.

"Liz." My sister stood up from the barstool and walked behind the long, tiled island to give me a tight hug. "You're going to get through this. I know this is hard, but you are the strongest person I know. Grady would not have left you if he didn't think you could handle this."

I hiccupped a big, ugly sob and bent my face into her neck. She smelled like lilac and vanilla and like my sister. We'd been sharing hugs like this since she was born.

"Em," was all I could sniffle. The pain was too acute, too shattering right now. I looked around the kitchen with watery eyes taking in all the careful details Grady had done himself with his own, rough hands.

Before cancer, he had been a strong, smart, capable man that started his own construction company and built it into somewhat of a local empire. He went from working every job himself to having multiple crews and foremen. He built our house, brick by loving brick and designed the entire inside himself when we finally had enough money and enough good credit to leave the cracker box of an apartment we shared for the first years of our marriage.

31

We had lived here for a little more than six years. Other than Blake, all of our kids were born into this home. We had gotten to know our neighbors as they each built around us and we had gotten our dream home, our forever home, when we were only twenty-six. We felt unbelievably blessed here when Grady was still healthy.

Now I felt drowned in memories of him. His ghost haunted me from every room, and lingered over each piece of furniture and hand-touched detail. This place by the island was where he would kiss me each morning and take his travel cup of coffee from me on his way to work. The long, weathered sectional couch in the living room was where we would cuddle up each night and fight over my reality shows vs. *Sports Center*. Our backyard was devastated by memories of him grilling, teaching the kids to play catch and enjoying nice evening nights as a family around the fire pit.

A consuming ache gripped at the center of my being and fractured my soul right down the middle. I felt the cracking intensely as it fissured out to each and every part of me, shattering my already broken spirit to pieces. Again.

"What am I going to do?" I whispered, ignoring the concerned look from Lucy. "How am I going to survive this, Em?"

Emma was bawling too by now. My hair was damp and matted from where her messy tears had fallen. But at my questions she straightened and cleared her throat. Using her mature voice again, she said, "First, you're going to go take your run. I have to be back at the coffee shop by twelve to meet my study group so I don't have a lot of time. And then… we will figure this out together, Lizbeth. You are not doing this alone."

"Okay," I agreed with a pathetic nod. I could do that. I could run. It would help me feel better anyway. I could use the time alone and the time to focus on at least one coherent thought.

"Mommy are you sad about daddy again?" Lucy asked, naïve, as any four-year-old would be.

I nodded, unable and unwilling to show her exactly how deep the sorrow was rooted.

"It's okay to be sad, Mommy," Lucy promised on a know-it-all whisper. "But don't be sad all day. He only went on vacation. He wouldn't leave us forever. He loves us too much."

The tears immediately started again and in that moment I instinctively knew this day was only going to get worse.

Emma took that moment to ask, "Where's Jace?"

I listened for a second and heard only silence.

So, I immediately panicked.

Unlike Abby, there was no way Jace had left this house without sounding alarm bells or leaving clues to what he was trying to do. Jace, in all his two-year-old glory, still hadn't mastered the fine art of turning a doorknob. But he was dangerously quiet and that never signaled good things.

Emma and I raced through the kitchen and up the stairs. "He was playing in his room," I panted as we careened down the hallway in search of him.

His room was empty, and so was his brother's. There was a chance he was in Lucy's room, so we headed that way next.

Then we heard the toilet flush. We changed paths and backtracked towards the kids' bathroom, dread sending icicles of anxiety into every part of me.

There he was standing over the toilet looking down at a bowl filled to the brim with entire rolls of toilet paper. A mischievous smile played on his lips and he looked up at us with a giggle. His finger played with the flusher, as if he was getting ready to flush it again. Panic hazed my vision.

"Jace, don't even think about it," I threatened in a low voice.

Emma and I paused in the doorway, hands raised like he was a wild animal we were careful not to spook. He let out another devilish giggle and enthusiastically flushed the toilet.

Emma and I leapt toward him, watching in horror as the bowl filled with water and all the sacrificed rolls sloshed around in their sogginess. I shuddered at the mess and started to cry again when the water reached the brim of the white, porcelain bowl and spilled over onto the tiled floor.

My sister grabbed Jace so he wouldn't get soaked and we all hopped back out of the way. Jace just kept giggling and the water just kept gushing onto the floor.

My head fell into my hands and I moaned, "This is just not my day."

I thought Emma would agree with me, instead she said, "Go, Lizzy. Go run. I'll clean this up."

"Emma, I cannot leave you with this mess. Are you kidding?"

"You need the run," she shrugged, but her face was contorted in disgust at the mess the bathroom had become in just a few short seconds. "I'll have this cleaned up by the time you get back."

"I love you," I whispered, still not able to get ahold of my emotions, but anxious for the opportunity to bale on this latest catastrophe. If I didn't have to clean up just one of the many tragedies in my upside down life, it might be the difference between my sanity and a mental breakdown.

33

"Go!" she ordered. "Before I change my mind."

And I obeyed. While she calmly chastised Jace on his destruction techniques, I slipped on my tennis shoes and bolted out the front door. I ran away from the mess in the bathroom, away from children I couldn't control on my own and away from a house so saturated with memories of the man I loved, I couldn't breathe with him so close.

Chapter Three

I rounded the corner and the house came back into view. We lived in a cul-de-sac on the edge of town. The homes were all relatively new and custom built. The trees had some time to grow but they didn't tower over the houses like in the rest of town.

Still, I loved our little neighborhood.

The families were all sweet and lovely and we took care of each other.

I couldn't bring myself to move or to take my kids from their home. Even though there were times that I wanted to.

Like right now.

Looking up at white siding spotted with black shudders and boasting a bright red door, I saw my dream home. And I saw a lifetime of pain I would never recover from.

Grady, where are you?

I slowed my demanding pace to a measured walk. I told myself this was a cool down, but the truth whispered and echoed inside me. I could push my body to my limits when I ran, when I ran away from everything and everyone that needed me. But now that I was confronted with those same things, I couldn't bring myself to face them again.

As a mother, I had always felt this severe degree of failure. I had four kids. *Four of them*. Life was always crazy for us and I never felt like I was enough for all of my kids. Chaos ruled my parenting style, and because they were all two years apart, they were always in different stages of needs and demands.

Now, without Grady by my side, I had never felt like more of a failure at anything. This wasn't just a small failure either; this was the crash and burn kind of catastrophe that combusted into a million unrecognizable pieces.

That was what I was doing to my children. I was the pilot of their plane of life and I was about to dive-bomb us into the middle of the ocean.

"You all right?" A voice called me out of my silent pity party.

I looked up to find Ben Tyler at his mailbox. I didn't know how to feel about meeting him again, especially while I looked like this. Most of me still fizzled with anger about our altercation this morning. But there was this small part of me that felt extremely embarrassed that the only times he'd seen me were when I'd been in my underwear and braless tank top and now like this, sweaty, red-faced and panting.

This guy had to think I was a complete nutcase.

I tried to smile, but my worries, exhaustion and general bad attitude made it more of a grimace than a happy expression. "I'm fine. I just finished a run."

"I can see that." His smirk was annoying.

"Don't you have a job?" The words fell out of my mouth before I could censor them. *Oh, god, what was wrong with me?*

He chuckled at my rude question. He should probably snap at me and swear to himself never to talk to me again, but something told me this guy didn't have it in him to hate people.

Not even his bitchy neighbor.

"I do," he said. "I took a couple days off to get moved into the new place."

"Oh." Well, obviously. I was an idiot.

"Don't *you* have a job?"

I couldn't tell if this was sarcasm or if he was genuinely curious. When he raised his eyebrows expectantly, I gave him an answer. "I'm a stay-at-home mom."

"Abby?"

"And her three siblings."

"Wow," he whistled. "Four of them? You don't look like you have four kids."

Um... "Thanks."

"I heard about your husband," he blurted suddenly.

"What?" My voice was a whisper. I felt my bones become brittle and breakable as he grimaced with his knowledge of my grief.

"I'm so sorry," he gushed. "I don't know why I said it like that. I just... I didn't know how to bring it up. And I didn't want you to feel like you had to explain it to me."

After staring at him for several silent seconds, I said, "I wouldn't have felt like I needed to explain it to you."

He winced. "Liz, I'm sorry. The neighbor across the street shared your story and I just... I obviously have no tact." He laughed bitterly at himself and I wanted to change the subject.

I needed to change the subject.

"Mrs. Mitchum. She has trouble minding her own business."

His dark eyes softened a little. "I noticed." He rocked back on his heels, clearly putting his next sentence together in his head before he spoke it. I glanced up at my house and desperately wanted to escape there. Sure, five minutes ago, I'd dreaded walking through that door. Now, thanks to Ben Tyler, I couldn't wait to get inside the safety of my own place.

"Well, I guess, I'll see you-"

"If you need anything, you can always knock." He took a step forward when he interrupted me. We stood just three feet apart, but I swear I could feel his aura or something. He radiated this energy that grated against my skin. I had no doubt that he was a successful person, and not just from the size of the house he'd bought. He had this charisma that poured off him. It annoyed the hell out of me, but I saw that in real life he could charm whomever he set his sights on.

"Thanks," I answered simply.

"Seriously," he emphasized. "If you need anything, don't hesitate to ask."

"Okay."

"And my pool!" His words came out almost desperately. I didn't know if it was guilt pushing him into wanting to be friends with me or what, but it was getting to be a little much. "Any time you or your kids want to go swimming, the pool is yours."

I cleared my throat, "It's going to get cold soon."

"Well, until then."

"Honestly, I have too many kids for that. I can't watch them all. It's too stressful."

"Oh." His shoulders deflated some and I could tell he was disappointed with my answer.

Clearly he had never taken kids under six swimming before. Sure, Abby was a freak of nature when it came to water sports, but Lucy and Jace weren't even close to being water-ready. If I had someone else to go with me, it wouldn't be so bad. I could split up the two littles and Grady could have helped me keep an eye on the two older ones. But I didn't have Grady anymore, and I didn't trust a complete stranger to help me keep my kids alive.

Plus, it was just weird. We hadn't known each other for twenty-four hours yet. I wished he'd stop forcing his friendship on me.

"Liz, I have to go soon! Get your a-s-s in the shower now or you're going to have to wait until Thursday before you can take one!" Emma's voice called from the front porch. She held Jace on her hip and Lucy clung to her leg. Her wild blonde hair whipped around her face in the fall breeze.

She looked like the well put-together mom I would never be.

Of course, she wasn't a full-time, single mom and therefore had time for things like hair appointments and manicures. Also, her body had not pushed four bowling balls out her vagina, so she had that going for her too.

I snuck a glance at Ben to see him watching my sister intently. Yep, she did that to all men. Poor guy.

"I'll be right there!" I called back.

It was too late; she'd noticed Ben and now her curiosity had gotten the better of her.

"I guess I'll see you around," I said quickly to him in hopes I could escape before my sister wanted a formal introduction.

"Mommy!" Lucy slammed into my thighs and wrapped her short arms around me. "You smell icky."

My face flushed with embarrassment. No doubt I smelled icky. Ben tossed his head back and let out a loud bark of laughter.

"Thanks, Babe," I grumbled.

"You do smell icky, Sis," Emma chuckled on her arrival.

"That's why I need that shower."

She ignored me, her sparkling eyes already on my new neighbor. "I'm Emma." She smiled widely at him. Jace made a dive for me and I caught him before he tumbled out of Emma's distracted arms.

Ben reached out his hand and took her now empty one. "Ben Tyler."

"You're the one with the pool?"

He winced again. "Is everyone going to hold that against me?"

I looked down at my kids and thought *yes* inside my head, but I let my sister throw out a flirty, "Only until you redeem yourself."

"Hey," he joked, "my Pop-Tarts saved the day this morning."

I resented that on principle. "I would have gotten her out eventually."

He shot me an indulgent smile. "Sure."

"Sure?" I raised an eyebrow at him.

"Mommy, I want a Pop-Tart!" Lucy squealed.

"Pop-Tart!" Jace echoed.

I bit back a tired sigh. "Can I have just twenty more minutes, Em? I promise I'll be fast."

"Twenty," she said firmly. "Then I have to go. My study group will kill me if I'm late again."

"Twenty, I promise." I gave Jace a sloppy kiss on his cheek and passed him back to my sister. I told Lucy to wait with her Aunt Emma while I took off for the house again.

I left my kids and sister to chat with my new neighbor in hopes that they could repair some of the damage I'd created with just two interactions.

Part of me felt extremely sorry for Ben for having to put up with me. I didn't know what had come over me. Sure, grief and depression ruled most of my moods these days, but I at least tried to put on a show for the rest of the world. I'd managed to stay polite and cordial to almost everyone else in my life, except for a select few, and those people had deserved every last bit of my ire.

Ben Tyler didn't deserve ire or anger or bitchiness or anything else unpleasant. He had been nothing but nice since we crashed his pool and his morning. Still, there was something about him that just bothered me.

I snuck a peek through the frosted paned glass in my front door once I'd slipped inside. Emma laughed hysterically at something Ben said and he seemed absolutely captivated by her smile.

I wanted to be happy they had hit it off. I should be grateful she could represent my family with her own kind of charm, but I wasn't. Irritation and frustration bubbled inside my stomach and spread out through my arms and legs hotly. I didn't understand all this animosity for a man I'd just met.

And I hated that I let it get to me and affect what could be a perfectly comfortable relationship as neighbors.

Emma was still smiling when they said goodbye to Ben at the mailbox and turned back to the house. He watched her walk away from him, holding a letter absently in between his long fingers. I couldn't help but laugh a little as he clearly checked out her obviously swaying ass.

My sister, the hottie with the body.

But then his eyes flicked up to the house and I realized I had been standing there spying on them. I jumped away from the window and sprinted up the stairs. I now had only fifteen minutes to get through my shower and do something manageable with my shoulder length hair. I couldn't let Emma down again.

She did so much for me. Allowing her to get to her study group on time was the very least I could do. Besides, I desperately needed a shower. I needed to wash away the sweat and grime from my run and the weirdness and angsty feelings Ben Tyler seemed to bring out of me.

I tried to convince myself that having a neighbor in that house would be a good thing. He'd offered help and I knew without a doubt at some point in the future, hopefully far future, I would need it. I needed too much these days.

I just hoped by the time I had to ask him for it, I could get over whatever hostility I felt for him and could treat him with the grownup respect I should naturally have.

Or, at least not snarl every time I got within six feet of him.

Chapter Four

I finished buckling Jace in his five-point harness and pointed a finger at Lucy. "Stop screaming."

She didn't.

I pushed my hair out of my face and let out a frustrated sigh. We were late. Again. Only this time it was worse than usual.

I shoved Jace's blanket at him and wiped some of his tears away with it before hitting the button to close the door on my super-sleek minivan. I threw myself into the front seat and jammed my seatbelt into place.

The two kids screamed out their protests in a serious show of inflexibility and willpower. My head pounded with a nasty headache and my stomach churned with the task ahead of me.

I rushed out of the garage, careful of the side mirrors, and down the long, slanted driveway. Once on the street, I shoved the gearshift into drive and the engine gave a jolt of protest.

I didn't have time to care. And I really didn't have time to pacify my screaming children. With my eyes on the road, I pushed the right buttons and breathed a slow sigh of relief when I heard the screen slide into place behind me. The movie I'd listened to for approximately seventy-seven days straight turned on and the banshee shrieking died down.

I gave my new neighbor's house an assessing glance before focusing on getting out of the neighborhood. I hadn't seen Ben Tyler in almost a week, not since I'd returned his towels. He'd kept to himself after the day we met and I'd been too busy to notice. Over the weekend I thought we might run into each other, but he hadn't made an appearance and I decided to be thankful I didn't get another opportunity to make a jackass of myself.

The drive to the elementary school only took fifteen minutes, but we were already fifteen minutes late. I was supposed to be there right now.

Shit.

I had a meeting with the school counselor. I was sure she expected me to be late, but that didn't make me any less stressed. I hadn't been the best about getting places on time before Grady died. Now that I had no help getting out of the house or into the car, my punctuality had become a joke.

I sometimes tried to analyze why it was so much harder now than it was before. Even when Grady was alive, he hadn't helped me get the kids to school. He had to leave for work almost an hour before the kids got up. And I always picked them up by myself too.

Somehow the absence of his normal absence made everything worse and my occasional-tardiness had evolved into a perpetual inability to arrive anywhere on time.

Even though Grady hadn't helped me before, everything was just harder now. It didn't matter what. Putting mascara on felt a thousand times more difficult than it ever had, or getting dressed, or hell, even getting up. I just couldn't manage the way I used to.

I kept waiting for the day everything would snap back into place for me. Sure, there were things that would always be hard, always require more effort on my part without my husband by my side. But getting out of the house or up in the morning or those small things that had been mine in the first place should just happen like they always had.

Why did Grady's death spread to every aspect of my life? Why couldn't some things remain untouched by grief?

By the time I slammed on the brakes and shut the engine off in front of the elementary school, my two little ones had stopped sniffling and fighting their seatbelts. Two actual seconds of blissful silence passed before Lucy started fighting her restraints and Jace began crying again.

The end of school coincided with the end of his nap. The temper tantrum was something I was used to, but that didn't make it any easier.

I grabbed my purse, stuffed with diapers and wipes, double-checked that I put my keys and phone in there, then wrestled Jace from his seat. I got Lucy out next, with one hand while Jace sobbed loudly onto my blouse.

It was black, which hopefully hid the wetness, but could never disguise the snot I knew he left behind.

The door closed with excruciating slowness. I locked the van with the push of my thumb and hauled the children with me into the school building.

School would get out in ten minutes. The counselor had wanted thirty minutes with me, but she would have to settle for seven. I felt near tears by the time I shoved the office door open and stepped inside the frigid place.

The line of secretaries looked up at me with knowing, sympathetic smiles. I avoided the pity in their eyes and shuffled to the desk.

"I have a meeting with Ms. Conway," I told them.

The closest secretary slid the sign-in sheet toward me and handed over a pen. "She's waiting for you. You can go right in."

I finished filling in the necessary information and turned to the appropriate door. I tugged Lucy along with me and readjusted Jace in my arms. I flashed an apologetic smile at Ms. Conway and hoped I could charm her out of thinking I was the worst single parent alive.

No luck.

"Hi, Liz, how are you?"

"Fine." I grabbed the back of Lucy's collar before she could make a bee-line for the breakable animal figurines lining Conway's desk. Harriet Conway was ten years older than me and had been single her entire life. I hadn't heard of a man that had ever been able to pass her impossible standards for more than the first date. She had intimidated me before, but now, *now* that I was a useless parent, drowning in a sea of impossible expectations, she terrified me.

I often gave myself the I'm-a-grownup-too speech. The one where I tried to convince myself that I was her equal in all things and that she had no authority over *me*, only my children. I swore to myself there was no need to fear her because honestly, what could she do to me?

But every time I stood in front of her, I felt myself shrink back and cower. I couldn't help it. Maybe if I'd felt like I was doing something right, or could get the kids to school just once on time, I'd have felt like I could stand on my own two feet. But that wasn't the case.

Instead, she seemed to reflect all my failures back at me and demand more of me as a parent than I knew I could give.

"Have a seat." She gestured to the dated orange chairs in front of her desk and I obliged. I set Lucy up and reminded her to be quiet and then I made a sniffling Jace comfortable on my lap.

She waited patiently for us to get situated. "Sorry we're late," I told her.

She gave me a tight smile. "That's one of the reasons I called you in today. I know that it's hard for you now, but Abby and Blake have been late more times than they've been on time this year. We're not even through the first quarter, Liz. I've tried to give your family grace while you adjust to your new situation, but I can't let this go on without speaking up. Both Blake and Abby are the ones suffering from their tardiness. They rush into class and disturb the teaching already in progress and its encouraging bad habits. I know you are going through a rough time right now, but I think finding some consistent routine would be good for all of you."

I swallowed back tears, mild rage and a whole lot of indignity. My new situation? A rough time? This woman had no idea. She had no idea what it was like to lose the love of her life, let alone manage to get herself and four kids ready and out the door at a reasonable time.

If I didn't think my kids would never learn to read, I would have withdrawn them today and homeschooled them. Then we'd never have to get out of our pjs.

Except her words weren't just infuriating and hurtful, they were also true. They were like daggers in all my weak places. And they screamed arguments alongside everything I already knew.

"We're trying." I hated the tremble in my voice. I hated falling back on this again. My grief and our loss didn't mean anything to her and I honestly couldn't expect them to. "We're working very hard to find our rhythm; it's just been hard."

Her face softened with compassion. "I understand that. But I can't continue to turn a blind eye. The kids need to be here on time."

I nodded. "Alright. We'll try harder."

She offered me another strained smile. I didn't think she believed me.

The explosion of children's voices reached us through the open office door. I let out a slow sigh of relief. School was out; this meeting had to be over now.

Ms. Conway glanced at her door and back at me. "There's something else."

I gulped.

"Yes?"

"Abby has been acting up again."

The words hit me hard. I couldn't even respond to them. Frustrated tears welled in my bottom lashes and I willed myself not to break down in front of this lady. I could hold it together. I could hold it together for just five more minutes.

"She's been very talkative," Conway went on after it was obvious I wasn't going to speak up. "She's been caught bullying some of the boys on the playground at recess. And we suspect that she's stealing erasers."

"Erasers?" My surprise gave me the ability to speak through my emotion.

"White board erasers," Ms. Conway clarified.

Oh, Jesus. "You think Abby's stealing white board erasers?" Mouthy, talkative, bullying, yes, fine. All those things applied to Abby lately. But stealing? Erasers? That just didn't make sense.

Not that I didn't think she was capable of it... But really?

"We don't have proof that it's her yet. It's just a feeling that her teacher, Mr. Hoya has. He wanted a parent-teacher conference with you, but I said I would speak with you first. I told him you would talk to Abby."

"I will," I assured her. "I'll talk to her."

"And try to be on time?"

I swallowed back the bitter pill of needing to humble myself in front of this woman I didn't even like. Humility was never a strong characteristic of mine, but I knew that I was in the wrong here, which made it worse.

"Yes, and we'll make a better effort to get here on time."

She smiled patiently at me. "I make you promise to be on time, but then I've made you late to pick up the kids. How thoughtless of me."

I didn't say anything. By now Lucy's fidgeting had gotten out of control and Jace had finally woken up and grown curious. Sleepy Jace was easy to take places. Curious Jace was about as nightmarish as any two-year-old in a space with breakable objects could be.

"Thank you, Ms. Conway," I said on my way to my feet. "If there are any more problems, please don't hesitate to call."

"I'm sure we'll speak again soon," she replied evenly.

Meaning she expected more problems, many more problems.

I held it together as I made my escape from her office and the main office. I held it together while I dragged Lucy alongside me and balanced Jace and my purse on the other arm. I held it together long enough to pick up Abby and Blake from their teachers and classes standing in clumps along the school sidewalk. I held it together while I shoveled kids and backpacks in the car and buckled car seats and checked the older kids' seatbelts. I held it together as I waved to other moms picking up their kids and while I waited in line to exit the lot.

I held it together for approximately five more minutes as I struggled to keep the van on the road while my mind spun and spun and my heart felt crushed inside my chest.

Finally, I had to pull over. The tears had started to fall in messy, blinding buckets and I knew it was too dangerous to continue. I found a McDonalds parking lot and slammed into an empty space in the corner of the lot. I threw the gearshift into park and dropped my forehead to the steering wheel.

I could hear the kids cry out for me from the back, but my grief had consumed me by now. I was useless. I was an empty shell. I was pathetic and helpless and so utterly lost I didn't even know where to go.

The thought of getting my kids to school on time felt *impossible*. Dealing with Abby felt even worse. How could I get through to my little girl who had lost her hero? Her daddy? Her partner in crime? I knew I needed to do a better job with her, but I didn't know how!

It felt unfair of them to expect so much of me. Didn't they know how much I hurt? Didn't they know that it took everything I had to get up in the morning and face the day?

This pain inside me drowned me; it tore at me every second of every day until I thought I would shatter into a million worthless pieces just from the sheer pressure of it.

I couldn't do this.

I couldn't.

And I didn't know what to do about that because there was no one else to shoulder this impossible burden with me.

I was alone. And I had never been this alone before.

I just didn't know what to do.

Little hands landed on my arms and wrapped around my neck from behind. I felt hot tears drip from my two older children and land on my shoulders and neck. I immediately unbuckled and spun around in my seat to catch them.

Abby and Blake fell on top of me, tangling in each other and me. We sobbed together, sharing the anguish and the confusion of what our lives had become.

I felt the pain more acutely as they clutched me, the one person they were supposed to be able to count on, but the one person that was letting them down in every way. At the same time I felt the pressure on my heart intensify. I also felt the comfort that came with their unconditional love and understanding.

I soaked up their hugs and tears because they were the only other people on this planet that had any kind of idea what I was going through. They were the only other people that knew how much we'd lost when their daddy died.

They might be the source of some of my current problems, but they were also the only reason I had to keep going. They were my lifelines. My hope. My reason for breathing.

"I love you guys," I told them through a broken whisper. They whimpered and mumbled back the same sentiment.

"Why did school make you cry, Mom?" Blake blinked up at me with his extra-bright green eyes. I knew he tried to stay strong for me. I knew he tried to hold back his tears. But he was only eight. Watching him struggle to be the man of the house nearly broke me on a daily basis. But gosh, I loved this kid so much.

My chin trembled as I forced the words out. "I had a meeting with Ms. Conway." Both kids grimaced and I laughed even as more tears fell. "We *have* to be on time for school from now on."

They both nodded.

"Okay, Mama," Abby agreed.

"I'm serious, guys. We're going to be in big trouble if we're late again."

"Even you?" Abby asked.

"Even me. Especially me."

"Okay, we'll help you in the mornings," Blake said seriously. I couldn't help but feel some pride at the responsibility he was willing to shoulder. But I hated it at the same time. I hated that he had to grow up so fast. And I hated it even more that I had to rely on him so heavily.

"Thanks, kiddos." I hugged them again and held them against me. They smelled like kid-sweat and school. I inhaled the tangy, unpleasant aroma and counted my blessings that they were healthy and here with me. Life was tough right now, but at least we had each other.

I pulled back and let them wander to their seats. I stayed turned around and narrowed my clearer eyes at my oldest daughter.

"Abigail," I started. I watched her shoulders stiffen at the sound of her full name. She turned around and sunk down to her booster seat, eyes wide and suspiciously innocent. "Are you stealing erasers?"

"Erasers?" she repeated.

"Yes. White board erasers. Are you stealing them?"

She snorted a laugh. "Why would I steal white board erasers?"

I stared intently at her and tried to see through her words. Was she lying? Why would she lie about something like that? Why would she even steal the erasers to begin with?

I let out an exasperated sigh. "I have no idea. But if you are stealing them, you need to stop. I mean it."

"Mom!" she groaned. "I'm not stealing anything! I promise!"

"Mmm." I couldn't tell if I believed her or not. "Maybe not, but we're going to talk about some other things when we get home. You're in big trouble, little girl."

I watched her face fall, but this time I could see the guilt written all over her pretty face. She might not have been stealing, but she knew there were other things she had been up to.

I pulled back onto the main road and headed home. Today had been hard enough, but tonight would be worse.

I didn't know how I would get through disciplining Abby. Or dinner. Or bedtime. All of those felt utterly impossible. But I would have to find a way. They would happen whether I wanted them to or not. Whether I was ready for them or not.

My heart clenched again, but this time I wrestled back the tears.

I had to keep it together at least until I got them to sleep. Then I could lose it again. Then I could drown in my own tears if I wanted. I just needed to get through bedtime first.

Chapter Five

"Stay away from the street!" I looked back to my forward progress just in time to avoid running over a tennis ball and chopping it to bits. I wrestled the lawnmower around it, swooped down to scoop it up and then I retraced my path in chopping, unattractive lines that would have made Grady cringe. I paused completely to yell over the loud rumble of the small engine, "Blake, keep an eye on Lucy and Jace!"

He shot me a thumbs up and continued to play basketball. I stood there idling for long enough to make sure all of my children were accounted for and alive, before I went back to the task at hand.

Only another month or so of lawn care before I could call it quits for the winter.

Only, that meant snow removal and laying down salt and... was there anything else I needed to do?

Grady had always taken care of the lawn care and outdoor maintenance. He loved being outside and took great pride in our curb appeal. I had left it all up to him. I had never once been curious enough to find out what it all entailed.

And now I felt completely out of my depth. This was just one more task that I needed Grady for, one more reason his absence left this family devastated.

During the summer months, I'd paid a neighbor kid to mow for me. But selfishly he'd applied to universities out of state and eventually had to leave to start his freshman year. It seemed silly to hire someone else when there were only four or five more weeks to go before it would be too cold for grass to grow.

But with only a quarter of the yard mowed, I was starting to second guess my decision to take this on myself.

At least it was finally Saturday. I could enjoy my kids at home without worrying about evil glares from teachers or pitying glances from the other parents. I could gather my children around me and we could hole up in our cozy home without worrying about the outside world until Monday.

"Blake, let Abby play too! Abby, stop kicking Blake!" Of course, there were minor pitfalls to having all the children home.

I chucked the tennis ball over my shoulder, wiped my sweaty brow and went back to work. The sooner I finished the front yard, the sooner I could move the children to the back, away from the street.

It had been a long week. And I'd wanted nothing more than to sleep in until noon, stay in my pajamas for forty-eight hours straight and eat my weight in chocolate.

Unfortunately, the kids didn't care what I wanted. Except for maybe the chocolate. I bet they would be on board with the chocolate.

So, this morning, I'd forced myself out of bed, made the effort to get dressed in workout clothes and set the children free on what was really a beautiful day. The sun shone hotly in the sky, but the cool autumn breeze kept it from becoming unbearable. The kids needed to burn off some of their wild energy and as they ran around the driveway and yard, squealing and laughing and even fighting some, I was glad I'd made the effort after all.

I jerked the lawnmower to the right, noticing a tall patch of grass I'd somehow missed and then curved it back in front of me. I put a little too much momentum behind the beast of a mower and accidentally sent it careening to my left. A pair of sneakers jumped out of the way just before I made them the mower's next meal.

The sneakers were attached to legs and I let go of the mower so I could scream at the top of my lungs. *Where had he come from?* The mower sputtered and died without the bar-thingy held down to keep it going.

"Sorry, Liz! I called out your name," Ben Tyler waved sheepishly. His cheeks were flushed red from his near death experience with my manic mowing. I couldn't tell if his blush was from the surprising exertion of fleeing for his life or because he was embarrassed to have snuck up on me. Again.

"No, I'm sorry," I told him. "I didn't hear you walk up."

"That much is obvious." He chuckled a deep baritone sound that forced a smile from me.

I glanced over my shoulder and counted my children quickly before turning back to him. He stood there staring at me. So in turn, I stared back. I didn't know what to say or why he'd made the trek across the property line.

After a few more moments, I felt too awkward to let the silence continue. "Beautiful day!" I wanted to smack my hand over my face. Was there anything more cliché than breaking the ice with weather?

"It is," he agreed. He wore that arrogant smile he couldn't seem to get rid of. I didn't like that smile. And because of that, it made it hard to like him. It was just too cocky, too mischievous. I felt like he knew this great big secret about me that I didn't even know. "You're mowing."

It was a statement not a question and so obvious I couldn't figure out why he bothered to speak it. "I am," I conceded. I looked back at my progress and cringed. I was mowing, but not well.

"Looks, er, good." Ben cleared his throat.

I narrowed my eyes on him. "You don't have to lie. I'm a big girl."

He ran a hand through his dark hair and grinned at me. "It's terrible. I've never seen someone mow like this before. Is it your first time?"

"No! It is not my first time. I've been mowing all fall."

"I think you should give it up. Hire someone. You're devaluing my property and I just moved in."

I laughed before I could stop myself. I couldn't get over his nerve! Obviously, I was new at this. Obviously, my husband just died so maybe he should give me a break. My insides churned with a confusing mixture of resentment and humor. I was too shocked to be truly angry with him.

"I did hire someone over the summer," I defended myself, "But he went off to college and left me in the lurch. Selfish bastard."

It was Ben's turn to look shocked. That quickly turned into a bark of laughter. "What an insensitive moron."

"Thank you!" I glanced back at the kids. Blake had organized them into teams, boys against girls. The girls were winning because he had to keep chasing after Jace.

"They're all there," Ben assured me. I turned my attention back to him. "Four, right?"

"Yep. Four."

"They look like good ones."

I took a step back, surprised by the compliment. "Thank you. They are for the most part."

"You should let me take over."

"*What?*"

"The mowing." Ben laughed again. "You should let me take over the mowing."

"Oh!" I fidgeted in front of hIm. Usually, I would be running from the awkwardness of this conversation, but there was a lightness about Ben that kept me from feeling too self-conscious. I enjoyed that he didn't taken anything seriously. For the first time in weeks, I didn't want to banish all other humans from my life forever. "No, that's alright. I don't mind doing it, even if I'm not very good at it."

He stepped up to the mower and gripped the handle. "I don't mind either. And I'm actually good at it. Go enjoy your kids."

"Ben, seriously, that's really nice of you, but I can handle it." I stepped up to the mower too and grasped the handle in a show of authority and intent.

"Liz, I know you can handle it. That was never in question. Now go enjoy this beautiful day with your beautiful kids." He bent down and like a pro, started the engine.

It had taken me twenty minutes just to get this stupid thing running earlier!

Then he put his hand over mine and removed it from the handle. "Go," he smiled at me.

I stumbled back a step and then did as he asked or rather commanded. I walked over to my kids and Blake passed me the ball as if he already knew I would play. The lawnmower growled in the background, creating a roaring soundtrack to our game.

I took a shot and laughed with my kids when the ball flew over the backboard and rolled into our other neighbor's yard, the Kents. Blake and Abby raced after it, while Jace hung on my leg and Lucy skipped around in a circle.

I took a deep breath and enjoyed the moment.

When was the last time I'd done this?

When was the last time I'd just let go of all of my grief, my pain, and my stress and just enjoyed being with my children?

I was ashamed to admit, I couldn't remember. Even before Grady died, he'd been sick. I had been coiled tight for as long as I could remember. My lungs felt coated with rust and disuse as I tried to let go of the nagging feeling that I should be doing something else, that I should be working in some way.

It took several minutes of mental struggle before I could fully relax into this time with the kids. Even they seemed a little baffled that I had stopped what I was doing to play with them.

As soon as the grief ebbed away, guilt filled in the space. If it wasn't one thing, it was the other. I couldn't seem to find normal. Or balance. Or center. I was a battered ship in the middle of a perfect storm. I rocked one way, only to be flipped around and tossed in the other direction.

The basketball game resumed and the children's laughter and smiling faces helped ease the guilt eventually. I hadn't been good at this recently, but it wasn't too late. I could start trying to do this more often.

I was the only parent these kids had now, would ever have now. If I didn't do this right, they would never forgive me.

I would never forgive myself.

"Mom, who's that guy mowing our yard?" Blake held the basketball propped against his hip. I smiled at the way he watched Ben. It was hard to believe that my Blake was the man of the house now. At eight years old, he was hardly a grownup, but he took his role very seriously.

I ruffled his hair and pulled him against me. Man of the house or not, he was still young enough to wrap his arms around my waist and not push me away.

"That's our new neighbor. His name is Ben."

"He's the guy with the pool?"

I looked down into my son's mossy green eyes and tried not to burst into tears. He looked so much like his dad, right down to the smattering of freckles across the bridge of his nose.

"He is the guy with the pool. He promised to lock his gate from now on, but you help me keep an eye on the other kids, yeah?"

Blake looked back at his siblings who had all moved on to other outdoor activities. Lucy was pushing Jace in the umbrella stroller and Abby had pulled out her scooter. "Helmet, Abs!"

She rolled her eyes, but didn't argue. That was progress.

"Yeah, Mom," Blake agreed. "But Abby will probably figure out a way to climb the fence."

I tried not to smile; he was too smart for his own good. "Just tell me if she does, okay?"

"Okay." He dropped his arm and started dribbling the ball while watching Ben make progress across our yard. I could see the distrust in his expression and the tension in his shoulders. Blake had never liked strangers; he'd always been the shiest of my children. But this was different, I could feel the slight animosity he felt for Ben Tyler. I didn't necessarily blame him because I often had those same types of feelings, but I didn't like it on Blake.

"Oh, and Blake?" He looked over at me, his shoulders still rigid. "He said we could use his pool any time we wanted."

He instantly relaxed and his face lit up with a new brightness, a light, like he was shining from the inside out. I loved it when my kids smiled like that. It happened so little these days.

"For real?"

"For real."

"Today?"

"Probably not today. I can't take you all swimming by myself. We'll have to wait until Auntie Emma can come with us."

Some of that beautiful light dimmed in Blake's face, but he stayed easy and cool. "Okay."

I stepped out of the way so he could go back to shooting hoops. Abby still struggled to snap her helmet, so I stepped around the stroller and Jace and went to help her.

We spent the rest of the morning in the driveway, riding various bikes and scooters, playing catch and laughing. It was the most relaxing morning we'd had in a very long time. And all the while the sound of the mower kept us company.

Eventually Ben moved to the back yard. He disappeared from sight, but we could hear him the whole time. The sound was shockingly comforting. After being on my own for six months, I was pretty confident I would never get the hang of it. There were just too many things to do, too many responsibilities to juggle.

Ben stepped in when I desperately needed help and that meant more to me than I could share with him. I wondered where all of this gratitude was coming from. I'd never felt like this when the college kid mowed our yard...

But then again, he had done that for money. Ben did this because he genuinely wanted to help us. There was a difference.

"Hungy!" Jace tugged on my jeans and grinned up at me with a dirt-smeared face.

I reached down to rub at his chubby cheeks. "You're hungry?" He lifted his arms and jiggled his wrists. I swung him up into my hold and held him tightly against my chest. "Did you start snacking on the flower beds? You're filthy."

"He fell out of the stroller," Lucy offered matter-of-factly.

"He fell out? Or he got pushed out?"

She tried not to smile. "It was an accident!"

"Sure it was." But since Jace wasn't in tears, I didn't give her too hard of a time. Four-year-olds probably shouldn't be put in charge of strollers anyway.

"I'm hungry too!" Lucy tugged on my arm. "Starving actually!"

"Oh, boy. We can't have that. Put your toys away and we'll go inside for some peanut butter and jellies!"

Lucy ran off screaming her enthusiasm for peanut butter while I called to the other kids and threatened them until they finally started picking up.

I hadn't noticed the mower shut off until Ben rounded the corner to the house, pushing the now silent machine. He didn't look sweaty or fatigued, but I still hurried into the garage to grab a bottle of water for him. It was the least I could do.

When I turned around, he was standing right there and I nearly screamed again.

"You've got to stop that! You're like a ninja!" Jace squealed in my ear and tugged on my ponytail. That might have been the reason I didn't hear Ben's approach.

Ben grinned at me and eyed the water bottle, "Is that for me?"

I thrust it out to him. "I thought you might be thirsty."

"Thank you."

"No, thank you. Seriously. You saved me such a headache."

He stared at me intently while he unscrewed the cap and took a healthy drink. I looked away, pretending to supervise the kids as they brought their toys into the garage. I could feel him watching me though and I wanted to squirm.

I didn't know why it bothered me so much, but I was completely unnerved by him. Maybe it was because he was so completely male. He seemed to radiate with virility. His tanned legs were nothing but toned muscle behind athletic shorts and his forearms were just as cut and golden brown. His dark hair had been pushed back from his face and gave him this completely ruffled, reckless look. His cheeks had darkened from the sun and exertion and his full lips were now wet from the water.

He was unfairly gorgeous.

And that bothered me. I would have much preferred our new neighbor to be some stodgy old man that yelled at us to keep off his lawn.

Ben Tyler was the kind of beautiful that people openly stared at. And I didn't want to be one of those people.

I didn't think I was at risk of sending him the wrong signals, what with the dead husband and four children and all. But I didn't want to act like a swooning teenager around him either.

I wasn't usually intimidated by good looks. I didn't know why I had to start now with him.

"Is there anything else I can do?" he asked after long moments of awkward silence.

My focus swung back to him. "What do you mean?"

"Around the house?"

"Around the house?" I repeated dumbly. "No, thanks. We're, um, the mowing was great, thank you. But I can't ask anymore of you."

Dark eyebrows drew down over equally dark eyes and his usually-playful lips pressed into a frown. "You didn't ask. I offered."

"No, I know. I just… We're headed in to eat some lunch. So, thanks anyway. Seriously, thank you. You saved me from a hectic day."

"You already said that." His mouth had reformed into that arrogant twist I couldn't stand.

"Well, I mean it," I snapped and then hated my tone. "I mean, thanks, Ben. Thank you."

He chuckled at my flustered behavior. "Not used to accepting help?"

Not from perfect strangers that keep butting into my life when they should just stay out. "One of my many flaws." I flashed him a winning smile and herded the children towards the door. "We'll see you later."

"Have a good rest of the day, Liz," he called after me. "And don't forget my offer for the p-"

"Shh!" I spun around and held up a hand pleading for him to stop. "I remember, just…" I gestured at the little kids huddled around me. Blake had been mature enough to let the pool promise go, the rest of the kids would not be so forgetful. I wouldn't hear the end of it for days. "I'm waiting until my sister has a day off. Then you can count on us knocking on your door."

His eyes practically twinkled with amusement. "Emma, right?"

"Right."

He put two fingers to his forehead and gave a little salute. "Have a good rest of the day, Neighbor."

"You too… Neighbor."

I didn't wait for him to leave; I spun around and practically shoved my kids through the kitchen door that connected to the garage. I dropped Jace, careful to set him on his feet and then slammed the door behind me. I fell back against it and let out a long breath.

Ben Tyler was best taken in small doses. I hated the way he could unsettle me so completely without seeming to try or do anything other than talk to me. And everything about our interactions was so painfully awkward.

I doubted he would repeat his offer to mow the yard after that disaster. And that was okay with me. I didn't need him filling in for Grady. I didn't even need him to be a friend. I just needed not to be weird around him for once. And to run into him as little as possible.

God, I wished Grady was around to deal with him. Grady was so good with people; he would have easily made Ben feel welcome. And Ben seemed like the kind of guy Grady would have enjoyed being around.

Just one more reason to miss my husband.

The sadness and despair that came with that thought dumped on top of me as if I were standing underneath a waterfall of it. My knees buckled and I nearly collapsed.

"Mom, when are you going to make lunch?" Abby called from across the kitchen.

I forced my eyes open and pushed the tears back. I didn't have time to meltdown right now. These sandwiches weren't going to make themselves. "Right now. I'm going to start making it right now."

Chapter Six

The next day, Sunday, I had abandoned more plans to get fully showered and dressed and decided to focus on the inside of the house. I'd put on running shorts, an old t-shirt and threw my hair up into a ponytail. The kids and I had turned the radio station to oldies after breakfast and attacked the dishes. Well, I attacked the dishes; they danced around my legs and generally ran wild. Except for Blake, who had pulled out a tablet and sat quietly playing games. He watched the chaos in the kitchen with mild terror.

When the doorbell rang, all of us were stunned. I looked at the kids like they might know who would show up on a Sunday. They were just as clueless as me.

I dried my hands on a dish towel on the way to the door and prayed it wasn't a vacuum salesman. I had no patience for a hard sell right now.

Through the cloudy glass panes, I saw that it was, in fact, worse than a vacuum salesman. It was my mother-in-law.

And brother-in-law.

Great.

I shoved my long bangs back from my eyes and opened the door to meet the steely gray eyes of Katherine Carlson.

Shouts of "Nana!" could be heard as the rumor that grandma was here passed through the kitchen and before I could even greet this woman, my children had pounced on her.

She bent low to scoop them all up in one giant hug. They buried their little faces in her neck and she closed her eyes, relishing the moment.

It was an odd picture for me. Since the first time I met her, Katherine had been an intimidating figure in my life. She was rarely anything but serious and loved her two children fiercely, so fiercely that at times it felt like I had disappointed her expectations for her oldest son's spouse. Until Grady became sick, I had never seen her show any kind of emotion, good or bad. She was as stoic as they came.

Except with the children.

With them, she transformed into this very sweet woman that wore her affection on her sleeve. She had been that way with Grady too. She loved him deeply. His death had shattered her as profoundly as it had me.

She had already buried her husband. Grady's dad passed away while Grady was in high school, the victim of a drunken driving incident. And now her oldest boy. This woman was a pillar of strength and control, but I couldn't get past her icy demeanor long enough to form a real relationship with her.

At first, I had thought Grady's death would bring the two of us closer together. We loved him the most in the entire world. Surely, we could bond over our mutual loss. But if anything, she'd pulled back even more.

And so we tolerated each other for the sake of the children, but that was it. If Grady and I hadn't had children, I was positive Katherine and I would have parted ways permanently following the funeral.

The sight of her this morning did nothing but stress me out. Why hadn't she at least called first to let us know she planned to stop by?

"Hi, Katherine," I smiled down at her. "I wish you would have called first. My house is a mess right now."

Her cool gaze floated over my disheveled living room and staircase piled with stacks of things that needed to be taken upstairs. "Don't worry about that. We just wanted to stop by and see the kids." She stood back up and moved into the house.

"Hi, Trevor," I greeted Grady's younger brother who clearly resembled his mother's side of the family. His hair shone a honey brown and his eyes a somber blue. Grady was the spitting image of his late father from what I could tell from pictures. Trevor hadn't inherited any of the red hair or freckles. But his face still reminded me of Grady. They made similar expressions and they both had this draw to them, this aura of something real and genuine. People had always been attracted to Grady. Trevor had that same charisma about him.

Only he was unforgivably less mature than Grady. He was twenty-nine now, without a serious girlfriend or kids. This apparently set him back light years from where Grady and I had been when we were that same age.

"Hey, Lizzy." He patted my cheek as he walked by and I tried not to shatter. Grady called me Lizzy and Trevor picked the nickname up from him. It nearly killed me to hear that endearment from someone so much like Grady but I didn't have the strength to correct him.

I closed the front door and leaned against it. Katherine and Trevor followed the kids into the kitchen, but I couldn't find the motivation. Since these people showed up three minutes ago, my emotions hadn't stopped picking up speed. I felt wild. Out of control. I felt the fragile threads that held my sanity together pull and tear.

There had been progress last week. I had thought maybe I was finally pulling myself together. But just a few minutes with these people had undone every bit of headway.

"Mommy, I'm thirsty!" Lucy called from the kitchen.

I closed my eyes and let a lonely tear slip. Brushing it away, I squared my shoulders and pushed the rest of my emotion back. They wouldn't stay forever. I could survive this.

I joined the rest of the family in the kitchen and went to work getting drinks for everyone. Katherine sat at the small art table with the kids that I kept near the paneled windows. Trevor slid onto a bar stool and looked down at his hands.

His hair was tidier than usual and he wore something besides a t-shirt. The polo look was new for him. But so were the wrinkles around his eyes and the bags underneath them.

His pain hit me hard, like a punch in the gut. I loved Trevor like a brother, and he had lost someone he loved too. Unlike his mother, I could bridge the gap between us with shared grief.

Grady was my life, but he was also the sun that shone in his brother's life. Grady had been the one to pull Trevor out of trouble and stand up for him whenever someone doubted Trevor's worth. Grady had been Trevor's constant champion. He had believed in his little brother like no one else could or would.

He had believed in Trevor so much, that in his will, he had left Trevor his construction company.

Despite my concerns.

Despite my objections.

I received a paycheck from Trevor as if I were a partner, but Carlson Custom Construction was now Trevor's sole and permanent responsibility.

"How's business?" I asked while handing him a glass of iced tea.

He took it without looking at me. "Fine," he mumbled. "It's fine."

A sick nervousness fizzled through me. It wasn't just that I depended on the business doing well to feed my kids, but this company was Grady's baby. If Trevor allowed this business to fail, I would never forgive him.

I opened my mouth to ask him what exactly "fine" meant, but he spoke before I could get the words out. "I don't know how he did it, Lizzy." He finally lifted his dark blue eyes to meet mine. I sucked in a breath and forced myself not to look away. The lost look in his expression hurt my heart. My chin trembled and I started crying before I could talk myself out of it.

"Don't know how he did what, Trev?"

Tears shone in his eyes, causing them to brighten. "I don't know how he balanced everything. I don't know how he knew what was the right decision to make all of the time and which projects to take or not take. It's too much."

Trevor had worked for Grady since he graduated from high school and Grady had always treated him like his second in command. When Grady got sick and couldn't manage the day-to-day business or even when he got really sick and stopped being a part of the company completely, Trevor had stepped in and managed everything.

When Grady was alive, Trevor hadn't had a problem coping with the responsibility.

But in the last few months, I had watched Trevor's downward spiral and I knew the company suffered because of it. I hoped that this was just grief inhibiting him from being a smart businessman, but it could also be his lack of leadership abilities and his poor insight.

Grady had a natural knack for running a successful business. By now, I was fully convinced that Trevor hadn't inherited any of it.

There was a very real possibility that Trevor was going to run my husband's legacy into the ground.

I stepped up to the counter and wiped the tears away with the heels of my hand. I leaned on my elbows so I could look him in the eyes and he could see how serious I was.

"Yes, you do, Trev. You know exactly how he did it and what you need to do too. You worked at his side for a decade."

"Lizzy, it's-"

"Trevor, listen to me. Maybe the truth is, you don't know what *you* should do. Could that be it?"

He broke my gaze and ran his hands over his face. "Yeah, maybe."

"But you know what Grady would do. Just do that. Until you figure it out for yourself, just do what Grady would do."

He continued to rub the back of his hand over his mouth but some of the desolation in his somber   expression ebbed away. "Okay, yeah. I can do that. I could maybe do that."

I stood back up and tried to relax. Panic mingled with frustration and heavy doses of heartache swirled through me. I wanted my husband's business to succeed. I needed it to. I needed something of Grady's to live on, even while he didn't. But I was helpless. The business was Trevor's and I would do an even worse job than he ever could. It wasn't even an option for me to consider running the business.

Grady had left me with my hands tied behind my back. I couldn't do anything except watch Trevor crash and burn. I couldn't even give him worthwhile advice because I didn't know anything about construction!

If only Grady were here. He could fix this mess.

No, that's not true. He would never have let us get to this point. He wouldn't have needed to fix anything.

"It'll be okay, Liz. I'll figure it out."

"Grady left you in charge because he believed in you, Trevor. Of course, you'll figure it out." Katherine's voice cut through the kitchen like a knife. Her words seemed to rally her son, but they had the opposite effect on me.

"Can I get you something to drink, Katherine?" I forced the conversation to move on. I didn't want to talk about the failing business anymore. I wanted to pretend it wasn't a problem or I had a feeling I would not make it through a pleasant visit with my in-laws.

"No, thank you." She stood up from the kid table and walked over to the island. "The kids look good, Liz. Healthy."

She made it sound like there was a possibility they might not look good or healthy. "Thanks."

"Have the... how are they... are they still adjusting?"

I took a step back, surprised by her question. It was just so... so uncalled for. I glanced around at the kids to see if they understood what she meant. By the way Blake refused to look at me and his cheeks heated to a rosy red, I knew he got her meaning.

I swallowed down resentment and frustration and managed to clip out a response. "They're doing okay, Katherine. Thank you for asking."

"I know how hard it is for them, Liz. I had two young men when Thomas passed. They don't always know how to manage grief when they're this young. They can lash out or misbehave while they try to come to grips with their world changing."

My thoughts immediately flashed to Abby and her behavior lately. I knew that was why she misbehaved and acted out, but I didn't feel like sharing that with Katherine. This was just one more thing we should have managed to bond over, but couldn't seem to move past our personality differences.

Trevor saved me from trying to come up with a response, "Aw, Mom, we weren't so bad!"

She gave him an indulgent smile. "You, Trevor William, were the worst. And your niece is turning out just like you. I'm worried for her mother." She set her hand on Abby's head affectionately and every one of her features softened.

"Who, me?" Abby asked with a sly smile.

"Yes, you. Your Uncle Trevor is nothing but trouble. I'd stay away from him if I were you."

"No way!" Abby squealed and then attacked her uncle. The little kids followed suit and soon Trevor had all four kids hanging off his arms and legs. He made monster sounds and dragged them into the living room where they could wrestle.

There was a lot about Trevor that frustrated me, but I couldn't deny that he was a good uncle. The kids loved him. And he managed to wear out some of their constant energy.

"He misses Grady so much," Katherine said softly after they'd disappeared from our sight.

I kept my eyes focused on the doorway when I said, "Me too."

A cold hand landed on my bare forearm. "It will get easier."

I tried to give her a confident smile, but it wobbled. The truth was I didn't want it to get better. I didn't want to stop missing Grady. I didn't want this pain to recede because that would mean I would be over this. Over him.

And I never wanted to be.

He was the great love of my life and I was terrified to forget one small detail about him. Even now the touch of his rough hands and the sweet scent of his skin were only sensory memories. I couldn't capture those intangible things in pictures or on video.

And that *terrified* me.

Noticing my struggle not to lose it, Katherine lowered her voice. "It will, Liz. You'll learn to breathe again. You'll learn to live again."

The tears started falling, but she didn't offer a hug or more encouraging words. She'd said enough. And I was still trying to decide if she'd helped or hurt me more. I wiped them away again, thankful that I hadn't bothered with makeup this morning.

"I'd like to have the kids for a sleepover next weekend if that works for you? I was thinking I could pick up Jace and Lucy from your house before school gets out and then we'd swing over and grab the older kids before we went back to my house. Trevor is going to stay with me to help manage them."

"They would love that, Katherine."

She smiled at me. "Good. You can have a bit of a break and I get to spoil them rotten."

I found myself smiling too. This was the easiest it had been between us in as long as I could remember. The sounds of squealing children and roaring filled the house.

"Would you like help with lunch?"

I listened to the kids for another moment and thought of Ben's accusing words. Maybe he was right. Maybe I did have a hard time accepting help.

"I'd love some. Thank you."

Chapter Seven

By the time Wednesday rolled around, whatever good vibes I'd been feeling over the weekend had been smashed to smithereens. Every morning had been a battle to get the kids out the door and into the car before school started.

We ran out of milk in the middle of breakfast Monday morning and everything went downhill after that. I forgot Blake's first soccer practice Monday night and he came home from school on Tuesday completely devastated because he was the only one of his friends not there. I hadn't gotten along with Abby in days. She'd been unmanageable, disobedient and just difficult. Jace, well Jace was two. So he was always a challenge.

And Lucy had taken everything green from her room and lugged it down to the basement earlier this evening.

Her behavior hurt the most. I realized the purging of everything green was my fault. I hadn't meant to scar her little life so drastically. I had been angry and upset and I had included my four-year-old daughter in something I should have been protecting her from.

But my partner was gone. The man that I was supposed to run to when I needed advice, encouragement and support. The man that was supposed to listen to me when I needed to talk, when I just needed to get words out of my chest. The man that was supposed to tug me against his chest and promise that everything would be okay. That I would be okay.

He was gone.

He'd left me.

And I didn't know what to do now.

I made bad decisions. I yelled at my children more than I should. I forgot *everything*. And I couldn't seem to help this family get back to center.

Before bed, I'd set the kids up with a movie on my bed and taken Lucy to her bedroom alone so we could chat. I sat her down on her bed with everything she'd taken down to the basement on the floor in front of us, and I'd explained why the color green disturbed me so much right now.

I told her that it reminded me of her daddy, and his gorgeous green eyes. I told her how much I loved his eyes and how much I loved him. I told her that when I saw that color, I couldn't help but think of him and when I thought of him, I *missed* him. I told her how hard it was for me to miss him and that I wished he hadn't left us.

I told her that I didn't hate the color green after all, but that I loved it. I told her it was my most favorite color of all. I reminded her that her eyes were also green, just like her daddy's and that I loved looking at them too. I promised her that green wouldn't make me sad anymore, because it would help me remember how much I loved Daddy and how much he loved his family, how much he loved her.

We hugged each other for a very long time, while she told me how much she missed him too. We spent time together putting each item back in its place and picking up her room. She had needed alone time with her mother and I had needed to work through that with her.

By the time I tucked the kids into bed and kissed them all, Lucy felt better but I had never missed Grady more. I ached with my grief. I felt it in my bones. I couldn't think from the weight of it.

Everything reminded me of him. *Everything*. The house. The furniture. My room. My bed. My kids. My *own skin*. I couldn't escape this pain. And even though I didn't want to, not really... I needed a break. I needed just a small reprieve from the endless pressure of it.

So I'd waited for the kids to fall asleep, then grabbed the baby monitor and made sure the front of the house was locked up. I slipped out the back patio door and breathed in the warm night.

Grady had built a fire pit in the back yard and set some Adirondack chairs around it. He and I had never spent much time back here alone, which was why I chose this place tonight. I needed to escape his memory for a little while and this was the only place I could think of without abandoning the kids completely.

With four kids, we had always been too exhausted after the chaos of bedtime to trek out here when they finally fell asleep. We'd spent our nights cuddled on the couch watching our favorite sitcoms. Or if he had work to do, I would read next to him while he tapped away at his laptop. We always meant to come out here, but it never happened.

I relaxed into the chair and stared out at the dark backyard. A floodlight had clicked on when I first came out here, but it didn't offer light beyond the edge of our property. No houses stood behind us to bounce back any light. Beyond our fence sat a nature preserve of thin forest with gangly trees and the tiniest creek. The land grew wild for a few miles, keeping builders from purchasing the land and turning it into something habitable.

I had loved that about this neighborhood when we decided to build here, but now it felt lonely. I wanted activity to watch and fill my thoughts. I wanted to spy on my neighbors so I could occupy my head with assumptions about their lives and forget about my own.

The landscaping lights to Ben's backyard clicked on and I heard his sliding glass door swish open before his tall figure appeared in the frame.

"Liz!" Ben's voice boomed through the quiet night and my spiraling thoughts.

"Hi, Ben." I cursed the floodlight for destroying any hopes of invisibility. He probably wanted to go for a swim, but now felt awkward about it. My yard was at a significant slope. The part closer to the house was higher than his and that gave me a great view into his backyard, even though there was a fence.

"I didn't want to scare you again," he grinned at me. "I thought I should give you some warning."

"Thank you," I tried to laugh. It fell flat.

"Want some company?"

I could honestly say that was the very last thing I expected him to say. But how to decline politely? I *didn't* want company. I didn't even know why he offered.

"I have wine!"

Well, that changed things. "Alright," I conceded. "Bring the wine!"

He disappeared into the house and I had two minutes to severely regret my decision. I didn't want to spend my peaceful evening sharing wine with my weird next door neighbor! I didn't even want to spend tonight with myself.

I had come out here for escape. And now this...

This didn't feel like escape.

This felt like punishment for my reluctance to be nice to the guy.

Yet... I had been wishing for a glass of wine. Desperately.

Damn, why was I such a lush?

I heard the gate open and the crunch of his feet as he padded his way over. He paused when he reached me, looming tall and dark, waiting for me to acknowledge him.

I looked up to his smiling face and felt myself relax just a bit. I didn't understand my reaction. He usually made me so uncomfortable that my rudeness was unforgivable. But tonight, he felt like relief. He felt like... a breath of fresh air.

Maybe I had been more afraid to spend time with the thoughts in my head than the harmless man that lived next door to me.

He held out a stemmed glass. The floodlight glinted off the shiny surface. I twirled the glass in my fingers while Ben pulled a corkscrew from his pocket and went to work opening the bottle. The glug-glug-glug of wine pouring into my glass was the only sound that broke our silence.

Eventually he pulled the bottle back, after a very generous pour, filled his own glass and slid gracefully into the seat next to me. His long legs extended in front of him and he draped his arms over the chair as though he'd sat here hundreds of times before.

I gave him a double take before I allowed this reality of him to set in. He was the cool kid in school, the cool kid wherever he went. He had the natural ability to feel at home wherever he was. I could see that about him. And now the arrogant grin made sense.

"Thanks for the wine," I finally broke the quiet that he didn't seem in any hurry to end.

He looked over at me and smiled. "You looked like you could use some company."

"Yeah, I guess. Mostly I just needed the wine." I grinned back at him and took a sip of a very nice red. I didn't know what it was and it was too dark to read the label from this distance, but Ben had great taste in libations.

"The cupboards are bare?"

I shook my head and laughed lightly. "Have you ever taken four kids into a liquor store?"

"I cannot say that I have. But I could only imagine the stress for all parties involved."

"Exactly. Luckily my new neighbor is very generous." I took another sip and settled back into the comfortable chair.

"Luckily."

We sat in comfortable silence for a few more minutes before I couldn't stand it anymore. I wasn't very good at sitting contemplatively, especially when there was another person around. I needed to fill the space between us. I needed to put something in the air and add to the peaceful evening.

"So what do you do, Ben? I don't know anything about you other than you have good taste in houses, great taste in wine and you eat Pop-Tarts for breakfast."

"Not every morning!" His foot slid over and kicked me playfully. I pulled my legs back and tucked them underneath me so he couldn't do that again. If he noticed, it didn't seem to bother him. "You caught me on a bad morning."

"Sure, I did."

He chuckled. "Those were the early days. It was either Pop-Tarts or cold pizza. Your child needed luring. I thought I would fare better with the toasted breakfast pastries."

I turned to face him and let myself be humbled by his confession. "Thank you for that, by the way. I don't think I ever truly thanked you for baiting her from the pool. We could have been in there all morning."

"She's *fast*."

It was my turn to chuckle. "She's now on a swim team. I decided to use her powers for good."

"She's like five? They make swim teams for five year olds?"

"She's six. And she's a little young, but one of the high school teams helps run a youth league. They let her try out. They were thrilled to see what a freaky little fish she is in the water."

"Huh." Ben crossed his feet at his ankles and stared down at his wine. He seemed to be chewing over my words with some degree of thoughtfulness, but I couldn't figure out what I said to make him think so hard. Finally, after I'd gone back to enjoying my wine and watching the soft sway of leaves float on the long, bent branches, he said, "That was a good mom thing to do."

"What was?" I had lost him.

"Putting her on a swim team. If that had been me when I was her age, my mom would have threatened my life if I ever tried it again. You gave her an outlet to use a talent that she obviously excels at. I think that's great."

Whatever easy response I wanted to give him stuck in my chest. The compliment, even though it felt out of nowhere, meant more to me than I could ever tell him. I hadn't heard something positive about my parenting since Grady died.

There was no one around to tell me I was a good mom. When my parents called, we had a lot to talk about, but never that. And when I was forced to interact with Katherine, I tried to speak as few words as possible.

I would never have expected this much-needed encouragement to come from Ben Tyler.

"Thank you," I whispered, struggling to hide my emotions.

"Lawyer," he blurted suddenly.

"Hmm?"

"Lawyer," he repeated. "You asked what I do… I'm a lawyer."

"Wow." That would explain how he could afford the house next to me. "Impressive."

"Not really." The deprecating tone he used didn't seem to fit. "It's my father's firm. I'm really just inheriting the practice."

"You sound super enthusiastic about that." The wine buzzed in my head. I hadn't had something to drink in a long time. Since the night after Grady's funeral, I realized. My parents flew in and stayed with me for a couple weeks to help with the kids. Emma had brought over a bottle of tequila and we decided to drink instead of cry.

We'd ended up doing both.

He grunted. "I am."

I turned to face him, sliding my knees toward my chest and making myself very comfortable in the slatted chair. I probably wouldn't have been as relaxed around him without the wine, but now I was curious. I couldn't help but meddle.

"No, really! What's with the attitude?"

"Attitude?" He swiveled in his chair so he could face me too.

I rolled my eyes. "Come on, I'm a mom! I can hear attitude a mile away."

The floodlight revealed a small smile playing on his lips. "Ack! Fine. I'll share my deepest, darkest secrets."

I laughed again, "You hate your day job. That's hardly a secret."

"From the woman that stays home all day. You basically live a life of leisure."

My mouth dropped open. I could not believe he just said that! "I can't believe you just said that!"

He tossed his head back and laughed. "I'm kidding," he promised. "And besides, you started it!"

"Oh, my god. You're as bad as my children."

"No, not that bad! I have wine, remember?"

"Yeah, yeah, yeah. Now spill your guts, Tyler. I have to go to bed soon." I ignored the flush of disappointment I felt for needing to end our evening. I really did have to get to bed. I just didn't expect to enjoy Ben this much.

"Do you know that I rarely get to court? Most of my job entails paperwork and settlements. I imagined something more... *Law and Order* when I signed up."

"Hmm." I looked down at the little bit of wine left in my glass. I swirled it around and bit back my objection. Ben's words sounded like deflection and not even a little bit like truth. But I would let this go for now. We barely knew each other. It wasn't my place to dig around in his life.

"We should do this again."

I looked up at his suggestion and didn't know what to say. "Sure. We should do this again... sometime."

"It will have to be tomorrow night."

I laughed, surprised by his enthusiasm. "Why's that?"

"I have a date Friday."

"Oooh, a date. Who is the lucky lady?"

"Friend of a friend. It's only the second date."

"So you're nervous? I mean, obviously." I plopped my chin into my hand and got a little more comfortable.

He shook his head at me like he couldn't quite figure me out. "Why would I be nervous?"

"Because you want to impress her!"

"Why wouldn't she be impressed with me?"

What a guy thing to say. "I honestly have no idea."

He smiled at my sarcastic tone. "Should I be nervous?"

"Just don't offer her Pop-Tarts."

"Noted."

We sat there for a few more minutes while I finished my wine. The quiet became easy and not forced.

I didn't know if it was the wine or Ben, but I finally felt more contented with myself. Some of the racing of my mind and spirit settled and my lungs took easier breaths and my heart beat easier beats.

I had dreaded Ben coming over here, but now that the night was over, I was glad that he had.

"Thanks for the wine, Ben. I enjoyed our little chat."

"Hey, me too."

We both stood up and I walked him to the gate. He paused to say goodbye and I awkwardly shoved the wineglass toward him. "Or should I keep it and wash it?" I regretted the question as soon as I asked it. Why did I have to make a big deal out of a stupid glass? I shouldn't have said anything.

"No, it's fine. I'll take it."

"Thanks again."

"Sure." He hesitated a little bit longer and I started to lose whatever peace I'd gained. "So, tomorrow night, then?"

"Tomorrow night?"

"For wine. I thought… I thought you wanted to do this again?"

"Oh, I didn't-"

"I just thought because the bottle was already opened and that way we could finish it. If you already have plans-"

"Ben, stop!" I held up my hand and laughed at the ridiculous turn our conversation had taken. "Tomorrow night is great. I'll be here. Bring the wine! I'll provide the glasses next time."

His easy smile returned. "It's about time you started pulling your weight around here."

I stared at him in wonder. Was I really considering this? "Same time, same place, yeah?"

"Yeah."

We finally parted ways. It wasn't until I stepped inside my house that I realized I was smiling. I locked up and made my way to bed, thinking about Ben the entire way.

He really was adorable. I had probably judged him unfairly at first.

And that grin of his.

He was too good looking for his own good.

And single!

Sure, he had that date on Friday, but a second date wasn't even exclusive territory yet.

There was obviously only one thing left to do: Set him up with my sister.

Chapter Eight

"I brought booze!" Emma called from the front door.

"How was study group?" I leaned over the kitchen island to catch a glimpse of my sister as she slammed the front door behind her.

"Long," she sighed. "I didn't think it would ever end! It's Friday night. Don't these people have anything better to do with their lives?"

I pulled the hummus from the refrigerator and finished setting up our dinner as Em swept into the kitchen in all her wild hair, grad-student, bohemian glory. She plopped two bottles of cheap Sangria on the countertop and flashed me a brilliant smile.

"That's a hangover in a bottle."

"When did you become such a snob?" She stuck her tongue out at me and went about retrieving two wine glasses from the dish drainer.

Since Ben Tyler introduced me to all of his fabulous wine. I kept that thought a secret. I didn't feel comfortable telling Emma about the last two nights or how Ben and I had started a friendship built on late night conversations and good grapes.

It felt wrong to say those words out loud. I couldn't help but feel guilty for spending time with him.

During my entire marriage I had kept my distance from the opposite sex. I had never been tempted to be anything less than faithful to Grady and I had never wanted to give off the wrong impression.

It seemed a little strange that over the past ten years, I had never been alone with another man for long periods of time. Unless it was Trevor, but he didn't count.

It felt awkward to admit my new friendship with Ben to my sister.

No, that was wrong. I didn't feel awkward... I felt guilty.

This friendship felt like a betrayal to Grady.

Nausea washed over me and I tried to ignore the disappointment that fizzed in my stomach. Disappointment because I'd let Grady down.

And disappointment because I would have to give up Ben and his good wine.

It shouldn't be hard though. We'd spent two nights chatting; there wasn't a whole lot of foundation there.

"Liz!" Emma shouted and I jerked back to the present. "Are you okay?"

I looked up and met her stormy blue eyes. I smiled weakly and tried to reassure her with a confident expression. "I'm fine. Just thinking."

"About Grady?"

Actually, for the first time in a long time, it was not about Grady. And that was more reason to end whatever this was with Ben.

Not that it was anything.

God, why did I keep doing that?

"Should we eat?" I knew that was a deflection, but I also knew my psych-major sister would allow it.

"Yes, I'm starving!" she groaned.

We settled in around the island and dug into the random appetizers I'd set out. Our mother had never been a very good cook, so Emma and I had learned to pick at food, rather than sitting down to full meals. With my own children, I tried to be better about serving complete dinners. But when Em and I got together we fell back into the routine of our childhood.

"Me too." I loaded up my plate with hummus, crackers, jarred bruschetta and some bread. I took a sip of the sugary sangria and decided I wasn't that much of a snob.

"So Katherine took all of the kiddos?"

I nodded around a bite. "She picked up Luce and Jace right after naptime. She plans to keep them through lunch tomorrow."

"That's nice of her."

"The kids were really excited."

"It's kind of weird though, isn't it? I mean, it's so quiet here."

"Yes! I could not wait to have the night off, but now that they're gone, I can't stop missing them! There's something wrong with me."

Emma laughed and shook out her hair. "There is nothing wrong with you, Elizabeth. You're just addicted to children. Okay… maybe that's not exactly normal. But I'm sure with a little therapy and maybe we can get you some Xanax and-"

"Okay, stop! You big brat." I gave her a dirty look and tried not to smile. "We just haven't been apart very much over the last few months. I'm not used to having the house to myself."

"Well, we'd better make the most of it!" Her blue eyes twinkled with the possibilities. "Should we turn on some rap music and dance around in our underwear? Or ooh! We could pop some popcorn and watch terrible TV that you would never turn on when your children are home!"

"Wow, Em, your ideas are truly inspired."

She did not appreciate my sarcasm. "Alright, sister dearest, what's your brilliant plan for the evening?"

A thought struck me. "Let's go swimming!"

"Swimming?"

"My new neighbor has a heated pool! And he said I could use it whenever I wanted."

"*The* new neighbor?" Her eyebrows rose with interest. "The hot new neighbor?"

"Ben," I offered.

Her interest died and she crinkled her nose. "Right, Ben. But won't it be weird if we just walk over there and jump in? What if he has people over?"

"He's not there. He has a date tonight."

"A date?" She shook her head slowly like she had trouble figuring this out. "How do you know so much about his social life?"

"I'm playing nice," I told her. The guilt swarmed again and I wondered if saying the words out loud would make it go away. Now it felt like I was hiding something illicit from her. Which was ridiculous. I needed to rip this Band-Aid off and face her judgment. "He helped me mow once and I've seen him a few times since then."

"Oh," she sounded honestly surprised. "That is nice of you."

"I can be nice."

She didn't say anything.

"So do you want to go swimming? You can borrow one of my suits."

"It's heated?"

"It is! I've already been in it once, remember?"

"Sure, sounds fun! We'll take our wine over there. Actually, it's starting to sound amazing."

By the time we finished picking at our dinner and put the leftovers away, we had finished the first bottle of sangria. We left the dishes and wandered upstairs to pick out swimming suits from my limited supply.

Emma wasn't impressed with my offerings, but she found one that she deemed "could work."

I slipped into my choice, a simple black two-piece, and couldn't help but feel extremely naked. I stared at my body in the bathroom mirror and wrapped my arms around my middle.

I hadn't been self-conscious about my image since high school. When I got to college I really grew into my own skin and decided to start loving who I was. Then I met Grady. If I had been okay with what I looked like before, his adoration for my body gave me a whole new sense of confidence.

Throughout our marriage, whatever insecurities I had never lasted long with his appreciative gaze and sweet, whispered words. He made me feel beautiful. He built up a confidence in me that I had hoped was unshakeable.

I didn't want to be the kind of girl that found her value in other people's words, and I didn't think I was. But his constant reminding had made it easy.

I still had the same body; in fact, I was much more toned now than I had been in my marriage. I had been soft from happiness and four pregnancies. I hadn't been fat, just soft.

Now, after months of running, my muscles were toned and my stomach had some definition. And yet, staring at myself in the mirror, I missed the easy way Grady made me feel sexy. I missed the way he would stare at me as if he couldn't believe that I was real.

I could hold those memories close, but they could never do for me what his actual presence did.

"You look hot! Let's go!" Emma smacked my booty, pulling me back to reality.

"I haven't been in a swimming suit in a while."

"I can tell." Emma circled her bikini area and I had a mild, embarrassing panic attack. But I was fine. Whew. She cackled at my expense and then tugged on my arm. "Come on, Sasquatch, it's just you and me."

We left the house wide open and carried our towels barefoot across the lawn. Ben's house stood completely dark and without signs of life. A twinge of nerves pinched inside of me that he might come home early. But I brushed it aside; he was the one that had extended the offer. After getting to know him the last two nights, I knew he wouldn't care.

We walked through his back gate and spent a little time searching for a light.

"All of the switches must be inside," I told Emma, finally giving up.

"Then I'm getting in! I'm freezing!" She walked to the side and slid in gracefully. I set my towel down on one of Ben's loungers and walked over to the edge. She popped out of the water and splashed warm water on my legs. "It's nice in here. Don't be a baby."

I dove into the deep end and felt the warm water wrap around my skin. My hair floated around my face and I felt weightless.

I came up for air and then dove under again. I closed my eyes and drank in the absolute darkness. I couldn't hear anything. I couldn't see anything. I didn't have any kids to worry about for the night. And I had actually had a good time with my sister. We hadn't spent the night weeping over my loss and the uncertain future. We'd just hung out and enjoyed each other.

Now submerged underwater, I drank in the isolation and let my heart seize with grief once again. It didn't seem fair that I kept living while Grady didn't. It didn't seem possible.

I kept waiting for Grady to come back. I kept waiting for him to walk in the door and wrap me in his arms and promise me that everything would be alright now. I couldn't let him go.

I didn't want to let him go.

Letting him go meant acknowledging that he would never come back. And I just couldn't. I needed him too much.

I loved him too much.

I kicked to the surface once again, desperate for air and escape. I couldn't sink into those thoughts again. I couldn't go there now or I would drown in them. The pool water felt especially poignant as I raced away from that dark place.

Emma reclined against the side and stretched out both of her arms to keep her body anchored. I swam in front of her and treaded water to stay afloat.

"This is really nice," she murmured her approval, tipping her head back and resting it against the patio. "We need to take Ben up on his offer more often."

"We can just hope he goes on a lot of dates."

She picked her head up and looked at me. "Does he go on lots of dates?"

"How would I know? I just know he's on one tonight."

"Girlfriend?"

"I don't think so. He said this was only their second."

"So he's still technically single?"

"I'm pretty sure."

"Big house for a single guy."

I laughed at my sister's not-so-subtle inquiry. "He's a lawyer."

"Oooh, single and stable. I like it."

"I'm glad he meets your standards."

"Have you seen him? He could be unemployed and live with his parents and he would meet my standards."

I splashed her in the face, "Please don't say that! You two would end up moving in with me and then I would have to take care of six children!"

"Liar. You would love having a live-in babysitter."

"Okay, that's true."

She grinned at me, but it faded some when she said, "You and Grady were poor in the beginning. You were still happy. It's not about money with me."

I cleared my throat and tried not to get overly emotional. "We were happy," I whispered. I shook off some of that sadness and smiled, "But you're more materialistic than me."

It was her turn to splash me in the face. "Am not!"

I pulled my arm back to splash her again when the patio lights blinked on and Emma and I were suddenly spotlighted in the middle of Ben's pool. The patio door slid open and he walked outside, speaking in low tones to a gorgeous brunette with inhumanly long legs.

Humiliated and feeling obnoxiously frumpy, I made a squeaky sound and plummeted beneath the surface. Then I felt silly for trying to hide in the pool, which was obviously impossible, so I swam to the side and resurfaced.

"Liz?" Ben sounded incredibly surprised to find us in his pool.

"Hey, Ben." My skin burned with embarrassment. "Sorry, we were, um, going for a dip."

"I can see that." The mild irritation in his tone could not be misinterpreted.

I swatted my sister's thigh to push her into action. She had been momentarily speechless and just as embarrassed as me. We swam for the ladder and pulled ourselves from the water.

There was just no subtle way to get out of the pool. I felt Ben's eyes on me the entire time and couldn't help but feel like a teenager caught red-handed. Emma and I moved to our towels quickly, neither of us making eye contact with Ben or his date.

"Liz, you don't have to go. You and your sister are welcome to stay and swim. We were just going to have a glass of wine. We can do that inside."

I whirled around and looked at Ben in his black pants and pressed blue dress shirt, holding a bottle of wine and two stemmed glasses. A wave of irritation rolled through me. I shook it off and forced myself to feel embarrassment again. "No, I'm so sorry. I didn't expect you to be home so early." It was his date's turn to blush. She took a step away from him and looked down at her pretty black stilettos. "I didn't mean to say that you shouldn't have come early. Or that you couldn't come home early. I just, what I meant to say, was that I expected your date to last longer." Oh, god. I slapped a hand over my eyes. "No, that's not what I meant either. Obviously, your date is still going on. I… I… I'm going to stop talking now."

"Probably for the best." I could hear the grin in Ben's voice so I refused to look at him.

"Hi, I'm Liz," I said to his date instead. She probably hated me by now, but I felt the need to explain my presence. Hopefully that would help Ben regain whatever footing I'd caused him to lose. "I live next door."

"Hi, Liz. I'm Megan." She reached out politely to take my hand. The towel hung awkwardly in front of me and when Megan took her hand away it was wet from mine.

"I'm Emma," my sister said brightly when she shook Megan's hand next.

"Hi, Emma," Ben greeted in his smooth tone.

"Hi, Ben," my sister giggled adding to my humiliation even more.

The four of us stood there rocking on our heels for another minute and the tension was painful. I finally met Ben's dark gaze and pressed my lips together to keep from cringing from the force of it. A slow smile spread across his full mouth and I knew I was forgiven, but I still felt bad about this small interruption to his date.

"Well, we'll get going!" I announced in a rush. "Ben, I'm so sorry! I should have thought ahead."

He shook off my apology with a jerk of his chin. "It's fine, Liz. I'm the one that offered my pool. Use it any time."

"Thanks." I started walking backwards. "Thank you." Emma moved with me. We were almost to the gate.

"I'll see you tomorrow night?" he called after me.

What? I might have panicked when I replied, "I can't tomorrow! We'll talk. I'll talk to you later." Then I turned around and basically fled for my house.

Emma hurried to keep up with me. "Oh, god," she groaned miserably. "That was so awkward!"

"I know!" I hissed. "I didn't expect him to bring her home with him!"

Emma threw her head back and laughed. "That's because you haven't been on a second date in like fifteen years!"

"It hasn't been fifteen years!" Only twelve. The difference between Ben Tyler and me punched me in the side and I lost my breath. He was on a second date and hoping to get lucky. I would never be in that position again. He was at the very beginning of his love life and I had watched mine wither and die. He was free to date whomever he wanted and I had buried the greatest love of my life.

I stumbled in the cool grass, nearly crippled by the weight of that realization. Emma was in the same place as Ben, but for some reason it had never bothered me when I thought about her dating life or future with a man.

Ben's differences stood out painfully from mine. He spotlighted the finality of my husband's death and the depressing loneliness I had to look forward to from now on.

Ben would eventually find a girl, maybe Megan, fall in love, get married and go on to live in blissful matrimony.

From this moment on I would grieve Grady, there would never be anything else for me.

"Liz, what was Ben talking about? Why did he want to see you tomorrow night?"

I looked at my beautiful, young, carefree sister and desperately wished I could trade places with her for just a few hours. I closed my eyes against the agony of my grief for just a moment before I met her curious gaze. "No reason," I told her hoarsely. "Just neighbor stuff."

"Sure, neighbor stuff. Because that's a thing."

I didn't say anything and she didn't push me. Emma always knew when not to push me. We dried off and put on our regular clothes again. The rest of the night was spent drinking the second bottle of sangria and watching reality television.

And I tried not to think about Ben Tyler and the date that I nearly ruined.

Stage Two: Anger

Denial came first. Then anger.

I thought working through denial was the hardest thing I would ever do. *It had been crippling.* But the problem with coming to terms with something as heartbreaking as losing the love of my life is that now I had to live with it.

This is my reality.

This.

This is who I am. Grady's death made me this. A widow. A single mom. Heartbroken and lonely and frustrated and overwhelmed and *gutted*.

And more than everything else, angry.

I'm only thirty-two years old. I shouldn't have to go through this at thirty-two. I shouldn't have had to face Grady's illness or the horror of his treatment or the traumatizing experience of watching my husband fade away.

I shouldn't have to figure out how to raise four children on my own, without a partner, without the daddy they loved and looked up to. I shouldn't have to comfort my sons who lost their hero or my daughters who lost the man that they should compare all others to.

I shouldn't have to hurt like this. Weep like this. *Long* like this.

But I have no other choice and that made me *so very angry*.

While my heart and mind continue to work through my loss, life around me continues to go on. It moves without my permission. It propels me forward without my consent.

I need time to process everything, to work through these five stages and deal with each as they come. But that isn't possible.

Time doesn't stop and the days keep ending and beginning again and I move from denying that my husband isn't coming back to feeling absolutely furious that I will never see him again. Never be with him again. Never touch him or look at him or breathe him in.

I can't even be satisfied that I get to move beyond denial.

I am far too angry to care.

Chapter Nine

"Abby, hurry up! Your cereal is getting soggy!" I whirled around, armed with orange juice and a spoon for Lucy. There was a possibility we would be on time for school today.

"Mom, I have a game tonight, don't forget."

"Chuck!" Jace squealed. I pushed his toast back in front of him.

"Please don't forget," Blake pleaded.

I looked at my eldest son and felt pangs in my chest. When had he gotten so old? So mature? His burnished red hair needed a trim, but the tousled look suited him. His bright green eyes were sleepy still and I swear he had grown two inches in the last month. My heart ached watching him become a bigger kid and slowly turn into an adolescent.

"I'll remember," I promised him. "It's on the calendar."

He grunted into his cereal bowl. "I packed all of my stuff, so we can go right after school."

"Blake, the game isn't until 4:30."

"Well, buy us ice cream or something first. This one's important."

I felt a mixture of irritation and amusement. "I'm not going to buy you ice cream right before an important game. But it's probably a good idea to go straight from school. We'll think of something to do."

"Chuck!" Jace shouted.

Abby rushed into the kitchen like a tornado of energy and mischief. "This trash stinks!" She pinched her nose with two fingers and ambled over to the table.

"Chash Chuck!" Jace squealed.

A nagging feeling pulled low in my stomach. *Oh, no.*

"What day is it?" I asked out loud. The kids just looked at me. They had no idea.

The groaning, screeching of a garbage truck pulled up in front of our house. *Oh, no!* I jumped over to the trash can, grabbed it in its entirety and ran to the garage door. The trash can was ridiculously heavy, a stupid wooden thing that I'd wanted because it looked nice, could hold a hell of a lot of trash and the kids couldn't knock it over. I had to drag it down the stairs. By the time I opened the garage and lugged the thing to our already overflowing garbage bins, the truck was already pulling out of our circle.

"No!" I screamed. "No, no, no!"

I couldn't believe this had happened again! Anger bubbled up inside of me and hot tears threatened to spill. In my frustration I kicked at the monstrous outdoor trash can with my bare foot and then grew furious all over again when that crushed my toes.

I hopped around cursing the trash and the trash men and Grady for leaving me this horrific responsibility.

The trash had always been Grady's thing. As far as I was concerned, Grady might as well have been a magical fairy that made my full trash bags disappear and new ones reappear. Even when he was sick, he still managed to take care of the trash for me. I had done it sometimes if he had to stay in the hospital, but he had always reminded me when the trash needed to be moved to the curb.

Now he was gone and I had no one to help me with this monumental task. It seemed so silly that I couldn't remember this one thing. We had plenty of trash to keep my mind on it. I had to take the trash to the garage at least once a day, sometimes two. It was really amazing how much trash the five of us could accumulate.

But I couldn't remember. And it infuriated me.

I had forgotten last week too, so now both of our huge outdoor receptacles overflowed. The indoor trash can at my side mocked my efforts. How could we go another week with this much trash sitting around here?

Thankfully, at the beginning of November it was finally cold enough that I didn't have to worry about making the entire neighborhood smell. Just my house.

I kicked out at the trash can again, blind with my frustration. I had never felt rage like this before. I was usually a calm, rational person. But I couldn't stop this tide of fury from swelling. It rose high over my head and then crashed down on me with disconcerting strength.

"God, you're such an asshole!" I screamed at it. "I hate you!"

"Are you talking to me? Or the trash can?" A calm voice called me out of my darkness.

I looked up to find Ben Tyler watching me. He leaned against the garage frame casually in a very nice navy blue suit. I had never seen him dressed for work before. We must usually leave for work at different times every morning or I was too busy with kids to notice him.

His hair had been combed back, more professional than he usually wore it. His shoes were polished and his shirt was nicely pressed. He looked like a lawyer this morning. I thought this image of him might be difficult for me to reconcile with the usually laid-back version of him I experienced, but this morning, despite my trembling frustration, I found it easy to put this label on him. I could now picture him in a corner office, barking orders at a pretty secretary and charging ungodly amounts of money per hour for his time.

He really was a lawyer. And if clothes measured any kind of success, he was probably a good one.

"The trash can," I finally answered his question. "I hate it." That pointless admission made me realize how ridiculous I was acting. I pushed my hair out of my face and stared down at my feet. I realized for the first time how cold they were against the icy garage floor.

"I hate it too," he said seriously. "God, have you heard what an asshole it's been lately?"

I lifted my eyes to meet his dark ones. They twinkled at me, forgiving my crazy outburst. He should be judging me right now. I was acting insane. But instead, I saw only gentle understanding.

"I forgot to set the trash out," I confessed, although I was certain it was obvious. "And I forgot to set it out last week. I'm frustrated."

"I can see that." He walked forward until we were only a foot apart. "I haven't seen you around lately."

His topic change startled me. I found myself looking away again. It was true, we hadn't really seen much of each other since Emma and I had interrupted his date a few weeks ago. We had said hello in passing and I spoke to him briefly at the mailbox one time. But I had been trying to keep my distance.

Seeing him on a date with a young, beautiful woman made me realize how different we were. Friendship between us would never be more than awkward and complicated. I had decided that night that I didn't need any more complications. Ben Tyler and I were better kept at a distance.

"We've been really busy," I said softly. "The kids have had so much going on with school and their activities. I feel like I've been running nonstop for weeks."

"You should take a break then."

I put my hand to my forehead, "That's a nice thought. But it probably won't happen."

"There's no time for late night wine? There's *always* time for late night wine."

I smiled at his confidence. "How did your date go the other night?" If he could change the subject, so could I.

"Date?" His brow wrinkled with confusion.

"Megan?"

A surprised chuckle shook his shoulders. "Megan? Is that why you've been avoiding me? Liz, I told you the pool was yours, any time you wanted."

"I haven't been avoiding you! I told you we've been busy. Look! I can't even get the trash out on time. That's how busy we've been."

He gave me a frown that said he knew the trash had nothing to do with our schedule. "My date went fine. Even with party crashers ruining my game."

"I am sorry about that."

"And I am kidding, Liz. I swear. Megan and I didn't end up having all that much in common. We haven't been out since, but it had nothing to do with you and the pool."

"Oh." My mind spun a little with his words. "So are you dating someone else?"

His eyebrows dipped low, "No. I'm not seeing anyone."

"Then I should set you up!"

"Excuse me?" He looked startled. I hadn't meant to scare him.

I put some excitement into my tone, trying to sell the idea. "With my sister!"

If possible, he looked more surprised than ever. "Liz, I don't think that's a good idea."

"Why not?" I demanded. I thought about calling the doctor. My mood swings were slightly terrifying. I felt sorry for Ben. He always seemed to get the worst of me.

He sucked in an exasperated breath, "Well, don't you think that might be awkward? What if Emma realizes what a terrible person I am and tells you. You'll be stuck knowing all of my embarrassing habits."

"You're not a terrible person."

"How do you know?"

I smiled gently. "I know. Ben, we might not know each other well, but I know enough to see what a good person you are. I think you would really like Emma."

"Liz…"

"Please? Just one date?" I blinked at him with wide, hopeful eyes.

"What if she doesn't want to go on a date with me?"

I played with my hair in an attempt to hide my knowing smile. "That's always a possibility. But it doesn't hurt to ask."

"I guess not," he agreed.

"So is that a yes?"

He smiled slowly at me, "I suppose it is. I apparently cannot say no to you."

"This is a good thing, though. You'll love Em. I promise." He didn't say anything in return, so I felt like I had to continue to sell the idea. "I'll call her today and see what she thinks. I'm sure she'll be up for it. She loves it when I set her up." She hated it when I set her up. But I hoped she wouldn't mind a date with Ben. She had obviously found him attractive before.

He pulled out his cellphone from his pocket. "If you give me your number, I'll text you. Then you can pass my number along to your sister. If she's actually interested, she can text or call me."

"Sounds good!" I recited my cell number and watched him punch it into his phone. When he lifted his eyes to meet mine again, he wore a cautious smile. "You're going to have so much fun."

"I'm sure we will."

Uncomfortable with his intense gaze, I went back to wrestling the trash bag from the inside trash can.

"Here, let me," Ben cut in. His hands brushed over mine as he moved to take the bag from me.

"Oh, no, it's fine. You don't want to get your suit all dirty." I looked down at my workout leggings and plain black active long-sleeved T, clothes I used to hide all of the kid smudges and stains that happened all day long.

"Liz, seriously, this bag weighs more than you do. Go back to your kids."

"My kids!" I gasped. "I have to get them ready for school! We're going to be late again."

His expression turned amused again and he waved me off. "Go, Liz! I'll take care of this."

"You're a saint, Ben Tyler."

"Go!" He pointed toward the door, this time I obeyed.

I rushed back inside and went to work washing little hands and little faces, making sure hair was brushed and their outfits looked decent enough for school.

By the time we had backpacks and lunches together and had piled in the van, Ben was gone. I didn't pay attention to the trash because I had more important problems on my mind, like arriving at school in the next three minutes, but the garage seemed bigger for some reason.

It wasn't until later in the day that I realized why my garage had felt so much larger than usual.

I had been in and out of the garage all day with the little kids. Between dropping off and picking up Lucy from pre-school, grocery shopping and running some errands in town, I had never realized that the garbage cans were missing.

Jace, Lucy and I picked up the big kids after school and grabbed some smoothies before Blake's game and then cheered him on to win. He scored a goal and everything! I was so proud.

By the time we got home, the kids were starved again and I had at least an hour of homework to look forward to before bedtime. The day, like most others, had been exhausting.

And yet when I pulled up the driveway, I couldn't stop the relief that rolled through me. In front of my closed garage sat my two outdoor garbage cans. The lids were closed, not propped open from too-many bags and my forgetfulness.

I parked the van, and ran to check out the cans. They were both empty.

Ben had fixed my trash problem!

I didn't know how he did it or even want to consider the amount of work it took to solve this problem. It had to be disgusting dealing with all of those bags filled with moldy leftovers and dirty diapers.

But he had done it for me anyway. What a good guy.

I re-parked the cans in their rightful place against the far garage wall and smiled at them. I would remember next week. I wouldn't let Ben's kindness be for nothing.

I helped the kids from the car and made sure we brought in all of the various school bags, lunch bags and soccer bags. But I did it with a lighter spirit.

Dinner was easier too that night. And bedtime didn't seem quite so chaotic.

By the time I crawled into bed not long after the children, I was still amazed at how Ben's small act of generosity had impacted my day. Was I really so easy to please?

Dark thoughts followed those good ones.

I settled into my huge, empty bed and let my hand reach over to Grady's side. It shouldn't be this hard for me. I should have Grady here to help me.

Tears started falling at the simple mention of his name inside my head.

"Why did you leave me, Grady?" I whispered to the darkness. "I can't do this without you." Anger bubbled with the grief and made me feel sick.

This was impossible without him. These kids, this house, my life was impossible without his help.

I turned to my side and hugged one of his pillows. I let my tears soak the cotton that no longer smelled like my husband or bore his imprint.

It was nice that Ben had helped me, but what I really wanted was to not need Ben's help at all. What I really wanted was my husband here with me to help every single day.

Chapter Ten

Emma picked up on the third ring, "Hello, sister dearest."

"Are you ready?"

I heard her muffled sigh on the other end of the phone. "This is not my first date, Liz. I'm ready."

I had convinced Emma to give Ben a chance when she helped take the kids trick-or-treating a couple weeks ago. We'd canvased the neighborhood with Blake as the Hulk, Abby as Michael Phelps's little sister, Lucy as a princess and Jace as a pirate. Emma had filled in for Grady. After we put the kids to bed, we'd spent the night crying together over buckets of Halloween candy while scary movies played in the background.

It hadn't been one of my finer moments.

But after we stopped by Ben's house and he passed out full-size Twix bars to all of the kids, Emma had finally agreed to text him about getting together. They had flirted in the doorway while I stared at the candy bars thinking what a bachelor move. Who passes out fifteen grams of sugar to a two year old? Single men in their thirties. That's who.

The Twix bars never made it to the morning. They were part of my Grady therapy. Somewhere around midnight, I retracted my negative feelings for Ben's naïve generosity. And then enacted them again after I got on the scale the next morning.

"I know, I'm just nervous," I confessed.

"*You're* nervous?"

I chuckled at her incredulous tone. "For you! I just want this to go well."

She laughed with me. "What if Ben's a total weirdo? Like he has a collection of doll heads or he brings his mom to dinner? You'll have to come rescue me at the restaurant. Then you'll have to move away from him."

Even the mention of moving out of this house hurt my chest. "He won't bring his mother to dinner. We've sort of seen him on a date before, remember?"

"No defense for the dolls' heads?"

"Well, I've never actually been in his house. There's no way for me to know for sure."

"Liz!"

"I'm just kidding, Em. He's so nice. You're going to have a great time."

"He'll at least be nice to look at." I nodded my head, even though she couldn't see me. That was true. "What are your exciting plans for the night?" she asked and sounded genuinely interested.

"On a Friday night? What else is there to do besides pop a bag of popcorn for each of us and cuddle up on the couch?"

"Oooh, what's on the queue?"

"*Sword in the Stone*. It's one of the few movies all of the kids can agree on."

"I love that movie," Emma sighed. "I kind of wish I was hanging out with you guys tonight."

"What? No way! You're going to have so much fun."

"You're being pretty pushy about this date."

I bristled a little at her comment. "I am not."

"You are."

"I just want you to be happy."

"I am happy. I don't need a man for that."

"You know what I meant. Why are you fighting this? He's a good guy! You said it yourself, single and stable." Emma and I used to argue, before Grady died. Just about little stuff, small tiffs or snotty remarks. Nothing long-lasting. We were sisters; we usually found something to disagree about. But we hadn't had a single disagreement since Grady had gotten really sick over a year ago. I knew my sister had been walking on eggshells around me and that our relationship wasn't so evolved that we would never fight again. But tonight, her irritation with me only made me more irritated with her.

"I just think, if this doesn't end well, it's going to be awkward for you. I'm trying to protect you," she insisted.

"I don't need you to protect me, Emma." I took a breath and closed my eyes, trying to dispel my frustration. "Listen, if you don't want to go out with Ben, then don't. But don't let your worry for me bother you. Ben and I are barely friends, so there isn't much to worry about between us. And if things don't work out between the two of you, there are other options besides keying his car and taking a baseball bat to his windshield."

She laughed again, sounding infinitely more relaxed. "Yeah? Like what?"

"Like being grownups, for instance. Like acting maturely."

She sighed for effect, "You just have all the answers, don't you."

"I'm older," I reminded her. "And infinitely wiser."

"Sure you are. Okay, he's here. I'll call you after!"

"Have fun!"

"Love you."

"Love you too."

I clicked off with Emma and turned back to pouring the popcorn into bags. I opened a box of Capri Suns, bought especially for family movie night and set them on the tray. A memory hit me so hard that my knees nearly buckled. I grabbed the counter for support and dropped my head.

I stood in this same place, doing this same task. Grady's arms wrapped around my middle and he pulled me back against his hard chest. His face nuzzled in the crook of my neck and he inhaled my skin.

"Friday nights used to be date nights," I reminded him. The kids had been overwhelming that week. Jace was just a baby and not sleeping through the night. Abby and Lucy were into everything and constantly fighting over toys. Blake hadn't wanted to hug me that morning when I dropped him off at school. My world felt tough and exhausting, it was easy to dream about the early years with Grady- how simple they'd been.

"That's true," he whispered against my skin. "Now they're family nights."

"I need a break, Grady. I'm exhausted."

"I'm here to help, Babe. Tonight will be easy."

I yawned in defiance. He squeezed me tighter and pressed a hot kiss against my skin. "If you say so."

"We'll spend some time with the kids, put them to bed together and then I'll spend the rest of the night helping you relax." His gruff words vibrated over my skin and sent tingles spiraling low in my belly. I loved how he did this to me, how his voice could put me at ease and he could soften my perspective. "We'll watch something later, just the two of us. You pick it out. I'll rub your feet."

"Mmm," I moaned when his kisses trailed up my neck to taste my earlobe. "You've wooed me."

His chuckle brushed his five o'clock shadow over my ear. "That's usually the goal."

I spun around in his arms and let him continue to woo me. We kissed long and desperately until Blake wandered in the kitchen looking for us.

"Ew!" he groaned. "That's gross!"

Grady pulled back from me and looked at his oldest son, "Take notes, Blake. This will come in handy someday."

I swatted his chest but laughed, unable to find my frustration from earlier. Grady wiped it clean and filled in all of my flaws with the best parts of him.

"Mom, can I have one?"

I looked up to see Blake reaching for a bowl of popcorn. The jolt from the memory of Grady and the reality of an older Blake in front of me felt like a physical shock. My chest seized in agony and my stomach flipped with heartsick nausea.

"Please?" I reminded Blake with a broken voice.

"Please," he whispered back. Instead of grabbing the bowl of popcorn, he walked around the island and wrapped his arms around me. I kissed the top of his head and inhaled his little boy smell.

He was growing up so fast. He was taller than ever and his body had started to fill out with muscle. He wasn't my baby anymore. While that made some part of me cry out with protest, most of me was just so proud of the young man he was becoming.

"Family movie night is hard for me too, Mom," he sniffled into my shirt.

I blanched with new grief. I had never stopped to think about how family movie night might hurt my children. I had wanted to keep their routine and help maintain Grady's memory. I had waded through my own heartache and forced myself to endure a night that I dreaded all week long.

And why?

So we could all be sad together?

That just didn't seem worth it.

I pulled back so I could look Blake in the eyes. He blinked rapidly and tried to avoid my gaze. My heart shattered into a million pieces.

"Let's do something different then."

"What?" He finally looked up at me and the sadness started to chip away. "What do you mean?"

"I don't know, it just seems like if this movie night thing is making all of us sad, we should try something different, something that might make us happy."

"Mom, are you coming?" Abby bounced into the kitchen with Lucy on her heels. Jace toddled in after them and hugged me too. His little arms wrapped around my leg and he looked up at me, babbling about juicy.

"I don't know, Abs. Blake and I were just talking about changing up the Friday night line up."

She tilted her head, "What does that mean?"

"What if instead of watching a movie tonight, we played games instead."

"Like Candy Land?" Abby asked.

"Not Candy Land!" Blake whined.

I smiled at him again. "How about we play a couple games? You can both pick one."

"And me too!" Lucy demanded.

"Sure, Luce. You too."

"Me! Me! Me!" Jace joined in.

I moved the kids to the kitchen table and set them up with popcorn and juice. I ran down to the basement and pulled out some games that had sat on a shelf for too long.

An hour and a half later, we had laughed our way through Candy Land, Chutes and Ladders, UNO and Old Maid.

The night hadn't been easy. Jace had been a handful and destroyed more than one of our attempts at playing. Abby had plenty of attitude to throw around and wasn't always satisfied with the outcome of the game. Okay, honestly, she was a terrible loser. I would have to work with her on that.

The night tried my patience and made me question if getting out all of these games was really better than just cuddling on the couch during a movie. Movies were so much easier, but infinitely more painful.

By the time I had them tucked in, I'd decided that I would make this our new tradition. I had been waffling up until bedtime. I was exhausted from the evening, but so were the kids. They went to bed happily. They brushed their teeth calmly and jumped into bed, ready to end the day.

I knew their better behavior was more than their level of exhaustion. They felt fulfilled for the first time in a long time. I wouldn't always be able to fill the role of both parents, but tonight I'd given them the attention they needed and the focus they craved. I hadn't punished them for their unruly behavior by taking away the games; I'd worked to refocus their energy on some friendly competition instead. And they needed that.

The sharp burn of humiliation seared over my skin. I couldn't believe it had taken me this long to realize how hard our movie night tradition was for them. I'd been too busy wallowing in my own grief to notice theirs. What a selfish mom I could be.

I walked back downstairs in my pajamas, wanting to clean up the games and the kitchen and then collapse face first in bed. And I knew I looked as tired as I felt.

The holidays were coming up. We'd somehow waded through the first few months of school and now had Thanksgiving to look forward to next week.

I looked down at scattered UNO cards and knew I had to do something like this for us during the upcoming holidays. We would not survive

Thanksgiving and Christmas if we had to relive every tradition Grady had helped us build.

Last year at this time, Grady had been admitted to the hospital. We'd spent our holiday season piled onto his narrow bed, promising each other that he would get better and be with us next year. Those memories cut like a knife, digging into my sternum and flaying me open. I couldn't even think about those final days without an overflow of tears and instant heartache.

We still had hope then. We still believed the treatment would work and that we would get Grady back as he used to be. We trusted that the children would have their father home with them again, that I would have my husband back.

Maybe it was because that hope now felt like an awful betrayal or maybe because I still desperately longed for that hope again, but those weeks, when we still believed he could get better, made me furious.

My hands shook as I pulled the piles of scattered cards to me and tried to straighten them. Wet tears plopped onto my hands and the table as the well of grief and frustration bubbled over. My chest hurt, my bones hurt... my soul hurt.

How could he leave me? How could he let me believe he would pull through? How could I have thought that there was enough hope and prayer and determination in the world to make my husband better again?

I was impotent then and just as helpless now.

I sunk down into a chair before my legs gave out and I collapsed to the ground. I dropped the cards back onto the table and buried my face in my hands. A strangled hiccup of a sob exploded from my chest and I gave in to the agony.

I poured myself onto the games as if they were an offering for healing my soul. I let myself bleed out onto that table and embraced the anger that now tainted every thought and emotion. I shook from the rage that seemed to boil up inside of me and threaten to take over.

I had never felt so utterly alone before. *So abandoned.*

The rational side of my brain argued that Grady didn't abandon me, that he would never have done that. He had fought as hard as he could to survive his illness. Unfortunately, my emotions weren't ruled by logic and understanding. They could only feel. They could only project what my heart felt.

And right now I was more pissed off than I had ever been.

I didn't know if this anger would ever deplete. It consumed me. I sat there, still and unmoving, while it burned away at my insides and spilled acid eating at my soul, inch by slow inch.

My phone buzzed in my pocket. It was probably Emma texting at the end of her date.

The last thing I wanted to do was face someone else's happiness, but that's why I forced my fingers to pull the phone out of my pocket and read it. I needed to climb out of the pit of despair I'd sunk into and let some light into my shattered world.

I had to get some perspective and fast or this might never end.

I sniffled and had to wipe at my eyes several times before I could read the words on my screen. The text wasn't from Emma after all. It was from Ben.

I know you're dying of curiosity. Emma is a fun girl.

How did he know that about me? It was obviously true, but I didn't think I was that obvious.

I thought about not answering him, but he was right, curiosity was killing me. *Best date of your life? You better have treated her well.*

He replied right away, *I took her to a live sex show and then we stole a car. Is that good enough?*

My face heated when I read, "sex." It was stupid of me. But I hadn't had this kind of relationship with a man since Grady. Most men were more serious around me. I had a husband of ten years and four children. I was kept at a distance.

Well, with everyone except Ben Tyler. He apparently didn't feel the need to handle me with kid gloves.

It took a couple of minutes to finally decide on the right response, but eventually I said, *Emma probably loved it.*

Don't lie- you would have loved it too.

I blinked at the text with no idea how to interpret that. It almost seemed like flirting... but he wouldn't flirt with me, right after he got home from his date with my sister. Besides, he just got finished telling me what a good time they had.

I didn't want to answer him, in case he thought I was flirting with him. But I didn't want him to think he made me uncomfortable enough not to answer either.

Why was texting other people so hard?

My personality felt rusty and misused when I finally tapped out my reply. Something awakened in my chest and spread its muscle-sore wings.

I couldn't define the feeling or say exactly what it was, but I knew it felt liberating. It felt relaxing.

That's the best you can do? Kind of boring if you ask me. I swiped off my screen and finished cleaning up the games.

I shut down the first floor of my beautiful, hand-crafted house that represented Grady almost as much as his children and walked upstairs with slow feet.

Crawling into my bed was something I dreaded every single night.

By the time I brushed my teeth and washed my face, my phone had buzzed twice. I didn't check it again until I was in bed and snuggled under warm quilts.

You, Liz Carlson, are a surprise.

When I hadn't answered after several minutes, he had texted one more time to say, *Goodnight.*

"Goodnight, Ben," I whispered to my phone as I shut it off and turned around. After my earlier breakdown, I had dreaded going to sleep tonight.

I could never seem to fall asleep after that kind of emotional trauma. There was a bottle of sleeping pills in my medicine cabinet that had been given to me right after Grady had died. I'd taken them a few times when my parents stayed with us because I felt safer with them here to watch over the kids.

I kept them just in case I was desperate. And during my breakdown I had contemplated using them. Just for tonight.

But Ben's text message had helped calm my frantic spirit. He'd managed to pull me out of my darkness and shine a bit of light on me. I closed my eyes and drifted easily to sleep, thankful for my sister that indulged me and for my next door neighbor that could make me smile when I thought I would never smile again.

Chapter Eleven

Thanksgiving.

Had there ever been a more awful holiday?

In fact the entire day set me on edge.

I didn't want to wake up grateful for the things I still had or spend time counting my blessings. I didn't want to remember why I was so blessed or teach my children to count every little thing as a gift.

I wanted to stay in my three-day-old pajamas and wallow in self-pity. I wanted to drink myself through the day and eat my weight in Ben and Jerry's. I wanted to pull all of my children into my big bed and fill it up for a change, and then I wanted to hold them close and weep.

I hadn't cried since last Friday night. The week had passed quickly and the kids had been out of school yesterday. I enlisted them to help bake some holiday goodies and we'd turned on Top Forty and danced around the kitchen- anything to keep the shadow of our first major holiday without Grady out of their heads.

This morning I'd woken up early to Abby having a terrible nightmare. She'd screamed at the top of her lungs. I rushed to her, terrified something was wrong. She hadn't even woken up when I crawled into bed with her and wrapped my arms around her tiny waist. She nuzzled against me and immediately quieted down.

I whispered soothing words for another hour before she woke up for good.

"Mommy?" She was so sleepily confused that I couldn't help but smile. Her curly hair was riotous around her freckled face and her green eyes had trouble focusing. She could be a handful, but she was *my* handful. I loved this little thing.

"You had a nightmare," I told her.

"I know," she whispered back.

"Do you want to talk about it?"

She shook her head and hugged me tighter. "It will make you sad."

I hadn't pressed her. Maybe I should have. Maybe I should have encouraged her to talk about it, get it out of her head and help her process. But I was afraid she was right. I didn't want to be more depressed than I already was. The idea that Abby had a nightmare about losing her daddy paralyzed me with grief. I couldn't do anything but hug her and promise her that it was going to be okay, even if I didn't believe that ugly, empty promise.

I couldn't lie to her about anything else though. So I didn't bother telling her she wouldn't have another nightmare or that she would feel better soon. I just made sure she knew that I was there for her, that she could come sleep with me anytime she was scared and that I would always be here for her if she couldn't sleep.

I didn't know if my words helped or hurt her in the long term, but frankly I didn't care. This was the best I could do.

Abby and I stayed in bed a long time, just holding on to each other for dear life. Eventually the other kids trickled in as they woke up and we added them to our pile.

We didn't have to be at lunch until eleven and so it wasn't until Jace couldn't stand being hungry anymore that we dragged ourselves from the warmth of the bed to the sustenance in the kitchen.

Now we stood on the stoop to Katherine's quaint, all-brick house and I had started to contemplate throwing the kids back in the car and driving to the nearest Denny's.

"Why are we just standing here?" Blake reached for the doorbell.

"I just want to make sure we're ready," I sighed. My children looked at me like the crazy woman that I was. Jace tried to jump out of my arms and dive for his nana's house. Blake pushed the doorbell to get us out of the cold.

Trevor opened the door and mayhem ensued. The children attacked him and he wrestled them into the living room.

I set my purse down and went back to the car for the pies the kids had helped me make. I balanced the apple in one hand and the cherry in the other as I stepped over kicking little feet and Trevor's arm as he played dead for the kids.

Katherine stood at the stove, checking the various casseroles in the oven. She looked over her shoulder when I greeted her and gave me a soft smile.

"Happy Thanksgiving," she said.

"Happy Thanksgiving to you too."

She examined my pies and immediately my hackles rose, maybe unfairly, but it didn't matter. "Did the kids help you make those?"

"Yes."

"I admire you for baking with so many children. I only had the two boys, but I couldn't seem to manage them in the kitchen."

I gave her a tight smile while irrational anger burned low in my stomach. I didn't have a choice. I didn't have two kids and I didn't have the luxury of help. She knew this. I didn't know why she felt the need to point it out.

I decided changing the subject would be better for both of us. "Do you need any help?"

"Thank you, Liz. You could fill the water glasses on the table; we're just about ready to eat."

And eat we did. Katherine was an excellent cook and she served a spectacular meal. Usually she invited cousins and aunts and uncles to celebrate the holiday as well, but she'd offered to keep it small for this Thanksgiving.

It was the only reason I agreed to come over.

Honestly, the idea of facing all of Grady's extended family without him by my side sounded like the inner circle of hell. They were overwhelming to begin with, but after Grady's death the day would consist of nonstop questions about how I was doing or how the kids were doing or how we were managing or how I thought Trevor was handling the business.

I would have dragged Emma along, but she had flown to Florida to spend the holiday with our retired parents. She had been hesitant to go, but I had encouraged her, thinking I would be fine at my in-laws.

Dinner was as chaotic as it always was with four children to serve and maintain, but relatively low key since there were so many adults to help out.

"Should we all say something we're thankful for?" Katherine's cheery voice grated on my nerves. I tried to smile at Abby, encouraging her with my expression, but I couldn't make it believable.

"Do we have to?" Abby groaned. "I'm not thankful for anything."

"Abigail," I hissed at her. I could see the pain written all over her face, but the mom in me couldn't stop from chastising her.

"What are you thankful for, Mom?" Her dry sarcasm could not be missed.

"I'm thankful for you," I told her honestly. "For how fun and adventurous you are." That seemed to calm her down, so I moved on. "And I'm thankful for Blake too." I looked at my oldest son, "Thankful for how helpful you are and for always remembering everything I forget." He gave me a shy smile and went back to pushing his green bean casserole around.

"What about me?" Lucy shouted.

"I'm thankful for you too, Luce. I'm thankful for all of your hugs and kisses. And I'm thankful for all of the pictures you make for me." I tousled Jace's floppy red hair and kissed a cheek painted in mashed potatoes. "I'm thankful for you too, J. I'm thankful that you are sleeping through the night again and that you always know how to make me laugh."

My mother-in-law dabbed at her eyes with a cloth napkin, "That was beautiful, Liz."

I shifted in my seat and looked away. It was shockingly unnerving to watch her tear up in the middle of dinner. It also had an intense effect on me. I wanted to cry too just watching her and then to think that it was my words that had made her emotional really choked me up.

Trevor sighed adoringly, "Ah, Ma. You're making Liz uncomfortable."

She flashed me a watery smile. Her trembling hand reached forward and rested on the white tablecloth. "I always thought the kids were so lucky to have a father like Grady," she admitted. "But I'm realizing they're really lucky to have a mother like you."

I should have heard the compliment in her words. I really should have. But all I could hear was the disappointment she felt for me up until this point. It had taken her son dying for her to see that I wasn't such a letdown after all.

I could feel the bad place I'd been trapped in. I could feel how poisonous these feelings were for my mind and soul. This anger that ate at my insides and spread toxin through my blood was dangerous and awful. I wanted it gone, but I couldn't make it go and that only made me angrier.

"Thank you for saying that," I managed to say although my words felt cold and false on my tongue.

It wasn't until Katherine disappeared into the kitchen to bring back the pie that I finally found a moment alone with Trevor. I hated the idea of other people asking the question, but I needed to know. This business was my living too.

"How are things, Trevor? With the company?"

He shrugged his shoulders and shifted in his seat. "Slow with the season." He wouldn't look me in the eye. He bounced nervously and reached for some water to gulp it down quickly.

My hand twitched. For the first time in my life, I wanted to stand up and slap someone.

"How bad is it?" My voice had become a low rasp of frustration.

His eyes lifted and he finally met my gaze. "Bad."

I felt that one small word like a punch to the gut. The room tilted sharply and then started to spin.

"I'm not sure what we're going to do. Things are bad," he continued.

I felt my heavy Thanksgiving dinner churn in my stomach. *How could he do this to me? How could he take Grady's gift and destroy it so flippantly?*

Didn't he care?

I had kids to feed! Bills to pay? Didn't he care about me?

"How are you going to fix it?" My words came out measured and labored, betraying the fury burning through me. I wanted to stand up and scream at him. I felt like I had finally tipped over the edge of insanity with the sheer volume of rage spiraling through me.

In a choked voice, he admitted, "I don't know if we can." He ran a hand through his dark hair and turned his head toward Blake.

"How dare you." My voice scared even me. I hadn't expected to react so violently, but I couldn't help it. "How dare you take my husband's company, his gift to you and run it into the ground."

Trevor jerked back in his seat, shocked by my accusation. He reached forward with a timid hand, "Liz, wait…"

"He trusted you," I spat out. "He didn't die suddenly. He died slowly! He had time to reflect on his company. He could have sold it and made a lot of money, Trevor! But no! Grady wanted to give it to you! He wanted to give you a future. He wanted to give you a job! And you've destroyed it! That was his dream. Do you know what that meant to him? Do you know how hard he worked to build his company and make a name for himself?"

"I know what he did, Liz. He was my brother."

"Then act like you give a damn!"

Katherine chose that moment to walk back into the room, although it might have had something to do with my hysterical screaming.

Jace and Lucy both started to cry. Lucy jumped out of her seat and ran to my side. She wrapped her little arms around my waist and held onto me tightly.

I was too ashamed to look at Blake or Abby. My kids had never seen me behave this way. They had been through enough; I didn't need to put this on them too.

And yet, I couldn't stop.

"I do give a damn!" Trevor shot back, just as infuriated as me. "You can't even imagine how this is *killing me*! How much of a failure I feel like because I can't make this one thing work. The *one thing* I want to work most *in the world*! You don't think I know how much Grady loved this company? You're wrong! I worked with him every day for nearly a decade. I watched him build it from the ground up! I know that the only thing he

105

loved more than that place was you and his kids. So don't think for a second that I would intentionally run this thing into the ground. But I am not Grady, Liz. I'm not even half the man he was." Trevor ran a rough hand over his eyes but couldn't stop his angry, hurt tears from falling.

I felt like the worst person in the world for making him feel that way, for making him admit things I didn't even think were true.

Katherine collapsed in her seat. Silent tears ran down her face, but she didn't' try to wipe them away.

When Trevor spoke again, his voice was broken, a picture of what I knew had happened to his spirit as well. "I want to try, Liz. I want to make this business run as successfully as it did when Grady was alive. But I can barely get myself out of bed in the morning. I know you lost your husband. I know how hard this hit you. But you've got to know that I lost my big brother. He was my *best friend* and now he is gone. I can barely walk into that office without breaking down and losing my goddamn mind. I want to do this right, Liz, but I am just so *sad*."

His last words were what finally broke me. I had had enough. I couldn't take it anymore.

I couldn't take Grady's mother looking at me with pity. I felt Katherine's eyes on me constantly. I felt her waiting for me to break. I could feel her just waiting for me to lose it.

Well, maybe I finally had.

And Trevor was so much worse. He didn't just look like his older brother, he acted like Grady too. And Trevor was in the middle of his own pain. I could see him suffering. He was a shell of the man he used to be.

I loved Trevor like a brother, but watching him like this made my grief double. I couldn't hurt for both Trevor and me. I couldn't hurt for all of us and expect to be able to breathe through this pain.

I pushed back from the table, taking my clinging kids with me. "Trevor, we're all sad. We all miss Grady. But you're killing him all over again by killing his company. And the first time is hard enough. I will not grieve him twice. Figure something out or I'm going to sell it."

His face went white and Katherine jumped to her feet, knocking over a glass of water as she went.

"Liz, you don't mean that."

I whirled on her. "I cannot watch that company implode, Katherine. I won't do it. Grady trusted Trevor, but he didn't want this." I turned on my other two children. "Get your shoes on, Guys. It's time to go."

"But we haven't had dessert!" Abby complained.

"Abs, we'll have something when we get home. Let's go."

Katherine looked absolutely distraught. "Liz…"

"I'm sorry, Katherine." I felt sick to my stomach. I was not a confrontational person, but I hadn't been able to stay quiet. "I really am. I didn't mean for that to… Or say… I think it would be better if we left now."

"Okay," she whispered.

Trevor dropped his face into his hands and I had to turn away when his shoulders started shaking. I couldn't watch him cry. I couldn't watch a grown man breakdown because of me and my stupid words.

But I couldn't make myself apologize either.

I'd meant them. Every word.

Getting in the car took longer than I wanted it to. The kids were not motivated to leave their nana's house. Katherine insisted we take the pies back home with us and I didn't have any energy left to fight her.

She helped me pack the kids into the car and load up some leftovers. We said clinical goodbyes and promised to call each other.

She kissed all the kids and then just as I had climbed into the driver's seat and she stood in the side door saying her last goodbyes, she said, "Grownups fight sometimes." I spun around to watch her smooth things over with my shaken children. "That doesn't mean they don't love each other. Your mommy and Uncle Trevor love each other very much, but they also loved your daddy. It's hard for them without him here. You'll forgive her for yelling at Uncle Trevor, won't you?" They must have nodded. "I love you all. I'll see you soon."

She stepped back and I closed the door before she could say another word.

It wasn't until we had pulled into the garage at our home that I had finally calmed down enough to offer them the apology they deserved.

I turned the car off and turned around. "I'm sorry I ruined Thanksgiving."

They all looked at me and let my words settle over them. Jace and Lucy had already moved on, but the older kids would remember this.

Finally, Blake unbuckled and walked over to me. He threw his arms around my neck and said, "Mommy, it was already ruined without dad here."

Tears started flowing again. He never called me mommy. I looked over his shoulder at Abby and asked, "Forgive me?"

"Is Uncle Trevor really going to ruin daddy's job?" she asked thoughtfully.

"Not anymore," I promised her.

"Okay." She hopped up and opened the door so she could jump out. Apparently that was all the affirmation she needed.

Blake let go and helped get the little ones out so I could carry the pies inside. We spent the rest of the day cuddled on the couch, eating pie and ice cream.

By the time I tucked them into bed, both pies were gone and I should have felt a lot guiltier than I did. They kissed me with sleepy smiles and didn't bring up my fight with Trevor again.

I didn't know if they would remember this into adulthood; maybe it would be one of the reasons that sent them running to therapy or maybe they would forget about it before the morning. But I did know that I had behaved inappropriately today and they deserved better than that.

Better than that version of me.

So did Trevor and Katherine.

I felt myself falling apart, crumbling into irreparable pieces that would be crushed into ash. I couldn't recognize myself anymore. I had become some angry, ugly creature and I didn't know how to go back.

That wasn't true. I knew how to go back to whom I used to be, but I couldn't. I couldn't go back to the person that I was before Grady died and I couldn't bring Grady back to me.

I had ruined Thanksgiving, but Grady's death had ruined me.

Chapter Twelve

I opened the pantry and then slammed the door closed. There wasn't anything in there! Damn it. Where had all the food gone?

"Mom!" Blake and Abby called from the entryway at the same time.

"What?" I attacked the refrigerator and searched through every drawer.

"There's a guy at the front door!" Blake yelled again.

I stood up and spun around. I stared at the stove. If I stared long enough would something magically appear?

"Who is it?" The staring trick was not going to work. I needed to figure out something fast for dinner or my kids were going to mutiny. Grilled cheese?

"The guy with the pool!" Abby shouted as an explanation.

"Ben?"

"Yeah," Blake confirmed. "Ben!"

"Let him in!" Poor Ben had probably heard every single word exchanged between us, but there was nothing I could do about that now.

Dinner needed to be made ASAP.

I heard the front door open and a low voice greet my kids. Jace ran for my feet, hiding between my legs. I opened the refrigerator again. There had to be something in here.

"I'm in here!" I yelled for Ben's sake. Lucy and Abby started fighting over something. Girlish screams erupted from the kid craft table.

"I just followed the deafening sounds. I found you."

I whirled around to greet Ben face to face. He looked like he'd come straight from work. His tie had been pulled off, his top button undone and his cuffs rolled to his forearms. His dark hair was more tousled than usual, as if he'd run his hands through recently.

"Hi," I smiled at him.

He stared at me for a few long seconds. "Hi."

His gaze unnerved me so I went back to searching through the cabinets. Nope, no dinner waiting for me in the Tupperware drawer.

"Is this what it's always like over here?" he asked on an amused chuckle.

"Always," I said with my head back in the pantry.

"I like it." From the tone of his voice, I could tell he actually believed he liked it too.

"Give it some time," I warned. Blake and Abby started fighting about which pencil they were supposed to use for homework. "Blake you have the orange Ninja Turtle, Abby you have Raphael!"

"What are you doing?" Ben asked in a genuinely interested tone.

I glanced over my shoulder to see him leaning on the kitchen island. "Trying to stop the fighting. It will only last a second though. Just wait."

He grinned at me. "No, I meant in there. What are doing to your kitchen?"

"Oh! I'm, er, trying to come up with dinner. I need to get to the store, but I just... haven't gone. So, now I'm trying to figure out what kind of meal I can make from a bottle of ketchup, parmesan cheese and frozen peas."

Ben made a sound in the back of his throat and said, "Please don't try to make anything with those three ingredients."

"What's in your refrigerator, Mr. Bachelor?"

"A bottle of Ranch and a six-pack of beer."

"No judging." I whirled my finger at his smug smile. "At least I have peas."

The three oldest kids started fighting again over pencils and homework and I had to abandon my conversation with Ben to break them up. Then Jace decided he would rather stand on the craft table then sit around it and color, so I had to deal with him.

By the time I got back to Ben, he was just ending a phone call.

"Alright," I teased. "Let's pool our resources. What can we make if we combine your bottle of Ranch with my bottle of ketchup?"

"No, need to try to figure out that perplexing puzzle. I just ordered pizza."

My brain refused to accept his words. "I'm sorry, what?"

"Your children seem hungry." He waved at the hooligans who had just broken out into a fight over an eraser. "You seem hungry."

"But I-"

"And I really am hungry. I'm afraid of a dinner that consists only of condiments. I thought I would solve both of our problems."

I was too overwhelmed with his generosity to protest anymore. "Thank you, Ben."

His smile softened with friendly affection. "It's my pleasure, Liz. I'm happy to help you."

"You didn't just help me, you saved my life tonight."

He leaned forward so that we were only a few inches apart and he could look directly into my eyes. "Elizabeth, any time I can save your life

110

by ordering pizza, please let me know. It's a sacrifice I am more than willing to make."

"I, er, um, thank you." My words were a rushed whisper. I whirled back around to busy myself with something, *anything*, in the kitchen. "So what did you really come over for? Unless we're so loud that you could hear us over at your place?"

"I brought some of your mail. A few pieces got mixed up with mine. Thought you might need your water bill." He waved a couple envelopes in front of him before setting them on the counter.

"Oh, wow, thank you! That would have been bad. My kids can eat peas and ketchup for dinner occasionally, but they cannot go without baths. They are surprisingly smelly."

"I don't think that's surprising," he countered seriously.

I laughed and watched Abby try to pencil in a mustache on Jace's wiggling face. He was probably right about that one.

"Abby, be careful of his eyes!"

She squinted studiously at Jace's upper lip. "I know, Mom!"

Turning back to Ben, I caught him looking at me, not Abby. "I thought you came over to talk about Emma!" I blurted when panic burst to life inside of me.

"Oh, no. Uh, I didn't come over here to talk about that, or, uh, her."

"She says you haven't called her. I thought you said she was fun."

His eyebrows bunched together. "I've called her. She's called me too."

"What? She told me you two hadn't really talked since the first date."

"Oh, right. Well, we haven't been on a second date .Maybe that's what she meant."

I narrowed my eyes on the giant boy-man in my kitchen and realized he was a terrible liar. "Why not? You said she was fun!" I knew I was repeating myself, but I couldn't help it. What was his deal with my sister?

He broke into an amused grin. "Yes, she was fun. But that was it. We had a good time. I knew that night I wasn't going to ask her out again and I know she didn't expect it to go any further either."

"How do you know that?" My tone lashed out, a whip biting at the air around me. The rage monster had taken up residence under my skin again. I couldn't stop my overreaction from happening even though I desperately wanted to.

"Because she told me."

"She did not." My hands gripped the counter top so tightly my knuckles turned white.

"Liz, she did." His voice gentled. "Your sister is smart, funny and downright gorgeous. But she is not into me like you want her to be."

I whirled around, unable to face him. His words spun around in my head, trying to land in one place long enough for me to make sense of them. But I couldn't. Emma and Ben were perfect for each other. And even though he put this on her, like it was her decision, I couldn't help but blame him.

I threw open the refrigerator again and yanked out the last of the milk. "Damn it," I cursed as I poured just enough into four small cups.

"What's the matter?" he stepped forward and took the empty milk carton from my hand.

"I need to go to the store."

"I can see why that would make you angry."

His teasing words only pissed me off. "Do you know what it's like to go to the store with young kids, Ben? I don't have the time! And I really don't have the patience for the headache. And my sister is perfect for you!"

His big hand landed on my shoulder and turned me toward him. His other hand came next and directed my chin so that I had to look at him. His touch confused me in the worst ways. No man besides Grady had ever touched me like this. Not with this kind of command and intimacy.

I couldn't pick one of my feelings out of my tumultuous head that would make sense. I couldn't even figure out why Ben's touch felt intimate or invasive. But the warmth of his skin seeped through my thin blouse and wrapped around my bones.

I hadn't been touched by another man besides Grady, but I also hadn't been touched by another man since Grady.

I missed human affection, a strong man's touch. My body awoke in ways that had been dormant for a very long time, even before Grady had passed.

My brows furrowed and I pressed my lips together in a frown. These feelings couldn't have been more inconvenient or ill-timed. I desperately needed to get control of my body and thoughts.

But then Ben spoke in a low rumble of authority and I knew I had no defense against him in that moment. My only saving grace was that I knew nothing would come of it because Ben was Ben and I was the hot mess that I was. We were friends and we were becoming good friends, but that was all that there was between us.

"Liz, I admire how much you think of your sister. I think she's great too. But you have to understand that we had a great time, there just wasn't that spark between us. We make great friends though. And we plan on staying friends. She's even going to help me pick out some furniture this weekend. I didn't break her heart or treat her badly. And I swear to you, she is not sitting around waiting for my phone call to ask her out. Please believe me."

I swallowed beyond the lump in my throat. "Okay," I whispered.

His hand that gently held my chin dropped to my other shoulder. He stood up to his full height but took a step toward me.

He stared down at me with those deep, dark eyes and for a moment I got lost there. I fell into him in a way that scared me. He held my gaze and dipped his head. For a crazy second I thought he wanted to kiss me.

After long seconds, he finally spoke, breaking the spell that had settled over the two of us. "You're a very aggravating woman." The doorbell rang just as I opened my mouth to defend myself. "I'll get it," he said instead. "They'll need my signature for the pizza."

He took his hands off me and left the kitchen. I collapsed against the refrigerator with weak knees. *Who was this guy?*

I looked over at my kids, but they were blissfully unaware. They'd settled into their drawing projects, not paying attention to me at all.

"Go wash up," I told them. They finally looked up at me. "Ben ordered some pizzas, go wash up and we'll eat dinner."

"Who's Ben?" Abby asked.

"The pool guy," I told her.

The kids watched in wide-eyed fascination as Ben reappeared with four large pizzas and two boxes of breadsticks.

He set the food on the counter and smiled sheepishly at me, "I didn't know how much would be enough."

"That's, um, plenty," I promised him, trying to process that amount of food.

He leaned forward and in a low voice, as if it would offend the children, said, "You have a lot of kids."

I suppressed a smile; he was trying to help. "Go wash up!" I reminded the kids. "And then come eat pizza!"

"Pizza!" They squealed, rushing off to the half-bath in the hallway.

Ben helped me set out paper plates and the milk. I decided to make this dinner as easy as I could. I opened the boxes to find that he'd picked a cheese, pepperoni, supreme and Thai from our favorite pizza place.

He somehow managed to walk in here tonight and not only save dinner, but order perfectly for us. I started to wonder if maybe he wasn't real. Maybe he was only a figment of my imagination.

The kids monopolized his attention at dinner, asking him a hundred questions about his job and house, if he had a wife, why didn't he have a wife, if he had pets, why didn't he have pets, when would he fill the pool up again.

He hadn't found the right girl yet. Lots of girls he liked, no girls he loved. Yet. My curiosity had been sated.

He stayed for a few minutes after we finished, helping me pick up and even wiped down the table. I shooed the kids upstairs to get ready for baths and walked him to the door.

"Thank you. For tonight and for the pizza."

He looked down at me with a burning warmth. I felt it all the way to my toes. "I'm glad to help," he promised. "Thank you for forgiving me for genuinely liking your sister."

"You're a very brave man to bring that up," I warned with little real anger.

"I genuinely like you too." His words shocked the hell out of me. "But I think in a completely different way than Emma."

"I don't know what that means."

He grinned at me. "That's okay with me."

"Goodbye, Ben."

"Bye, Liz."

I watched him walk across my yard to his own. His long, confident gait ate up the distance quickly. He turned around just once more to wave at me and disappeared into his dark house.

I closed the front door and moved upstairs to get the kids ready for bed. I smiled through bath time and story time, thinking about how Ben probably never expected to spend the evening with us. His dinner plans were most likely vastly different than sitting at a crowded table, sharing pizza with four wild kids.

Just as I tucked Jace in and kissed him one last time, there was another knock on the door.

"What now?" I muttered to myself as I bounced down the stairs.

I could see Ben's tall figure through the mottled glass. I glanced toward the kitchen wondering what he forgot.

"Hey," I smiled gently when I opened the door for him. He held out a paper grocery sack. "What's this?"

"I called Emma, like you wanted me to." I rolled my eyes at his accusing tone. "She's going to come over tomorrow morning around ten so that you can go grocery shopping alone. If you ever need a few things, I can always stop on my way home from work."

"Ben, I can't-"

"Liz," he cut me off, "You have people that care about you, that want to help. Let us." He wiggled the paper bag, so I took it from him.

I looked into the bag to see a gallon of milk, a box of brown sugar Pop-Tarts and my favorite K-cups. Emma must have told him my preference.

Tears glistened in my eyes, when I lifted my head to meet his intense gaze, "Thank you."

"You'll call me if you need anything?"

I nodded. Yes, I would. Ben had proved himself to be someone I could trust.

Someone I could rely on.

"Have a good night, Liz."

"You too."

This time I didn't watch him walk away, I was too absorbed in the little miracle he'd left in my arms. A gallon of milk might not seem like much to anyone else, but to me it was the difference between getting through the morning tomorrow and crashing and burning in a blaze of failure.

He had saved me tonight.

And I couldn't figure out why.

Chapter Thirteen

I walked in the house, arms laden with groceries. Emma sat at the kitchen island with Lucy and Jace making some kind of structure out of Duplos.

The kitchen had always been our most loved room. It was open and spacious, with plenty of room for my dream kitchen, an island for the kids to sit at, a table for informal dinners and a window nook for the kid's fun table. Grady had designed this with all of my hopes and dreams in mind. The mud room walked straight out to the garage and had plenty of storage for coats and shoes, backpacks and whatever else we could pile in there. The kitchen opened up into our dining room on one side and the entry way, leading to the front door and living room, on the other side.

I loved walking into our house, even after the stress of the grocery store. It just calmed me. It was only one of the reasons that I would never sell this place, even though it reminded me so very much of Grady.

He had built this for me. I couldn't imagine living anywhere else.

The sight of Emma at the counter with my two littlests warmed my heart. Whenever she was with them, she engaged them completely. They just ate up every bit of attention she focused on them.

"Ook, Mama!" Jace held up a tower of Legos. "Me did this!"

"Wow, J! I love it!"

"Auntie Emma and me are building a castle," Luce told me excitedly. "It's for princesses only."

"It looks like a princess only palace."

Lucy beamed at me and went back to her project. Emma continued to watch the kids while I brought in all of the groceries and put them away. I was amazed at the peace we maintained during the entire process.

I was also amazed at how relaxed I felt after only an hour to myself.

The grocery store had been blissfully quiet. I walked up and down every aisle slowly, savoring the freedom I had to browse and compare prices. It was a mother's dream come true.

Comparable only with the illusive and annual pedicure.

"Are you starving yet?" I asked Emma after the last of the groceries found their home and the plastic bags had been tied up nicely and stored for whatever uses I found for them later.

"I don't know. Are we starving?"

"Yes!" the two littles cheered.

I pulled out ingredients for sandwiches while they cleaned up the Legos.

Finally, the kids were happy with their lunch and Emma and I had a minute to talk to each other.

"Thanks again, Em. I needed to get out."

She leaned forward and rested her elbows on the white-tiled countertop. "You could have called me. You know I want to help out as much as I can."

"I know." I let out a weary sigh. "But I already ask so much of you. I know you're gearing up for the end of the semester. I didn't want to add any stress." I cleared my throat and amended, "Any more stress to your busy life."

She reached out and put her hand over mine. "Stop thinking you're a burden. I love you. I will always do what I can to help you. And I love your kids like they are my own. You guys are not extra stress. You're my family."

I turned my hand over and squeezed her fingers. "Then I'm sorry Ben had to call you. I didn't ask him to."

She pulled her hand back and waved it dismissively in the air. "I know. He told me."

"When he called you."

She picked up her sandwich. "Obviously."

"Even though you told me he hadn't called you yet! What is that about?"

Her cheeks heated with embarrassment. "I didn't lie to you!" she blurted in a rush. "He really hadn't called me like you wanted him to call me!"

"Why didn't you just tell me that you two wanted to be friends?" Emma could be flakey when she wanted to be, but her lie still bothered me. It felt like she wanted to hide something, but I didn't understand what or why.

She let out a small breath of indecision. "I don't know... I guess it was a little humiliating. And you had such high hopes for us. I didn't want to disappoint you."

"Why was it humiliating?" Blood rushed to my head and fingers, hot and ready to defend my little sister.

"Because it was so obvious he wasn't into me. From the very beginning, I could tell his feelings for me would always be neutral. It messed with my vanity."

I smiled at Emma. She was absolutely gorgeous with her wavy, wild blonde hair and piercing blue eyes set against perfectly creamy skin and full lips. And her nose, her stupidly cute and adorable nose was so much smaller than mine. She hadn't experienced a whole lot of rejection in her life.

"I'm pretty sure your vanity is going to be okay."

She grinned at me. "I met someone in the library over the weekend. He's taking me out tomorrow night."

I rolled my eyes. "I'm glad you're defining your self-worth by the number of guys that ask you out."

She snorted into her sandwich. "My self-worth is just fine. But a little attention from the opposite sex doesn't hurt."

"So what's up with Ben? Do you think there's something wrong with him?" I bent nearly in half to plop my chin in my hand. There had to be something wrong with him if he didn't like my sister. Right?

Emma tipped her head back and laughed before leaning over to lay her cheek on the top of Jace's head. "There is nothing wrong with him! But I love your loyalty."

"Okay, but he's thirty-five years old and doesn't even have a serious girlfriend. Plus, you said he wasn't interested in you from the start. He eats his fingernails or something. I know there is something wrong with him."

"That was part of it I think. He's thirty-five. I'm twenty-six. That gap between us is pretty big. It might work for some people, but right now he and I are just too different. He looks at me like a kid sister."

I frowned. "I didn't think about that, the age difference I mean. I guess you are in different stages of life." I let out a long sigh and forced my loyalty to accept that reason. "But still, he's a catch. He should have found *somebody* by now."

"He is a catch," she said thoughtfully. "We had a really nice time hanging out. I definitely like him."

"There has to be something. What about weird tics? Did he chew with his mouth open? Not a good tipper? Did he check out other girls all night long?" When she wrinkled her nose at me, I cried, "Come on! I need dirt." It bothered me how many questions I had about Ben. But it also bothered me that Emma had been on a date with him and seen this side of him I never had. We had only known each other a couple of months, but there was something about him that made me feel comfortable to count him as one of my friends.

And ever since Grady died, those had been very few and far between.

Well, basically just Emma.

I had other friends before Grady passed away, but over the past ten years of our marriage my close friendships had more or less dissolved into casual ones. We all had families to take care of now and the time we made for each other had lessened year after year.

Sure, there were still girls I could talk to, but since Grady's funeral, I had pretty much been a weepy mess of a human. Nobody wanted to deal with that or listen to how hard things were for me now. I knew most of my friends were afraid to even bring Grady up. And I was too apathetic about those shallow friendships to care.

If I didn't have Emma though...

I couldn't even think about that.

"Honestly, I think he's interested in someone else." Emma sounded completely perplexed.

"He's never mentioned anyone to me," I told her. I was a little surprised too. If he had his eyes on someone else, why had he agreed to go on a date with Emma?

Her eyes narrowed a bit and her eyebrows bunched together. "I think it's you, Lizbeth. I think he likes you."

An unbelieving laugh bubbled out of me. "Now who's just being loyal?"

"I'm serious! He asked approximately three thousand questions about you during dinner. He smiles whenever he so much as says your name. He's clearly smitten."

I felt sick suddenly. The sandwich churned unforgivably in my stomach. "He thinks I'm crazy. He smiles because he's trying not to laugh at me."

"I think he has a crush."

I pressed my lips together to keep from demanding Emma to take it all back. How could she think that? "Emma, be serious. I am not the kind of girl men have crushes on. He's seen the chaos of my life and he knows about Grady. The last thing he has is a crush on me. He feels sorry for me. That's it." As soon as I said the words, I hated them. The thing I appreciated about Ben so much was that he didn't feel sorry for me.

Or at least he didn't act like it.

"He does not feel sorry for you, Elizabeth. He likes you."

"As a *friend*."

A full minute went by where neither of us said a word. We stared at each other, waiting on the other to admit that she was wrong. I felt myself grow hard with determination. She was wrong about this.

Finally, she gave a defeated sigh and said, "I'm sorry I said anything."

"I'm sorry I freaked out."

She looked at the clock on my stove. "I should go anyway. I have to get ready for class."

I deflated immediately. I wrapped my arms around my waist and curled my shoulders in. I didn't want her to leave like this. And over something so stupid! Why couldn't I stop fighting with every single person I cared about? I hated that I kept lashing out in the ugliest ways possible.

I walked her to the door and found myself near tears. I threw my arms around her before she could get too far. "I'm sorry I snapped at you."

She returned the hug and squeezed me tightly. "I'm sorry I suggested you're hotter than me."

I giggled into her neck and sniffled back tears. "I didn't realize that's what you were doing."

She pulled back and hit me with her baby blues. "Lizzy, you're thirty-two-years old and smokin' hot. It's a compliment if you can manage to catch a guy's eye with your wild kids running around."

"I like Ben. He's been super nice."

"So what if he has a little crush on you? It's harmless."

"Because it would mean that he's crazy. You know what my kids are like! You know what *I'm* like. And he's seen us all at our worst. He would have to be completely bat shit to find anything about this remotely attractive." I waved a hand down the length of my body and tried not to make a face.

It was my sister's turn to burst into giggles. "You don't see yourself, Liz. You never have." That was her goodbye. She kissed my forehead, turned around and skipped to her little Jetta. I waved to her, feeling more lost than ever.

It wasn't that I didn't see myself. I *did* see myself. Very clearly. Which was why I knew that she was wrong about Ben.

He wasn't interested in me. He couldn't be. I absolutely believed that I was well beyond the years of catching anyone's eyes. If it wasn't the four kids that turned them off, it was the dead husband. And if those two weren't enough to put me completely in the untouchable category, I was half-crazy with grief and more than overwhelmed with life.

I had become the kind of woman that men ran from. And men should run from.

Ben was smart and funny. He had a great job and a gorgeous house. He was maybe the nicest person I had ever met and so giving. Finally, he was great to look at. Basically, Ben could have his pick of females. The last one he would turn his dark eyes on would be me.

Emma's words bounced around in my head throughout the rest of the day. In between naptime, picking the kids up from school, taking Abby to swim team, Blake to basketball, rushing them back home to feed them some semblance of a healthy dinner, finishing up homework and getting them all to bed, my thoughts had ping-ponged back and forth with frustrating thoughts about Ben's real motivation for helping me.

By the time I walked downstairs again at eight-thirty, I had come to the conclusion that insanity ran in my family and Emma was out of her damn mind.

That was the only thing that made sense.

I had almost made it to the kitchen when someone knocked on my door. I turned around and couldn't bring myself to feel surprised when I saw Ben's figure blurred through the glass, as if my spinning thoughts had conjured him.

I opened the door and greeted him with a smile, "Hi."

He held up a bottle of wine, "Hi."

"What's this?"

"Well, I figured since you didn't have time to grab milk this week, chances were you didn't have time to grab wine either."

"I went to the store by myself today, remember? Someone called in emergency babysitting for me. I bought four bottles."

His wide grin made his eyes sparkle. "Good. You owe me."

He pushed the door open and stepped inside before I could invite him. I followed him to the kitchen, reflecting on how quickly he'd made himself at home.

"So your plan is to show up and drink all of my wine? How neighborly."

He flashed a smile over his shoulder and started rummaging through my cabinets. "I'm going to share. It's too cold to sit outside now, even if I built a fire. Glasses?"

"Next to the fridge."

He moved over and finally found what he had been looking for. He surveyed my small wine rack that sat on the side cabinet. His lips pressed into a frown as he picked up each bottle and read the label.

"We'll drink mine," he finally decided.

"Snob! There's nothing wrong with my wine."

He gave me a look that contradicted my opinion. "I'll teach you. You get out of the house so little, you need my help."

"You have managed to invade my privacy, insult my taste in wine and call me a recluse in the span of three minutes. I'm honestly impressed."

He started opening and closing drawers, looking for the cork screw. I pulled it out of the right drawer and handed it to him.

"I don't think you're a recluse," he told me with his concentration fixed on the bottle of wine. "I think you're busy. And I think I have better taste in wine."

"Both of those things are true," I finally conceded. I slid onto the bar stool and tried not to be charmed by his smug grin.

He handed me a half-filled glass and watched my face as I took my first sip. Then he poured his own.

"How was your day?" he asked after a few minutes of comfortable silence.

His words floated over my skin, warm and smooth. I felt my heart swell with friendly affection for this man that barely knew me, but cared enough to ask about my day- my day that was filled with kids and mess and craziness.

"Actually, pretty good." I tucked some hair behind my ear and took another sip of wine. "I enjoyed my trip to the grocery store. Thanks again for calling Emma."

"My pleasure." His gaze stayed focused on my face. "My day was good too, thanks for asking."

I shook my head at him. "Put any bad guys in jail?"

His warm chuckle filled the room with an easy grace. "Not today. Let's see, I had a mediation, a couple contracts and one last will and testament. I told you, no *Law and Order* for me. It's all paperwork."

"You're really pretty boring, aren't you?" I dropped my chin into my hand. "No wonder you have such a hard time getting dates."

His eyes narrowed playfully. "I don't have a hard time getting dates."

"Oh, just keeping them?"

"I'm going to take my wine back."

I gulped a big swallow and then grinned at him. "Let's hear the gory details, Ben. Where's Mrs. Tyler? Emma said you were perfectly normal. You didn't make any disgusting mouth noises or try to get out of paying the check. How is it that you're still single?"

He swirled his wine and stared at it contemplatively. "There's not a big mystery here, if that's what you're looking for. I've had girlfriends off and on over the years, but no one that I really felt a deep connection to. To be fair though, I have been pretty focused on my career lately and before that, school. It wasn't until recently that the idea of finding someone to settle down with entered my mind."

"Oh." Well, that was a normal enough answer. "You're a workaholic then?" I teased.

"My dad's a workaholic," Ben explained without any hint of humor. "I've spent a large amount of my life chasing his high expectations."

"Oh," I repeated. This was the real reason he didn't like working for his dad. "You don't seem to still struggle with that?"

"A year ago, he had a pretty severe heart attack. It really shook him up, helped him realign some of his priorities. It also helped me realize how short life can be. I spent the majority of my life chasing after this impossible goal he had set for me. He was a mostly miserable man, always focused on work and building his practice. And he wanted me to be the same and to dedicate my life to the same pursuits. Then he had the heart attack. I walked into his hospital room, saw him lying on the bed, attached to machines and monitors, barely breathing on his own and I realized I didn't want that to be me. I saw an empty shell of a man that had nothing to show for his life's work. At least nothing that mattered. He had a son that couldn't stand the sight of him and a wife that barely tolerated his existence. No friends, no co-workers that cared enough to show up. He was alone. I decided then that I wouldn't spend every minute of my life pursuing things that would never care about me too, that would never love me back."

It seemed that every time Ben spoke, I admired him even more. "How is he today?"

"He's better," Ben answered softly. "His health is better, and I think he realized a lot of the same things I did. We've been working on our relationship. It's not perfect. And it hasn't been easy for him to change. But, slowly… we're getting there slowly. It's not the lost cause I once thought it was."

"And your mom?"

"She's great. You would love her actually. She's full of life, very funny, pretty much the opposite of my dad. They're working on things too. I think they've lived together being miserable for so long, they're not sure how to go forward. But they're trying. That's part of the reason I can learn to respect him now. I couldn't stand the way he neglected her… ignored her. He washed-out this effervescent woman until she became a shadow at his side. I just… I couldn't tolerate that."

"But things are better now?" It seemed he needed to be reminded. I could see how hard it was for him to accept this change and I didn't blame him. His dad sounded like a piece of work.

"Things are better," he agreed. He took a deep breath and leveled me with another intense gaze. "Alright, your turn."

"My turn for what?"

"Serious questioning. You got down to the bottom of me, now I want to hear about you."

I fortified myself with another gulp of wine. He was right. It was only fair, even if I didn't want to go into details. If I really wanted a friendship with Ben, I owed him this.

He started with a relatively easy question though. "I worked on a will today and it got me to thinking, are you okay in this house? Will I be getting a new neighbor any time soon?"

"Wow, starting with financials. How classy of you."

He made a growly sound and demanded, "Answer the question, Liz. I like having you as a neighbor. I'm going to be pretty distraught if I come home one day and see a for sale sign in your yard."

My heart jumped in my chest. "I'm sure you'll survive."

"Answer the question, you aggravating woman."

I gave him a dramatic sigh, but admitted, "The house is paid for. We won't be moving, so rest your weary head. Grady owned a construction company and used his infinite resources to build as economically as he could. He also had a trust from his dad, who died when he was in high school and I had money from my grandfather. We didn't want to worry about a mortgage on top of business debt, so we paid off the house."

"And his life insurance is enough for you to stay home full-time?"

I felt a little strange opening up to someone outside of my family, but I didn't see the harm in answering his questions. "He had a large policy. So do I. With four kids, there's no other way to do life insurance. There's more than enough to get me through these next few years while the kids are little. I have an education though. I'd like to go back to work after Jace goes to school."

"That's nice how that worked out for you," he said softly. He must have seen my expression crumble from his words because he quickly added, "Not nice, obviously. But I'm glad for your sake you were prepared." With a rueful twist of his lips, he added, "I'm glad you're taken care of, for my sake."

"Your sake?"

"I get to keep my neighbors. That's good for me because I like them."

"Just wait until I start throwing keggers. And Blake and Abby shoot out your windows with their BB guns."

He walked around the island and stood over me. I could smell his pleasant, masculine cologne and feel the heat of his body. He had completely invaded my personal space and seemed very unapologetic about it.

His thumb rubbed at my upper lip. "Wine," he explained. "If you start throwing keggers, I hope I'm invited. And if you ever decide to buy Blake and Abby BB guns, send them to me so I can teach them how to use them properly."

"Grady had a brain tumor! I mean, technically tumors, plural." The words exploded from my mouth. He was too sweet, too close. Emma's words screamed in my head and his touch tingled against my skin. I had to do something. Ben took a quick step back and practically fell onto the nearest barstools. "That's what killed him. Or, um, cardiac arrest actually killed him. But that's what made him sick. He fought for two years. We went through as many treatments as we could. Surgery wasn't an option. We tried the regular drugs, experimental drugs, chemo, radiation. We did everything we could, but it didn't matter. He… he couldn't…" Tears dripped down my cheeks as I tried to explain my husband's sickness to this man.

"Liz," he whispered.

"March," I croaked. "He's been gone since March." I buried my face in my hands, unable to look at Ben anymore.

"Oh, Liz."

His arms wrapped around my torso, tugging me tightly to him. His warmth completely enveloped me, completely immersed *me* in him.

His nearness felt more comforting than anything had in a very long time and that confused me. I cried harder, battling within myself whether to let him hold me or pull away and ask him to leave.

Eventually I gave in and sunk into his hug. I kept my hands over my face in a silly attempt to keep my makeup from running all over his gray t-shirt. He held me close to his chest, my ear resting against the heavy beats of his heart.

He whispered soothing words that I couldn't hear above the roar of my internal war and never moved away from me, not until I had calmed down enough to pull back.

"I'm sorry," I said, embarrassed by my outburst. "I didn't mean to leak all over you."

He had no patience for my flippant attitude. His hands brushed from my shoulders, up the line of my neck until they cupped my face. He tilted it upwards to look at him and smoothed his thumbs beneath my eyes, wiping away the flood of tears.

"Don't ever be sorry for that, Liz. You can cry on me anytime you need to."

"Why are you so nice to me? You barely know me."

A soft smile played on his lips, "But I like what I know so far. And I am excited for what else there is to find out." He stepped back to refill our wine while I reeled from his words.

He settled back onto the bar stool and started conversation again about our nosey neighbor, Mrs. Mitchum, who had brought over an olive loaf for him the other day and made him give her a tour of his house.

We talked for another two hours, enjoying the wine and learning more about each other little pieces at a time. By the time I walked him to the front door, it was past my usual bed time and I knew I would be more tired than usual in the morning.

But I fell asleep easily and without tears.

Ben had been a therapy of sorts. And I couldn't make myself regret the time we'd spent together. I decided to ignore Emma's words completely. I knew Ben better than she did and I wasn't ready to give up this new friend I'd only just made.

Stage Three: Bargaining

I survived denial.

I crawled my way through anger.

And now I would battle bargaining.

Before this happened to me and before I became a clinical study on what it's like to lose someone important, I had always thought of bargaining as the easy stage.

It's so much easier to wish someone back than admit that they're gone. It didn't seem like a difficult process before I had to go through it myself. But I had never known real grief before, so I couldn't picture myself pleading for my husband's return or desperately begging God to bring him back to me.

And that is the crux of it right there. Desperate. Desperation. *Desperately* willing to give up anything if I could just see him one more time, speak to him one more time. Kiss him one last time.

I have become so desperate in my grief that I can't be reasoned with. The pain continues to slice at my chest like a deadly knife, digging deep and making wounds that I am convinced can never be healed. The sheer intensity of it only worsens as the days go by. There is no end in sight. No reprieve or fast breath of relief.

There is only sadness and tears.

In the middle of this agony, I begin to think of Grady less and less. My life moves on. The kids keep me busy. School days fill my time and practices hoard my nights. I am becoming more self-sufficient every day and for the things I cannot do myself, I now have a sturdy support system that swoops in before I ever need to ask.

At night I lie in bed and force myself to think as much about Grady as I can. I constantly worry about losing all of my memories of him, of not being able to remember things just as they were. I do whatever I can to shove thoughts of everyone else out of my head and think only of Grady.

Because he is not the only person I want to think about. And I hate myself for that. I hate that my thoughts won't stay loyal to my husband.

I will do anything to ease this guilt and misery, to tape my broken heart back together. I will do anything to think of Grady as my husband. Even still. Even beyond his death.

And to think of Ben as only a friend.

Chapter Fourteen

"You guys shouldn't have let me sleep in! I could have gotten up!" I wandered into the kitchen, following my nose and the smell of freshly brewed coffee.

My parents had arrived from Florida the day before. They were from this area and had raised Emma and me here, but took their retirement some place warm.

After the four inches of snowstorm we got last night, I didn't blame them. They were lucky it didn't start until after we got home from the airport. It had been a very mild fall. New England had one of the prettiest winters in the country and I was excited to finally have snow on the ground.

This was our first real snow of the season and it was just in time for Christmas. The kids had been off since last Friday and I appreciated the snow for them and for my parents.

Christmas would be hard enough this year; it helped that it would at least be pretty.

"No, grandparents are supposed to wake up early, Lizbeth. That's why we came." My dad sat hunched over the kids' table with his knees pressed to his chest and a princess crown on his head.

My dad, Matthew Ferris, looked like the banker he used to be even in his late sixties, except for the tiara perched atop his head. His strong nose and angular jaw gave him the visage of a man in charge. Until his grandchildren surrounded him. Then he turned into a big puddle of grandpa and spoiled them rotten.

My mother, Julia, stood next to my Kuerig, already brewing me a cup. She looked sleepy still, hugging a cup of her own coffee and dressed in her fuzzy pink pajama pants.

"I thought we would wake you up." She passed the hot coffee to me and I inhaled deeply. "We were so loud down here. Did you take a sleeping pill?"

"No," I told her. "I haven't taken one in a long time. I've started to sleep better lately."

"Oh," her soft voice pulled on my heart. My mother was the sweetest woman I knew and she had been incredible during this time. Both of my parents were great actually. They loved each other deeply. One of the hardest things for them about Grady's death was that I wouldn't get to grow old with him. They felt they had something unique and beautifully special. They had wanted the same thing for me.

I looked out the windows to the snow-covered backyard. "I should go shovel the drive before we need to go anywhere."

"You didn't hire it done?" my dad asked while he pulled Jace onto his long legs.

"No, but that's a good idea." I wondered if Dillan, the kid I hired to mow over the summer, was back for Christmas break. I could give him a call...

"Then who's out there shoveling it? I thought you paid a man or I would have done it myself."

"What do you mean?"

"Liz, there's a man out there shoveling your walk right now."

My stomach flipped as I hurried to the front door. My family room had a nice view of the front yard and part of Ben's yard, but I had to go to my front door to see the driveway. I held my coffee carefully in my hands so not to spill it, but I had to confirm my suspicions.

I opened the door and stepped out onto the shoveled porch in just my slippers. The cold, icy air bit at my skin and blew up my thin pajamas. I shivered in the morning air as I took in the sight of Ben working his way up and down my long drive.

"Hey!" I called out to him. His head lifted to face me, and even though he wore a stocking cap and a scarf that covered half of his face, I could see his eyes brighten with a smile. "I hope you're not expecting a tip!"

His shoulders shook as he laughed at my joke. He stuck the shovel into a snowbank and walked over to me, tugging his scarf down as he went.

"No tip? I quit."

"You can't quit!" I squeaked. "You're only halfway finished."

He grinned at me. "And it doesn't look like you'll get out here anytime soon, lazy bones. Did the kids let you sleep in this morning?"

I handed him my coffee without thinking. He took it and held it in front of his face for a minute before taking a healthy drink.

"My parents flew in yesterday," I reminded him. "They let me have some peace. Well, after Jace, Abby and Lucy all woke up and got out of my bed."

"Oh, that's right. They're the ones responsible for ruining wine night."

I shook my head at him. "I'm sure you survived."

"Well, I drank the wine, if that's what you're implying."

"All of it?"

He laughed into my coffee, "I'm teasing. I saved it for you."

"Of course you did! I'm so much more fun than drinking by yourself."

"Yeah, our two glasses of wine once a week, really blow my mind."

"You're so full of yourself today. It must be the snow. It's gone straight to your head."

I reached out and tucked a stray strand of hair back into his stocking cap. It had fallen over his eyes and was undoubtedly adorable, but I knew it had to bother him while he tried to work.

His skin was so cold to my touch. I pressed my hand against his face, hoping to help warm him up.

I watched his eyes darken at the gesture and my stomach flipped again.

"I missed you last night, Liz."

His rumble of words hit me straight in the belly and caused tingles to ripple out from my center. I took a steadying breath and tried to banish my hormones.

This had been happening more and more lately. He had somehow infiltrated my life in as many ways as he could. He ate dinner at our house often and came over after the kids were in bed to talk over wine or popcorn. He helped me around the house and in the yard and even helped Blake with his math homework occasionally.

I had gotten used to seeing him almost every day and when our schedules didn't line up or we spent our evenings apart, there were always text messages to exchange or short phone calls to check in.

I wasn't surprised to see him out shoveling my walk without asking him to do so, but I was so grateful that he chose to help me. I was like this never-ending charity case for him and he was my mega hot Good Samaritan.

I knew our relationship was unconventional, but I couldn't stop myself from drawing closer to him. He had saved me more times than once. And more than that, I really enjoyed spending time with him.

"Liz, is everything okay?" My mom's voice saved me from replying to Ben's sweet words.

"Hi, Mom." I sounded ridiculously breathless. My cheeks heated with a mixture of shame and embarrassment. "I, um, I'm just talking with Ben. Ben this is my mom Julia. Mom, this is Ben, my next-door neighbor. He's the one shoveling the drive."

"Hi, Ben." My mom extended her slender hand, only to be swallowed up in Ben's big, gloved one.

"Hi, Julia. It's a pleasure to meet you."

"Thank you for shoveling for us. That is very generous." I watched my mother assess Ben from head to toe and I felt guilt all over again. I didn't know what this looked like to her, but I could only imagine the thoughts running through her head. Especially because Ben still held my coffee cup.

"He's just being neighborly," I explained quickly. "Ben is the best neighbor. He helps out a lot."

Ben's face flashed with irritation and I immediately regretted my words, but it was too late now. I should be able to explain Ben to my mom without feeling this sick to my stomach. Ben and I weren't anything but friends. I didn't understand where this acidic feeling of indignity came from.

"Just being neighborly," he repeated with a very unamused voice.

"We're friends too," I blurted. "We've become friends. Good friends. The kids love him." *Oh, god, I needed to stop.*

"Then I should thank you for that too," my mom offered. "Liz's father and I have been so frustrated by how far away we live. It eases my mind that there's someone close by she can count on."

"Liz can definitely count on me," Ben told her. "Like she said, I'm the best neighbor."

Oh, good grief.

The kids started screaming in the background, fighting over something or other, probably my dad. My mom excused herself to go check on them.

"I'm so sorry," I whispered as soon as she disappeared. I didn't even know what I was apologizing for; I just knew I owed Ben some kind of explanation.

"What's there to be sorry for, neighbor?" He handed me back my cup that had cooled considerably from the winter wind.

I shivered on the door step, unsure how to proceed with Ben. "I'm an idiot. You're obviously more than my neighbor."

"A friend, right?" But his words tasted bitter.

"Ben, I'm not sure what-"

His fierce expression softened and his shoulders relaxed. "I am your friend, Liz. We're good friends."

"Right," I whispered against the clenching feeling in my chest. "Good friends."

My dad appeared behind me suddenly. "Matthew Ferris," he all but shouted. He stuck his hand in Ben's face and exerted his lifetime of distinguished authority figure. "I hear you're the one we have to thank for the driveway."

Ben graciously shook my dad's hand. "Ben Tyler. It's nice to meet you, Matthew."

"And what do you do for a living, Ben?"

"Really, dad?" Ben was never going to talk to me again after this morning. If he hadn't thought of me as a head case before this moment, then he would have no choice but to now.

But Ben was apparently used to crazy people. He gave my dad a charming smile and said, "I'm a lawyer."

That settled dad down some. But I still felt the need to explain, "Ben's dad is going to retire in a few years, so Ben is transitioning to take over their firm."

"Oh," my dad muttered, unable to come up with a legitimate reason to hate Ben based on his occupation. "Well, that's... good for you, son. I'll just go find your mother now, Elizabeth, and see what she's up to."

"Good idea, Dad."

"Nice to meet you, Ben." My dad practically ran into the kitchen.

"Are your parents scouting me?" His earlier irritation had disappeared and been replaced with his usual amusement.

I shivered and looked toward the kitchen. "Something like that. I haven't mentioned you before; I think they're beyond curious."

He let out a frustrated sigh that made me turn to meet his dark gaze. "Have I told you before that you can be aggravating?"

"Once or twice."

"Will I see you at all this week?"

I shook my head and stared into my coffee, ignoring the sinking feeling in my stomach. "My parents are staying with me through New Years."

"Mmm," he acknowledged. "I'd better get back to shoveling. And you should get out of this cold."

I looked up and braved his warm gaze. "I'm going to miss wine night," I whispered.

His eyes heated up and whatever tension had been left from our awkwardness earlier floated away. "Call or text me. I, at least, want to hear that you remembered to buy milk."

My heart jumped in my chest. "Miss me that much?"

"Miss you more than that much."

My lips parted in surprise, but as usual he left me to stare after him. He readjusted his scarf to cover his mouth and walked back to his shovel.

I hurried inside, suddenly aware of how cold I was. I carried my cooled coffee back to the kitchen and rinsed it out in the sink. I had just started a new cup when I felt my parents' presence fill up the space behind me.

"He's your neighbor?" My mother's voice sounded incredibly suspicious.

I turned around to face the inquiry. What were they thinking about me? I immediately imagined the worst.

What kind of woman made friends with other men nine months after her husband died? What kind of woman flirted with another man nine months after her husband died?

I winced internally. Not a good woman. I knew that much.

"Yes, my neighbor. He moved in a few months ago. He's been... honestly, he's been great. The kids love him. He's helped out so much. I just... he's just a really nice guy."

"He seems like a nice guy," my mom admitted softly. "He also seems very interested in you."

My dad looked between the two of us, carefully gaging our tension. His heavy arm wrapped around my shoulders and he pulled me into the sanctuary of his embrace. This was the safest place I knew of now that Grady was dead and I couldn't help but feel small and childish wrapped in my daddy's arms. But it was a good feeling. "He'd be crazy not to be interested in you."

I smiled through blurry tears. "We're just friends." I had repeated that simple line so many times that it had started to chafe my throat whenever I forced the words out.

My mom reached out to squeeze my arm. Her voice never rose above a whisper, "It's okay to move on, Lizzy."

"No, it's not," I hiccuped on a broken sob.

"It is," my dad rumbled against my temple. "Grady never would have wanted you to be alone for the rest of your life. You have too much on your plate. I'm not saying that this is the man to move on with. I just want you to open up to the possibility. You don't have to do this alone. We all understand."

I loved my father, but I hated his words. Didn't he know how much I loved Grady? I'd said vows that would last forever. I promised to love one man for the rest of my life.

And those were not empty vows. I meant them the day I got married and I still meant them today. Nobody could compete with the man that Grady was.

I didn't even want to try to find a man as good as the only man I'd ever loved.

Ben was a great guy and I enjoyed spending time with him. I could admit, even if I didn't want to, that I even enjoyed flirting with him occasionally. But I had never thought about him seriously like that.

We were neighbors. We were also friends. But there were no other feelings between us.

"It's too soon," I cried to my parents. "It's way too soon to even think about that. I can't... I couldn't... I could never do that to Grady."

"Oh, Sweetheart." My mother's arms wrapped around my back and I felt her hot tears fall on my shoulder. "Grady is gone, Lizzy. He's gone forever. You're not doing anything to him. He would never begrudge you for falling for someone else. You have got to give yourself some forgiveness. Don't tie yourself up in his memory for the rest of your life and miss what else could be out there."

"Are you telling me to find someone?" The disbelief in my voice echoed through the room.

"No," my dad huffed quickly. "We are not telling you to go out right now and start looking. But we want you to be happy again, baby girl. We want you to find happiness somehow. And we want these children to find happiness again. Don't shut yourself out to the possibilities, even if they go against your grief."

I cried harder into his chest for long moments. The kids ran crazy around the house, but the three of us couldn't bring ourselves to separate.

I was a thirty-two-year-old woman, with a family of my own, but there was no place I felt more comfort and acceptance than in my parents' arms. Even now.

Emma burst into the kitchen on a gust of outdoor air. "Hey!" she called, completely oblivious to our moment. "I saw Ben outside shoveling. He's freezing. Liz, you need to take him some coffee or something..." her voice trailed off and then changed completely when she asked, "What did I miss?"

"They met Ben," I sniffed.

"Oh, so you saw how in love with her he is and how hard she's trying to deny her feelings for him."

"Emma! None of that is true!"

"Emma!" my mom gasped.

She started ripping off her outdoor gear. Her hat landed with a slap on the island, then her scarf and gloves. Her coat followed in a messy heap of winter wear.

"What? Did you meet him? He's so obvious!"

Sometimes it was very hard to imagine my sister as the future counselor she aspired to be. Sometimes it was hard to imagine her as anything but the bratty six-year-old she acted like.

"He isn't in love with me. Stop."

Emma rolled her big eyes. "He's one of my closest friends, Liz. I think I would know."

"No, he's one of *my* closest friends, I think *I* would know."

Emma snorted. "Don't tell him that. I doubt he'd appreciate the fact that he's been friend-zoned."

Ben's earlier irritation echoed in my head. I shook away the memory immediately. It didn't matter what my sister thought or suspected, I had told my parents the truth. It was way too soon to even consider the possibility of moving beyond Grady. I couldn't stomach the idea of being with another man outside the boundaries of friendship. And I trusted Ben enough to believe he would never try to make me.

"We're just friends, Emma. I need you to understand this."

She opened her mouth to argue, but Blake and Abby ran into the kitchen with a flurry of motion and panic.

"Jace found Papa's shaving cream!" Abby shouted.

"He's painting his room with it!" Blake shouted over her.

The race up the stairs ended all adult conversation for a long time. For the first time in my life, I was grateful for Jace's destruction.

Chapter Fifteen

Christmas Eve I had invited Katherine and Trevor over to share the holiday with us. My mom, Emma and I had cooked an elaborate spread and Katherine had brought the desserts this time.

My parents were familiar with Grady's family by now, so the only awkwardness that existed that night was between my in-laws and me.

Trevor and I had not talked since Thanksgiving. I suspected we both kept our distance because we were too ashamed to confront the other person.

My chest ached when I remembered how terribly I'd acted that day and how rude I had been to him. I knew the depth of my own pain; I knew how debilitating it could be. I should have had more grace for Trevor. I should never have said those things to him.

I had managed to avoid him for the last month, but now that we were face-to-face I knew I needed to apologize.

If for no other reason than Grady would have been so completely disappointed with me if he were still alive. He would not have tolerated this behavior from Trevor or from me.

"Hey, Trev, can I talk to you for a sec in the kitchen?" I asked gently after homemade cheesecake had been served.

He hesitated for a few seconds by looking everywhere but at me. Just as my nerves truly began to twist, he shrugged casually and said, "Sure." He stood up and walked into the kitchen without looking at me.

Once we were both in the kitchen, I started looking around for a better place to talk. Everyone could hear us in here and I wanted to give us enough privacy so that we could both say what we needed to say.

I walked to the mudroom and beckoned for him to follow me.

Once we were alone in the garage, I clicked on the light and stood shivering in the cold air. Trevor shut the door, walked down the three steps and stared at my car without saying anything.

Okay, so he wasn't going to make this easy on me. I deserved that.

I cleared my throat and gathered some courage. "Trev... Trevor, I am so sorry for what I said at Thanksgiving. I wasn't myself and I hate that I just unloaded on you like that. I've been under so much stress ever since Grady. Well, you know that. I guess, I'm just... I'm heartbroken. I don't think I've had a single clear thought in over a year. I was rude and hurtful and what I said was uncalled for. Please forgive me. I hate that there is this distance between us."

He didn't say anything for a long minute. I held my breath, waiting for him to explode at me or agree with me… or I didn't know what. I braced myself against his retaliation though. I'd picked at his flaws and the weak point that had been magnified by Grady's death, but I knew I had plenty of my own. He could rip me apart if he wanted to, shove all of my shortcomings in my face and remind me what a terrible mother I had been in Grady's absence.

But he was a better person than me. Instead of doing any of that, he took a deep breath and pulled me into a tight hug.

"I get it, Liz," he promised. "You're right. I was… I was messing things up. And I'm sorry. It's just that sometimes I miss him so much… you know? I don't even know how to get out of bed some days or how I'm going to survive another day in that office. It hurts down to my bones. Losing my dad was something else, but I've never known anything like losing my brother."

His words ripped and tore at my chest, puncturing my heart with the agony I heard in them. "I know, Trev. *I know.*" We both sniffled, desperately trying to hold ourselves together.

It wasn't just Christmas that had left me emotionally raw and fresh with grief. I hated having anything between Trevor and me. Other than my kids, Trevor was the closest thing to Grady I had left. Sometimes that hurt more than it helped, but I knew that I wouldn't always feel this way. One day, my grief would soften and I would be able to enjoy Trevor because he reminded me so much of my husband. I couldn't imagine not having him as a big part of my life.

After long moments, we pulled back from each other. I felt his forgiveness slide into place between us. Most of my spirit and heart were still in complete upheaval, but with the closure of this conversation, I felt some of those important pieces return home.

"I bid on a new job," he told me conversationally. "It's looking pretty good too. It's for a new strip mall near Hartford. Nice, long job with a great paycheck."

"That's great, Trevor! That's really exciting."

Trevor's smile faded some when he said, "You know, he really did teach me everything he knew. I like to pretend that I don't know what I'm doing because then I don't have to think about him, think about all the time he spent grooming me to take over. But I am prepared for this, Liz. I *can* do this and do it well."

"I never doubted you, Trevor. Grady believed in you and he had every right to. You're one of the smartest men I know."

"I've always felt the same way about you, Lizzy. From the first time I met you, I knew that if Grady chose you, then you were someone worth knowing."

Hot tears pooled in my lashes and I couldn't swallow around the lump in my throat. "He was the greatest guy. I just miss him so much."

Trevor pulled me into another hug. "Me too. But we're going to get through this. I know we will. We have each other. He didn't just prepare us to run his business or raise his kids; he prepared us to go on living without him. We can't let him down in any of it."

I nodded against his broad chest but couldn't bring myself to say anything. I had lashed out at Trevor for letting Grady down, but what about me? How had I been as a mother? As a grieving widow?

Failure.

I felt the word brand itself on my skin. It burned hot and final.

Trevor stepped back, patting my shoulder one last time. "We should get back, yeah?"

I nodded, "Thanks for not hating me."

He chuckled good-naturedly. "Never, Lizzy."

He led the way back into the house. We joined the rest of the family seamlessly. There was a subdued excitement buzzing through the air. The thrill of the season was with us, but we restrained it out of respect for Grady.

Abby and Blake had the hardest time. They couldn't help but look forward to the morning, but the painful ache for their daddy held them back.

By the time we moved to the living room for the traditional opening of grandparent presents, Abby had started shaking, struggling not to cry.

"Abs," I whispered just loud enough for her to hear it. She looked back at me and I beckoned for her to squeeze onto the couch with me.

She jumped at the invitation. She snuggled into my side and wrapped her arms around my waist. I kissed the top of her head and stayed there a moment, breathing in her wild red curls. Her hot tears started to fall on my forearm and then she sucked in a gasping sob.

Blake had been staring intently at the tree, but as soon as Abby's cry broke the silence, he whipped around and leapt to join us on the couch. His face was haunted with grief. I could see the battle inside of him not to cry, not to ruin this happy night. But it was no use.

Lucy joined us next, tears streaming down her freckled cheeks. Jace crawled on my lap too, making himself at home on top of the pile. His chubby little arms wrapped around my neck and squeezed tight. He didn't mourn for Grady the same way we did. He had been too little when Grady died to remember much of his daddy. I hated that for him. I hated that he couldn't have the memories that the rest of us did.

It was a little awkward, breaking down like this in front of my parents, my in-laws and my sister. We had a lovely dinner and even though my make-up with Trevor was emotional, it was nothing like this.

This was our grief and pain at our deepest. This was our hearts and souls scraped raw. This was desperation so intense I felt it in my bones, in the broken places of my soul. And that my children shared this grief made it so much worse.

I didn't know how to deal with their pain. Their little bodies trembled against me and I was soaked with their tears. The worst part was that I couldn't do *anything* to stop this hurt.

In that moment I would have done anything to stop the moment. I would have given up anything and everything to have Grady back with us. I would have traded places with him in a heartbeat if I could just give my children their daddy back.

"I have an idea," I finally announced when the worst of the crying ebbed. "Before we open presents, why don't we share something we miss about daddy? It's hard not having him here with us, but maybe if we share our memories, it will feel like he's not so far away."

"That's a lovely idea, Liz," Katherine agreed in a soft voice. I looked up to see her face wet from her own tears. She nodded at me graciously.

"I'll start." I wiped at my face with the back of my hands and tried to speak words that would hurt like physical blows. "I miss how he used to come home from work with Christmas-themed baked goods or ornaments he spotted and had to buy. He always wanted to add things to our house. He started a new tradition every year. He just loved Christmas so much and he wanted the kids to experience every single thing they could. Last year, we had to give up most of them because he was so sick, so he had the kids and I bake about three hundred sugar cookies and then he took us around from room to room passing them out and giving them to nurses. I burned half of them. I was a mess last year. Not that I'm any better this year..." I wiped at my face and rubbed my nose on my sleeve. My mom stood up and handed me a tissue. "I was so mad at him. I didn't want to think about other people. We were hurting so much, I just couldn't take anymore. But by the end of the evening, he had made me laugh so many times that I had forgotten why we were there. He turned that horrible time into a week filled with happy memories. Memories that we will keep with us forever."

142

Blake lifted his head and laughed, "Remember when that old guy made us sing to him."

I chuckled too, thinking about the dying elderly man that had wanted a Christmas carol. "I think he regretted asking us. Your dad couldn't carry a tune for anything."

Lucy and Abby started giggling too, remembering the terribly off key rendition of We Wish You a Merry Christmas Grady made us perform.

"I didn't know you did that," my mom hiccupped.

I nodded, it was just one of many things Grady had done to make Christmas special last year. "It was the week before you came up."

"Remember when we built that monster snow fort?" Blake sat up with excitement. His green eyes were bright from tears and memories. "It was so big! He made tunnels and it had different rooms! It took us forever, but it was so cool when we finished it."

"It did take you forever. You guys worked on that for days. You were just a little thing, Luce. You could stand up and walk right through it." She smiled at me, not remembering the actual fort, but loving that she was included.

"He got stuck in the door," Abby added. "He didn't make the hole big enough!"

We laughed again. He had nearly collapsed the entire thing trying to get out of it.

"One year when we were kids," Trevor started. "He wanted to build the biggest snowman on the block. He was always like that, always building things, always wanting them to be bigger and better than everyone else's. So he enlisted me and the help of two of the guys we used to run with, Johnny Gillette and Bryan Fall. We spent all day working on that thing, building the base and then the middle part. It was huge. I mean..." Trevor held out his arms wide, "huge. But by the time we got to the head, we were all too tired and cold to put much effort into it. So the head ended up about the size of a baseball, sitting up on top of this monstrous body. It didn't even look like a snowman. It was just this big old blob of snow."

On and on the memories went. We couldn't seem to stop. Everyone had a great memory of Grady, even my parents.

By the time we opened presents, we all had to dry our eyes, but there were smiles on our faces.

I hadn't remembered Grady like this yet. Whenever I thought about him over the last several months, I had been too racked with grief to let my thoughts be good ones. And I couldn't remember a time when any of us had spoken so openly about him, remembering the great man that he was instead of the man we all wished was still alive.

My kids smiled and laughed and screamed for joy while they opened presents. Most of the gifts were still hidden away in my closet, bought online and shipped straight to my house. All of the years before, Grady and I had made special shopping dates to pick out presents for the kids.

This year I had nearly given up before I even started. I was too overwhelmed with the responsibility of making this holiday happy for my kids. I hadn't felt the desire to celebrate anything.

But just like all the years before, it was never me that made this holiday special. It was Grady. It was always Grady. Even in death he put smiles on our faces and love in our hearts.

This holiday was especially hard because he wasn't here to celebrate with us and yet, we could make it through today and tomorrow and all the days after because of the memories he had given us that would stay with us forever.

I closed my eyes, completely overcome with devotion for a man I would love forever and beyond. Thinking about Ben in this same context seemed silly. How could any man compare to the husband I'd loved and lost? How could I even entertain those ridiculous feelings? They were so incomparable to what I felt for Grady.

After presents and more cheesecake, my parents took my kids upstairs to help them get ready for bed and I walked Katherine and Trevor to the door. Trevor threw his arms around me and squeezed me in a tight hug before hurrying to the car to warm it up for his mom.

"That was really a lovely evening," Katherine told me as she put her coat and gloves on. "I have been dreading today for so long, I just... I never expected to enjoy it so much."

"I know exactly what you mean. What are your plans for tomorrow?"

She hesitated with her hand on the frosted screen door. "Trevor is going to come over in the morning and then we'll go to my brother's house. Clay has five children of his own and sixteen grandchildren. It should be busy enough to keep us entertained."

"Thank you for spending tonight with us, Katherine. I know things have been strained lately... I just wanted to apologize for my behavior on Thanksgiving. I should never have said those things to Trevor. And I feel terrible for ruining your meal and-"

"Liz, please don't bother apologizing to me." Her gloved hand landed on my shoulder. I lifted my eyes to meet hers wet with new tears. "I know how hard it is now that Grady is gone and I know how frustrated you must be with my son's behavior. But do you know what I saw on Thanksgiving?"

I shook my head; I couldn't even imagine what she saw. A woman crazed with grief? A hot mess that should seriously consider therapy? I wasn't sure I wanted to know the answer.

"I saw you treat Trevor like family. And even though you were furious with him, I saw that you still love him. He doesn't have Grady anymore, but he still has you."

"Katherine, of course. You are my family still, even if Grady isn't here to legally tie us together."

She smiled warmly at me. "When my husband died… well, I didn't see much of his family after that. We all got too busy or moved on or I don't know what, but it hurt me that his parents didn't reach out more or spend time with their grandchildren. Now, I can see that they were probably too torn apart by their own grief. Besides, my boys had been much older. They were teenagers and difficult to connect with. I suppose I've been waiting for you to pull back too." She cupped my face affectionately. "I couldn't bear it, Liz. The idea of not just losing Grady, but you and the kids is too much for me. So, yes, please yell at Trevor as often as you'd like. Ruin as many holidays as you want to. Just don't shut us out of your lives, please."

I threw my arms around her and hugged her tightly. "I won't," I promised. "You are my family. Grady brought us together, but I'm going to keep us together."

We hugged each other for a couple long minutes and then separated ways. It was easier tonight than it had been in the past. We were both hurting, but she was right, we were family too. And we would help each other get through this together.

Chapter Sixteen

By lunchtime the next day, I had thrown away at least three thousand feet of wrapping paper, dealt with approximately six hundred batteries and cried too many times to count. But we survived Christmas morning.

It helped that my parents and Emma had come to share the holiday. I didn't think I could do this without them.

My kids endured a large part of their grief last night and the excitement of Christmas morning overrode their sadness, for which I was eternally grateful.

The morning had been insanity, as usual. But things had quieted down now that we'd enjoyed a great Christmas morning brunch and they all had brand new presents to occupy their time.

I finished up the dishes and then checked my phone for the first time all day. I had bunches of texts from various relatives wishing me happy holidays, but one stood out above all others, a text from Ben.

Merry Christmas. He had texted about an hour ago.

Merry Christmas to you too. Hope you had a great morning! I wrote back.

I moved to the couch in front of the tree and tucked my feet underneath me. There were lots of things I should be doing, but I couldn't find the motivation. And this time it wasn't because grief had weighted me down.

For the first time in a long time, my children were happily occupied and I had a couple minutes to myself in my own home. I decided to take full advantage and enjoy this quiet moment in front of my beautiful tree before I had to take it all down.

It was a fake one, but still pretty with all the lights and ornaments hung around it. When Grady was healthy, he would make a big night out of going to pick out a real tree- the perfect tree. Then I would spend the next month vacuuming up needles. Of course, he didn't care. He loved the fresh pine smell and the wide-eyed wonder the kids had the night we shopped for it. And to be honest, I loved it for those reasons too.

Last Christmas, when he was too sick to leave the hospital, Emma and my parents had surprised me by decorating my entire house while I was at the hospital. They had enlisted my kids' help and had outdone themselves by making every room festive. They'd bought the fake tree because we'd all been too busy going back and forth to the hospital to deal with a real one.

I was thankful for it this year, when the same thing was true, but for different reasons.

My phone buzzed on the cushion next to me. I picked it up to find another text from Ben. *I'm celebrating with my parents tonight, so my morning has been pretty lazy so far.*

I grinned when I texted back, *Pop-Tarts?*

You got it. But they were the sugar cookie kind, so that's festive, right?

You should have come over for brunch with us. My stomach dipped after I pressed send. Why had I told him that? How inappropriate! My fingers started shaking. I had to stop sending him the wrong messages. At least it was over now though, so I didn't have to worry about following through with the offer.

Thankfully, he didn't acknowledge the invitation. Instead, he wrote something even more perplexing. *Are you busy now? Or do you think you could spare a few minutes?*

I debated how to answer, but curiosity got the best of me. *The kids are pretty quiet right now. Lots of new toys to play with. What do you need?*

You.

His one word answer caused my heart to spiral into overdrive. I felt my face heat with a flush and a shiver tingled down my spine.

But then the rest of his text came in and I forced myself to calm down.

You to come over. I have something for you.

What is it?

I'm not sure you understand how Christmas works.

I smiled at his teasing words. *You want me to come over to your house?*

Yes...

"Who are you texting?" Emma plopped onto the seat next to me and pulled her knees to her chest.

I looked up, immediately feeling guilty. "Ben."

I expected her to jump up and do some kind of victory dance, but she kept her neutral expression. "Is he having a good Christmas?"

"I don't think his has really started yet. He's seeing his parents tonight."

"Gotchya." She reached for a pillow and hugged it against her chest.

"He wants me to go over there," I confessed in a rush of words. "He says he has something for me. Did he get you something?"

"Yes, he did."

"What was it?"

"A scarf that I picked out and sent him the links for." She smiled shamelessly.

God, I loved my sister.

"Well, I didn't pick out anything for him to buy me. I can't imagine what it is."

"Go find out."

I chewed undecidedly on my bottom lip. "I didn't get him anything." My gaze bounced around the room as I tried to figure out something I could wrap quickly and re-gift.

"I doubt he is expecting anything, Lizbeth."

"What did you get him?" Curiosity about Emma and Ben's friendship burned oddly in my stomach. I couldn't figure out why it bothered me that they were so close. Ben and I were close too. I shouldn't feel jealous about what they had together.

Jealous?

Did I really feel jealous?

"A wallet," she told me. "He picked it out and sent me the links."

I laughed at their silly gift exchange. "Maybe he got me the same scarf. Different color?"

"Maybe," my sister shrugged. "It's a very cute scarf. I guess there's only one way to find out..."

I didn't move a muscle. My phone screen had darkened so I couldn't see Ben's invitation anymore, but I felt it all over my skin and low in my belly.

"Go!" Emma encouraged. "I'll make sure the house doesn't burn down."

"I won't be gone long," I promised, jumping up from the couch.

"Don't worry about it if you are."

"Okay, but I won't be."

"Whatever, just *go*!"

I tucked my phone into the pocket of my black skinny jeans and slipped on my boots. I had dressed up a little for Christmas in a red, silky shirt-style tunic and gold bangly jewelry. It was the most effort I had made since Thanksgiving. I pulled on my coat as I slipped out the front door.

I hurried from my house to his, making long, dragging footsteps in the snow across our lawns. It was cold outside and I was anxious to see this present.

I raised my hand to knock on his door, but it swung open for me instead. My hand hung there while he took his time raking his eyes from

149

my toes to the top of my head. He nudged the screen door open and I slid by him into his house.

Ben had never invited me over to his house before. He always came over to mine, for obvious reasons.

He had good taste though. The rooms I could see were decorated with rich browns and aged wood accents. I could picture him stretched out on the chunky leather couch, watching something on his massive TV mounted to the wall. There was a small tree set on an end table with a few gifts wrapped professionally beneath. The only thing I could find fault with was that his beautiful house felt a little empty. It was such a big space for only him.

"I like your house better." His low voice came from behind me. His fingers landed on my shoulders and tugged at my coat. I let him help me out of it.

"Yours is gorgeous," I told him a little breathlessly. The pads of his fingers trailed down my arms as he removed my coat. I slipped out of my boots quickly to put space between us.

"Mine is lonely," he said. "Yours is full of life."

I spun around to face him. I would have never described my house like that. To me, my house felt full of death. Full of ghosts. Full of memories that ate at me day and night.

"Why did you buy such a big house for only you?" Changing the subject seemed like the wisest decision.

He took a step towards me and I took a quick one back. He smiled a little, amused with my jumpy behavior.

I couldn't help it! This was the first time we had ever been alone, truly alone. The kids weren't asleep in the other room or running around at our feet. It was just he and I and this great big house.

Nerves skittered over my skin and pooled in my stomach. I didn't know how to handle all of these feelings and sensations, especially because my reaction seemed so silly.

Ben saw me as a friend, not anything more, but not anything less either.

"Well, I didn't think I would always be the only one living in it," he admitted.

"Oh." I sidestepped his couch and looked into the kitchen. Sure enough, a box of Christmas Pop-Tarts sat on the counter. "Mrs. Tyler and the kids, you mean?"

I turned back to see him shrug. "I don't know. Maybe when I first bought it, I thought that. But, I'm not sure this is the right place to raise a family anymore."

"You think you'd move?" I hated the sinking feeling that washed over me, a heavy wave that threatened to drag me under a new surface of sadness.

He watched me carefully, when he said, "I would move for the right woman."

His words hurt in a way I never expected them to. Talking about Ben finding the woman he wanted to marry was one thing, but facing the reality that I could lose him completely someday had never occurred to me. My heart squeezed with confusion and resistance.

I didn't want that to happen. I wanted to keep Ben to myself. Selfishly, I didn't care about his happiness or desire to get married and have kids. I wanted him always, just like we were.

"Liz, I... I want to... I have your gift." He walked over to the small tree and pulled a perfectly wrapped present from beneath it.

An ivory card sat against the red plaid paper and gold bow. My name was written in his slender scrawl.

"Are you going to tell me what it is?" I looked up at him with shaking hands, almost too afraid to see what he had thought to buy me.

It didn't feel like a scarf.

"How about I watch you open it instead."

"I didn't buy you anything, Ben. I'm so sorry; I barely got the shopping done for my kids-"

"Liz," he said in a soft voice, cutting off my rambling. His warm hand wrapped around my trembling one. "I never expected one in return. I bought this because it reminded me of you. You've become someone that means a lot to me and I wanted to... to show you how much I care for you."

I stared at the prettily wrapped present in my hands and debated handing it back to him. I didn't want to know how much he cared for me.

"It's not going to bite," he nudged gently.

I looked up into his dark brown eyes and it hit me. I might be afraid of what this present represented on his side, but I would open it up anyway because I cared for him. I couldn't hurt him by refusing this. I wouldn't hurt him.

I carefully untied the bow and slid my finger beneath the seam of the paper. He took it from me so I could hold a black box without a label.

My heart jumped to my throat. I could only imagine one kind of gift in a box like this and I didn't want it. I didn't want jewelry from Ben. I didn't know what jewelry from Ben even meant!

I swallowed my fear and opened the box. I gasped at the thoughtfulness behind this surprise. Relief rushed over me and I nearly stumbled from the force of it.

In the box, wrapped in shiny red tissue paper, sat a snowflake ornament made out of wine corks. A shimmery blue ribbon had been fastened to the outer edge and gave it some color.

It was a perfect gift. I loved it.

"I love it," I told him on a whisper. I picked it up and held it delicately in my hands.

"They're ours."

I looked up at him, confused by what he meant. He stared at me intently, watching my reaction. "What do you mean?"

"It was an accident at first. I would put the corks in my pocket after I opened a bottle at your house and I never seemed to get them in the trash. They piled up on my dresser. Then I saw a little knickknack a coworker had bought, made out of corks. She told me she bought it at a craft fair. I tracked down the person that made them and had her make this for you."

Awe and pleasant surprise warmed me all over. "You went to a lot of work."

"I like how it turned out." He reached for it, running his hands over the corks.

"We drink a lot of wine."

He grinned at me. "We don't always finish the bottle in one night." He took a step closer to me, closing that confusing space that separated us. "These corks represent a lot of good times. It's hard to believe we've only known each other a few months."

"Are you saying it feels like longer?" I teased.

"I'm saying it seems like it took too long to meet you." He took another step closer. I could feel the heat of his body and the brush of his gray sweater on my hands.

"Some days I don't know what I would do without you," I whispered, surprised at my courage. But these words were true and in the isolation of his quiet house I felt safe enough to speak them.

"Then I'm glad you have me."

I looked down at the snowflake ornament, too unsettled by his words, only for him to recapture my attention when he said, "Liz, look up."

"Why?" But I did.

"Mistletoe," he murmured.

Then he kissed me. His soft lips pressed against mine in a gentle kiss that lasted only a second. I barely had a chance to let my eyes flutter closed before he stepped back again.

I blinked up, but there was nothing there. The only thing that hung from the vaulted ceiling was a ceiling fan.

No mistletoe.

My cheeks burned and my stomach flipped. He'd kissed me. Ben had just kissed me.

How could he? I was still married!

No, that was wrong.

Technically, I was now single, but not the kind of single girl looking to be kissed.

Still, it wasn't an open-mouthed kiss or even that intimate. A friend could give a kiss like that. Right?

I pressed my lips together, trying to sort out all of the sensations that had erupted inside of me. Nerves tingled beneath my skin and I heated all over.

I wanted to forget that ever happened, but I couldn't stop replaying the nearness of his body or the smell of his cologne. I still felt his lips against mine and my heart still raced with the thrill of his boldness.

"I should go," I croaked.

He looked at me affectionately, as if those words were the most adorable thing he'd ever heard, and said, "I figured."

"What do you mean by that?"

"That you have a family that needs you. I figured you had to get back to them."

I narrowed my eyes on him. I didn't believe that was what he meant at all.

"Thank you again for the gift." I settled it back into the box and replaced the lid. "I can't wait to hang it up on the tree."

"If you need to get away from your parents, you can always come back."

The desire to take him up on his offer seared through me without my permission. I wasn't supposed to want to come back to his house. I shouldn't want to spend more time with him.

I shouldn't still be thinking about his kiss.

"I probably won't see you until after they leave."

His smile faltered, "I forget not everyone dreads spending time with their parents."

"You love your parents," I reminded him.

"They're growing on me."

"One day I'd like to meet them."

His eyes darkened and he spoke in a low rumble, "You should probably let me take you out on a date first."

"Excuse me?" I practically choked on the words.

But then his eyebrow rose in that cocky way he had and I realized he had been joking. I was the one that read too much into it. "Isn't that how it usually goes? I was just kidding."

I cleared my throat and attempted a smile. "Merry Christmas, Ben."

"Merry Christmas, Liz."

I stepped into my boots, grabbed my coat and practically bolted from his house. By the time I had shut myself back in my own house I had managed to convince myself that his kiss and his flirting didn't mean anything. He was a friend. And he thought of me as a friend.

I looked down at the box in my hand, then clutched it against my pounding heart.

He was just a friend, I decided concretely.

And because I willfully came to that conclusion, I didn't bother to examine my actions when I tucked the ornament inside my bedside table instead of hanging it on the tree where it would be stored away with all of the other Christmas decorations in just a few short days.

Chapter Seventeen

"Ms. Conway will see you now," the school secretary informed me.

I stood up from a chair lined against the wall and walked toward Ms. Conway's office. This time I thought ahead and called Emma to babysit the two little kids while I had my meeting with the school counselor.

When she called last Friday to ask me to come in on Monday, she'd made it clear that this was a very serious meeting and that I should be serious about it.

I figured the call was meant to scare me into leaving my gaggle of children at home.

I walked into her office and steeled myself against the immediate chill. I hated being called in here. I hated that she had the ability to reduce me to fear and panic attacks.

Before Grady died, I had been the poster mom for volunteering and school spirit. Now I was the cautionary tale whispered about in carpools and PTA meetings. *This is what happens when you have too many kids and lose your mind. You turn into her.*

These women had once relied on me. Now they couldn't meet my eyes because they didn't know what to say to me.

Maybe it was unfair to cast them all with the same dye, but beyond some initial casseroles after Grady's funeral, I hadn't heard from one of them.

"How are you, Liz?" the counselor asked me from behind her desk.

"I'm alright, thank you."

"Please, have a seat." I followed orders. "Do you know why I called you in here today?"

I tried not to feel like a ten year old again. "No, the kids haven't said anything."

She pressed her thin lips together and looked down at some papers in front of her. "But you know Abby has been having problems in nearly all of her classes? She's been acting out, disrupting lectures and not turning in her homework?"

"We've been working on all of that." I suppressed the urge to run my hands over my face with frustration. "She's had some difficulties since Christmas."

"What happened at Christmas?" Ms. Conway gasped as if waiting for some piece to this unsolvable puzzle that was my second born child.

"We celebrated it without her father for the first time. It's been hard on all of the kids, but Abby is my only one that reacts disruptively with grief. She isn't processing this well."

Ms. Conway let out a short, irritated sigh, as if my daughter's pain irritated her. "Well, it's the beginning of February now, Liz. I know that Abby is going through something tough, but she is causing major problems for all of her teachers. If she doesn't change her behavior soon, we're going to have to take disciplinary action."

I shook my head, trying to make her words disappear. "Ms. Conway, I know that she can be a handful, but she's been through so much. She's not a bad kid; she's just a little girl that misses her daddy. We're working through her pain, but it takes time."

"I know you think I'm the bad guy here, but I'm just trying to help her. She has to learn that even through rough times, she still has to follow the rules at school and in society."

"She *will* learn that," I promised. "I'm working with her at home and she's opening up more. I am hoping she's processing Grady's death more maturely now. She just turned seven a few weeks ago. That might be part of the problem and part of the solution."

"What do you mean?"

I clasped my hands together in my lap to keep from fidgeting. "Abby's birthday is in January, so between the holiday season and her birthday, she had to face a lot of important, special family events that her dad couldn't be at. That was very hard on her. On all of us. But she is seven now. She'll grow up some in the next few months, she'll mature. This has been a tough year for her, but I know she's getting better. Just give her a little bit more time."

"Liz, we're nearly to the end of the school year."

"We're also nearly to the one year anniversary of Grady's death. That might have something to do with her behavior too."

"When is that?"

"Middle of March."

She let out another long sigh. "Alright, I understand. I know this is hard for your family. I get it. I do."

"Thank you."

Her cold eyes lifted to meet mine. "But she cannot keep disrupting class and lunch. Yesterday she had all of the kids in the lunchroom chanting, "Yum!" at the top of their lungs."

My eyebrows shot to my hairline. "Yum?"

Ms. Conway started pounding her fists lightly on her desk in time to illustrate, "Yum! Yum! Yum!"

"I can see why that would cause so many problems."

"Ms. Carlson, they were extremely loud. The teachers couldn't get them to settle down."

"Give her just a little more time to struggle through this. I promise I will have a talk with her and she will get it together for the rest of the school year."

"We just have a few more months," she offered sympathetically.

"We'll make it, Ms. Conway. I will get her through this year and then by next fall you will see a different kid. A healthier kid."

"Alright, Liz. Alright."

The bell rang for school to be dismissed and we both stood up. I said goodbye and walked out to meet my kids.

"Abby, we are going to talk when we get home," I told her.

I wasn't as irrational as I had been at the beginning of the year, but I knew my daughter needed discipline. I could only blame myself for so much and Grady's death was a reality we had to learn to live with.

She couldn't keep getting into trouble like this and Ms. Conway was right about her school work. Although she was only in first grade, she had all but given up trying to do well on anything.

"Am I in trouble?" she squeaked nervously.

I gave her a look, my mom look. I had perfected it over the years. She shrunk back. She knew the look all too well.

The ride home was silent. I let Abby stew in her fears of what was to come, but I didn't exactly know what I was going to say either. I needed to work that out.

I had no idea where to begin with my daughter when her entire life had been shattered. She was my wildflower, my free spirit. Abby couldn't follow rules before Grady died. How could I expect anything less of her now?

"Hey!" Emma greeted happily. "How was school?"

"Ask Abby," Blake mumbled and then took off to find a snack.

"What's wrong?" Emma asked me.

"Hey, can you stick around for a little bit longer? Like another hour?"

"What's up?" Emma stepped close while Abby hovered nearby.

"I'm going to take Abs for some ice cream," I whispered so the other kids didn't overhear. "I need to talk to her."

"One hour." She held up her finger to accentuate her point. "I can give you one hour, but no more."

"You're a saint, Emma." I kissed her cheek and then shuffled my wayward child out the door.

We drove to McDonalds where I bought us both vanilla milkshakes and parked in the corner of the lot. I invited her to sit in the front seat with me before turning the radio off and getting down to business.

Once she'd crawled to the front and situated herself with ice cream in hand, I began, "Abs, you cannot keep doing what you're doing. It is not working."

"What do you mean?"

I gave her a look. "At school. In the lunchroom. With your homework. Baby girl, you cannot behave the way you are behaving any longer. This behavior and this attitude are just not okay. You are not acting like the Abby I know."

She opened her mouth to defend herself, but couldn't find the right words. Her shoulders slumped and she stared down at her cup. "It's not fair," she mumbled. "It's not fair that other people have dads and I don't."

I knew this was coming… I knew all of the reasons for her behavior problems and issues at school. Still, nothing could have prepared me for that.

"Abby," I cried and then pulled her across the center console and into my lap. I buried my face in her wild hair and let out a choked sob. "I don't think it's fair either."

"Why did he have to leave us, Mommy? Why did he have to die?"

"I don't know, Sweetheart. He didn't want to die. He tried his hardest to stay with us, but his sickness was too bad."

"Why did he have to get sick? My friends at school have dads and none of them have gotten sick and died." Tears streamed down her pretty face and her little nose ran. She sniffled and wiped her rivers of snot with the back of her hand.

I cupped her face with my hands and kissed a few of her freckles. I couldn't give her answers to those questions, at least not any answers she would understand. "Abigail, your daddy got sick and because he got sick, he had to die. And now where is he?"

"Heaven," she whispered.

"And did he love you when he was alive?"

She nodded, "Yes."

"Did he love you with his whole heart?"

She nodded again and hiccupped a sob. "Yes."

"And did he stop loving you when he went up to heaven?"

"Did he?" she asked in the most frightened and innocent voice I had ever heard.

"No," I promised immediately. "No, of course not. He loves you just as much now as he did when he was alive. He's just in a different place now."

"Will I ever see him again?"

"Of course you will. *Of course.* One day you will see him again, but it might not be for a very long time."

Her chin trembled as she struggled to hold back more tears.

I took a breath and pressed on, "Abby you cannot keep getting into trouble at school. I know you miss your daddy. I know that. I miss him too. But honey, you are a good kid. It's time you start acting like one."

"Mr. Hoya doesn't think I'm a good kid."

Mr. Hoya was her first grade teacher and at his absolute wits end. "Then show him, Sweetie. You've given him a headache all year. Prove to him that you know how to listen and pay attention. Show him that you do know how to read and write. He's not even sure if you know your own name!"

Abby laughed like I wanted her too. "He knows I know my own name! He's always yelling it!"

I couldn't help but smile at her. "I need you to try, Abby. Okay? I really need you to be the good kid I know that you are."

She let out a long-suffering sigh, "Fine. I'll try."

"And if you don't try?"

"I don't know." She shrugged her shoulders and picked up her milkshake again.

"You're in super big trouble, that's what. This is the last time I ask you nicely. Got it?"

She slid back to her seat. I could feel her struggling not to roll her eyes. "Okay. Got it."

"I love you Abs. I love you more than the whole world. I know you can do this."

"I love you too, Mom."

I asked her about her day yesterday and we laughed about the incident in the lunchroom. Maybe that made me a bad mom, but I still couldn't believe it happened.

It was an hour and a half before we got back home and Emma's car was nowhere to be seen. I shut the car off and jumped out of my seat, racing inside and checking my phone for a missed text at the same time.

I found Ben sitting at the island going over Blake's homework with him. Lucy was at the craft table coloring and Jace was sitting on Ben's knee eating a banana.

"Hey," he greeted me easily, as if he had done this a hundred times before.

"Hey."

"Ben!" Abby screamed and ran over to give him a hug. "Will you help me with my homework? Mommy says I have to start doing it. And you do Blake's for him. Can you do mine too?"

"Get it out, kiddo. But you have to write all of the answers so your teacher doesn't know it was me." He looked up at me and winked.

"Where's Emma?" My mind spun with conflicted feelings. Should I be upset that Ben was here? Alone with my kids? Or did I trust him enough to leave him unsupervised and in charge?

"She had to go. She called and said a bunch of things really quickly. What I got out of it was that you told her you'd be gone an hour? And it was longer than that? She asked if I could hang out until you got home. I've only been here... maybe twenty-minutes? I put chicken fingers in the oven. The kids were getting hungry. Is that okay?"

And just like that my spinning thoughts slammed to a stop.

I trusted Ben.

I trusted him completely.

"That's great," I told him.

"You're okay?" he asked next. "Abby?"

"We're fine. We just went for a little drive and had a little talk."

He nodded like my answer mattered to him. "If the kids eat the nuggets, I could order us Thai food."

"That sounds good."

"Are you sure you're okay? You look a little jarred." I watched him twitch as if he wanted to walk over to me, but he had too many kids around him.

I smiled at that. I smiled because it relaxed me to see that my children trusted him and that he seemed to genuinely like them too.

"I'm good, Ben. I'm really good."

It wasn't until after dinner, when I sent the kids to the living room to watch a little bit of TV before bed that Ben and I had another opportunity to talk.

He stayed after dinner and helped clean up the cartons of Thai and what little dishes there were to do. He filled my dishwasher while I wiped down the table and then he filled up the water on my Keurig for tomorrow.

"That will save me some aggravation in the morning," I told him gratefully. I leaned back against the sink and smiled at him. He moved to stand next to me.

"We should do this again." His low voice was barely louder than a whisper.

I tilted my head so that I could look up at him, "Dinner?"

"Yes, but not here."

"What do you mean?"

"We should go out to dinner," he clarified.

"With the kids?"

He shook his head slowly as if he couldn't figure me out. "Just the two of us. You and I should go out to dinner."

I shot up and practically jumped across the room. "Like a date?" I gasped.

He nodded, hitting me with one of his slow smiles. "Yes."

I started shaking my head rapidly. "Ben, are you serious? You can't be serious."

Doubt flickered over his face. "Valentine's Day is coming up. Neither of us has a date. I don't know, I thought it would be... fun."

"That's sweet, really. But, I can't. I cannot go on a date with you. I can't. I... can't."

"It was just a thought," he shrugged casually.

I ignored the expression on his face. I couldn't read it right now and frankly I didn't want to know what it meant. "You don't want to go on a date with me anyway. You don't. I'm... I'm broken, Ben. My husband hasn't even been dead a year. I'm done with dating. Forever. I'm sorry; I didn't mean to make this awkward between us. I just care about you. I didn't think you thought of me that way."

His hands cupped my shoulders and held me still so that he could look into my frightened eyes. "Liz, you didn't make things awkward between us. This isn't the right time, I get that. Don't feel bad. I'm not in a hurry. It's alright. I can wait."

"No, Ben, that's not what I m-"

He leaned down and pressed a lingering kiss to my cheek. I shivered at the contact and whatever I had wanted to say to him dissolved into thin air. When he stepped back, my body swayed toward him.

"Goodnight, Liz," he told me sweetly. "I'll talk to you tomorrow."

"Thanks for dinner," I squeaked. "And for babysitting."

He gave me one more charming smile when I walked him to the door. I didn't watch him walk to his house or wait for him to get inside. I closed the door and locked it as soon as he was through it.

I had to shut him out, shut him out of my house, my thoughts and my heart.

I climbed into bed that night more upset than I had been in a very long time. I reached out and clutched at the sheets on Grady's side, desperate for him to be here.

"I don't know what is happening to me, Grady." The words fell out of my mouth as a frantic prayer. How could I love my husband so very much and still have these feelings for Ben? It didn't make sense to me. "I *need* you, Grady. I need you to *come back to me*. I hate that you left me to do this on my own because I don't know what to do. Come back to me. *I would do anything to have you come back to me.*"

Chapter Eighteen

March fifteenth. The one-year anniversary of Grady's death.

I woke up that morning before the kids and stared at myself in the mirror for a long time.

I couldn't find myself through the haze of grief and heartache. In the mirror I saw a stranger, a person I didn't know and couldn't tolerate.

Every once in a while I would glimpse a glimmer of my old self, but it was only a flicker, an echo of life and light.

Part of me accepted that this was the person I was now. I could never go back. I would never find my lost self. That part of me knew I could only go forward and I would have to discover this unknown person as the days went by.

And that same part was okay with finding this new version of me. I couldn't go back, but I also didn't know if I wanted to go back. The other Liz had been happily married to Grady. She had been a good mother that had things under control because she had the help of a good man. She built a life that revolved around her husband and her children and that was enough for her.

But I could never have those things again. And so moving forward I needed to let them go.

Yes, I still had my children and I would always do everything I could to give them the best life possible. But I wasn't the mom that volunteered twice a week in their classrooms now. I wasn't the mom that baked up a storm for fundraisers and teacher appreciation week. I wasn't the mom that remembered every practice and had healthy meals on the table every single night.

I was just me. A widow struggling to keep them bathed and clothed.

And you know what? It worked for us. We survived a year without Grady. A whole year. Maybe it wasn't pretty. Maybe our lives weren't tied up perfectly with bows. But we still loved each other. And we were still alive.

There were dark times over the last year, but it hadn't been all darkness. There were days I never thought I would live through and moments when I was convinced that it was the end of us. But we'd pushed through and we'd kept on living.

Best of all, it wasn't all depression and hard times.

Somehow, we hadn't just managed to go on living, but we'd managed to smile through some of it too. Our hearts hurt and our souls ached, but there was plenty of love and happiness left for us.

I pushed my blonde hair back from my face and made a mental note to make a hair appointment. The lines near my eyes were definitely more pronounced and my youthful complexion wasn't so youthful anymore.

At almost thirty-three-years-old, I could say that I was happy with how I'd aged. I hadn't found much time to run through the winter. I hoped to remedy that this spring. Still, I was in better shape than I ever had been before.

What mattered most to me about looking at myself for so long was that I could finally recognize some of what Ben saw in me.

I knew Grady loved me. I knew without a doubt he thought I was sexy. He told me I was beautiful nearly every day. But he had been married to me. We had spent ten years together. At some point he had made a conscious decision to see me that way and to continue seeing me that way. I had no doubt that he believed all of those things, but part of that was because he never looked any other direction. I was it for him, just like he was the end all, be all for me.

Ben had started as a complete stranger with absolutely no obligation to me. Our relationship had developed into a strong friendship and I was happy with that. Although, I knew he wanted more. He had told me so more than once.

I thought it might be awkward between us after he asked me out and I turned him down. I shouldn't have ever worried.

Ben would never let something as little as rejection stand in the way of our relationship. Not even more rejection. He'd continued to ask me out as another month passed.

He was never forceful about it. He had this gentle way about it that always made me feel comfortable enough to say no. And I always said no.

I should have ended things with him in every way. I didn't want to lead him on. I cared too much for him to play games with him.

But I was also too selfish to let him go and he seemed in no hurry to escape me. He meant more to me than nearly anyone else. And if I was honest with myself, I knew I had feelings for him.

I just could never explore them.

I still loved my husband as fiercely as the day he died. It wouldn't be fair to Grady, my kids or Ben for me to say yes. Besides, I knew Ben and I would not last long after a first date. Where could that possibly go? Marriage was out of the question. A long term relationship was out of the question. Sex was so far out of the question it made me laugh, and then seize up in fear and anxiety immediately after.

We had no future as a couple.

I didn't want to mess up our friendship. It was too important to me.

I decided to keep the kids home from school today. It was a Tuesday, so the rest of the world went on as normal. I just couldn't make them go.

Our world had stopped being normal a year ago.

No, longer than that. After Grady's first diagnosis, things took an abrupt turn into the abnormal. And we'd pretty much set down roots there.

I got dressed and put on some light makeup. I made my way downstairs in a still quiet house and went about making breakfast.

The kids trickled into the kitchen, sleepy-eyed and tousled. I loved this picture of them. I loved their sleep-rumpled pajamas and lazy smiles. I loved that they walked straight to me and wrapped their arms around me as soon as they saw me, as if the very first thing they needed every day was my touch.

I kissed their wild hair and turned on some cartoons so I could focus on a great big breakfast of pancakes, bacon, scrambled eggs and pre-made cinnamon rolls.

This day was going to be tough no matter how it went; I figured we should start off by glutting ourselves.

We ate quietly, except for Jace, who didn't understand the significance of this day. He was just excited to have his siblings all home with him.

After breakfast, I bathed them and dressed them in nice clothes with bows for the girls and shiny shoes for the boys. And then I took them back downstairs and I gave them each a present.

I gave them all something of Grady's.

I gave Blake his daddy's basketball. Grady would often play Saturday morning ball with his guy friends at the local Y. He kept it in a gym bag in our closet and I hadn't touched it until I thought about giving it to Blake. It smelled like leather and sweat. It smelled like Grady when he would come home after a few hours of playing, dripping wet and exhausted, but alive with an energy he only found with good friends and hard play.

For Abby, I found a boxset of The Hardy Boys in hardback. They were Grady's from when he was a kid. His mom had brought them over when we first moved into this house and he had kept them on a shelf in the den. Abby was just now able to read well by herself and I thought she would love the mysteries and adventure, and even more, reading something that her daddy loved at her age.

Lucy was the hardest to find something of Grady's that would mean something to her. But digging around in the den, I found a box that he had made in high school woodshop. He had stained it and carved his initials in the top, then attached the lid with hinges. It was hard to part with something that meaningful to him. He had kept it with him all of these years and I knew he was proud of his work even back then. My heart had screamed to keep it for myself, but I knew Lucy would grow to love it and treat it with as much care as he had. I told her we would put it some place safe and when she wanted to look at it, I would help her get it down.

I wanted to find something symbolically Grady, so that when Jace was older, he would know it was his dad's without being able to attach a memory of him to it. But I couldn't find anything that represented Grady without taping a picture to it. And then it hit me. Jace needed a picture of his daddy. I had one of my favorite pictures blown up and framed. Ben said he would hang it for me later in Jace's room. The picture was of Grady sitting on a bench at work a few years ago. His chin was tilted high while he laughed at something off film. His green eyes sparkled with life and his tousled hair blew in the wind. He was breathtaking to me. I had been the one that took the picture. I had taken much younger kids with me to see where daddy worked and brought him lunch. I remembered rushing to capture the shot and falling in love with him all over again in that moment. It was an image of Grady I would always remember because it was so quintessentially him. Jace needed to see his daddy like that.

I knew the little ones wouldn't understand the significance yet, but one day they would and they would learn to appreciate the value of what I gave them. I now had totes for each of them, compiled with gifts from Grady that I planned to give each year.

The totes gave me a sense of peace I hadn't expected. I had left this house completely untouched after Grady died. His clothes still hung in the closets and his work boots still sat in the mudroom. They weren't just his earthly possessions, they were pieces of him that I couldn't imagine parting with.

Well, until now.

Now that his most important memories were packed away and waiting for my children, I thought it might be time. Maybe I could pack up his clothes and give them to someone who needed them. Maybe it was time to put his shoes away and empty the bathroom of his toiletries.

Maybe.

One thing at a time.

The children stared at their gifts for a while, all of them except Jace, who toddled off to get into the box of toys we kept in the living room. Abby and Blake both cried over their new gifts and soon Lucy joined in. Jace came back to see what the commotion was about, so I picked him up and cried with him too. I lead my children to the couch and let them all snuggle close.

Yes, things were better, but they were still hard.

A knock at the door forced me to move. Looking at the clock on the wall, I knew it was time anyway. I gave all of the kids kisses and one last hug.

Ben stood on the other side of the door, holding a large bouquet of pale pink orchids. Before I could greet him, he stepped through the open door and crushed me in a hug. He smelled like him, like the scent I'd gotten used to over the last several months, and the flowers he held against my back.

My arms wrapped around his waist and I held on. I had been the rock all morning, the steady one, the one that held us together. But now I needed someone to be my rock. I felt myself crumbling to pieces, sand that washed away every time a new wave rolled in or ash that scattered in the wind.

"How are you holding up," he whispered against my temple.

"We've survived so far." I took a step back, realizing that embracing Ben might be inappropriate in front of the kids. He held out the flowers and I took them, dipping my head to enjoy their fragrance. "These are gorgeous. Thank you. Orchids?"

He gave me a small smile. "Roses felt... inadequate."

I didn't know what to make of that, so I busied myself with putting them in water. Emma showed up a few minutes later and we all piled into my minivan.

The ride to the cemetery wasn't long enough. Ben drove for me because I didn't think I had the strength.

I hadn't been here since they put in the headstone. And the only other times I visited his grave was right before the funeral when I picked the plot out, then of course, during the funeral.

It just didn't seem right. His body rested here, but his soul was gone. This was an empty place for me. It didn't hold the Grady I loved and it only represented his death.

I didn't want to remember him in death.

I wanted to be with him in life.

The cemetery I'd chosen was a beautiful piece of land with huge trees and rolling hills. His plot sat on the top of a hill, nestled into a view of the sunset at the right time of day and overlooking the rest of the grounds.

At some point during the funeral preparation, I had designed his tombstone. I hardly remembered what I'd picked out, but it was simple, stately, to the point but with a little bit of whimsy.

Like Grady.

Katherine and Trevor met us there. We had arranged to spend time around the grave, remembering this day together.

After Ben parked the car and we piled into the wet March morning, I realized how inappropriate it was for Ben to be here.

I looked at my sister in panic, but she was busy talking to Abby.

I took calming breaths and tried to sort out my feelings. It shouldn't be awkward. We were just friends. I shouldn't feel the need to justify his presence to my mother-in-law or to my husband's empty body.

But I did.

The breath left my lungs. Why hadn't I thought this through before now? I had asked Ben to be with me today because I knew I needed him. But now it seemed… *wrong*.

I couldn't help the feelings of guilt and shame that bubbled over me. I'd made a huge mistake. And there was nothing I could do about it now.

Ben's hand landed between my shoulder blades where he rubbed a soothing path. I relaxed some but that only irritated me more.

"Who's your friend, Liz?" Trevor demanded with harsh eyes and a firm mouth.

A sickness rolled through me. I closed my eyes and steeled my courage. "This is Ben, Trevor. He's a good friend. Ben, this is my brother-in-law, Trevor and my mother-in-law, Katherine."

Ben stuck out his hand and greeted them politely. They did not seem charmed.

After an hour of standing in the drizzle, mostly silent with our own thoughts, we decided to go for some lunch. I chose a kid friendly place that the adults could enjoy too.

The meal was spent remembering Grady, sharing our memories and tears once again. We talked for the first time of details about the funeral. I realized that all of us had been in a daze during that time period, going through the motions, but not mentally present. Among us we were able to piece together a lot of the details and some really great moments from that time. The kids were wild, wound up after a subdued morning, but we didn't mind their chaos. In fact, it broke the last of the graveside tension.

The peace only lasted until Ben excused himself for the restroom. He had been silent throughout the meal, taking in our conversation with thoughtful attentiveness. His hand had rested on the back of my chair throughout lunch and when he left, I felt his absence more than I should have.

"How did you meet, Ben?" Katherine asked softly. "I've never heard you speak of him before."

Trevor glared at me while I answered, "He's my neighbor. He moved in early September and over the last six months we've become very good friends."

Trevor grunted derisively. I gave him a pleading look, begging him to understand that my actions weren't done out of disrespect to his brother or lack of love. I had needs too. I had lonely places inside of me that needed a friend, that needed someone to care about me.

"He's very nice, Liz," Katherine smiled at me. "I'm glad you have someone you can lean on."

I jerked back, surprised by her gracious reply. "Me too," I whispered.

Katherine paid for lunch even though I tried to convince her to let me. She waved me off, not caring how much more right I had than she.

We parted ways in the parking lot. I hugged both Katherine and Trevor, warning him to be nice. He growled at me.

I couldn't help but laugh. That was so Trevor. And like Katherine said at Christmas, he was treating me like family, like I was his little sister and he was my overprotective big brother. Or like the brother of my dead husband. Either way, his concern made me feel loved.

Emma helped the kids into the house while I walked Ben to the edge of the garage. I had a lot of time to think today and more time than usual to spend with Ben.

He stepped close to me, shielding me from the biting drops of cold rain. I let him invade my personal space, completely used to it by now. When he turned to me and said, "Go out with me, Liz. It's okay for you to move on now."

I finally agreed with him. I didn't know if it was visiting the grave and once again realizing how empty it was, how far gone Grady was from me or if it was that I realized today I didn't want to be without Ben. I didn't know what my feelings for him meant or how deeply they went, but I did know they mattered to me in a profound way.

He mattered to me in a way I couldn't ignore anymore.

"Okay," I whispered.

The smile that broke out across his face made my stomach flutter and my skin buzz with anticipation. "Okay?"

I nodded, "Yes."

He tucked a stray strand of hair behind my ear, leaned down and kissed my cheek. "Get a sitter for Friday."

I watched him walk away, baffled by his words and his attitude. I always expected him to treat me as though I were fragile… thin glass that would shatter with just the slightest bit of pressure, but he never did. He pushed me beyond being delicate, into a place I had never thought I would go again. He made me strong. He demanded that I be anything but weak and broken.

Which might have been the reason I finally said yes.

But oh, god. I said yes.

The happy feelings were replaced with absolute panic. I had a date.

On Friday.

With someone who was not my husband.

Chapter Nineteen

I attacked Emma as soon as she walked in the door. "Oh, my god, he's a psycho isn't he? He has to be. That's the only explanation!"

"Elizabeth Grace, what are you talking about?" My sister went white-faced at my panic attack. "Are you okay? Is everyone okay?" The kids swarmed her legs and demanded she pick them all up.

"Ben!" I shouted over them. "Ben is a psychopath! He has to be!"

"Wait. *What?*" She scooped Jace up into her arms and bugged her eyes out at me. "What are you talking about?"

"Emma, I have had four children! *Four of them!* Do you understand the state of my vagina? What kind of man goes out on a date with a woman that has *four children*?"

"Oh," she sighed. "You're just panicking."

"Of course, I'm panicking! What else would I be doing?" I took a second to catch my breath. "What have I done? I cannot go out with him. He's got to have like a... a... fetish or something. Or maybe he's not a lawyer at all. Maybe he's a conman trying to steal all of Grady's life insurance money. Or maybe-"

Emma cut me off, "I'm going to stop you right there. First, you know he's a lawyer. And you know he's not a liar. Well, or really mostly not a liar, because you know, it's iffy when you're a lawyer and... Anyway, I've been to his office! I can vouch for him. And he doesn't really seem like the type to have a fetish. But hey, if he does, just go with it. It could be fun!"

"*Emma!*"

"Elizabeth, it's one date. You can never talk to him again after this if you want. Or you can go back to being friends. Really, how is this any different than one of your wine nights? He comes over for dinner all the time. Just think of this like you two hanging out casually. He'll bring you back home before you turn into a pumpkin and you'll go to sleep in separate beds. This is no big deal."

Emma's words calmed me considerably. I took a slow breath and picked up Lucy to cuddle. Cuddling always gave me comfort.

"This is a date?" Blake asked with one eyebrow raised.

Shit. "No," I said at the same time Emma said, "Yes." I gave her another frightened look. "Don't lie to them, Liz! Be honest!"

My sister, the grad school counselor.

But she was right. I didn't want to lie to Blake or Abby. And I really didn't want to have to come back later and explain myself.

"Emma's right, Blake. This is a date. Ben asked me to go to dinner with him and I said yes."

He absorbed the information and then with maturity I didn't know he had in him, he said, "Cool." I stared at his bouncing head as he moved back into the living room to pick up his game controller.

My gaze swung to Emma. "See?" she said. "I told you."

"Mommy?" Abby asked and her face revealed more of the reaction I had expected.

I sunk to my knees in front of her, ignoring the cold press of the wood floor against my bare legs. "It's just dinner, Abs. Ben asked mommy to go with him alone. He, um, he wants to spend time with me. Is that okay?"

"I like Ben," she mumbled. "But…"

I found myself using Emma's words on my daughter. "It's just dinner, Sweetheart. If I come home and you don't want me to do this again, I won't. Okay?" That was probably the worst parenting ever, but I couldn't help myself. I wouldn't put my kids through another traumatic experience because I was too selfish to ignore my volatile feelings.

"You're coming back tonight?"

I shivered at her question. "Yes, I'll be home in a few hours. Promise."

She threw her arms around my neck and kissed my cheek. "K!"

I stood up and faced my sister again. "Do I look okay?"

"You look smokin', sweet cheeks." When I rolled my eyes, she gave my shoulder a little shove. "You're gorgeous, I swear it. But how long are you going to make it in those heels? When's the last time you even wore heels?"

I looked down at what were once my favorite pair of black peep-toe stilettos and frowned. "The funeral."

"Well, don't think about that now!" Emma cried.

"You're the one that asked!"

"Liz, look at me." I did. She grabbed my shoulders and shook me hard, wrinkling the silk of my black lacy cocktail dress. "Ben is the best thing that ever happened to you." She winced, "After Grady. Do not mess this up."

"I've already messed it up, at least a hundred times. I have no idea why he thinks this is a good idea. I'm not even sure why I said yes! I should call him and cancel right now. I should-"

The doorbell rang.

He was here.

Son of a bitch.

"Emma, I can't do this."

172

Her expression softened and she whispered, "Yes, you can. You can because you want to do this, because you'll regret not doing this. You care about him, Elizabeth."

"It doesn't matter, Em. It doesn't matter how I feel about him. This can't go anywhere."

"Just worry about tonight. Then decide about the rest tomorrow."

"You're going to make a great shrink one day." Heat rushed my eyes, I was near tears.

Emma fanned at her face. "Elizabeth!"

"I can see you both standing there!" Ben called through the door.

That dissolved our emotional moment. Emma rushed over to the door and yanked it open. I had a half second to take a steadying breath before Ben stepped into the house and knocked the breath out of me.

The low evening light burned behind him, setting off his dark hair and darker eyes. He stood in the doorframe wearing gray dress pants with a matching gray vest, a white dress shirt with the sleeves rolled up and a black tie. He had his fancy watch on and his hair had been styled away from his face.

He looked... incredible.

I felt lost looking at him, completely out of my depth and so far beyond casual feelings for him that I couldn't breathe right.

And yet when his eyes stopped traveling over my body to finally meet my gaze, I felt found. His heated stare held so much affection but I managed to take courageous breaths and clear my mind of the sharpened panic that had sent me into a tailspin.

I managed to put all of my grief, heartache and craziness aside for this moment and focus only on him and how he made me feel.

"Liz," Ben breathed. "I'm not going to be able to stop looking at you."

I blushed fiercely from his compliment. I had never been admired so openly by anyone other than Grady. I didn't know how to react or even accept the praise.

"Thank you," I barely whispered.

The kids attacked Ben, asking him where we were going and when we would back. Blake wanted to show Ben his game and the girls wanted to play with him. He looked up at me for help, smiling affectionately at the hooligans latched to his legs.

"Can I come over tomorrow to see the game?" he asked Blake. "I promised to take your mom to dinner and I don't think I can keep her waiting much longer."

"Why not?" Blake asked like it didn't matter if I had to wait or not. Such a typical response from my oldest.

"Look at her, Blake." And that was all he said. Blake had no idea what he was talking about. Ben closed the distance between us and reached for my hand. "Are you okay?" he asked gently.

I nodded. How could I be anything but okay with this man? "Yes."

"Ready to go?" I nodded again. "Then kiss your kids and let's get out of here."

I did exactly as he said. I gave all of the children big hugs and kisses one at a time. They hugged me back but let me go, excited about their night with Emma.

I let him lead me to his car. He helped me into the passenger's seat and then took his place in the driver's. He had already told me that he planned to take me to dinner, so I had known what to expect.

"We won't be out late tonight," he said once we were driving through town.

"Okay." I tried not to sound too disappointed.

His hand reached over and squeezed mine. "I want to ease you into this. I don't want to scare you away."

Something tingled down my spine. I couldn't put a name to the feeling. There were too many mixing together for one to stand out. Fear? Maybe. Irritation? Possibly.

Anticipation? Definitely.

"You sound pretty confident. How do you know you haven't already scared me away?"

He pulled up to a red light and turned to give me a very serious, very heated look. "It's okay to be a little bit scared, Liz. We're just getting started."

I nearly snapped my neck turning to look out the window. "You're so full of yourself," I croaked.

His chuckle filled the car and wrapped around my skin. *Oh, boy.* I took a deep breath and let myself stay present in the moment.

If I thought about this too much I would fall apart.

But here, in this moment with Ben, I felt more alive than I had in a very long time.

He pulled up to one of the nicest restaurants in town and handed his keys to the valet. We let the waitress lead us to our table. When we were seated we glanced over the menu quietly.

Nerves jumped around inside of my body. I had only ever really dated one man in my life. There had been guys in high school, but it had never been like this.

And when Grady and I had started dating we were so young. God, it felt like a lifetime ago.

So now, on this date, with this older man, I had no idea what to do or say or think. I felt the tension start to creep back in and my muscles lock up. My breathing stopped functioning properly. I was a mess.

I tried to hide behind my menu, staring at it but not seeing a damn thing. His fingers appeared on the top of it and pushed it down so he could see me again.

"Liz," he said in a deep rumble. "It's just me. Nothing has changed."

"Okay," I squeaked.

He took my hand again and rubbed his thumb over my palm. "It's wine night, alright? It's just you and me and a bottle of wine. We're just talking. You're just being you and I'm just being me and we're just going to have a conversation that will make us both smile. It's going to be the best part of my day, just like all of our other ones. And I'm really hoping it's going to rank up there on yours. Maybe? Right after the kids?" He closed one of his eyes, scrunched up his face and gave me an adorably hopeful expression.

"Maybe," I agreed on a shaky laugh.

His face relaxed and he broke into a grin. "I like you, Liz. I've liked you for almost as long as I've known you. And every time I spend time with you, I just like you more. You're an incredible woman that I can't imagine not seeing every day, listening to your stories, listening to you laugh… listening to the bad things and the good things. I know this freaks you out. And it should probably freak me out too. But it doesn't. It feels right. You and I *feel right*. So stay with me for just tonight. I promise to return you home in one piece, both inside and out. Can I have this? Just tonight?"

"Yes." The word left my lips in a confession of feeling. Yes, he could have this night. Yes, we did feel right. And it did freak me out, but I couldn't make it stop.

A soft smile played on his lips, "Will you tell me about your day?"

I looked into his dark eyes and felt myself center again. I felt tethered to something again. "My day? Oh, it was so boring. It started off with Jace dumping a whole box of Fruit Loops onto the table and then moved on to getting a call from the cable company. Apparently I've forgotten to pay them the last two months and then it ended with Lucy getting Cheeto prints all over the first dress I tried on tonight."

"Well, at least that's something to be thankful for."

"Why is that?"

"Thanks to Lucy, I get to see you in this. I don't know what the other dress looked like, but I am pretty happy with this one."

I resisted the urge to throw my napkin at him. "The other one was super slutty. Boobs everywhere." I waved a hand in front of my minimal cleavage to demonstrate.

His eyes darkened as he smiled at my joke. "Now you're being cruel."

"I thought this was a regular wine night. I'm just trying to stay in character."

He stared at me intently for a long moment before saying, "I'm glad you said yes." He let that settle over me while he flagged down the waitress to bring us some wine.

We spent the rest of the evening laughing and talking over good food and great wine. Ben was right; there was no difference between here and at home. I enjoyed him as much as I always did.

I was surprised when he pulled into my driveway and I didn't want the night to end. I had imagined racing from his car, barricading myself in my house and avoiding him for the next four months.

But he had made this night amazing and so casual that I hardly noticed it was anything more than one of our usual nights in my kitchen.

It wasn't until he walked me to the door that I truly remembered that this was a date. At the restaurant there had been a table separating us. And even though he would put his hand on my back when we walked to or from the car, he always did that so it wasn't anything new.

On my porch, he lingered.

This was new.

And my nerves noticed it immediately.

I looked up at him, trying to decide what to do and how to end the night. "Thank you, Ben. I had a lovely evening."

"I'm glad," he murmured and stealthily took a step forward. "I had a nice time too."

"The food was great."

He ignored my trite comment. "You'll do this again with me?"

I forced myself to hold his steady gaze. "Ben, I don't-"

He had no patience for my refusal. One of his hands wrapped around my hip and jerked me against his hard body. His mouth descended on mine before I had a chance to panic.

His rough, demanding intensity pulsed around me, but his mouth moved sweetly, gently, as if he were savoring every single second of this.

Soft lips against soft lips, his tongue swept out along my lower one and then I found myself opening for him, letting him taste me completely. I kissed him back, unable to make coherent thoughts or think of anything beyond this moment.

My heart pounded ferociously in my chest. My hands slid up his vest and wrapped around his neck. His other hand pressed against the small of my back until we were chest to chest, tightly held together.

He kissed me for a very long time, longer than any first kiss I had ever had. He didn't seem to want to stop. He would nibble on my bottom lip and then delve his tongue back into my mouth.

I gasped for air and sanity, but he filled every breath and sense.

Finally, just as our kisses became frantic and our touch more desperate, he slowed down. He ended our make out with the sweetest, lingering kiss. He pulled back just a little but rested his forehead against mine while his breathing steadied out.

"I have wanted to do that for a very long time." His words were worshipful whispers.

I started trembling. I couldn't form words or share the same sentiment. I had never thought about kissing Ben.

Not once.

"I'll call you tomorrow," he promised.

I nodded, still unable to speak.

He let me go and I groped for the door handle. I couldn't look at him as I fled inside the dark house. I shut the door behind me and flicked the deadbolt over. My back slammed against it and reality came crashing over me.

I started sobbing; it seemed there was nothing left for me to do. The cries came straight from my heart, soul-wrenching sobs that were so deep they didn't make any sound at first.

I slid to the ground, completely bereft.

What had I done?

I betrayed Grady. *I betrayed him.*

I sucked in a gasping breath and whatever barrier had been left completely dissolved. My cries were loud now, ugly and desperate. I held my hands over my face and wept while my soul shattered apart.

Emma came running into the room completely frightened by my breakdown. "Oh, Liz," she gasped when she found me on the floor.

I felt her arms wrap around me so tightly it hurt as she slid down next to me. She held me against her chest like a small child, rocking me back and forth. Her tears mingled with mine and she mourned with me even though she couldn't begin to know what a horrible person I was.

When I had finally settled down some, she asked, "Was it horrible?"

I shook my head as more tears started to fall. "It was wonderful," I confessed.

"Then why are you crying?"

"Because it was wonderful. And because he kissed me!"

"You didn't want him to?"

"No," I shook my head and my face scrunched as hot tears poured from my eyes. "I didn't want him to stop."

She finally understood my inner conflict. She pulled me into her arms and I stayed there as both of us cried for the husband I'd love and the husband I'd buried.

Emma couldn't possibly understand all of the emotional turmoil that beat on me, that stirred up my insides and ravaged my heart. But she knew that this hurt me. That it both killed me and somehow sewed me back together.

I didn't know what to do about Ben or if there was even anything to do. The only thing I knew that night was that it had been one of the best of my life.

And one of the worst.

Stage Four: Depression

There has been this faint hope inside of me that while I work through these stages of grief, they would become easier along the way.

I pictured myself healing as I waged war with each stage, gradually building armor that would protect me from the hurt, heartache and despair.

That hope is a lie.

Grief doesn't get easier with each stage. Grief becomes harder, more difficult to face, more consuming with each breath that I take.

I am adrift in a sea of confusion. I am lost in a desert of heartache.

I am broken.

And now I must face depression.

This is the last of the great miseries. I am supposed to find acceptance after this stage, but I don't think it will happen.

I can't help but believe I will be lost in depression for the rest of my life.

The only light I can find, beyond my children, is in Ben and he brings his own private agony that rips at my chest with claws as sharp as knives.

He is both comfort and pain. Both freedom and shame.

The relief I feel when I am with him is at odds with my private guilt. Guilt that I try to ignore.

Grady has been the only life I know.

But can there still be life in death?

If I chain myself to my dead husband, will I ever truly live again?

And yet how can I let go of a love and a man that still mean everything to me?

There is too much on my heart, too much weighing on my shoulders. Depression comes in fast and fiercely, without apology and without reprieve.

Depression leaves me feeling heartsick and hopeless. Ben is the only fresh air in my stale, stagnant thoughts. Yet I will eventually have to let him go too.

And then my depression will become twofold. Once for the man that I will always love, but can never be with again. And once for the man that I will have to choose to never be with in the first place.

It is agony to live like this.

I love one man and I am falling in love with another.

I am grieving and I am celebrating.

I find moments where I am truly happy.

But at the end of the day, when I am alone and left to my thoughts and my grief, I find that I am so very depressed. And that is the very beginning of me and the very end.

I am nothing but depressed.

Chapter Twenty

Five days passed before I saw Ben again. True to his word he had called me the day after our date. And when I hadn't answered, he had texted asking me to call him back.

I hadn't done that either.

I managed to avoid running into him over the weekend and into the school week. My kids kept me busy. Soccer season was in full swing for both of the older kids, and Lucy and Jace had started swim lessons. I had signed them up weeks ago, hoping we would be able to use Ben's pool during summer.

Now the lessons felt like little digs at my heart, painful reminders of what I'd ruined between us.

I couldn't face him again. I couldn't look into his eyes and remember that kiss and not fall to pieces.

Worst of all, I didn't want to give that up. *Him* up.

I wanted there to be more.

When I lay in bed at night now, I reached over to Grady's side and felt the crushing weight of his absence. But then I would close my eyes and remember the feel of Ben's lips against mine, the hard press of his body, the firm grip of his hands as he held me tightly to him, as desperate for me as I was for him.

My mind would spin and my thoughts would crash into each other. My heart couldn't figure out where to settle, whether to feel guilt or elation, shame or joy. It was too much for me. I walked around those days with tears I could not stop and a sick feeling in my stomach.

I tried to convince myself that if I felt this ill about Ben, then I shouldn't be with him. A relationship couldn't be built on emotions as volatile as these.

But in the depth of me, in my very center, I knew that it wasn't Ben causing this trauma. It was my refusal to acknowledge my feelings for Ben that had me tied up in knots. It was the suppression of my real feelings that made me ill and heartbroken.

I knew he would get tired of my avoidance. Ben wasn't the kind of man that ran from problems. He faced them head on and like with everything else, he challenged me to do the same.

But I desperately hoped he would give up on me. I needed him to walk away and find someone that could actually give back to him what he wanted... what he needed.

Late Wednesday night, a knock at my door warned that the time had come to face Ben.

I sat curled up on the couch, a book lying listlessly in my hands. I had been planted there for an hour and hadn't read a single word.

I looked through to the door, heart already pounding, breath already shortened. I couldn't bring myself to move from the couch. How would I face him? How would I tell him I couldn't do this?

My brain warred with my heart. My soul argued with my intellect. I knew what I should do, but I couldn't bring myself to do it. I was forcing myself to lose someone I cared about all over again, only this time there was no one to blame but myself.

When I agreed to his date, I had been so worried that I would ruin things with my awkwardness and emotional unavailability that he wouldn't want to continue any kind of relationship with me. Not even friendship. But it had been easy to be with Ben. So easy.

And after that kiss... I knew that I was the one that would have to end things with him.

He had shown me a truth that I wasn't ready to see. He'd revealed a part of me that I had denied for a long time. Those things scared me.

Terrified me.

He had become the friend I could always count on, but so much more than that. He had become the man that I needed. That I wanted.

I wanted more and being near him without having more would be torture.

He was my slow death.

He knocked again, harder this time. I couldn't help but smile at his persistence.

I pulled myself off the couch and dug deep for courage. I was an adult. I was a grown woman with grownup responsibilities. I could face Ben Tyler.

My hand shook as I turned the door handle, calling me a liar.

He stood there with one arm bent at an angle against the doorframe. His forehead rested on his wrist while he stared down at his shoes. My heart squeezed, he looked miserable.

His eyes lifted to meet mine and I noticed he hadn't shaved in a few days. The rough growth suited him and tugged at something low in my belly. I ached to run the palm of my hand over the stubble, wanting to know what it felt like against the pads of my fingers.

"You're ignoring me now?" he rasped gruffly. His dark eyes flashed fiercely.

I shook my head immediately, denying his accusation. "No."

He stood up to his full height and pushed by me into the house. "I knew this was going to be hard, Liz. But you could talk to me about it. You could tell me how you're feeling. I could help you work through this."

Fear turned to anger, "So we're just jumping right into this then? I'm fine by the way, thanks for asking."

"I know you're fine. As fine as you can be," he ground out. "But I'm not."

His words punched at my resolve making my breath puff out of me. "Ben-"

"We're right for each other, Liz. The other night... that was a damn good night."

"Maybe... sure, it was a good date, but that doesn't mean there can be more. I don't even know why we bothered. We should never have tried anything beyond friendship."

He ignored me, "And all the other nights before that one? Also damn good nights. Every time I'm with you, I feel it, Liz. I feel it here." He pressed his hand to his heart and I swayed from the ferocious emotion swelling inside of me. "I know that I need to be careful with you. I *want* to be careful with you, but I need some of that same respect in return."

"I don't know what you're talking about."

"Return my calls, Liz. Tell me what's going on. Share your thoughts once in a while! I am trying here, but I can only do so much on my own. You have got to help me out or we're not going to go anywhere."

"Ben, I can't do this. You're not listening to me! I don't want this to go anywhere! You're asking too much of me."

"I'm not." He stepped right up to me. His chest heaved with his frustration and something else... something I wasn't ready to acknowledge yet. "I'm going to be gentle with you, Liz. We're going to treat this delicately. I'm going to let this happen slowly, let us fall slowly. But I am not asking too much of you."

"This will never work!" I snapped at him. "We're doomed from the start. I'm in love with another man, Ben! A man you will never be able to compete with because he's dead!"

Ben's hands reached up to cup my face. His thumbs rubbed over my cheeks, wiping away tears I hadn't realized I'd started to shed. "I don't want to compete with Grady," he murmured. "And I don't ever expect you to stop loving him. But whether you want to admit it or not, we've started something great. You don't have to prove to me that you have room for two men in your heart. You've already made room. I think it's time you realized that so we can move forward."

I stumbled back a step, ripping myself away from his touch. His words made my skin tingle and my heart flutter. How did he know how to say such perfect things? How did he know how to reach inside of me and pluck my fears from my chest and my hesitation from my soul?

How had we gone from casual friendship to this? This felt earth shattering... soul-shaking... fundamental to my very existence.

I stood at a crossroads. I could continue on with my life the way it was, grieving Grady and refusing to take control of the life I had left to live. Or I could try this thing with Ben. I could acknowledge that not everything in life made sense and that Ben was right.

I loved Grady, but I cared deeply for Ben. I hadn't thought it was possible to care for two men, but my heart had already made room.

This seemed ill-timed and impossible, but this incredible opportunity stood in front of me in a very nice package that I had come to believe I could not live without.

"What do you expect to happen between us?"

A tender smile touched his lips, "I expect us to take this one day at a time. I expect you to be difficult and for me to be patient and understanding and so, so gentle. I expect us to enjoy each other, Liz. And not much more. Not yet."

"I already enjoy you," I glared at him, hating that he was able to get through to me.

I had to be crazy to even consider this!

"I know you do."

I let out a sigh of frustration, "This isn't going to work, Ben. We're both going to end up hurt."

"You're already hurting, Liz." He stepped toward me again and tucked a stubborn piece of hair behind my ear.

"That's what I mean." My chin trembled as I struggled not to cry again. I hated that I couldn't keep a lock on my emotions. I hated that losing Grady had broken me so severely that my eyes constantly leaked and my crazed emotions always floated near the top. I needed to normalize. But looking up into Ben's eyes and taking in his handsome, pleading face, I knew it wouldn't happen any time soon. "I can't take anymore heartbreak," I confessed on a broken whisper.

"Then it's a good thing I'm not going to break your heart." He leaned down and pressed a kiss to my lips. His mouth felt warm and hopeful.

He kissed me like I was a delicate, fragile thing. He kissed me with care and an aching sweetness that touched the bitter places inside of me and brought them back to life. I came to life in his arms, with his lips against mine. I awoke from the dead and bloomed into something so beautiful I felt awed by the sight of it, something that had not existed until Ben Tyler walked into my world.

He pulled away before I was ready, but I couldn't admit that. Not even to myself.

I met his unwavering gaze again and asked the question that had been burning brightest. "Why me, Ben? You could have anyone. You could have your pick of uncomplicated girls without kids and without dead husbands. You're the whole package. Any girl would be lucky to be with you. I just… I don't understand why you chose me."

He didn't hesitate. One of his hands came to rest on my waist, the other wrapped around the back of my neck. "You were not the only one that was lost when we met. I found something in you I had been looking for for a very long time."

"What was that?"

"Myself," he whispered.

I closed my eyes and struggled not to be swept away in his wake. "Ben…"

"Liz, I didn't expect to fall for you, not like this… not so completely. And I never expected for you to fall for me too. But here we are. Let's see where this goes. Let's see how far left there is to fall."

I nodded, unable to make the words form on my lips.

He pulled me against him. "Really?"

"I can't say no to that."

A satisfied grin broke across his face. "I figured."

"You're unforgivably cocky. You know that?"

"I have you to remind me."

I have you… His words wrapped around my heart and held it together as the frantic pounding of it threatened to tear me apart.

His eyes darkened again and his lips turned down into a serious frown, "When this becomes too much *tell me*. All you have to do is tell me how you feel and I will help you, Liz. I know this won't be easy. I know we're asking a lot from each other. But I also know that it is worth it. We are worth it. But it will never work unless I know what you are thinking and how you feel. Alright?"

I nodded again, "Okay."

"Tell me when it's too much and I will back off. I promise you that."

"Okay," I repeated.

He watched my face for a few long moments before he dipped his head and trailed his nose along the curve of my jaw, placing a tender kiss just below my ear. "Okay," he whispered against my skin.

And then he ravished me, right there on the cold tile of the entryway.

Just kidding. Then one of my children screamed bloody murder from the top of the stairs.

"I have to go check on her." He took a step back and nodded. "Wait for me?"

His entire body relaxed. I watched him turn from carved stone to a man that could slay me with one of his heated looks. His shoulders relaxed and his limbs became tensile and familiar. "I'll wait," he promised on a low rumble.

I shivered and tried to ignore the fluttering feeling that I hadn't felt in a very long time. Turning from him quickly, I raced up the stairs to check on Lucy.

She turned to face me when I flipped the hallway light on. Her little arms lifted, begging for a hug.

I scooped her up in my arms and pressed a kiss to her sweaty forehead. "Did you have a nightmare?"

She nodded against my cheek. "I miss my daddy!" she cried. "I want him to come home! I want my daddy!"

I tried to swallow against the lump in my throat. I had no words for this little one. I had no hope or promises to offer. All I could do was hold her tightly to my chest and cry with her.

I closed my eyes and snuggled back against her headboard. She changed positions and threw herself over me, wrapping her arms around my neck. "I want my daddy!" she continued to wail. "I want him to come home to me!"

"Shh," I sung against her forehead. "Shh, Luce."

"Mommy, *where is he*? Where did he go?"

"Lucy, you know where he went. You know this."

She shook her head roughly against mine. "No."

My sweet, sensitive Lucy. She had waited for Grady to come back for so long. But she had turned five over the winter and with that little bit of added maturity, reality had settled in. It was like grieving all over again as she slowly accepted the truth that her daddy was gone forever.

She ended up in my bed most nights now. Sometimes she had these awful nightmares and sometimes she woke up already in tears. I hated that she had to go through this again. I hated that my little Luce had to come to understand that her daddy was gone forever.

"Tell me where your daddy is, Lucy Kate," I coaxed.

She continued to shake her head, her hair getting tangled in her tears. "In heaven," she hiccuped. "He's in h-h-h-heaven."

"And is he ever coming back?"

Lucy cried harder, but we'd gone through this enough times by now that she did know the answer, "No!"

"But, Luce, does he still love us? Even though he's way up in heaven?" My voice trembled and my tears mingled with hers. I hugged her tighter to me, needing her comfort as much as she needed mine.

"I don't know," she sniffled.

My chest ached as I rubbed her back and tried to force the words from my mouth, "He does, Lucy. He loves you so very much."

"Then why did he leave?" she hiccuped.

"Oh, baby girl. He wanted to stay. So badly. But he got sick. And the doctor's couldn't make him better. He tried so very hard to stay with us. He did everything that he could." Lucy cried harder as I rocked her gently.

Ben's tall frame darkened the door. I didn't look at him for a very long time. This had to be extremely awkward for him. He had just convinced me to date him and then he had to find me with one of my children, crying over my dead husband.

He walked over and sat at the end of the bed, jolting me out of my fear. He watched Lucy and me with a beautiful intensity. His furrowed brows and concerned frown tugged at my heart.

I had expected him to tell me that he was going to take off. I thought he would look at the two of us and be repulsed. If the child in my arms and the responsibility she represented wasn't enough to scare him away, then it would have to be my tears. I was a wreck and I couldn't make it stop or pretend like I had it together.

Yet, his hand squeezed my knee and settled there to offer some comfort. He didn't run at the first sign of difficulty, he jumped in and held tight.

And somehow he managed to give me courage that I didn't know I could find and he settled my spirit in a way I didn't know was possible.

"Do you know that he loves you, Lucy?" I whispered to my little girl. "Do you know that he will always love you?" She nodded for the first time, sniffling and whimpering against my now-soaked t-shirt. "He loves you more than anything. He always will."

"I miss him." Her tiny voice was a broken whisper.

"I miss him, too." Ben squeezed my knee again. I took a steadying breath and felt little pieces of my heart mend themselves back together. "But he's still watching over us from heaven. He'll never be far away. We just can't see him anymore."

Lucy wiggled in my arms until she lay cradled against me. She had gotten so big this year. Her legs dangled over the side of the bed, kicking a soothing rhythm. She reached up to play with some of my hair, wet from both of our tears.

"Is that why Ben is here?" Her words completely stunned me. My mind went blank. I tried to come up with some kind of explanation or excuse for why he'd walked into her bedroom late at night, but her next question proved that her thoughts were on a different track than mine. "Did Daddy send Ben to take care of us?"

My heart took on a frantic rhythm, pounding so loud I could barely hear my own voice when I answered, "Yes."

Chapter Twenty-One

"Abby told me she's the sun tonight?" My mom's amusement rang clearly through the phone.

"I think it was her teacher's idea of a joke. He cannot wait to get rid of her."

"That cannot be true," my mom tsked defensively. I loved her grandparent vision. But really... I was convinced that Mr. Hoya was counting down the minutes until he could officially be finished with Abby.

I had joined him. I couldn't wait for the summer just around the corner. I could stop worrying about needing to get the kids to school on time and homework in the evenings. Our scheduled activities would all but disappear, except for a few fun leagues the kids wanted to play in with their friends.

I planned on using Ben's pool as often as I could and actually getting a tan this summer. I had three months to cherish my children as they were until we started a new school year and they managed to grow up without me noticing. Summer always felt like a freeze frame. I could watch them closely and keep them near. When school started, it was a race to keep up with them.

And next year, Lucy would be starting kindergarten. Because obviously she had stopped loving me. Otherwise she wouldn't go; she would stay home with me forever and not force me to watch her grow up.

"Sorry, Grandma; despite popular belief, Abigail is not a model student."

My mom snickered on the other end, "I know better than that, don't I?"

"You've got your grandparent goggles on again," I laughed with her.

She paused for a moment, sucking in a fortifying breath. Finally, she said, "You sound happy, Lizbeth. You sound... okay."

I stopped near the banister and gripped it so I wouldn't tip over. She hadn't said something like this to me since long before Grady died. She had known better.

But now her words rang out through the miles that separated us and I felt them inside of me, blooming with new life and a whole heart.

Was I happy? Somehow I was.

There were still bleak moments of darkness, moments I thought I could not survive. There were still tears shed and difficult decisions to make. There were still times when I failed... completely; when my children didn't have what they needed or I didn't manage to fulfill all of my responsibilities.

But this May was vastly, incomparably different than last May.

"I'm dating someone," I whispered, afraid of her judgment.

I could feel her shock as if it were a physical thing. She didn't say anything for a very long time and I started to worry that I should have dropped that bomb a little more delicately.

"You are?" she whispered back after another minute.

"I am."

"The neighbor?" she guessed. "The snow shoveler?"

I smiled, "Yep, the snow shoveler."

"Wow, Liz… Wow." I waited patiently for her to come to terms with this. Ben and I had been dating for going on two months now and I still hadn't come to terms with it. I couldn't expect my mother to be okay with my new relationship after only a couple minutes.

There hadn't been a lot of dates in our short relationship. I had four kids after all and Emma was my sister, not my nanny. Still, there had been nights when we'd snuck away and grabbed dinner or a movie.

The majority of our relationship happened around my house. He spent a lot of time with the kids and me during the evenings and on the weekend and he came over after the kids were in bed most nights to spend time with me alone.

I would worry about our time together and decide that I needed space, but then he would have work to do and I wouldn't see him for a couple nights and I would realize how deep my attachment for him had grown.

I missed him when I wasn't with him. My fingers itched to text him or call him and my spirit would wait for him to show up.

And when we were together?

He had been right. It was damn good.

We weren't perfect people and our relationship was far from utopic, but he had been true to his word to be careful with me, to go slow.

Although slow was hard.

Very hard.

Sometimes I felt like a teenager again with how desperate his kisses could make me. He never pushed beyond that point though, never asked me to make our physical relationship as deep as our emotional one.

And most of the time I was thankful for that. But then he would kiss me into a frenzy. He would tease my senses and awaken desires I thought had gone dormant forever.

He would bring me back to life in every way and then he would settle me back into lazy contentedness, a lingering passion that made me stretch out like a happy cat and nuzzle into him.

I smiled a secret smile, remembering the feel of his hard body lengthened against mine, of his sensual hands exploring my body, of his breath mingling with mine as he tasted my lips and skin.

He was taking this slow, but my feelings for him seemed to accelerate with every minute spent with him. I should be afraid of that. I should be afraid of our connection and my deepening need for him.

But I couldn't make myself stop this. My mom was right, I was happy. And I didn't want to give up being happy to return to the darkness I had just escaped from.

"When did this happen?" she asked breathlessly.

"End of March," I confessed. "We're taking this very slow. But, I don't know mom... This isn't something I ever expected. I just... I like him."

She sounded nothing short of awestruck, when she said, "You do?"

Guilt nagged in my gut, "I don't want you to think that I stopped loving Grady or anything. I mean, obviously I still love him and I... it's not like... I haven't forgotten him or tried to forget him, I just-"

"Elizabeth," my mom interrupted in a way that only my mother could, "I know. I know that this has nothing to do with Grady. I know you too well to bother with worrying about that. I'm just pleasantly surprised. That's all."

"Pleasantly surprised?"

"You're so young, Lizzy. And those kids need a father figure. I just worried about you being all alone. I'm glad you've been able to step outside of your grief and get back to the land of the living."

"I don't think I ever left the land of the living," I tried to joke, but it fell flat and lifeless.

"Sweetheart, you did. You checked out. And I don't blame you for that. But I can feel your light again, your warmth. I don't know Ben very well, but I'm thankful that he gave it back to you."

"You know, we'll probably break up at some point and I'll drop dead again. You shouldn't let your hopes get too high."

She chuckled lightly, "I don't think you would have started this if you expected that to happen. No matter what happens, your father and I will be here. We love you, you know."

"I love you too, Mom. I've got to let you go though or Abby is going to miss her debut on center stage."

"Give the kids kisses from your father and me!"

"I will. Talk to you soon."

I clicked off the phone and sunk down onto the step. My mom's words prickled at my skin. Was she right?

I knew things would eventually end with Ben. I expected them to. Eventually, he would want things from me that I couldn't give him. We were just too different.

He wanted to start a family, but I already had one.

He wanted a wife, but I had already been one.

Ben wanted a fairytale, but I had been living in a nightmare.

We couldn't work for much longer. So what then?

My blood turned to ice as I tried to process my life without Ben now. I couldn't do it.

When Grady was first diagnosed, I had lots of horrible thoughts about what it would be like to lose him. Throughout his treatment and as the brain cancer worsened, I would often find time to simply sit and picture my life without my husband in it.

They weren't pleasant thoughts by any means and they mostly left me furious and feeling lost. But eventually, I had to come to terms with those thoughts becoming reality.

Now, as I did the same thing and imagined my future as a single woman again... I couldn't do it. My brain refused to picture my life without Ben in it.

My heart started pounding as I struggled to force myself back to those dark months when Grady was gone and I had no help, no hope and nothing to look forward to.

They must have traumatized me too much, because my conscious mind refused to go there. I laughed a little hysterically. It was crazy to think that Ben could have such an impact on me and my family.

I cared about him, but I didn't love him like I loved Grady. I didn't love him at all.

Right...?

"Mom, I can't get this stupid thing on!" Abby called from upstairs, shaking me out of my spiraling confusion.

"Don't put it on!" I shouted at her. "You'll never fit in the car!" I ran up the stairs before she could rip apart her spring play costume and caught it halfway over her head. "We'll throw it on as soon as we get there," I panted as I tried to wrestle her out of the awkward costume. "Besides, isn't it hot?"

"Duh," she groaned. "It's the sun."

I pressed my lips together and failed at holding back a laugh. "And what a beautiful sun it is."

She crossed her eyes at me until I tweaked her nose. Suddenly, she was thoughtful, "Do you think Mr. Hoya is punishing me for making him so mad this year?"

I leveled her with my best motherly gaze and prepared to say something inspiring. Instead, the truth came out, "It's a very real possibility, Kiddo."

She sighed, "I can't wait for summer."

"You and me both."

Ben showed up five minutes later and helped me pack the kids into the minivan. Abby had won the non-speaking part of the happy sun while Blake had been given a more prestigious part. He had been cast as the poky little puppy in the elementary school's rendition of *The Poky Little Puppy*.

We had been practicing lines for a month now. He was always confident and relaxed, but tonight he was obviously nervous. And I was just as nervous for him.

My heart clenched wishing that Grady could be here. Blake needed someone to give him some encouraging words. I didn't count. Whatever I said was ignored because, well, I was the mom. And I needed Grady to be here to get me through this night. Both of my kids would be on stage. This seemed like something their father should see.

Ben dropped the older kids and me off at the door because we were running a little late- no surprise. I rushed them backstage, gave them big kisses in front of all of their friends and left them to the charge of teachers who got paid to yell at my kids.

"Hi, Liz," a mom from Blake's class stopped me in the hallway by putting her hand on my forearm.

I jerked to a stop. "Hi, Melissa," I smiled at her. Blake and her son, Tanner, were good friends. A year ago, she'd had Blake over several times in an effort to help me out and distract Blake from his grief. Blake couldn't be distracted and every time she saw me, I had been a walking train wreck. The playdates had stopped over the summer.

I hadn't talked to her all year.

"How are you?" Melissa asked in that nasally, dragging tone people think sounds sympathetic.

"I'm alright," I answered honestly. "How are you and the family doing?"

"Oh, we're good," she smiled brightly. "Tanner is so excited for summer. I can hardly get him to focus on homework!"

"I know what you mean." I tried to stay engaged, but something had happened to me after Grady died. And I supposed after I forged my friendship with Ben. I had very little patience for superficial these days. I simply couldn't stomach it.

These lives we lived were a gift and precious and so short. I wanted to spend my time authentically, surrounded by people I truly loved. I knew there was a time and place for small talk and it wasn't as though I wanted to get into something deep with Melissa before the play... but it was hard to listen to her fake laugh while my family waited for me in the auditorium.

"So, listen," Melissa started. "I know we haven't seen a lot of Blake lately, but Tanner has been begging to have him over now that he's, well, you know... better. So I was thinking-"

"There you are," Ben appeared at my side. He slid his long arm around my shoulder and pulled me against him.

My cheeks bloomed bright red and I tried not to be skittish. "Hey, where are the kids?"

"With your sister. Katherine and Trevor got here early to save us seats." All of his attention focused on me. His sincere eyes watched my face carefully; his arm wrapped around my body and shielded me from the dangers of elementary school parents.

If I cared about Melissa's opinion of me, I would have desperately wanted to explain this to her. And I couldn't deny the shame and embarrassment that mingled in my chest. I wanted to run away or shove Ben out the front door and tell him to wait for me in the car.

I closed my eyes and shook my head. It wouldn't make sense to anyone else that I had seemingly moved on already.

But the truth was, I hadn't moved on. I couldn't have explained it to others if I wanted to. I still very much grieved Grady. Ben was just... Ben. A man I couldn't say no to and a relationship I didn't want to let go.

And Melissa was not my friend nor did she deserve an explanation.

That did not lessen my urgency to get to my seat where she could stop judging me with her curious eyes.

"I'm Melissa," she interjected anyway. Her hand shot out to take Ben's. "I'm the room parent for Blake's class."

"Hi, Melissa." Ben shook her hand but didn't offer any more details about himself.

Melissa's wide gaze shot to me. I nearly laughed. "I'll call you about the play date," I told her. I left her to watch after us as we walked back toward the entrance to the auditorium.

I groaned as soon as we were far enough away from her and leaned into Ben, pushing him sideways. "She's going to go run and tell all the other mom's I brought a gigolo to the spring play."

"Do I look like a gigolo?" Ben sounded truly alarmed.

I started laughing, I couldn't hold it back. It started in my stomach and worked its way through the rest of my body. I had to stop walking and prop myself against the wall, too hysterical to hold myself up on my own.

Ben put his hand on my shoulder and chuckled with me, although his wasn't quite the full-body laugh that mine was.

"Are you okay?" he asked after another minute. "I didn't mean to make you the center of gossip. I can go tell that woman I'm your cousin from out of town if that would help."

"Oh, god, don't do that!" I stood up and slid my hands to his waist. "That would severely back fire on me. Can you imagine if we're still together next fall? Then they'd *really* talk. I can only imagine those rumors."

"We will be." His voice was so serious that I had to look up at him. He stared at me intently, searching my eyes and my expression for something I didn't know if I could give him. "Liz, this isn't a fling. You know that, right?"

"I know you think that, but-"

He slid his fingertips along my cheek until he cupped my face with one of his big hands. "Liz, I know this isn't a fling." He dipped his head, bringing his lips only an inch from mine. "And you do too."

My eyes fluttered closed when he kissed me. I couldn't help it. This was the worst place for him to kiss me, but we were mostly alone in the hallway. The rest of the hustle and bustle had moved into the auditorium, ready for the play to start.

I had too many doubts to believe that Ben and I could be long term. Until he kissed me like this. His tongue swept across my bottom lip and then dipped into my mouth for a sweet taste. Our mouths pressed together in a sensual meeting that left me breathless and warm even though it was brief.

He pulled back and hit me with one of his intense looks. "Not a fling," he reiterated.

I bit my lip, hoping to savor him for just a moment longer and shook my head at him. I couldn't analyze his words or his kiss or the fact that he

195

had just very publically kissed me. We might not have had a large audience, but we had enough. Word would spread.

I didn't know how to feel and so I decided to think about it later. I wanted to enjoy my kids tonight, not obsess over potentially negative thoughts. And so I decided to enjoy this moment with him and not stress.

Well, until we turned toward the auditorium and found Katherine waiting for us near the doors. My stomach plummeted while I tried to read her gaze. Ben's hand reached for mine and squeezed tightly, urging me to be brave... to be confident.

I tilted my chin and promised myself I would talk to Katherine about Ben... soon. If she brought it up.

She didn't say a word to me or Ben as she led us to our seats. In fact, she didn't say a word to me for the rest of the night.

I might have been able to suppress my concern of Blake and Abby's friends' parents finding out I was seeing someone now, but I could not ignore Katherine's cold stare or icy behavior.

Luckily, there was enough going on to distract me. Blake played an amazing Poky Puppy. He remembered all of his lines and hammed it up to the audience. His dad would have been so very proud of him.

And Abby played her part as the sun exactly how I thought she would- grumpy. She snapped at the flowers and kicked a bone all the way across stage. She was awful. And it was so adorable I stood up at the end of the play and gave her a standing ovation. Mr. Hoya got exactly what he asked for. Abby's dad would have been so very proud of her too.

Although you could never get me to say that out loud.

Chapter Twenty-Two

The school year ended in a blink of an eye and summer flipped by in lazy days of late mornings and reckless play. June was a month filled with outdoor barbeques where Ben would grill and I would fill the patio table with paper plates and corn on the cob. The kids loved to eat outside and it wasn't too hot to enjoy the summer evenings.

Some nights Ben would watch the kids for me while I went for a run. They loved their Ben-time without me to take away his attention. And I loved my alone time.

On the weekends we would spend hours in Ben's pool. With two of us it made watching the kids simple. Emma would join us whenever she didn't have other plans.

Ben rarely spent a night away from us. And when he had to be away, it wasn't just me that missed him. The kids wanted him with us, at our dinner table, in our house, a part of our lives.

The Fourth of July had been spent at the lake, where he supervised small fireworks and I managed s'mores. We invaded his parent's cabin for the weekend and it was the first time I allowed him to sleep over.

Not that he did anything more than sleep. Still, that was a big step for me.

By the middle of July, I was already dreading the school year and simultaneously looking forward to the kids having a more structured life. Lucy couldn't wait to go to kindergarten and Abby had settled down just enough that I thought maybe her second grade teacher might be able to survive the year.

With the right amount of prayer.

Before I thought too seriously about school though, I decided we needed a lot more days at the pool. Because it was Saturday, Ben could join me and the children could survive the day.

"No running!" I called after Abby and Blake as they raced around the side of the pool and fought to see who could make the bigger cannonball splash.

Lucy had her floaties on and had no trouble puttering around the length of the pool and Jace was enjoying his froggy inflatable that sat him upright near the shallow end. All children were safe for the moment.

It was a good day.

I spread my arms along the edge of the pool and let the baked cement warm my skin. I blinked up at the bright sun and soaked in these blissful few moments.

"We need another date," Ben murmured, floating up to me. His firm torso was exposed for my viewing pleasure, the water crashed against his chest as he moved closer to me. My fingers twitched, desperate to run over his taut muscles.

"Why's that?" I snuck a glance over his shoulder to make sure all of the children were safe… and also distracted. My fingers cut through the water until they brushed against his ribs.

His hands mimicked my movements. I squirmed a little as they trailed over my skin under the water, causing my breath to hitch and his eyes to darken.

"Because I need you and this bathing suit all to myself." His lips dropped to my collarbone where he trailed hot kisses dripping with cool water to the tip of my shoulder and back down. I dropped my head back and closed my eyes. A small whimper escaped the back of my throat and his gentle grip became fiercely needy. He clutched my sides and slid his thigh between my legs. With the little bikini bottoms I had on, his leg pressed to my core with shocking pressure.

I lifted my head and opened my eyes, only to come face to face with the purest picture of desire I had ever seen.

I stopped breathing and my heart stopped beating. A blush swept over me from top to bottom. His intentions were so clearly written on his face that I had no doubt of the thoughts that ran through his head.

We had been dating for five months and this had never become a topic of conversation for us. I had been too terrified to bring it up and he had been too much of a gentleman. But surely he thought about this… wondered what would happen.

I certainly did.

But mine always ended with a big buzzer sounding and an announcer declaring that we were out of time. I couldn't get past my own humiliation to even think about the good stuff.

I had always thought Grady would be the last man to see me naked. And I had liked it that way. I couldn't fathom undressing in front of another man. Not after ten years of marriage to the same man.

And let's not even discuss my destroyed lady bits. *Thank you my darling children.* You didn't exactly leave me in tiptop condition.

So, no. Sex was a nonissue to me because it would never happen.

Ben would have to break this off with me if he ever wanted to get laid again. And guessing from the heated look in his eyes that sent shivers racing up and down my spine, he was going to have to break up with me soon.

Or I was going to spontaneously combust into a million pieces.

Ben continued to press kisses along my jaw, the shell of my ear and finally my mouth. My hands slid around his neck and our bodies came together naturally.

"Ew!" All of the kids shouted at once.

We pulled away laughing. This hadn't been the first time we got caught.

"How about that date?" He waggled his eyebrows at me and put a safe distance between us.

"I'll talk to Emma."

"Maybe we should think about finding another babysitter. A girl that is more available? Maybe a high school kid or someone we can pay?"

We can pay. We should think about finding another babysitter.

Ben's words stripped away my easy smile and poked at my motherly instincts. I didn't know how I felt about Ben's suggestion or his insinuation that we were so coupled.

What did it mean for us to both pick out a babysitter? Did that mean he had an actual say and I had to listen to his opinion? Did he care enough about my children to find someone that would truly take care of their needs and make my home a fun and safe environment while maintaining some kind of order? Was he offering to pay for the sitter? Or did that responsibility remain entirely with me?

He misread my expression, "I love Emma, Liz. Don't get me wrong. She's just so busy. I'd like to find someone who can come over weekly. You need a break and I need you alone."

I gaped at his insightful words.

"How much of a say do you think you have in this?" I followed a droplet of water with my finger as it trickled down his chest.

He captured my hand and brought it to his mouth for a chaste kiss. "A lot of say," he grinned at me. "So much say."

"I'm not so sure..." What I really wasn't sure about was inviting another person into our lives. I liked how we had things right now. I didn't want to upset the fragile balance we'd struck.

"I love these guys. I want the best for them too."

"I know you *say* that..."

"And I mean it." His voice was a serious timbre that made me want to sit up straighter. "I love those kids, Liz. More than I ever thought I could love anybody. If we are going to take this relationship any further, don't you think I should start working with you to make decisions that affect the whole family?"

He talked about my kids like he was already a father figure for them and about the family as if he were already a part of it.

I didn't know how to feel about that.

Frankly, he left me a little breathless.

Or, er, rather largely breathless.

I opened my mouth to say something although I didn't know what. I needed to politely ask him to back off until I could catch up with him. I didn't think I wanted Ben to become so involved. If he stepped into Grady's shoes that meant Grady would be pushed out.

And I didn't want Grady to leave.

But I didn't want Ben to leave either.

"Uncle Trevor!" Abby squealed before I could put two words together.

Lots of splashing ensued as my children scrambled from the pool to attack their uncle with wet hugs. He laughed and let them drip all over his work clothes. I held my hand up to shield the sun and silently thanked Trevor for interrupting at just the right time.

I pushed beyond Ben to climb out of the swimming pool too. Once I had a towel securely wrapped around me, I walked over to my brother-in-law to see why he'd tracked us down.

After my initial relief that he'd interrupted a tense moment between Ben and me, I now felt disastrously ill. Trevor didn't seek me out on his own. There had to be a problem with the business.

"Hey, Trev," I greeted.

He looked up at me with a very perplexed expression and explained, "I followed the screaming. I could hear these monsters from the driveway." They all laughed and screamed louder, proving his point.

"Is everything okay?" The words were out of my mouth before I could think of better ones. I was too nervous to wait for him.

"Can we talk?"

I cleared my throat, feeling more nervous as the seconds ticked by. "Sure."

"Alone?"

"Yes." I nodded enthusiastically and pointed toward my house. "I forgot the sunscreen anyway. Walk with me?"

"You got it." He bent down to kiss the top of the kids' heads and offer promises about taking them to the arcade.

I looked back at Ben and tried to convey my concern with raised eyebrows. We hadn't been dating long enough for him to read all of my facial expressions, but I hoped this one was pretty obvious. "Can you keep an eye on everybody? I'll be back in a few minutes."

200

Ben moved to the ladder and climbed out with agile grace. "Who needs a snack?" he called to the wild things. They agreed with more shouting and cheering. "That's great!" he told them as he herded them toward his sliding glass door. "Because I've got three different kinds of Pop-Tarts I need to get rid of." I froze in place. He had to be kidding. He looked over and shot me a sly wink. *That man.*

Trevor and I walked in silence up to the house. I opened the front door for him and stepped into my super-cooled entryway. Or maybe it just felt that way after lounging for hours in the hot sun. I hadn't bothered with flip-flops so my grass-covered feet felt every inch of cold wood as I led him into the kitchen where I'd left the sunscreen on the counter.

"I haven't seen you in a while, how have you been?" The truth was, I hadn't seen much of Trevor or Katherine over the past couple months. I knew she was avoiding me after she caught Ben kissing me in the hallway and I felt too guilty and too ashamed to reach out to her first.

Trevor was a casualty of Katherine and my avoidance.

Although, there was a very good chance that he was avoiding me on purpose too.

"I've been great," he breathed on a sigh that sounded good- so much better than the last time I saw him.

"Really?" The question was out of my mouth before I could process why I asked it. I thought maybe I expected more bad news. It was stranger to me that Trevor could possibly be okay than if he would have said he was filing for bankruptcy.

He smiled at me, "Really. Summer has been good for me and good for the business too."

His words filled me with hope, "How good?"

"Liz, we might be back on track. We haven't lost money in three months and we're booked out through the fall. I think it's going to stay this way too. I finally feel like I have my feet underneath me and a handle on what Grady had been doing."

"Trevor, that's amazing! I knew you could do it!"

His smile grew into a proud grin. "I kept waiting for Grady to come back and put someone else at the head of his business," he confessed. "I just couldn't believe that he meant to put me in charge. I am not Grady. I *will never be* Grady. And yet he left me so much to take care of. I felt like he made a mistake."

"He didn't."

Trevor's smiled died and the bright light in his eyes dimmed. "I am still struggling to believe that. But what you said at Thanksgiving, about how I was killing him all over again, that really made me start to think."

"I shouldn't have said that!" Regret churned in my stomach. God, how cruel I had been! "It wasn't true, Trev. I was just so angry and-"

"It was true, Liz. And I needed to hear it. I needed a fire lit under my ass."

I smiled and shook my head at him. "I'm still sorry."

"And I've already forgiven you." He looked around the kitchen, taking it in again. "I don't really like that guy you're dating."

His words sucked the air from the room. I wasn't expecting them and I didn't know how to reply. I stood there awkwardly playing with the spray can of sunscreen.

"But Grady would have."

My heart dropped to my stomach and I struggled to speak above a whisper, "What?"

"Grady would have liked him," Trevor repeated finally meeting my eyes. "He never wanted you to be alone, Lizzy. He never wanted to leave you with everything. It's been hard for me to come over here ever since he… died. Not just because everything in this damn house reminds me of him, but because watching you do this on your own killed me. I love those kids, as much as I've ever loved anything. They need a dad. You need help."

"Trev, Ben and I aren't serious. Not at all. I'm hardly thinking of him as a replacement for Grady."

He smiled patiently at me, as if he knew something I didn't. "But if you have to have a guy around, he's a good one."

"You don't really know him."

"Are you trying to convince me not to like him?" Trevor laughed. He ran two hands through his tousled hair and took a deep breath. "When Grady first told me about you, I was still in high school. He called me up to tell me he was going to bring a girl over to meet mom. I was too young to know that might mean anything, so I made some off-color joke that he didn't like. I remember that he got serious, right away. He didn't yell at me though or lecture me. He just said, 'When you meet Liz, you'll get it. She burns bright, Trevor. I need that kind of light in my life.'"

"Trevor…"

"He didn't want that to end with him, Lizzy."

Through a thick throat, I said, "He said something like that to me near the end."

"He always thought of you first. *Always*. And he always wanted what was best for you and the kids. That's why he worked so hard. That's why he built what he did. He just couldn't even imagine giving you something less than he thought you deserved. He was the best guy I have ever known."

"It's hard to imagine settling for anybody else. I think whoever they are will always feel like second best. Or second string or whatever."

Trevor barked out a surprised laugh. "Yeah, maybe. But whoever they are will have a lot to live up to. So maybe don't worry about that. Maybe just keep doing what you're doing and trust that it will all work out."

"When did you get so wise?" I looked at my brother-in-law from across the kitchen and saw him differently. He'd grown up over the last year. He wasn't the same immature kid that followed his brother around, desperate for guidance and Grady's approval. He was a man. And somehow he'd become a good man. Grady would have been so proud of him.

Trevor ran his hand through his hair again and shrugged one shoulder. "Guess my brother convinced me to grow up after all." He blew out a long breath, "Damn, I miss him."

"Me too."

I walked him out to his car and said goodbye, promising him that I would text soon about having him over for dinner. I watched his car pull out of the cul-de-sac and stood there wrapped in my towel for a long time, thinking about our conversation.

When I finally turned back to Ben's house, I realized it was the first time Trevor and I had ever talked about Grady when I hadn't cried.

Chapter Twenty-Three

"I don't know why I agreed to this." I looked at the well-manicured, two-story house that Ben grew up in and felt sick to my stomach. What had I been thinking?

"Are you nervous?" Ben settled back in the driver's seat of his Lexus and watched me fidget.

"Of course, I'm nervous. It's never easy meeting someone's parents."

"They already love you," he reminded me. He had been telling me this for weeks as he tried to get me to agree to this dinner. I had avoided it for as long as I could before I started to irritate him. "You don't have anything to worry about."

"It just feels so... final, you know? It's what people do in serious relationships." I played with the hemline of my flouncy navy blue skirt and refused to look at him.

A chill filled the car when he said, "Liz, what is it that you think we're doing?"

My heartbeat picked up, but not in a good way. "Ben..."

"We're serious."

I sucked in a quick breath. This was the wrong place and time to have this conversation. "That's not what I meant."

"What did you mean then?" His hand reached over the console to intertwine with mine. "What do *you* think we're doing?"

"Making out a bunch?" I dragged my gaze up to meet his and watched his lips twitch.

"That is not what we've been doing," he disagreed seriously. "We're not fifteen anymore."

He could be so exasperating. "Then what would you call it?"

"Foreplay."

His body slid gracefully from the car so he could walk around and open my door. I felt the blood drain from my face while a fire lit low in my belly. Something deliciously lustful rolled over my skin at the same time I struggled not to panic.

I swallowed against a lump in my throat and tried to steady out my breathing. By the time Ben opened my door and offered his hand, I had started to tremble.

He pulled me from the passenger's seat and settled his hand on my waist. He nudged me to the side so he could close my door, but backed me against it, caging me in with his body.

"Liz, you mean a lot to me. I've come to care for you deeply." His hand brushed over my jaw and his gaze bored into mine with staggering intensity.

"I care about you too." I hated the quiver in my voice, but there was nothing I could do about it. I was obnoxiously stunted when it came to this relationship. I felt more immature about my feelings for Ben than anything else in my life. But I also didn't know how to solve that. I wasn't ready to be anything more than casual with him. I wasn't ready to let go of Grady and accept that my feelings for Ben were real and significant. I had started my cycle of grief all over again only with this relationship. Currently I had settled into denial.

I liked denial.

Ben's expression did not soften when he said, "I'm exhausted with pretending that this thing between us is anything less than serious. I want more from you, Liz. I want more from us."

My heart kicked into overdrive, "I don't know if I can give you more. I'm... I'm just trying to keep up with what we already are."

"Then meet my parents," he coaxed gently. "That's all I'm asking. Live in this moment with me and we'll get to the next moment together. I'm not going to make you do this on your own."

My hands glanced over his chest to wrap around his neck. I needed him to hold me together, to keep me together. He wrapped his hands around my waist and pulled me tightly to him. My heart pounded against his chest, but when I breathed in his familiar scent I couldn't help but relax.

I closed my eyes and let my spirit return home.

"Don't leave my side," I ordered him.

"I won't, Liz. Not for anything."

He squeezed me tighter and I felt his promise burrow inside of me and chain itself to my heart. I didn't want to face the fact that we were serious, but we were. Ben had become an immovable part of my life. He cared about me and I cared about him. He cared about my children and they loved him in return.

I had to let go of this denial. I needed to face the reality of our relationship. What I didn't have to do was decide what that meant. A permanent future together was still impossible, but I couldn't give him up yet.

So that meant I needed to meet his parents.

"Okay," I conceded. "Take me to dinner."

He pulled back to press a sweet kiss to my lips. "I can do that."

Taking my hand, he led me to the front door of his parent's stately two-story house. This looked like the kind of place a successful lawyer would live. And yet, I had to laugh because it was so vastly different than Ben's current home.

Ben's house was modern, the most modern in our circle. This house had all of the character that he'd described his parents with, colonial with cream stucco siding and beautiful flower beds that wrapped around the house. I felt a thrill of anticipation. I suddenly couldn't wait to meet them and to see the kind of faded environment Ben had grown up in.

His relationship with his father improved daily, but he'd shared some of the hurt from his childhood and I knew it was still hard for him to accept that his father wanted to change, to salvage whatever they could of their tattered bond.

We walked through the open front door and Ben called out, "Mom, we're here!"

She rushed into the entryway, a ruffle-trimmed apron tied around her waist. "Ben, hi! And you must be Liz! I'm Sharon, it's so great to finally meet you." A beautiful smile lit her happy face. She was everything I expected her to be from the pictures hanging in Ben's house, but so much more in real life. Her dark brown bob fit the shape of her face stylishly, no grays anywhere in sight, and she held her slender frame with a dignified grace that I recognized in the way Ben held himself too. She looked between Ben and me with a shocking amount of affection. I didn't know how to accept her immediate approval of me.

Katherine had been so distant my entire marriage to Grady. I had expected much of the same with Sharon.

A burning irritation rippled through me. I couldn't help but hate that I had to go through this again. It had been bad enough with Grady, but what was I doing here with Ben?

His hand squeezed mine and I tried to step out of my bad mood. "It's nice to meet you too, Sharon. Ben has told me so much about you." I smiled politely and squared my shoulders in an attempt to push my negative thoughts away.

She looked at her son adoringly, "Has he? He hasn't shut up about you and the kids. It's too bad you couldn't bring them with you. I'm so anxious to meet them."

"I... Well... I, uh, thought it was probably better if they stayed home tonight. They can be... a little much."

She waved a hand in front of her face as if dismissing that very true fact. "Oh, I don't believe it. And if they are, I'm sure it's in the best way. Ben speaks so highly of them; I know they are very special kids."

I tried to contain my surprise when I said, "Ben is a little biased." I had never imagined Ben speaking well of my kids to others. The thought had literally never crossed my mind. And if I had maybe stopped to think about what he would say, I assumed it would be of how chaotic my life could be or how overwhelming we were. It left me a little breathless that he didn't seem to feel that way at all.

"Ben loves you. Of course, he's biased," she grinned at me. And then, as if her words had not just completely shattered my entire world, she waved us toward the dining room. "Dinner's ready and Mark will never forgive me if I learn anything more about you without him."

She turned her back to us and started walking toward the dining room. I froze in place. I couldn't pick up my feet or find energy to follow her. My body had become fragile, my skin had grown thin and brittle, my heart a piece of delicate glass.

"Do not freak out," Ben's words were a whisper against my ear.

All I could do was press my lips together and shake my head.

"Liz," he rumbled before pressing a kiss against my jaw. "She's my mom and she's never seen me this happy before. Of course, she thinks I love you."

I braved a look at him. "And do you?"

"If I deny it, will you be able to get through dinner?"

I nodded, ignoring the thin veil of his words over the truth I didn't want to accept.

"Then I don't love you. You're the most aggravating woman I've ever met. I can barely tolerate you."

"And my kids?"

"Oh, no," he chuckled. "I definitely love them."

"You do?" An aching affection flooded my body, filling in all of the cracks that fear and uncertainty had left me with. An emotional heat bubbled in my chest and wrapped my stiff limbs with something like hope.

"Yes, I do. But they agree with me about you. You aggravate us all."

"Are you two coming? The roast is getting cold."

He pushed his hand against my lower back and led me to a dining room that had been set up for an elegant evening. I marveled at the china place settings and the silver cutlery. Sharon knew how to entertain.

I felt severely unprepared for the evening ahead, but it had very little to do with the table set up.

Ben's dad stood up when we entered the softly lit room. He was an imposing figure with a broad chest and impeccably coiffed silver hair. He held out his hand to me with a small smile warming his expression.

"Liz, it's so nice to finally meet you. We've been looking forward to this evening for a very long time."

"It's nice to meet you too, Mark," I smiled at him. "Everything smells delicious."

"Then let's eat it," he grinned.

We took our seats and started passing dishes. Mark and Sharon threw question after question at me, seeming intrigued by every single aspect of my life.

I felt out of breath through the entire meal, trying to keep up with them. They were genuinely nice people that just wanted to know more about me. Still, their interest in my life was disconcerting. I had four kids. I was a widow. I was the very last person they should want their successful son to fall for.

Ben shared stories of the kids and they laughed as if they knew them. Sharon told anecdotes from Ben's childhood and I found myself laughing along with them. Mark was more reserved than his wife, but I could see the effort he put into getting to know me.

I could picture him as the distant father Ben had known most of his life, but he wasn't that man anymore. I found myself extremely satisfied with this realization. I was proud of Ben for loving his father through the rough years and working to cultivate this new relationship they had begun to forge.

"Liz, we'd love to meet the kids," Sharon announced over store-bought lemon bars- I appreciated that about her. She was a very good cook, but she claimed desserts exceeded her limitations. Apparently this was Ben's favorite. And I liked that even more. I liked knowing this about him. I liked that he had a favorite and I'd found out this way.

I tried not to analyze that too much.

"Sure," I told her. "We don't start school for a couple more weeks, so we're pretty available."

Sharon looked at her husband and then turned back to me. "We were thinking about taking everyone to the lake. We thought we could go for a weekend? We'll bring the boat this time."

"The kids had so much fun over the Fourth. They would love that." I answered as Ben's hand landed on my bare knee under the table. His thumb trailed a path up along the outside of my thigh. I shivered from the touch, but felt the encouragement he meant to give me.

"He told us," Sharon grinned. "We cannot wait to see for ourselves."

"I have to admit that I'm surprised you're both so… accepting of me and all my children." The words slipped out before I could think better of them. I internally winced when I saw Sharon glance at Ben uncertainly.

I knew they were just doing their best to make me feel welcome and maybe ease the awkwardness of an unexpected situation. I doubted they hoped their only child and heir to the family firm would ever become serious with a woman like me. With a woman who had as many children as me.

"Oh, Liz…" Sharon sounded heartbroken at my words and I wished I could shovel them back in my mouth and swallow them whole.

My chest stung with a pain that I had caused. I opened my mouth to explain, but Mark beat me to it.

"I have to admit, Liz, that we were surprised when Ben told us that you two were dating, but only because you finally said yes." His teasing smile helped shift the atmosphere back to friendly again. "From the first day he met you, we have heard stories about his next door neighbor and all her kids. Slowly those stories took on an affectionate note and then grew into something more. We've always known how Ben felt about you and your family. We just didn't know if you would ever feel the same way after everything you've been through. We couldn't be more thrilled that you're here tonight, Liz. We couldn't be happier to see our son so happy. You have to understand that Ben has never given us much of a say in his life. He does pretty much whatever he wants and we respect him for that. He makes wise decisions. And I can't help but see that he made a brilliant one with you. Of course, we accept you and all of your children. Anything that could make our son this happy is more than worthy of our approval."

Ben's hand left my knee to slide over my shoulders and rest around me. He pulled me closer to him and pressed a kiss to the top of my head while I tried to control my emotions.

"See?" he teased. "They're not so bad."

I blinked up at him and gave a watery smile, before turning back to Mark and Sharon. "Thank you. That means a lot to me. Thank you."

Mark winked at me, "Whatever he's told you about me, I only live up to about half of it."

I laughed lightly, enjoying his sweet humor. "I can see that."

Sharon waved a hand in front of her face and dabbed at the corners of her eyes with her napkin. "No, you're worse!" she cried at her husband. "You weren't supposed to make me cry over dessert! Nobody should cry over dessert!"

"She's never going to come back if you keep it up, Mom." Ben's hand played with the sleeve of my white and yellow printed blouse, feeling so familiar that my body and soul couldn't help but notice. "You've ruined lemon bars for her forever."

"That's not true!" I gasped. "This night has made lemon bars for me. Forever."

We settled into easy conversation after that and I could truly say I enjoyed my evening. By the time Ben parked in his driveway and walked me to my front door, I couldn't stop smiling. His parents were great. He was great.

And sometimes, I was great too.

At my door, I turned to face him and his hands settled on my arms. He pulled me into a hug and sighed contentedly.

"I really like your parents," I confessed into his chest.

"Good," he breathed. "Thank you for going with me tonight. I know it wasn't easy for you."

"Well, I'm not easy for you, so I figured I owed you."

His chuckle vibrated through his chest and made me fall for him just a little bit more. I tried to hold out, I tried to stop this fall... but I was helpless against this man that had wiggled his way into my life and made me need him, made me want him.

"You do owe me," he murmured, dipping his head to capture my mouth with his.

I fell into the now familiar rhythm of our kissing. His lips molded against mine, tasting and savoring each brush and nip. His tongue swept over the seam of mine until I opened my mouth for him and gave him a deeper touch.

His hands fell to my hips and held me tightly to him. His fingers tugged at my blouse until he could slide them beneath the silky fabric and caress my bare skin.

My breathing hitched as one of his hands slid higher, nudging the underwire of my bra. His kiss intensified, heightening each of my senses and causing me to drown in lust for him. His lips moved over my jaw, down the column of my neck and across my collarbone.

"Liz," he whispered as he pushed me against the door, trapping me against his hardened body.

I gasped as his kisses turned slowly sensual. His mouth returned to mine and I felt overwhelmed with the sensation of him, with his virile touch and his consuming worship of my body.

He grew increasingly desperate as we continued to kiss in the shadows of my entryway and the light of the moon. His thumb brushed over my nipple, hidden behind my lacy bra, and I thought I would collapse. My knees weakened and my thighs trembled. I hadn't expected to feel this much with him. I hadn't expected to become so intensely turned on from his seductive touches and mind-blowing kisses.

He caught me by sliding his thigh between my legs. My desire hitched even higher and I dropped my head against the glass screen door, completely lost to Ben and whatever he wanted to do to me.

His lips moved back down my throat, licking a sensual path. His tongue delved into the hollow of my throat and I whimpered. My usually cluttered mind completely emptied and all I could do was feel.

The porch light flicked on and we jumped apart, both of us breathing heavy. I planted my hands on the glass behind me and tried not to melt into a pool of lust.

Ben watched me with heavily-lidded eyes. His chest breathed raggedly and I could feel his desire from a foot apart.

I wanted him too.

And I didn't know what to do with that.

"I'm going to ask Emma to watch the kids overnight next weekend."

His words hit me with a punch of reality. I stood up straight and tried to keep from panicking.

"I don't think that's a good idea."

He reached out and tangled his fingers with mine. His touch was so light, barely there, but I felt it to my toes. My mind swam with lust and fear, with heady desire and breath-catching anticipation.

But I couldn't go that far with him. I couldn't take those finalizing steps.

I had so many feelings for him and I'd given up so much of my heart. This… sex… felt like it was the only thing Grady still owned completely.

Maybe that was a harsh exaggeration, but it was the only tangible thing I had left to save.

"We don't have to have sex," he rushed to explain. "But I want one night where I don't feel rushed to leave you. I want one night where I can kiss you for as long as I want and not worry about having the police called on us or one of the kids walking downstairs."

"Ben…"

"We won't have sex." He ran a hand over his jaw and some of the drowsy hunger cleared from his gaze. "Okay? We won't. I'll turn down your advances. I won't let you seduce me." I couldn't help but laugh at him. "Just spend the night with me," he pleaded gently. "Stay with me one night."

"Okay," I heard myself whisper without any hesitation.

His lips broke into a staggering smile. "Good."

The door opened behind me and Emma found us staring at each other like moonstruck teenagers. I blinked back into reality and untangled my hands from his. "Thank you for introducing me to your parents, Ben. I had a great night."

"I thought you might." He leaned forward and placed one more kiss on my forehead. "Goodnight, Liz."

I stepped inside and Emma and I watched him walk back to his house.

"Sorry," she groaned. "I didn't realize it was you at the door."

"It's okay."

"Did I interrupt anything naughty?" Her singsong voice did nothing to disguise her hopeful tone.

"Not tonight."

She pushed my shoulder until I faced her completely. Her eyebrows rose comically and her eyes bugged, waiting for more information.

"He wants me to spend the night next weekend."

Her screaming excitement, excitement I had yet to feel, woke Jace and Lucy.

Chapter Twenty-Four

Friday came too fast like a train barreling down the tracks that I could not stop.

We only had a couple more weeks until school started, so I had been filling up our days with as much activity as I could fit in.

And maybe I had been trying to avoid thinking about tonight.

Ben had been as much a part of our lives as usual, only now, when the kids were asleep in their beds, his touches would linger, his kisses would push boundaries and his intentions were made clear.

I had given him permission when I agreed to spend tonight and he had spent the last week building my anticipation and preparing me for what was to come.

But he had promised no sex and since I knew without a doubt that I wasn't ready for sex, I bound his words against my nerves and tried to be brave.

"Good luck tonight," Emma whispered when she showed up a few minutes before Ben.

"Nothing is going to happen," I whispered back. She gave me a "yeah, right" look. "Seriously, Emma. Even if... even if I thought we were ready for that, I just can't be intimate with someone else. It's too weird."

"Give me a break," she sighed. "You deserve a night like tonight. Relax and have fun. Forget about the other stuff."

"You're a terrible sister. You're supposed to support *me*, not Ben."

"I do support you!" she hissed. "And I support the very clear reality that you need to get laid!"

Ben walked in the house without knocking, which was now his way, and we shut up.

"Everything okay?" he asked, glancing between Emma and me.

"Yep!" Emma practically shouted at him. "We're just peachy."

My body flushed from my toes to the top of my head. I tried to smile at Ben, but I had to look half-deranged.

Ben's eyes darkened with concern. "Is this your bag, Liz?"

"It is," I croaked.

"I'm going to take it outside. Come out when you're ready?"

I nodded, anxious to have another moment to myself. The kids were happily eating dinner, but when they realized Ben was here, they chased him out the door to say hello. With a few moments to ourselves, Emma put her hands on my shoulders and got right in my face.

"You will survive this night," she promised.

"I'm not sure that I will."

"You will. Ben will be there to walk you through it."

"Will you be disappointed in me if we don't do anything more than sleep?"

She shook her head and let her blonde waves bounce around her chin. "Never," she promised. "I just want you to be happy again… however that happens."

I nodded, acknowledging that I had the best sister in the entire world. "You'll call if there are problems?"

"Obviously."

"If I text you *code red*, you'll call and make up a problem?"

"Lizzy, I will set your house on fire if you need me to. Now go!"

"Okay, I'm going." I paused in the doorway and turned back to her, "Em, no matter what I text, do not set the house on fire."

She rolled her eyes and waved me off.

The three of us wrestled the kids back inside so I could give them each a kiss and a hug and then Ben set us off on our date… our date that was supposed to last us all night long.

"Where do you want to get dinner?"

I looked up at him, startled by his question. "Oh."

His mischievous grin brought all kinds of fluttering feelings to life inside of me. "You did want to get dinner, didn't you?"

"I-I, um, yes."

He took my hand and swung me around to face him, pausing on the sidewalk between our two houses. "Or did you want to go straight to my place?" He dipped his head to place a slow kiss along my jaw, sending shivers racing down my back.

"Dinner is good," I squeaked.

His dark chuckle did nothing to help prepare me for the night ahead. "We're taking tonight at your pace, Liz. We can do whatever you want tonight. I promise not to ravish you before you're ready."

As if those words were going to calm me down. "I know."

"You're shaking," he pointed out.

"I'm nervous."

He pulled back so that I could stare into those fathomless dark eyes. He held my gaze, long enough for me to know that he was serious. "Do you trust me?"

I took a breath. "I do."

"Then trust that I want you anyway you'll let me have you. There's nothing else to worry about tonight."

Those words were all I needed. We climbed into his little car that was free of fast food wrappers on the floor and stickers stuck to the windows. He took me to one of my new favorite restaurants, one that he had introduced me to.

We had a fantastic meal and then took a long walk through downtown, admiring the summer night and holding hands.

Everything with Ben was new and thrilling. Sometimes my mind compared him to Grady without my permission, but for the most part, this man next to me was so very different than my first husband that I could keep thoughts of them separate.

When Grady held my hand, it was the feeling that had been with me for a decade. It was a love that had grown from a seedling into a mature, unbreakable bond.

With Ben, we had started at the beginning with something fragile and small, but what we had was never like what Grady and I had. Our feelings for each other didn't start as a seed, they started as an ocean. I felt as though we were separated by miles of rocky, turbulent water that could drown both of us or either of us with the wrong step. And as we'd spent time together, as we'd opened up and shared in each other's lives, that ocean had shrunk. The waters between us had grown smaller and less frightening. The distance between us had all but disappeared.

We had grown into something different... something profound, but I couldn't put a name on it just yet. I couldn't think of the right words to claim it.

At the edge of downtown, Ben leaned against a building and pulled me into the curve of his body. "Can I take you home now?"

I stared at his chest and breathed, "Yes."

"Do you still trust me?" he asked, tilting my chin with one long finger to meet his depthless gaze.

I nodded, unable to speak through my fears.

We drove home in silence. Ben asked me if I trusted him and I did, without a doubt. But it wasn't him that I had to worry about. It was me. Did I trust myself?

I didn't trust myself to keep my hands off of him. And I didn't trust myself to finish something if I were to start it. I was a mess of anxiety and lust, unable to separate the two from each other.

Ben pulled his car into the garage and opened my door for me. His garage was so empty compared to mine. He had one bike parked along the wall and a set of tools. There was a kayak hanging from the ceiling and some storage boxes piled on shelves. But he lacked the overflow that kids managed to accumulate with multiple bicycles and tricycles and balls and outdoor whatever. Normally I would have expected this from someone single like Ben, but it felt wrong on him. He had become such a huge part of our lives that I expected his garage to be filled with kid things too.

My footsteps seemed to echo through the empty expanse as I followed him into the house. His house, that had seemed so perfect for him a few months ago, now felt wrong and ill-fitting.

I set my purse down next to my bag that he had brought in and joined him in the kitchen for a glass of wine. The delicious red helped calm some of my frantic nerves and I tried to focus on him... on just being here with him in the quiet of his home.

"This is good," I said to fill our silence.

"Is it weird that I brought you back to my house?" Ben asked, appearing pulled from deep thoughts. "I thought a hotel room might seem... presumptuous."

"It's not weird."

"I want to know how you sleep," he kept going, not seeming to hear my answer at all. "That is definitely weird. I know that." I opened my mouth and then closed it without anything to say. It was a little weird. He pushed on with an explanation, "I just... I know so much about you. I know how you like your wine and how you like your food. I know what you look like when you're angry at the world and angry at your children. I've watched you laugh and smile, cook a meal and fold a basket of clothes. I've seen you cry and I've seen you sit in silence, so lost in your thoughts that the rest of the world doesn't exist. But I've never seen you sleep, Liz. It's important to me to share this with you."

"Okay."

He set his wine on the counter and walked over to me. "I told myself that I would go easy on you tonight." His cautious smile melted whatever defenses I still had raised. "I have wanted this for so long, but I'm having a hard time believing that it's real. That you're really here with me."

I set my wine down so that I could press my hand to his heart. "I'm here, Ben. I'm with you."

He laid his hand over my heart and held my gaze. His eyes said something that my heart refused to accept. I had a moment of panic where I knew I should run, but he started speaking before I could convince my body to move.

"Liz, I've fallen in love with you." I said nothing. The silence rang around the room as I waited for more from him, a qualifier or an excuse or anything other than those words. He smiled patiently and his fingers brushed over my cheek and finally an explanation of sorts came, "I tried to fight this attraction for a long time. And then I thought I could be satisfied with just the little bit that you were comfortable giving to me. But, the more I get to know you, the deeper I fall. And it isn't just you I've fallen in love with, but your family, your chaotic life. I cannot imagine my life without you and the kids in it. I don't expect you to feel the same way about me. I know that Grady will always be there with you. But I wanted you to know how I feel. I don't have anything holding me back, Liz. I fell for you because that was the only way for me to go... to feel."

"Say it again," I whispered, surprised by my strong reaction to his words. I expected to hate them if he ever said them to me. I expected to run from them as fast as I could, but they felt *right*. They felt like salve against my wounded soul, like glue to my shattered heart.

They felt like home.

"I love you."

I didn't say them back, but I couldn't just stand there either. I wrapped my arms around his neck and pulled him down for a desperate kiss.

Our mouths crashed together with all of the depth and intensity wrapped up in those beautiful words. I held him tightly to me, letting him worship my mouth with the emotion I could now name. His hand blindly moved the glass of wine out of our way before he gripped my hips and tossed me on the counter.

I wrapped my legs around his waist as he stepped into me, letting me feel the strength and masculinity of his hips. His hands moved over my body with skilled seduction.

I was helpless against the blazing fire he built inside of me.

I felt dizzy with lust. My fingers shook as I worked the buttons on his oxford. He patiently let me unhook them all. My hands brushed over his bare chest, relishing the feel of his hard muscle and pounding heart. I peeled the shirt back from his shoulders and he worked the wrists loose until it was a pile on the floor.

His kisses moved down my neck and over my throat and chest. He kissed me through the thin material of my plum dress. I shivered when his hot mouth pressed against my nipple.

His fingers played with my zipper, teasing me with his desire and uncertainty.

"Yes," I panted.

"Liz." His breath hitched as he pulled the zipper down slowly, teasing me into blind passion.

I bunched my shoulders and the sleeveless dress fell past my wrists to pool at my waist. Ben gazed with hooded eyes at my body, my breasts hidden behind a lacy bra and my hips marked with pale stretch marks. He bent low to remove my heels, taking care to tug them off with slow, intoxicating touches. Then he placed his hands against my bare waist and helped me to the floor. My dress dropped to my feet and soon I stood there in nothing but underwear I'd ordered online just in case of this moment.

He took a step back and rubbed his fingers roughly along his jaw. "Beautiful," he breathed.

And in that moment I didn't feel like a used woman or a mother of four children. I didn't feel mid-thirties with gravity working against every part of me.

I felt beautiful. He breathed that word into existence and there had never been a purer, more honest moment than right then.

I stepped out of my dress and ran my fingers over his stomach, settling them on the waist band of his jeans. I played with the button, shocked at my courage and at the undeniable need I felt for this man.

I watched my fingers move as I remembered how to unfasten a man's pants. I pushed them down to his ankles and he stepped out of them in only boxer briefs. My eyes traveled the length of him, memorizing every inch of his body, every part of this incredible man that had changed my life so profoundly.

"Are you sure, Liz? I only want to do this if you're sure."

"I am," I promised him. "I'm ready."

He scooped me up into his arms and carried me to his bedroom. With a needy toss, he dropped me onto his massive bed. I had little time to take in his room, his king sized bed, a large TV mounted to the wall, soft, silky sheets.

His body covered mine and his mouth began to taste all of the skin he had never had access to before. The little bits of clothing we still had on disappeared and our hands began to explore places we had managed to avoid until now.

He asked me once more if I was ready for this and when I agreed, he pulled a condom from the bedside drawer and put it on. I marveled at his body while I waited, taking in the rippling muscle of his abs and chest, the powerful strength of his thighs, resting on his heels. I watched as he crawled back over me and tried to breathe through new fear.

He leaned forward and kissed my hip. I jerked, shaken by his touch, but he was not deterred. He kept kissing me, across my belly and over my breasts, up the line of my throat until he finally landed on my lips. There he took my mouth leisurely, seductively and when he pressed against my core, it felt only natural.

Ben pushed inside of me and I felt bursts of pleasure dance through me. We moved together, learning each other, knowing each other in a way that I had never thought to know another man.

He took his time, both desperate and relaxed, both lost and found. I let him carry me away. I let him erase all of my doubts and fears and grief and anything else that stood between us. I let him help me realize exactly how I felt for him, without anything else clouding my thoughts.

When it was over, he rolled next to me and gathered me in his arms. He held me there with a sweetness that moved me. For three minutes, I simply lay there, completely absorbed and abandoned to him.

His fingers rubbed a lazy path along my spine and the scruff of his chin tickled my forehead. Neither of us spoke. I couldn't find adequate words to describe my feelings and I had no idea what Ben was thinking.

But then that started me thinking. And the more I thought the faster my mind spun. The haze of lust and fulfillment fell away and I was left only with the reality of what I had done.

I had just slept with another man.

I had sex with another man.

A man that was not Grady.

The sob hiccupped in my chest before I could stop it. The grief crashed around me again as I reeled from the consequences of my actions. I grasped for sanity and stable ground but I could not find any.

"Liz?" Ben sounded concerned and I couldn't blame him.

I launched myself from the bed and raced for his en suite bathroom. I barely made it to the toilet before I heaved up all of my dinner and my regret.

I stayed there for endless minutes, crying hysterically as my body physically reacted to what I had just done and the commitment we had made.

Ben followed right after me and stayed there with me. His gentle fingers held back my hair and his soothing words helped ease the crippling pain of my betrayal.

After a long time, I collapsed onto the floor. He did not hesitate to pull me into his arms again and hold me against his chest.

I didn't deserve his kindness or his understanding, but without it I was positive I would have broken into a thousand jagged pieces. I would have been truly broken, *permanently shattered*.

221

We sat there for so long that my arm fell asleep and I ran out of tears. Ben had put on his briefs before he came in after me and covered me with his robe that hung next to his shower.

His thoughtfulness opened up new wounds inside of me and when I finally spoke, my voice was filled with raw honesty.

I had come to terms with who I was now tonight. And I had also admitted the reality that Grady was gone forever. That he would never come back. And that in some ways, I had moved on.

But that I was not healed.

I had ruined something beautiful between Ben and me, something that should have been sacred and protected. I couldn't help how I reacted or how I had behaved since then, but there was one simple thing I could do to salvage this night.

I could tell Ben the truth.

With my head against his chest and my fingers curled over his heart, I whispered, "Ben, I love you too."

He held me tighter, crushing me against his warm body. He didn't say anything. He didn't need to say anything. I knew how he felt and now he knew, good or bad, how I felt.

Chapter Twenty-Five

Eventually Ben and I left the bathroom floor. I grabbed my overnight bag so I could brush my teeth and wash my face. Then I pulled on some new underwear and a cami. I brought pajama pants, but they seemed a little pointless. Ben stood in the doorframe, leaning against the door, watching me.

"Is this interesting?" I asked around a mouthful of toothpaste.

"I like this, Liz. I like being domesticated with you."

I dropped my gaze to his sink and focused on finishing the job I started.

I crawled beneath his comforter and snuggled into one of his pillows. His bed was better than mine, and not just because it was absent of Grady's ghost.

Ben curled behind me and wrapped his arms around my waist, holding me impossibly tight to his warm chest. I expected my mind to race with the events of the night, of sleeping with Ben, of betraying Grady, of saying I love you to a man that was not nor would ever be my husband.

But Ben's even breathing and protective touch lulled me into a cozy place that was absent of haunting husbands and sweet regrets.

"I would apologize for puking after sex," I teased, "but I bet that happens to you a lot."

I felt his body still, surprised by my joke. "You think you're clever."

I looked at him over my shoulder and through mussed strands of hair, "I know I'm clever."

I squealed when he started tickling me. How was that a fair response! I jerked and struggled to get away from his torturing, but it was no use. I flopped to my back and he pinned me down by straddling my waist. I was laughing so hard I wasn't making any sound.

"Stop!" I gasped, bucking against him. Stop!" I tried to pinch his nipple in retaliation, but he caught my hand and pinned it to the pillow beneath my head.

His nose ran a slow trail over mine. He stopped tickling me in favor of running his free hand over my side, across my stomach and along the curve of my breast.

"That was mean," I panted. He was still driving me crazy, but now his touch had turned sensual and my breathing panted for a different reason.

"Mmm," he murmured as he nipped at my bottom lip. "But so worth it." His thigh slipped between my legs, parting them until he could slide between them.

This time, I did not puke. This time, when it was over, he pulled me into the curve of his body again and we fell asleep, tangled in each other.

And when I woke, I knew that I was with Ben and not Grady.

I had been afraid that I would forget, that my memories would collide with my reality and I would truly wound Ben by not remembering that I was in his bed.

But I came awake with Ben's familiar scent filling my nostrils, not Grady's. And it was Ben's leaner, longer legs that overlapped with mine, not Grady's.

I woke with a clear sense of who I was with and what we had done.

And I was okay.

Mostly.

Ben made us a big breakfast of eggs and hash browns over toast. It turned out Pop-Tarts weren't the only thing he knew how to make. We laughed and talked over a shared pot of coffee and deliciously tingling feelings from what had transpired last night.

When he walked me to my door, he kissed me with the knowledge of a man that knew my body intimately.

"I'll stop by later," he said.

"Okay. For dinner?"

"Yeah."

With one hand on the door handle, I turned back to him and blinked in the light of day. I didn't have the courage this morning. I couldn't say the words again. They churned in my stomach, filling my chest with acid.

I wanted to say them. I wanted to believe that they were true… But I couldn't. The day was too bright, the morning too raw.

"I-I-I'll see you later," I told him instead.

"Okay, Liz."

I escaped to my house and shut the door behind me, locking out Ben and the feelings and sensations he brought with him.

My children attacked me with cries of "Mommy!" I brought them all into a hug and held them tightly to me.

Emma stood over us with a hopeful expression on her face, "How did it go?"

I looked up at her and blinked away tears that I refused to cry. "Good," I admitted. "Really, really good." She grinned, blinding me with her brilliance. "And bad," I continued to confess. "Really, really bad."

Her eyebrows drew down in confusion. "What happened?"

"He, uh, he told me he loved me." I mouthed the last part to her so the kids didn't hear. Her eyes grew huge and her mouth dropped open. "And I... um, told him the same thing."

If possible Emma's expression grew even more surprised. "Oh, Lizzy," she whispered. She stepped close to me and wrapped me in a tight hug.

I didn't cry this time. I wouldn't let myself have an emotional release. I deserved this pain. I deserved this heartache.

Unlike Grady's sickness and death, I had done this to myself.

My heart felt ripped in two. One part would forever stay with Grady, loyal to my first love and my husband. The other part ran to Ben, to this new love.

Emma asked me if I was okay probably forty times before she left me for the day. I told her each time that I would be. I didn't believe my lie and I knew she didn't either.

By the time Ben came over for dinner that night, I was wound tight.

He walked in the house without knocking. He had been doing this for a while, but this time it caused my anxiety to spike. The front door happened to be open this time, but if it hadn't been, he had a key. He had access to my house, my family and now my heart. And I'd just given it to him.

I'd given it all to him.

So now how did I get it back?

"Ben, when are you going to move in with us?" Abby asked over tacos.

I dropped my fork. "What?"

"I asked Ben when he was going to move in with us," she repeated, as if it wasn't the most absurd question in the entire world.

Ben chuckled, clearly more level-headed than me, "Why do you ask that, Abs?"

Blake kicked her from under the table. "That's such a stupid question. Why would he move in with us? He has his own house. And it has a pool."

Abby's expression flashed with fury, my little hot head that couldn't keep her temper under control. "It's not a stupid question!" she shouted at her brother. "Ben loves mom! I heard her tell Aunt Emma. He loves her! So why wouldn't he move in with us? People that love each other are supposed to live together!"

"It's different!" I rushed to tell her. "Some people that love each other live together, but other times they just live... next door." I wanted to face plant into my refried beans.

"Why?" Abby asked innocently.

225

"Well," I cleared my throat and struggled to regain some of my composure. "Sometimes people that love each other live together. Like us. I love you so much that I don't ever want you to move out. You can live here forever and ever and ever." She giggled at me and Blake groaned. The two littles cheered for that idea. "But sometimes," I went on, "people that love each other have to live apart. Like your Nana. You love Nana Katherine, don't you?" The four of them nodded enthusiastically. "But she lives in her house and we live in ours. It doesn't mean we love her less, it just means we live in different places."

"But when you loved daddy, he lived with us," Abby put in oh, so helpfully.

My heart plummeted into my stomach, "I still love daddy. I still love him very much, Abby."

Her nose wrinkled with confusion. "I thought you loved Ben."

I made a frustrated sound that rattled my chest. "Abby, you were not supposed to hear that. You can't just-"

"Liz," Ben interrupted with his deep, rolling voice. He gave me a pleading look to let him try this. I slammed back in my seat and raised my eyebrows at him. I blamed him for this. This was his fault. "Abby, do you love your mom?"

"Yes," she answered simply.

"And do you love your dad? Even though he isn't here anymore?"

"Yes," she whispered.

"Don't you think you'll always love your dad?"

"Yes. Forever and ever."

Ben smiled affectionately at her. "That's how your mom feels about him too. She loves him so much that she'll never stop loving him. And we don't want her to, do we? We always want her to love him."

The kids all nodded.

Ben continued, after taking a deep breath, "Is it easy for you to love both your mom and your dad? Even though one is here and one isn't, you can still love both of them, right?"

The kids nodded again. "Yes," Abby said.

"That's how your mom feels. She loves your dad very, very much. But she also loves me. And even though your dad is gone now, she will never stop loving him. She just also loves me now. We don't have to limit how many people we love. Our hearts make room for as many people as we want to let in."

My chest fluttered with his words. He had explained that perfectly to my kids. They all understood what he meant and accepted his explanation easily.

Even I found it easy to agree when he put it like that. I didn't want to accept that it could be so simple; my heart protested that he was wrong, but I couldn't come up with an argument to prove it.

"So are you going to move in with us or not?" Abby looked seriously at Ben, apparently back to business.

Ben looked to me. He watched my frightened expression and measured my obvious panic. Then he ignored all of the hot mess that I was and turned back to my daughter and said, "One day."

"Soon?" she said.

"If I get my way," he told her.

It was a miracle that I got through the rest of dinner. I simmered with frustration and anger. I wanted to kick him out of my house and deal with him later. But for the sake of my kids, I struggled through the rest of the night.

Ben stuck around after dinner and helped put the kids to bed. He had to know I was pissed at him, but he didn't seem to care. At least not enough to leave without me telling him he needed to.

I gave the kids extra-long hugs and kisses, escaping to their bedrooms so I could avoid Ben for as long as possible. He'd moved back downstairs after they brushed their teeth, so I had a few minutes before I needed to face him.

I went to Blake's room last because it was closest to the stairs. I found him lying on his back with both hands tucked beneath his head. He was staring up at the ceiling deep in thought. It wasn't until I sat down next to him, that he looked over at me.

"Do you really still love dad?" he asked quietly. His green eyes held tears that hadn't fallen yet.

"Yes," I promised him immediately. "More than anything else."

"Is Ben really going to move in with us?"

"No!" I rushed to assure him. "No, he's not. Ben is going to stay in his house and we are going to stay in ours."

He tilted his head to look at me. Somehow he'd gone through third grade, turned nine, been an all-star on his soccer team and become the man of the house all over the last year. He wasn't my little baby boy anymore. He had matured. He had become a kid that made me so very proud. He'd become a kid that would have made his dad proud.

"It would be okay with me, Mom. If he moved in."

227

Blake's words shook me to my very core. "He's not, Blake. Please don't worry about it. It's not happening. He's not going to move in."

"Okay." His gaze moved back to his ceiling and I could see the disappointment written all over his body.

Great.

I kissed his forehead and turned off his lamp. I stopped feeling angry with Ben. Instead, I felt something incredibly more difficult. The truth of what I needed to do.

The weight of my relationship with Ben pressed down on me and threatened to crush me. I missed Grady with a fierce ache that fractured my heart and soul. I couldn't have both of these men.

I couldn't have either of them.

I walked downstairs and found Ben lounging on the sectional. He was stretched out, flipping through the channels with one hand propped behind his head.

The image of him reminded me so strongly of Grady that my knees nearly buckled.

His eyes lifted to mine as soon as he saw me. A playful smile danced on his lips and his fingers twirled the remote casually.

This man should never have fallen in love with me. I was only going to destroy him.

"Hey, are you okay?" He sat up as I walked over. Tension seeped back into his shoulders and straightened his spine.

"No," I told him honestly.

He jumped to his feet and closed the distance between us. "What's wrong?"

I swallowed thickly and told him the truth, "I can't do this anymore, Ben."

"Do what anymore?"

"Us."

"Liz..."

"I can't," I sobbed. "I can't be with you. I can't love you. We have to stop."

"No, you have to stop." His voice had turned to rough gravel, dragging across my heart. "How can you say that? After last night? After everything we've been through?"

"After everything I've been through, you mean!" I struggled to keep my voice low enough so I wouldn't wake the kids. "I didn't want this, Ben. I didn't ask for you to come into my life and make me feel for you. I didn't ask you to become a part of our lives and take over where my husband left off."

"Liz, you know that I have never tried to take over Grady's place or be what he was to you guys. I have never once asked you to ignore or forget him. That isn't fair."

I went on like he had never spoken, "And now my kids are asking you to move in with us! You can't replace their daddy! You can't just move in and fill this void that he left behind!"

"I have never once tried to do any of that!" he growled at me. "Stop making this into something that it's not."

"Then what is it?" I shouted at him. I shook my head and lowered my voice again, "What is it? What is this?"

"This is us, Liz," he pleaded with me. "This is you and me. We're figuring it out as we go. Neither of us expected this, but it happened. We need each other. We… We love each other."

"So what?" I spat cruelly. "Where does that leave us? Where is this going?"

"Liz…"

"You can't move in with us. So that's off the table. I will not get married again. So that's also off the table. We can't ever be anything more than what we are right now and is that enough for you?"

"No." His answer was so immediate and forceful that I jumped.

"See!"

"No, I don't see. Why can't we move in together, Liz? Why can't we get married? What in the hell is stopping us?"

"Me!"

"Right!" He took a step closer to me and I felt the vibrations of his anger ripple around me. "You! But *nothing else.* Nothing else is standing in our way. So tell me, tell me right now, why you're putting a stop to this."

"Because I can't do this anymore!" I cried. The tears of the day finally fell as my world came crashing down around me for the second time in my life. "I cannot be with you when I miss him so much my body aches from it! I cannot be with you and make a life with you when all I want is for him to come back. I can't be intimate with you when it's his hands I imagine touching me, when it's his body I dream about. I cannot be with you when I will never stop loving him." I closed my eyes to rid myself of the image of Ben's broken expression and defeated posture. I couldn't stand that image of him. My confident, defiant, authoritative neighbor had been crushed because of me. I did that. I destroyed the second man that I loved. "I can't love you when I love him like this."

"You mean that?" he rasped. "You're done trying?"

"I'm done. I have to be done." I opened my eyes and blinked through the tears. I watched him accept my words, I watched them sink in.

"You don't have to do this, Liz. We could work through this together. I could share this pain with you and we could get through it."

I shook my head and delivered the final blow, "You can't help me, Ben. This is *my* pain. This is *my grief*. There is nothing you can do but let me be."

He nodded once before gathering his things and leaving. I watched the door close behind him and felt the avalanche of grief cascade over me. My dam of sorrow and sadness ripped open again and I felt the agony of losing someone I loved all over again.

I stumbled to the couch and did not get up for the rest of the night. I couldn't face my bed again, not after the night I had with Ben. I couldn't face Grady's empty side of the bed and come to terms with what I had done.

I curled up on my couch, in the place that Ben had just occupied and I cried myself sick. I stayed there until there were no more tears to cry, until the depression I had been in wrapped its skeletal claws around me and carried me into the grave it had been slowly preparing for me.

My husband was the one that died, not me. But it didn't feel that way tonight.

Not without Ben to help me wade through the pain. Not without this new love to soften the harsh, unforgiving blows.

We had been so active this summer, but after that night, I stopped moving. I lay on that couch for days. My kids ran around me and Emma came over to help take care of them, but other than that I stayed planted.

Never once did I go up to my room or look at my bed again without feeling intensely sick to my stomach. Never once did I pass by Ben's house that I didn't burn with new grief and heartache.

I didn't just stop trying.

I stopped living.

Stage Five: Acceptance

Grady is dead. Grady is not coming back.

These are truths I have come to terms with.

It has taken some time, more than a year, but I have finally reached the stage where I can accept this heartbreaking truth.

It took me a long time to get here and I learned a lot about myself along the way. There were times when I didn't believe I would ever reach this point. There were times I was convinced I would die first, times when I knew that this grief *would kill me*.

There were times when I wanted it to.

But, despite my heartache and difficulties, I miraculously made it to the other side.

That doesn't mean that everything is fantastic now. It doesn't mean that I feel great all of the time and that life is easy. It really doesn't mean that I have completely moved on and am okay with what happened to Grady.

I am not. And I still miss him fiercely. Daily. Hourly. Minute by goddamn minute.

I miss his touch, his smile, his laugh. I miss the smell of him wrapped up in our sheets. I miss the sight of him walking through the door after a long day at work. I miss his presence at the dinner table and the way he made each one of our children feel special and so loved.

I miss him. *I miss him so very much.*

But I have learned to live without him. I have learned to accept that he is gone. And I have come to terms with his absence.

Grief does not get easier. This is something I learned over this process. It does not get easier but it lessens in intensity.

As I move away from Grady's death, I think about him less, I miss him... less. But when I do think about him, the ache is still there, the heartbreak is always just as strong.

Maybe that doesn't make sense if you've never lost someone, but I'm not sure I will ever be able to think of Grady and our short time together without weeping. I am not sure I will ever watch our children grow without him there to experience it without hating his absence. I am not sure I will ever not miss him.

And that is the truth of losing someone you love. It always hurts. Always.

The same is true for Ben.

I lost him too. And the longer I try to live without him the deeper I realize my feelings for him go. I cannot take this pain. I cannot add his loss to Grady's and breathe through the day. It is too much.

Grady had to go. The world, his illness and fate decided that there was no other choice.

But I am the one that banished Ben and I am afraid I will have to deal with these consequences for the rest of my miserable life.

I miss Grady.

But I miss Ben too.

And Ben's absence is something I refuse to accept.

Chapter Twenty-Six

"Mom! I have a science project!" Abby called from the mudroom where she knelt digging through her backpack after school.

I had already set Blake up with his massive amount of homework at the island and Lucy had flashcards to work on. She hadn't stopped talking since we walked in the door, not-so-patiently waiting for me to finish with Blake.

When did fourth grade math get so hard? And why wasn't I smart enough for these story problems?

"What kind of science project, Abigail?" I had already decided that if her project took any more time than ten minutes, I was going to have to sell her on EBay.

Maybe I could use the money I made to pay a math tutor to help Blake finish elementary school.

Her bouncing red head popped into the kitchen and she held up an instruction sheet dated a week ago. I mentally went to the Craigslist browser. I could probably find an immediate buyer.

"I have to do a thing. On a vertebrate."

"What is a thing?"

"What is a vertabit?" Jace echoed.

"I diaphragm."

"Gram," I corrected quickly. "You have to make a diorama."

"Whatevs." She read over the sheet of paper. "And I have to write a report."

I took the instructions from her. "And color a picture. What is wrong with your school? This is too much work! You all have too much work! I've decided, starting tomorrow, we're going to homeschool."

Blake snickered, "Wouldn't you have to do all of the work then?"

"Since you're so smart, maybe you could teach it." He tapped his pencil on his psychotic math homework. I let out a squeak of frustration. "Okay, we're going to need to divide and conquer. Abby, your vertebrate is a monkey. Don't argue with me. Lucy, go get Mr. Puddles."

This instruction caused an uprising from the savages. "Abby, I don't care if you want to take Mr. Puddles or not! That's the only model I can think of to use. Lucy, you have to share with your sister! She will bring him back! Jace, get off the table!"

I wanted to curl up into the fetal position on the floor, but that wouldn't help solve any of these problems. I settled the kids down by working myself up and shouting at them- always an effective tool. They went off to their corners of the house to retrieve a shoebox, a skinny, bendy monkey figurine that Lucy had nicknamed Mr. Puddles after she dropped him in one, and I went to the computer to do a Google search on printable monkey pictures.

"Blake, I'll be right back! Just do what you can!"

"I figured it out!" he shouted back.

It seemed to take forever for the monkey pictures to print. My computer was slow and then my printer wouldn't connect wirelessly. By the time I had something for Abby to use, my kids could probably all curse with the best of them.

With the pictures printed and held victoriously in my hands, I walked out of the den and dropped them all over the entryway floor.

Ben stood in the doorway, looking slightly panicked and more than a little bit confused.

"What are you doing here?" I felt utterly breathless as I took him in. If possible he looked more gorgeous than ever. And up close his handsome face made my heart flutter and my stomach fizz. I had been watching him at a distance for two months now. I would watch him check the mail or mow his yard. I would look to see if his car was around on the weekends or if he had a date.

Of course, I never knew if he had a date or not. But I liked to speculate. Sometimes I would make Emma come over just so we could speculate together.

He had let his five o'clock shadow become a gruff beard that suited him. He had thick-framed glasses on that I had never seen before and his clothes were more rumpled than I could remember them ever being.

All in all, he looked like a mess.

Not that my limp ponytail and sweatpants were any better.

It was just shocking to see him so… disheveled.

"I got a text." He held up his phone so I could see the screen. "You said it was an emergency."

"I didn't text you."

His eyebrow quirked. "Liz, I was in a meeting. I raced over here. I was rude to a client."

"Ben, I'm so sorry. I… It wasn't me."

"It was me," the small voice came from the kitchen doorway. Blake looked ashen. "I didn't know you were busy. I'm sorry."

Ben looked from me to Blake and then back again. "Why did you text me, Blake? What did you need?"

"I need help with my homework and mom is busy. She's really busy and she keeps cussing. I just wanted to make it easy for her."

Ben's gaze swung back to mine, "You keep cussing?"

I felt betrayed by my oldest child. "PG-13 words! Nothing worse than that."

Ben and Blake both gave me disbelieving looks.

"Did I ruin your job?" Blake asked with a slight tremble in his voice.

Ben's expression broke and a grin finally made an appearance on his face. "No, no you didn't ruin it. I was only rude to my client because he was a jerk to me. I'll make it up to him tomorrow. He'll get over it. If you need help with your homework, I can help you. Then we'll both help make dinner so your mom stops cussing."

"I wasn't really cussing!"

"That's awesome! Thanks, Ben!"

Blake disappeared into the kitchen while I swooped down to gather the scattered pictures. "You don't have to stay, Ben. I have this handled."

"I'm sure that you do, Liz, but if you don't mind, I'd like to stay."

I steeled my nerves and met his hopeful gaze. "You would?"

"I've missed these kids," he admitted on a long sigh. "A lot. I've thought about coming over here at least a hundred times to see them, but I didn't want to make things worse."

"Oh."

"Ben!" Lucy squealed from the staircase. She jumped down four steps so she could run into his arms. "Ben! Ben! Ben!"

Abby followed and Jace raced over too. They attacked him with hugs, screaming his name and jumping up and down.

"Are you going to eat supper with us?" Abby asked excitedly.

"I'm going to make it for you," he told her which brought on a whole new level of screaming.

"Okay, settle down! Get off Ben or he isn't going to come back!" I tried to pry my kids off of him, but they wouldn't have it.

"You mean, he gets to come back?" Lucy wrapped her arms around me as a thank you hug for lifting Ben's exile.

Oh, gosh. What had I done?

"If he wants to," I told her.

She looked up at me with bright green eyes and said, "He does! I know he does!"

I patted her head and smiled down at her. I didn't think he did, but I couldn't tell her that. "Go help Abby find the crayons." Jace galloped after her.

When it was just Ben and me and miles and miles of distance between us, I said, "You didn't have to come over."

"I know," he said back.

"You don't have to stay."

"I know that too."

He tucked his hands into his pockets and stood there stoically. He didn't make a move toward the kitchen even though the kids were calling his name. He watched me instead, without saying anything, without seeming to want to say anything.

The quiet was too much for me. I couldn't look at him there without filling up this space that separated us in some way.

"How have you been?" I was thrown off by how much I wanted to touch him. I had broken it off with him in an attempt to end my heartache, but ending things with Ben had only worsened the pain. I had been a mess before Ben left, but now... now I was a disaster.

Maybe on the outside things had gotten marginally easier. We could make it to school on time this year. I didn't forget nearly as many after school activities. Dinner had fallen into a routine. My kids brushed their teeth twice as much as they did last year. But internally... internally I was a pile of ashes. I was broken, jagged pieces that cut and tore and damaged everything they touched.

One of his eyebrows rose in a challenge to my inane question. "How have *you* been, Liz?"

I cleared my throat and banished the tremble that threatened to give me away. "Oh, you know... holding it together."

He took four steps forward until he stood just a few inches away from me. His dark, stormy gaze hit me with the power of a hurricane. "Liar," he accused.

My lips parted, something was bound to come out of them. I just had to think of it first! He turned away from me and walked into the kitchen. I stared at his back and decided that was probably a good thing.

I didn't know what I would have said. I doubted it would have been kind. Or maybe it would have been the truth.

I missed him...

I needed him...

I didn't know how to reconcile my feelings for my husband and for him, but I wanted to try it again...

Those thoughts scared me more than anything. So, like the pro I was, I buried those thoughts as far down as I could and moved on to helping Abby with her science project.

While Ben helped Blake with his homework and talked to the kids about school and the rest of their summer, I made the best damn monkey diagram this world had ever seen.

Okay, it was probably a B+ effort. But we tried.

I worked with Lucy on her flashcards while Ben and Blake made dinner like they promised. We sat down to grilled cheese sandwiches and tomato soup as a family with the addition of our estranged next-door-neighbor.

"How are your parents, Ben?" I asked over the laughter of children.

He looked up from where he had just painted Abby's nose red with tomato soup. The wide grin he wore died as he looked at me from across the table. His shoulders stopped shaking with laughter and his entire demeanor grew serious.

He hated me.

And why shouldn't he?

"They're good, Liz."

Okay, that attempt at conversation was a bust. Apparently he didn't want to make this easy on me.

"How's work?"

He took a patient breath and said, "It's good, too."

I was too stubborn to give up. I should have stopped but I couldn't. "Lucy's art project is going to be featured in the school art fair next month."

His level gaze held mine, "I know. Emma told me."

Betrayal hot and sharp cut straight through me. "Emma?"

"Yes, Emma."

"When did you talk to my sister?"

He leaned forward, resting his elbows on the table. "Liz, Emma and I never stopped talking. We're still good friends."

"She never said anything." I couldn't believe my sister had kept this from me this whole time! I made her come over and eat boxes of chocolate with me just so I didn't have to face this alone and this whole time she had been talking to him?

"She was probably afraid of your reaction."

I glared at him, "I wouldn't have reacted."

"You can be very irrational. She probably didn't want to risk it."

He had a point. But I didn't want him to know that. "She's my sister. I will love her no matter what she chooses."

"That's funny," he said with the driest expression ever. "Because I feel the exact same way about *her* sister."

The breath left my lungs and I nearly knocked over my bowl of soup. "Ben-"

"Who wants dessert?" he asked loudly. "I saw popsicles in the freezer!"

I watched my kids jump around his legs as he pulled out the leftover boxes from summer, all but Blake who sat at the table pensively watching the excitement. Ben dealt with each kid patiently, making sure they walked back to the table with their icy dessert and had everything they needed. He held out the box to Blake and then pulled back just as Blake went to grab one. Maybe it was a little cheesy, but Ben got Blake to smile and that was all I cared about.

"Liz?" he held out the box to me. "Would you like one?"

"No, thanks."

"They look pretty good," he pushed. "Might help cool you off."

"I'm not hot."

He gave me a smoldering look. "Are you sure about that?"

I reached for an orange one.

My kids had asked about Ben every single day since our "breakup." That word... that whole idea... Breakup. It seemed so childish compared to what actually happened.

We didn't break up. I ended things between us and set my world on fire, burning what little remained to cinders. I removed Ben from our life and watched my heart abandon me completely.

He had never been my boyfriend. Boyfriend was a word used for girls who had never been through what I had. For girls that still believed in love. For girls that still believed in happily ever afters.

I knew better.

Ben had been my savior.

Ben had been breath back in my lungs. Beats back in my heart. Blood back in my veins.

Ben had been found instead of lost. Home instead of wandering. Life instead of death.

And yet there was still too much between us... too much that kept us apart. I couldn't just move on with him. I couldn't expect my kids to move on. Ben wasn't the answer to all of my problems. He might have eased the burden, but he didn't take them away.

Dinner ended and I shooed the kids upstairs for their baths. They couldn't go without giving Ben a hug first though. The sight of three of them clinging to his legs and waist twisted in my guts. Maybe the kids didn't need to move on before they could accept Ben.

Maybe he had been right. Our heart just accepted new love by expanding, not by being exclusive.

Blake didn't hug him or jump all over him, but he did walk over to ask when he was coming back.

"Do you need more help with math?" Ben didn't even glance at me to see if I approved. I would have told him not to worry about it at all, but he wouldn't look at me. He stared straight into Blake's eyes and let my oldest answer on his own.

"Mom's not very good at math," Blake confessed.

"I do just fine," I said to no one because no one was paying any attention to me.

"I'll come back tomorrow, yeah?"

Blake's mouth split into a big-toothed grin. "Yeah." He held out his fist to Ben and they did this silly fist-bump thing they'd worked out over the summer.

"Alright, ducklings, up the stairs you go! Go brush the Popsicle off your teeth!" After a few more minutes of wrangling, they finally listened.

I moved toward the door to let Ben out. We were alone again after several hours of screaming kids and other things to occupy our attention. I didn't know what to do with him except shove him out of my house.

"Thanks for helping Blake," I told him. "We would have figured it out, but it was nice to have the extra hands."

"Do you know what I keep thinking back to?" Ben asked seriously. I shook my head. I had no idea. I wasn't sure I wanted to know. "The time you tried to overpay for our dinner at Sullivan's. The waitress kept trying to give you the change back and you kept trying to hand her more money. It all makes sense now. You can't add."

A surprise laugh bubbled out of me. "I can add! I was confused that night! They write their receipts weird there! And Blake's homework is just insane. It's like they expect fourth graders to have nothing better to do with their time than work on math problems. I didn't learn that stuff when I was in school!"

"Don't you have a masters in education?"

"Well, look at you. Successful lawyer and math genius. Congratulations on being awesome."

"I miss you." His words killed our laughter. Murdered it. My breath hitched in my chest and any coherent thought I had left disappeared.

"Ben…"

"I'm not going to apologize for coming over tonight."

"I didn't ask you to."

"And I want to keep seeing your kids," he pressed on. "And you. I've thought about this for months, Liz. I've thought about coming over here night after night. I've thought about what you said and the space you needed. But I'm tired of it, Babe. I'm so tired of it."

"What are you saying?"

"I want to be a part of your life. However much you'll let me. We were friends before we were anything else and if that's all you'll give me then so be it."

My stomach fluttered, butterflies awakening from a dormant sleep. They stretched their wings in my belly and took flight, lifting their faces toward the sun for the first time in months. "You want to be friends?"

He laughed darkly, "No, Liz. I want to be so much more than friends. But if this is all I can have, then I'll take it."

"You should move on," I pleaded with him. "You are such a great guy. There are so many girls out there that would love to be with a man like you."

His jaw tensed and his eyes heated. "I don't want to be with other girls, Liz. I want to be with you." I opened my mouth to argue with him, but he held up his hand and stopped me. "Listen, I get that Grady was your first great love. I get that you had this incredible marriage with him and he was your soulmate. I understand that. And I would never want him to be anything else. Never. I have endless respect for him. For loving you the way that he did, for raising these amazing kids. I don't know if I can ever live up to the legacy that he left behind. I don't know if I want to. But Liz, he died. And you're still alive. And there is so much left of your life to live. I want to live it with you. I want to be a part of everything that remains for you, good and bad. I want to be there for your kids, for your stressful days, for your amazing days, for all of your nights and for every moment in between. We tried the time apart, but we are better together. Both of us. Yes, Grady was your great love, but you are mine. And if you would let me, I would be yours too. There isn't a limit on how much we can love, Liz. You had Grady. Now have me."

"Ben, I-"

"Forgive yourself, Liz. Give yourself the freedom to be alive again." He put his hand on the door and swung it open. I couldn't stop him tonight. I couldn't even make words to respond to that speech. He gave me a slow, hopeful smile and disappeared into the sleepy twilight.

I watched him walk across our lawns without looking back. He'd said everything he had to say. He made his point.

And like so many times before, he challenged everything I thought and believed and then asked me to believe it too.

Could I do what he asked?

Did I love him enough to give us a chance? A real chance without the walls I'd built around my heart or the ghosts of Grady's life haunting us?

Could I do as he asked and give up this buried existence that I'd entombed myself in and live again?

I would never forget Grady. He was my true love.

But maybe some people were allowed to have two. Maybe my love story didn't end with one man, but continued throughout the course of my life.

Maybe Grady had been able to love the woman that I was, but Ben would get to love the woman I had yet to become.

Chapter Twenty-Seven

I pulled the van to the side of the narrow road and slowed to a stop. I hadn't been here as often as I should have, but this place had a special familiarity I felt every time I came.

I turned the car off and sat in the still quiet of my car for a very long time.

I needed to face something today and I didn't necessarily want to.

Gravestones spotted the rolling hills on every side of me, making neat, evenly spaced rows. The grave markers came in every size and shape, but they all declared the same sad event- someone had died.

I had always thought gravestones were fascinating. Rarely were they designed by those that rested beneath them. They were in fact, made from the projected feelings of loved ones that remained alive. Or the nearest living relative. Or maybe by the state.

They said what we wanted them to. They represented a part of the deceased that we decided should be displayed.

Grady and I had talked a lot before he died. We had hours to plan his funeral while he wasted away in the hospital. We had long days to make decisions about the kids and their future. We talked about the past, the present and the future. We talked in hopeful tones and despairing ones. We whispered secrets and sweet nothings to each other. And we held on to each other as if our love had the power to keep him alive, to make him healthy again.

Not once did we discuss his gravestone or what would go on it.

After he died, it was the very first realization I had that I would not be able to do this without him.

The man had helped me plan his own funeral. He picked out the songs that would be sung and the people that he wanted to speak. He chose his pallbearers and the minister from his closest group of friends and relatives.

And yet, he had never mentioned what kind of gravestone he wanted displayed above his lifeless body.

When I sat down with the undertaker and he started asking questions about what kind of casket Grady would want to be buried in and what the stone should say, I completely lost it.

Emma and my dad were there to hold me as I collapsed on the floor and wept. The director handed my sister a box of tissues and excused himself from the room. It was obvious he had seen his fair share of grieving widows.

It took me six more hours before I could decide anything.

I cried the entire time.

I just couldn't bring myself to make such a lasting decision about Grady without him. The color of the stone... the shape... the words engraved into the smooth surface... No matter how much I loved that man, I did not feel equipped to write his final message to the world.

Even now, as I looked at the stone through my windshield, I didn't like it. It wasn't Grady. It was my pain and grief. The words weren't from Grady's mouth; they were from my broken heart.

This place didn't remind me of Grady and the life we lived together. This place reminded me of loss and misery. It reminded me of everything that had been taken from me.

When I wanted to see my husband, I looked at his children. I looked at the house he had built for me.

I looked in the mirror at the woman he had loved with everything that he was.

This morning, I had woken with the desperate need to talk to him. I had reached over in our bed and felt the searing slice of loss all over again. He wasn't there, but I couldn't shake the pressing urge to talk to him. I had questions I needed to ask him. I had thoughts I wanted to run by him. I needed him here.

I *needed* him.

Except I couldn't have him.

So, I had done the only thing I could think to do. I called up Emma and asked her for the millionth time to come watch my kids. For a split second I had contemplated bringing them with me. I dismissed the idea as soon as Jace knocked his full cup of water onto the floor.

I needed peace and quiet or this trip would be for nothing.

When I told Emma what I wanted to do, she canceled her plans and raced over. I told her she didn't need to do that, but she completely supported this mission of mine. She'd told me so at least thirteen times.

With a heavy sigh, I opened my door and stepped into the crisp morning. October had turned beautiful in the last week. The big trees rustled with bright yellow and orange leaves. The grass had turned brown beneath the layers of fallen leaves. The air smelled like football and harvest.

I pulled my jacket tighter around my waist and trudged toward Grady's plot.

There wasn't anyone else around on this Thursday morning. I had the place completely to myself. The only people around to keep me company were the ghosts of other lives.

I ran my fingers over the rough top of the gravestone for a few minutes, familiarizing myself with the feel of the rock and glittery surface. I walked to the front of the plot and began carefully removing the sticks and leaves that had cluttered up the space.

I walked the length of the plot and then back to the end. I stood several feet from the stone and tried to force myself to be comfortable here. I struggled to find Grady in this place, to feel him close to me again.

But he wasn't here.

He had departed from this earth more than a year ago and there was nothing I could do to bring him back.

He was gone forever.

I could accept that now.

I finally settled on sitting down. I tucked my long pea coat underneath me and leaned against the headstone. My legs stretched out in front of me and I picked up a rust-colored leaf to shred to pieces.

"I met someone," I began softly. I had a lot to say, but I was in no hurry to get it out. "Well, really, he met me. He lives next door. You know, in that house that took forever to sell? He moved in about six months after you left. His name is Ben." I stopped talking and listened for a response, some sign that Grady could hear me. The wind blew, the leaves skittered along the pavement, the sun shone brightly in the sky, but Grady did not answer me.

I went on, "I think I annoyed him at first. I was out of my mind for a long time, Grady. I couldn't keep it together. I was a walking catastrophe. One disaster after the next. Ben… Ben stepped in and cleaned up my messes. He made life easier for me. He became someone I could count on first. And then he became my friend. And from there… I'm still not sure when it happened or how it happened, but we seem to have fallen in love.

"I didn't mean for it to happen. In fact, I fought it for a long time. And I think he did too. It's not exactly easy to fall in love with a woman that has four kids. That's your fault by the way. All those kids… just the way you wanted it. Besides that, I can be difficult. You knew that better than anyone. So, I don't know what we were thinking. Or if we were thinking. I think it happened so subtly that neither of us knew to stop it.

"You were like fireworks. That's how I think of falling in love with you. One beautiful explosion after another. The first time you kissed me. The first time you made love to me. The first time you told me you loved me.

245

When you asked me to marry you. Our wedding day. As I watched you become a father and then a great father. Every step we took together felt monumental. I fell for you hard and just kept falling." I paused to wipe away heavy tears. "God, I miss you."

It took me several more minutes before I could continue, "Ben didn't happen like that. There were no fireworks or epic moments. It was just us, lost and wandering. It was like we were taking this journey, both of us, but separately. Until one day we started taking this journey together. Neither of us knew where we were going at first. Not until we met each other and started walking together. Then all of a sudden I knew I had a destination again, I had a compass. Our love happened as the miles passed and we felt a little less lost. It happened as the road became clearer and less lonely. He came in like a sigh, a soft breath of hope. He happened to me through tears and grief and missing you so much my body hurt. My heart hurt.

"But now I hurt for a different reason. I told him to leave and he listened. Grady, I love you. I don't think I will ever stop loving you. I can't. You're too much a part of who I am. But somehow I love him too. And I don't think I can live without him.

"I had to give you up. Against my will. But I don't have to give up Ben. Not if I don't want to. If you wouldn't have died, I don't think I would have ever gotten to know Ben. I think he would have stayed a neighbor, nothing but a passing acquaintance. I think he would have found someone else to love. And you and I would have lived out our happily ever after.

"But you did die. And Ben and I did get to know each other. Grady, you are the love of my life. That will never change. Except that because of Ben, my life doesn't have to end. Maybe he's the love of my second chance.

"You can't tell me how you feel, but I think I already know what you would say. And I'm going to tell you how I feel whether you can hear me or not. You're the one that made me promise to not let my light die out. Did you know this would happen? Did you expect me to meet another man? Or did you just know that your death would hit this hard? For a long time, I didn't think I could do this without you. Now I know I can do this because of you.

"I'm going to try it again with Ben. I'm going to see where this goes with him. I don't imagine that it will be easy. I'm still a pretty big mess. I still feel a little lost. I still miss you. I still love you. But Ben makes all that easier. He forces me to live life again and makes me smile. He fills in all of the cracks you made when you left me. I love you, Grady. I always will. Just please… please forgive me for not loving only you."

"Oh, Liz!"

I jerked, so surprised to see someone standing over me. I blinked through my tears and up at the sun to see Katherine sobbing. Her shoulders shook with the force of her tears.

I didn't know how I hadn't noticed her before, but I was more than a little embarrassed that she might have heard my speech to her son.

Before I could get up, she collapsed next to me and clasped me in a tight hug. Her crying continued, deep and soul-crushing. I held her back, refusing to let her go through this alone.

Finally, after a couple more minutes, she pulled back so she could look me in the eyes. Her gray bob whipped around her wet face and the front strands stuck to her cheeks. Her makeup had run and her soggy tissue was now useless.

"He forgives you, Liz," she cried to me. "Oh, Honey, he forgives you. He would never hold this over you or feel less for you because of Ben."

"How do you know?" My chin trembled and my tears started all over again.

"Because Grady knew what a prize you were. Oh, you should have heard him brag about you to me. He just thought the world of you. He knew he had something special, something that any man would be beyond lucky to have. And he knew that the beauty in you wouldn't die simply because he did." She reached out and clasped my hand in between hers. "Liz, Grady loved you enough to want you to continue living long after he was gone. And I think he would approve of Ben. I think he would be very happy for you."

"I thought you hated me." I wiped at my eyes, but it was no use.

"Why would you think that?" she gasped.

"You saw us at the spring play and... and... I was so ashamed. Trevor hated him. I thought you must too! And hate me because I had moved on so quickly after Grady died."

She shook her head forcefully. "No, no I never thought any of those things. Anyone that knows you can see what a struggle it's been for you to lose him, and not just because of the kids or the house, but because you are hurting. Honey, I *know* you loved my son. That didn't change because you met someone knew."

"But you haven't really talked to me in months! I thought... I thought we were making progress until Ben showed up and then..." I couldn't say anything more. I wanted her to fill in the blanks.

She let out a pained chuckle. "I stayed away for Ben, not because of Ben. He seemed like such a wonderful man and just like with Grady, I

247

could see how much he meant to you. I didn't want to scare him away from you. I didn't want him to be hesitant about a relationship because every time he came around, the mother of his girlfriend's dead husband was there. I thought I was doing you a favor."

I laughed through my tears as relief flooded me. I could never have anticipated that answer. Katherine was such a surprise. It was a shame I didn't find this out before Grady passed away.

"Ben isn't like that," I assured her. "He… he isn't afraid to be reminded of Grady. He isn't intimidated by my grief. He somehow manages to help me deal with the pain and add more to my life than I deserve."

"No, Sweetie…" She squeezed my hand, letting me know how serious she was. "You deserve all of the happiness you can find. That includes Ben. If you think you're ready for something with him, then I think you should go for it. Go as far and fast as you want to. Your happily ever after is far from over."

I blushed, realizing how much of my speech she had heard. "Thank you, Katherine."

"No, Liz, thank you. Thank you for keeping me in your lives and bringing such joy to mine. It makes me so very proud of my son to know that he could find such a treasure."

We sat there for another hour, talking about Grady and remembering little things he had said or did. We probably looked ridiculous sitting on the stiff grass, crying our eyes out. But we didn't notice anyone else. It was just Katherine, me and Grady's memory.

His ghost had drifted away and I was left with only the warm memories of a man I loved.

By the time we parted ways, I had a smile across my face and hope in my heart. I had also made a decision.

Ben was right. I didn't have to give Grady up to be with him. I just had to be with Ben and trust that my love for both of them only made my life better.

Chapter Twenty-Eight

I didn't have to wait long to see Ben again. He came over that evening after he got home from work just like he'd said he would.

I was a little more put together than the last night. I had a plan for dinner, there were no surprise homework projects and Emma had stayed long enough for me to get a shower. My hair was fixed, I had makeup on and my kids were mostly taken care of.

He knocked politely and Abby ran to let him in. I forced myself to wait in the kitchen for him. I wanted to talk to him, but I didn't want to do it in front of the kids.

We had things to say that they didn't need to hear.

Still, I had softened to him so much that I couldn't help but smile at him when he appeared in front of me.

He walked straight up to the counter where I stood chopping vegetables and greeted me first. I smiled at him, noticing that he had shaved and his clothes were more put together today.

He smiled back and said, "Hey."

"Hey. Want to stay for dinner again?"

He tilted his head to the side and tried to figure me out. Good luck, buddy.

"Am I invited?"

I looked back down at my chopped carrots, "I just invited you."

"Well, then I guess it depends on what we're having."

"Chicken pot pie."

"Sounds better than takeout."

"Depends. What kind of takeout?"

He frowned, "China Garden."

I made a face. "I don't know if it competes with China Garden. They have egg rolls."

He set his elbows on the counter and stole a slice of carrot. "That's true," he conceded. "But you have math homework and chocolate milk."

I leaned forward, closing some of the space between us. "Math homework does trump most other things."

"Mmm," he agreed. "I should come over here more often."

"You probably should."

"Ben, I need your help!" Blake shouted before Ben could fully absorb those words.

We both moved into survival mode as the dinner hour grew closer. The kids kept us busy and occupied throughout the meal. There wasn't any opportunity for us to speak to each other, but I could feel his eyes on me the entire time.

Ben could feel or see the change in me, but he didn't know what it meant yet.

He entertained the kids while I cleaned up the kitchen and by then it was time for them to head to bed. I pulled out the one purchase I'd made in town today by myself and set it on the kitchen counter.

He and the kids had started a mean game of hangman at the craft table, but when the wine appeared, Ben's focus immediately shifted.

"What's that?" he demanded. The flirting tone he'd been using all night disappeared. He didn't want to tease me anymore.

The wine signified too much.

"I thought maybe you wanted to stay for a bit? After I get the kids to bed?"

He pushed back from the small table and jumped to his feet. His long legs ate up the space between us in a few elongated strides. He picked up the bottle and read the label before setting it back on the counter.

"When did you get this?"

"Emma watched the kids for me today. I had something I needed to do."

"What was that?"

I looked up into his dark eyes and held his gaze with a confidence I had never felt around him before. "I went to talk to Grady. I had a few things to tell him."

"Like?"

I smiled, "Don't you want to wait until after I get the kids down? We could have privacy. It might be easier."

His hand reached out to grip my waist; his other steadied himself on the counter. "Don't make me wait, Liz. I don't want to wait."

My heart thumped frantically in my chest and my skin tingled where he touched me. "I told him that I fell in love with you. I asked him for his forgiveness, but then I realized I didn't need it. You were right, Ben. I can love two men. I can love Grady without holding back anything from you. And I can love you without betraying him. I don't want to be neighbors anymore. I don't even want to be friends. I just want to love you. For as long as you'll let me."

He lunged for me, crushing me to his chest and wrapping his arms around me. "I want that too," he breathed against my neck.

The kids erupted with grotesque sounds, not pleased with our public display of affection at all. He pulled back to give them some peace, but kept his hands on my back, holding onto me.

"You want to do this?" his eyebrows raised and his expression grew serious again. "You're willing to fight for this? It's not going to be easy."

"I know it's not," I told him. "But I love you, Ben. I can't stay away from you anymore. I don't want to. I wondered for a long time how I would fit you into my life, into our life. I know now that you *are* my life... as much as the kids and Grady. You brought me back to life. You gave us a future to look forward to again. I already lost one man that I loved. I cannot lose another."

His palm cupped my jaw and his thumb brushed over my cheek bone. "I love you, Elizabeth Carlson. As difficult and aggravating as you may be, I love you more than I have loved anything or anyone. I am with you in this. I am with you forever."

He leaned down and kissed me on the lips, slow and leisurely. The kids broke out with more disapproval and raucous laughter. I pulled away from him reluctantly to give them all the evil eye.

He pressed his forehead to my temple and whispered, "Let's get these kids to bed. We have more making up to do."

I made a needy sound I wasn't proud of and that was maybe highly inappropriate in front of my children.

"Mommy, do we get to keep Ben now that you love him again?"

I looked down at Lucy and felt my heart fill up to the top with love and affection for all of the people in this room. I hadn't been this filled with love in so very long. My grief and pain took a backseat to these beautiful feelings brimming at the top.

"Yes, Luce, we get to keep Ben. Ben might just keep us too." He squeezed my side to assure me that he would. I looked over at Blake, noticing that he had stayed silent. "Blake, how are you doing, Buddy? You up for this."

His cheeks heated with embarrassment, but he lifted his chin and gave us a brave look. "You're happy again, Mom. Ben can stay for as long as you want him to."

Ben chuckled, "That is a good answer from a good man. I might be able to learn a thing or two from you, kid."

Ben helped me take the kids upstairs and get them ready for bed. He stayed the night with me, in my bed. It took some mental adjusting, but... I didn't vomit.

And we didn't have sex.

He held me through the night and I adapted to a body beside me. A body that wasn't Grady's. I knew this would take time. I was okay with that. And Ben was okay with that.

It would be another year before he asked me to marry him. He would wait until the kids were asleep and then one warm fall night, he would lead me to my backyard where the Adirondack chairs still sat, and he would kneel before me and ask me to be his wife.

I would be ready by then. I would still cry and later that night I would cry again and say goodbye to Grady again, but I would also say yes to Ben.

By then he would know my parents and my in-laws and my sister so well that they would be his family too. And I would know his parents and my kids would know his parents and learn to call them Grandma and Grandpa.

Actually, they would call Sharon and Mark their grandparents long before they called Ben dad.

We would get married in my backyard in a small wedding with only our closest friends and family. I would move Grady's ring to a necklace that I never took off and Ben would place his diamond on my ring finger as my husband.

I would trade my married name for Ben's name and I would be proud to be Mrs. Tyler, even though my kids all kept Carlson.

We would put Ben's house for sale soon after that because he had always planned to move in with us.

Like he said, my house had always felt like a home to him. His house was just a house.

We decided to keep his bed though.

It was important that we didn't keep everything exactly the way it was in my house.

Ben would be the father that watched my kids grow up and the husband that would grow old with me. He would help me drop my children off at college and walk my daughters down the aisle when they got married. He would be the one that held my grandchildren and watched as my already big family expanded. He would be my second chance at love and happiness and a sequel to my happily ever after.

But most importantly, he would always be the man that gave me life after death.

The man that helped me through the five stages of grief.

I would always love Grady.

But I would always love Ben too.

Sometimes love didn't make sense. And that was okay. It was far better to know love and accept love than try to understand it.

I truly hope you enjoyed Liz and Ben's love story. Look for me on Facebook so we can recover together! The Five Stages of Falling in Love was my debut adult novel. While I have many young adult and new adult books already available, look for my next adult contemporary, Every Wrong Reason, September, 2015.

Acknowledgments

To God, always the first portion.

And then to Zach. Thank you for enduring my endless tears and for teasing me constantly. You are it for me. In every way. I love you more than life. More than anything. You have made this life beautiful for me and for our kids. Without you, I would be a fraction of the person I am. Thank you for always supporting me, for always loving me and for always putting up with me.

Mom, thanks for loving even this one. The five stages suck. I'm blessed to know such a strong, faithful woman. You're my hero.

To Carolyn, thank you for all of your hard work and sharp eye. Thank you for homophones and sentence fragments and for always being right.

To Caedus Design Co., thank you for the incredible cover! I am in awe of your talent. Cannot wait until you make me another one!

To Candice, thank you for reading this book as I wrote it. You put up with missing words and entire paragraphs that didn't make sense. But you fell in the love with the characters anyway. Thank you for your amazing friendship and for always wanting to read what I write.

To Sam, Shelly, Lila and Diana, thank you for reading about Liz and Ben before anyone else and for putting up with my panic and obnoxious questions. You girls are the best friends and I am so blessed to have you in my life. Thank you for encouraging me and pushing me to get over myself.

To my Hellcats, Samantha Young, Shelly Crane, Lila Felix, Amy Bartol, Georgia Cates, Angeline Kace and Quinn Loftis, thank you for your constant support and friendship. Thank you for being my safe place and the place I want to hang out at the most. Thank you for getting me. You are my tribe and I love you all to pieces.

To Rachel Marks of Mark My Words Book Publicity, thank you for your general awesomeness. You are incredible. My inbox and my To Do List love you dearly.

To my Rebel Panel. Girls. You have become a community of friends that I am so blessed to know. Thank you so much for your support, opinions and encouragement. I can count on you for so much and that means everything to me. Especially to Lenore, Caylie, Jocelyn, Amy and April for all of your extra work and insightful eyes. You made all the difference. Thank you so much.

To the Reckless Rebels, you girls are one kickass street team! Thank you so much for all of your hard work and endless hours of support. You make this fun and I love each and every one of you.

And lastly, to the readers. Thank you so much for reading and surviving this one. I know that it's so different from what I usually do, but I am so thankful you took a chance and tried something different from me! I am so grateful for each and every download. Thank you for taking the time to spend a few hours in Liz and Ben's world.

About the Author

Rachel Higginson was born and raised in Nebraska, but spent her college years traveling the world. She fell in love with Eastern Europe, Paris, Indian Food and the beautiful beaches of Sri Lanka, but came back home to marry her high school sweetheart. Now she spends her days raising their growing family. She is obsessed with bad reality TV and any and all Young Adult Fiction.

Look for more from Rachel in 2015.

Other books by Rachel to be released early 2015 are The Heart, the third and final installment of The Siren Series, Bet on Me, an NA contemporary romance and Every Wrong Reason, an adult contemporary romance.

Other Books Out Now by Rachel Higginson:

Love and Decay, Season One
Love and Decay, Volume One (Episodes One-Six, Season One)
Love and Decay, Volume Two (Episodes Seven-Twelve, Season One)
Love and Decay, Season Two
Love and Decay, Volume Three (Episodes One-Four, Season Two)
Love and Decay, Volume Four (Episodes Five-Eight, Season Two)
Love and Decay, Volume Five (Episodes Nine-Twelve, Season Two)
Love and Decay, Volume Six (Episodes One-Four, Season Three)

Reckless Magic (The Star-Crossed Series, Book 1)
Hopeless Magic (The Star-Crossed Series, Book 2)
Fearless Magic (The Star-Crossed Series, Book 3)
Endless Magic (The Star-Crossed Series, Book 4)
The Reluctant King (The Star-Crossed Series, Book 5)
The Relentless Warrior (The Star-Crossed Series, Book 6)
Breathless Magic (The Star-Crossed Series, Book 6.5)
The Redeemable Prince (The Star-Crossed Series, Book 7)

Heir of Skies (The Starbright Series, Book 1)
Heir of Darkness (The Starbright Series, Book 2)
Heir of Secrets (The Starbright Series, Book 3)

The Rush (The Siren Series, Book 1)
The Fall (The Siren Series, Book 2)
The Heart (The Siren Series, Book 3) coming February, 2015

Bet on Us (An NA Contemporary Romance)
Bet on Me (An NA Contemporary Romance) coming April, 2015

Every Wrong Reason coming September, 2015

Connect with Rachel on her blog at:
www.rachelhigginson.com

Or on Twitter:
@mywritesdntbite

Or on her Facebook page:
Rachel Higginson

Keep reading for an excerpt from Rachel's New Adult Contemporary, Bet on Us and
Impulsion by Jamie Magee.

Please enjoy an excerpt from Rachel's new adult romance, Bet on Us

Chapter One

I blamed this on Kelly Clarkson.

On Kelly-Freaking-Clarkson.

The angry man standing across the kitchen island looked like he was about to throttle me. I had visions of large hands gripped firmly around my neck shaking me like a rubber chicken. His eyes flashed with frustration and I cursed Kelly Clarkson straight to the grave.

Things started out so well this morning, so unbelievably, unnaturally well. I should have known better. But at the time, I woke up in my bed to the powerful chords Kelly Clarkson belted through my radio alarm, and laid there for the length of the song just to let her words sink in.

Stronger.

In fact, I started to think Kelly Clarkson was a genius. And like maybe we were soul sisters that survived something awful but came out on the other side of it *stronger*. I started to think maybe she got me.

Because the bed *did* feel warmer. And I *did* dream in color again. I never felt lonely when I was alone anymore and I really *was* standing taller. Kelly Clarkson had it all figured out.

Well "was" as in the seriously past tense because with monster-man looming over me, pissed off and yelling about money he wanted that I definitely did not have, I wasn't standing taller anymore. I was shrinking slowly into what I assumed would soon be the fetal position.

But this morning, even as the warm sun sifted through my bedroom window and heated my exposed skin, everything seemed possible. I felt strong enough to get out of bed today and conquer the world, or at least the closest Starbucks and my Econ class.

Which come on, that's close enough right?

And even though last week I missed a seriously important pop quiz in my post-break-up-cowering phase and now my grade was in some trouble... and then it started raining and I happened to be wearing a white t-shirt and red bra.

Who does that by the way? Me apparently, in my Kelly-Clarkson-gave-me-the-strength-to-be-a-skank-mood.

And then even after I came home to my roommate on her way out, for what she promised was just a bite to eat even though she was two months behind on her share of the rent, I believed today was the start of better things to come.

All thanks to Kelly Clarkson.

After setting my purse down on the kitchen counter because the entry hall table that I usually placed it on had been moved, I started to wonder if maybe Kelly Clarkson lied to me.

Well, okay, that's not exactly true. First I wondered if I was hallucinating. Then I ran through the possibility of being robbed. But my roommate's casual departure quickly negated that idea.

I blinked. And blinked again. And then blinked so hard tears formed in the corners of my eyes and I felt like I was trying to be the second coming of *I Dream of Jeannie*. If I willed all of my furniture and belongings to reappear, they would.

But they didn't.

And that was just the start of my disappointment.

Then there was the letter... The one that calmly explained my roommate had a clinically diagnosed gambling addiction and that she was thousands of dollars in debt. She explained that she had to sell the furniture, *my furniture*, to pay for rehab. Her family insisted on it. She had a real problem. A *real problem*. And I needed to understand that anything she had done to hurt me was her addiction and not the real her.

Well her addiction wasn't going to replace all of my furniture.

Her addiction wasn't going to come up with the other half of my rent!

And her addiction really wasn't going to explain to the man across the kitchen yelling at me that no matter who he thought I was, I did not owe him seven thousand dollars!!

I picked up the handwritten letter-of-crazy with a shaky hand and held it out to him.

"What's this?" He paused in his tirade to take the half sheet of torn notebook paper. I noticed my Biology notes on the back of it for the first time. Seriously, she couldn't even use her own paper???

"Um, see? I'm not the one that owes you money." I sounded confident, but inside I was a trembling, terrified puddle. And on second thought, maybe I didn't sound quite so confident...

"Who's Tara?" he grunted after skimming the note quickly.

"My roommate," I said simply and then thought better of it. "My *ex-* roommate. She's moved on to group therapy and the twelve steps, apparently."

"And who are you?" he asked carefully. His eyes swept over me in a way that made me feel like he had x-ray vision. Suddenly I felt very vulnerable and very naked.

Okay, more vulnerable.

And not really naked.

But feeling *more* vulnerable was a hard emotion to feel since he elbowed his way in here not even ten minutes ago and started shouting at me and threatening all kinds of legal action and at times bodily harm.

"I'm, uh, wait a second! Who are *you*? You're in *my* apartment!" I dug deep for some courage. I slammed my fists on my hips and tilted my chin in my best I-mean-business pose.

"Don't get cute with me." He sneered. I wanted to explain that I wasn't being cute. I was being tenacious. But I decided to stay silent when his full upper lip curled in frustration and his dark, chocolate brown eyes narrowed. "I'm the guy you owe seven *thousand* dollars!"

Ugh, he was still stuck on this! I cleared my throat and tried again, "How could I possibly owe you seven thousand dollars? I've never even met you before! I don't even know your *name*."

"You're really going to stick with this whole doe-eyed-innocent act?" he scoffed unkindly. He walked forward and placed two meaty hands on the kitchen counter slowly, like he was weighing his strength against a fragile surface. His broad shoulders tensed and stiffened and his entire body went rigid with frustration. I almost felt bad for him.

Almost.

But then I remembered I was not that person anymore. No more pity for people that didn't deserve it. No more sacrificing my time and money and energy for people that would just screw me over when they got what they wanted. This was the new me. The stronger me. The me that was soul sisters with Kelly Clarkson. The I-get-what-I-want-me! And right now, I seriously wanted this guy out of my life, or at the very least, out of my apartment.

"I'm not innocent," I spat back with my arms crossed firmly against my chest and my hip jutting out. I realized that maybe that wasn't my best defense but I pushed forward. "And I'm not doe-eyed!"

His face suddenly opened up in some shock and his lips twitched like he had to hold back a laugh. "I can't believe this." He rubbed two hands over his face in a sign of exhaustion and turned his back on me.

With his body more relaxed I saw him in a new light. He was less macho-Neanderthal in this posture and more holy-sexy-back-muscles-batman. Obviously the disaster that was my last boyfriend did a number on me if I was checking out the confused hit man pacing back and forth in my kitchen.

I mean, honestly, fantasizing about what his back could potentially look like under his thin t-shirt was seriously clinical, right? Maybe Tara wasn't the only one that needed medical observation and group therapy.

"I think there has been some miscommunication," I ventured, now that he appeared somewhat relaxed. "You think I am someone that owes you money, but I am not. Do I look like a drug addict to you?"

He swung his head back around to face me. "You think I'm a drug dealer?"

"Seven thousand dollars is a *lot* of money," I sniffed.

"Yes, it is. And you think the only way to go that much in debt is by drugs?" His eyes widened in disbelief.

Now that he was even calmer, I noticed his face wasn't necessarily menacing, but more chiseled and dignified. Actually when his dark eyes weren't bugging out of his head in rage, he looked more like a Calvin Klein model than Tony Soprano. And his hands weren't so much meaty as they were just large and connected to *very* defined arms. And okay, originally I was under the impression that his neck was the size of a redwood, but now that I was really paying attention it was more just a very strong, carved out piece of art, attached to an equally and artfully sculpted body.

To top it off, he had great hair. I just needed to admit that. He had amazing hair. Hair that I was instantly jealous of! Dark, rich coffee-colored hair that matched his eyes. Short on the sides, and just a little longer on top. It was stylish and trendy, not at all ex-military-renegade-private-security like I originally thought.

Wait a minute, I didn't think I liked that he was attractive... more than attractive, hotter-than-hot attractive. When I finally took in the scruffy growth across his jaw that partially hid too-full lips, I wanted to roll my eyes. Who *was* this guy?

"Well, it's one of the ways," I huffed impatiently.

He cocked his head back, seemingly surprised with my answer. "I actually have no argument for that. You're right, drugs are one way to go into that much debt." I smirked at him, momentarily satisfied until I realized he was really a drug lord and he thought I was his client! A client that owed him money! "But that's not why you owe me money. I'm not a drug dealer."

Oh, whew. Sure, I knew that.

"Okay, are you a bill collector then? Because I don't even have a credit card. Well, I have one credit card, but it's for emergencies only and I've *never* used it. Besides, it only has like a fifteen hundred dollar limit on it. And it's actually in my brother's name."

I grew more impatient the longer he stared at me. It was like all of the anger that propelled him into my apartment to begin with had evaporated somewhere between drug dealer and bill collector.

Now his chocolate eyes lit with amusement and his mouth did that annoying twitching thing again. "And my roommate gets calls from debt collectors all the time. *Phone calls*- have you heard of those? You seriously did not need to come all the way over here. I could have explained this to you over the *phone*."

"I'm not a bill collector either."

This time I could tell he was laughing at me. The corners of his eyes crinkled with humor and he held his hands up, palms out as if to stop me from guessing anymore. But I wasn't finished. If he wasn't a hit man, drug dealer or bill collector but wanted seven thousand dollars from me, that left only one option.

I gasped, "Oh, my gosh, is this about prostitution? Oh, my goodness, are you a *pimp*?" I shrieked and backed up three steps.

"What?" he burst out in a bark of confusion. "Are *you* into prostitution?"

"What? Me? Do I look like a prostitute?" I was back to being angry; I narrowed my eyes, cocked my hands on my hips, and scowled in a tight expression.

"Well, no, honestly. You look more like a missionary." He shrugged a casual shoulder and let his eyes travel over me.

"A missionary!" I spit the word out like it burned me. I clutched at my gray infinity scarf that covered my black and white cowl-neck long sleeve tee. Okay, maybe it was a little conservative, but he seriously did not need to confuse modesty with missionary.

"Would you rather look like a prostitute?" He asked, his stupid dark brown eyes laughing at me.

"Why in the world would you think that?" I demanded. This conversation had the disorienting feel that we were going backward instead of forward; I started to feel dizzy from all the circles and the way his mouth quirked up when he tried not to laugh.

Wait, scratch that. I was only dizzy from the conversation!

"Listen, honestly, I don't care what you are, I just want my money." Some of his amusement faded and a wave of exhaustion flashed across his face.

"So this isn't about prostitution?" I asked just to clarify. It was kind of important that this wasn't about prostitution.

"If you're not a prostitute and I'm not a pimp how in the *hell* could this be about prostitution?" he rumbled.

"Well, I don't know. I just need to be… sure," I finished lamely.

He ran a hand over his face again and growled out a frustrated sound. Then he pulled his cell phone out of his pocket and checked the screen. "This is taking up too much time. I just want my money and I'll be gone. I won't bother you any more, I promise. Although I strongly suggest that you stay away from anymore poker games. You are obviously not lucky enough to be as careless as you are with your money."

That got my attention. "Wait." I held up a hand like I was asking him to stop his vehicle. But then I didn't know how to go on. Gambling? This sounded way too convenient… way too coincidental.

A man comes to my door, demanding a seven thousand dollar poker debt minutes after my crook of a roommate robbed me blind and headed off to rehab for a *gambling addiction*? "Okay, I don't know what you're talking about, but why don't you tell me who you think I am. That might make things easier."

A smug smirk turned his mouth and he said with confidence, "Eleanor Harris."

That caught me off guard. Because he was right. "Um, Ellie," I corrected before he stuck to calling me Eleanor. Ugh! Even if he were here to murder me I would make him call me Ellie.

"Fine, Ellie Harris."

"Okay, you know my name, but you don't know anything else about me. Like for instance, I don't owe you any money!" I argued, still wondering how he knew my name.

"Alright, let's see. You're a sophomore, originally from farther up north. You transferred to La Crosse spring semester last year. You were originally at University of Wisconsin-Madison but you wanted to be close to your boyfriend who turned out to be a cheating douche bag. He broke up with you two weeks ago for another girl, and since then you've gone from being a straight A student with a nearly perfect attendance record to skipping all of your of classes, doing your best to fail out of school and now you've apparently acquired a gambling addiction with a side of pathological lying."

"What!" I would have made a terrible reporter. "I am *not* a liar! And I have never gambled a day in my life! And I'm *not* trying to fail out of school. A girl is allowed to take a few sick days after her three-year relationship ends! How can you possibly know so much and so little about me at the same time?" This was possibly the most exasperating conversation I had ever had.

"I make it a point to know all my players, Ellie. Especially ones that come into the game waving money around like you did," he explained patiently with that same cocky smile on his face.

I had the strongest urge to smack him. And I had never, not in my entire life, ever felt like hitting anything before!

"Clearly you have me confused with somebody else because I have no clue what you are talking about!"

"That is not going to work on me!" the anger simmered under the surface again. His eyes turned almost black with emotion.

"Okay, okay, okay," I backtracked quickly. "I can see that. So, just for fun, how about you explain to me exactly how I came to owe you all this money and then we can figure this out together. I want you to get your money just as badly as you do. I promise, alright?"

He seemed to think that over for a minute. His face relaxed back to movie-star-stranger instead of serial-killer-hit-man. It didn't take a genius to figure out which version I liked best.

"Alright, fine. We can do this your way. Especially if you promise you'll help me get my money," he said evenly and then waited for me to answer.

"Yes, I promise. I mean, I know *I* don't owe you the money. But if there is any way I can *assist* you with it, I'd be glad to help." What I didn't say was that as long as I didn't have to shoot, stab or bury somebody I would be glad to help. Really, I meant like a stern, authoritative letter I could put a stamp on and mail for him. Plus, these were mostly just empty promises until I could get him out of my apartment, lock the two deadbolts, slide the chain into place and call the police.

"About a week and a half ago, you contacted me about joining the game. I had heard your name around campus and knew that your request was entirely out of character. So I started to ask around about you and that's when I found out you just got dumped. It made sense then, why you would want to play. Even if I didn't think it was a good idea. I've been dumped before, I guess I could relate in a way."

"*You've* been dumped?" I scoffed before I could stop myself. He was gorgeous, all testosterone and muscles, standing in the middle of my kitchen with his gray t-shirt, loose jeans and flip flops. Plus, he was more than just a little intimidating. I could hardly believe a girl found enough courage to break up with *him*.

He seemed to find this more amusing than anything and actually broke into an eye-twinkling grin. Yes, his eyes twinkled. I was so shocked by the expression I had to look away. He was more dangerously good-looking than ever and a strange heat lit a fire in my belly. So obviously, I cleared my throat and pretended that never happened.

"Sure, I've been dumped." His smile turned wicked and I suddenly felt like he was laughing at an inside joke. "So I know what it's like to do something reckless after the heartache."

I snorted. "There wasn't that much heartache. Trust me. You were right when you called him a cheating... uh, you know."

"Douche bag?" he questioned.

"Yes, that." I blushed a deep red. I wasn't a missionary. But okay, sometimes curse words made me uncomfortable. Which was kind of surprising since I grew up with three brothers that basically existed with "R" ratings attached to them: strong language, violent behavior and sexual content.

He let out a soft chuckle at that. I was becoming unending entertainment for this guy and I was suddenly hit with a flash of irritation. He didn't know me!

Although... he kind of *did* know me. Or at least a lot of random facts about me and it was definitely weirding me out.

"Anyway, when you proved you had the buy-in, I decided to give you a chance. I mean, who was I to judge your methods of coping, am I right?" he asked and actually waited for my agreement.

"I guess so." But an ugly foreboding feeling started to unfurl inside my chest and I suddenly found it hard to breathe.

"In fact, if you remember, I even advised you to hold back some since I didn't want to see you lose everything at once."

"And you advised me how?" I clarified, trying to piece this together. Except I wasn't even sure what he was talking about. Buy-in? Game? None of this made any sense.

"Private message." When I gave him a blank look, he continued, "Online."

"Online," I repeated.

"Yes, online. But you didn't listen to me. And then you got in way over your head, lost big time, and now you owe me seven thousand dollars," he finished arrogantly; I almost expected him to take a bow.

"I lost in a game of..." I prompted slowly, so afraid of the answer my hands started to tremble.

"Five-Card-Stud." When I continued to stare blankly at him, he finally added, "Poker. Online poker."

"Oh, my goodness," I winced. Suddenly the puzzle was pieced together and in front of me. I was going to be sick. I was going to be *really* sick. I reeled in a circle, desperately searching for a place to sit down, but all of my furniture was gone.

Another wave of clarity rippled through me and my stomach actually lurched this time. I took off for the kitchen sink and gripped the stainless steel basin. I ignored the anal retentive voice inside me screaming about germs, not because I wasn't worried about them, but because thinking about them made it worse. I choked on a gag and dropped my head forward so I could breathe in and out deeply through my nose.

"You're not going to…? Are you going to be sick?" the guy asked from behind me. He didn't sound concerned, just really grossed out.

I waved an aggravated hand behind me, hoping he would get the hint and just *leave*. He didn't, or if he did, he ignored it and instead walked over to the fridge and opened it. I heard him rummage through the practically empty appliance.

My college-size budget didn't cover much more than a value pack of Ramen Noodles. I heard the telltale sign of a pop can opening, then the fizzy bubbles of ginger ale tickling my nose.

He placed the can to my lips and tilted it back before I could protest. I took a small drink and stood up before he could force anymore down my throat. The carbonated beverage settled in my stomach and coated the nausea with something soothing.

Okay, that felt all right.

I took the can from his hand, my fingers accidentally brushing over his before I took possession and sipped another soothing drink.

"That wasn't me," I finally choked out, squeezing my eyes shut.

"What?" he asked. I jumped by how close he stood.

I took a step back, opened my eyes to meet his and said more slowly, "That wasn't me. I didn't place a bet, or play a game or whatever. It was my roommate. She must have… stolen my identity! I swear to you, not even an hour ago, I found this note that said she had a gambling addiction and she was going to rehab. She owes me money too! "

A long, very still moment of silence stretched between us before he said, "She stole your identity?"

"Yes!" I squeaked. Even I could tell how high-pitched and annoying that was, but I couldn't help it! "*And* my furniture," I said with further emphasis.

"I *was* actually wondering about that," he said pensively.

"So you see? It's not me that owes you seven thousand dollars, it's *her*."

"But she's gone? To rehab? With all of your furniture?" His phrases sounded like questions, but they didn't *feel* like questions. It felt more like he was trying the words out, rolling them around on his tongue and deciding whether or not I was lying.

"Yes!" I answered anyway, hoping he would believe me.

"You can see why your version of what happened is hard to believe." He sighed and if I didn't know better, or if maybe I wouldn't have slapped my hands over my eyes, I would have been able to assure myself there wasn't a hint of amusement in his voice, or the sound of him smiling. Those things were all products of my delusional imagination.

"Yes, I could see why, but it's the truth," I promised, struggling to peek from behind my fingers.

"Regardless of what happened, your name is still signed on my contract. *You* still owe me my money," he stated finally.

"Contract?" I croaked.

"Online document, your initials were used. Unless you have a way to prove to me that it wasn't *you* who signed the document, I have to assume it was. I mean, that's a lot of money. It's not exactly like I can just look the other way."

"But it wasn't me! I'm sure I can prove it, I just need... time," I pleaded. My head spun with every kind of crazy thought to get out of this.

His hand went up to cup his chin in thoughtful silence for a while. His eyes roved over me again, taking in every piece of me as if to weigh it on his internal truth scales and decide whether to trust me or not. Finally, after several minutes of quiet, he said, "I'm a nice guy-"

"You're not a nice guy! You're a *scary* guy," I confessed honestly and probably a little frantically before I could think better of it.

A rush of laughter fell out of his mouth before he could compose himself, "You don't even know me!"

"You're right! I don't even know your name," I pointed out, suddenly realizing that should have probably been the first thing I found out.

"Ah," he stewed on that for a moment and said, "Finley Hunter."

I gulped. "*Finley Hunter*?" Okay, the online gambling thing made sense now. Because Finley Hunter, a senior track star, rumored to go through girls like Kleenex during flu season and ditch more classes than he attended, was also rumored to run an online on-campus gambling site the university had no idea about.

"Fin," he smiled at me. "You can call me Fin."

"You are a nice guy," I drawled.

His grin widened to wicked trouble. "So nice, I'm not going to make you give me my money tonight."

"You're not?"

"No, I have a solution that will help both of us get what we want," he announced confidently.

"You do?" I asked dryly with so much less confidence at the same time, I wondered what it was that he thought I wanted.

"Just don't forget, you promised you would help." The hard, authoritative look returned to his eyes and a shiver of nerves climbed up my spine.

I nodded because there was nothing left to do. I needed time to think this over, to hunt down Tara and strangle her until dollar bills popped out her eyeballs.

Please enjoy an excerpt from Jamie Magee's Impulsion

Chapter One

Harley Tatum was leading her prized eight-year-old dark bay gelding, Clandestine, into the main barn. Her thighs were burning and her shoulders and arms were tight, almost numb. Her trainer, Camille Doran, was hard-core, a woman that knew this sport inside and out. She could read the horses, the riders. There was little to no softness in that woman. She expected the best and trained the best, which was the only reason Harley's parents allowed her to be at Willowhaven Equestrian Center.

This was Harley's third year working with Camille Doran. Harley was barely fifteen when she began to train with her, and now at seventeen there was no doubt that Camille had brought forth the athlete and talent in both Harley and her ride. Yet, Harley still had a long road before her, for in this sport there is no end, only new challenges around each bend in the road.

The center was not only owned by Camille Doran and her family, but was also located just outside of the town of Willowhaven, a town that was near a thousand miles from Harley's home in New York.

Not that Harley would call the home she had in New York a home; she was rarely there, if at all. Her mother had placed her in an all girls' school from day one, and when she wasn't boarding at the school, Harley was chasing her passion in the equestrian world. An expensive hobby that her father, who was twenty years older than her mother, found no fault in supporting.

Her father, Garrison Tatum, may have been one of the nation's leading corporate finance bankers, but his blood was in the south. He grew up in Texas, and oil was in his blood—at least that was what he'd told his only daughter Harley more than once. He understood what it felt like to be outside, how it felt to be sore, hot, filthy—how satisfying and peaceful that could be. Harley's mother, Claire, was against this adventure from day one, and she argued her point as thoroughly as she could, but when it came down to it Garrison had the final say, and he had the final say because not many dared to counter him—not even his wife.

Harley was entranced with Willowhaven Farms for more than the obvious reasons. The family aspect was what took her breath away. Every night, dinner was served in the main house. Camille's two sons and one daughter, along with her husband, his brothers, and parents, were there. Harley had never seen her parents touch, laugh. She rarely saw them in the same room, and if she did, it was a social occasion, which included the holidays; for every event Claire Tatum made a social occasion.

Harley figured out long before she came to Willowhaven Farms that there was no love between her parents. Her mother had married up; even though she came from old money, she managed to find a man with older money, more money. And her father…honestly, Harley was not sure why he married, though she assumed it was because he wanted an heir. Harley was the only blood family he had left, at least that he claimed. At times, Harley thought she was the only one her father trusted and she did her best never to compromise that trust, the one, singular ally she had in this cold world she found herself being raised in.

Of course, all that did was cause more conflict when she was at home. Her mother was vindictive, saw everything and everyone as a threat, even Harley. There was little to nothing that would ever cause Garrison Tatum to turn his back on his daughter, shut her out of his life, his inheritance. Her mother? For all Harley knew, a shift in the wind would cause Garrison to leave his wife and not think twice about it.

Harley's heart quickened as she stepped into the grooming bay. Wyatt Doran, the eldest of Camille's sons, was there waiting on her with a secret smile. They had spent the last three summers together. There were only seven months between them, with Wyatt being the older of the two. He was tall, strong, and to say he was easy on the eyes would be a gross understatement; he was a walking heartbreaker. The sun of the summer always kissed his light brown hair, highlighting it perfectly, and his blue eyes, well, they simply gleamed. His skin was golden, pure.

Wyatt stole Harley's breath from the first moment she saw him. To this day, she had yet to understand the pull he had on her. No doubt his image alone was addictive, but there was more to it than that. He wasn't cold, a mold of his father focused solely on himself like most of the boys she knew, the ones her mother always placed her with during her famous charity events. No, Wyatt had a good soul, something that could be palpably felt in his presence.

Wyatt had a way of being strong and vulnerable at the same time, though she doubted many had seen that vulnerable side. The first time she saw him nervous was three summers ago down by the back creek, on the fourth of July, just before he leaned in and kissed her, a real kiss. A first for the pair of them. She was sure she was in love with him before that night ended. As that first summer moved on, as the nerves left those stolen kisses that they would fall into when there was no chance they could be caught—there was no questioning that notion. When the summer ended and she had to leave and it felt like her soul was ripped from her body, she knew without a doubt that she'd never get over him. Whatever souls were made of, hers and his were one in the same.

The summer that followed was hotter—in more ways than one. They dared to sneak away more, to explore more. To share more. They always held back, found a way to stop, to hold on to their virtue, their innocence a little longer.

Harley had told herself that this summer was going to change her life, that this summer she was going to give him something she could never take back, that no matter what, no matter where life took them, they would forevermore live in each other's memory. They were living in an immortal summer.

The first few weeks of this summer started like the rest, with her deep in her shell, uptight. It was hard for her to move from one lifestyle to the other, for her to let her shoulders down and breathe in, relax. Most times, she made it to Willowhaven Farms in mid-May and didn't leave until the end of August. Over Christmas break, she would fly in for a week just to ride, and if she was lucky she would find a way to spend at least part of her spring and fall breaks there as well. The time in-between was hard. Doran Farms possessed the two things she was sure she could not live without: her gelding, Clandestine, and Wyatt, the love affair that she had no choice but to keep clandestine.

Wyatt's mother would kill them both if she ever figured out there was something between them. Not because she didn't adore Harley, but because she was a woman of her word. She had sworn to the Tatum's that she could safely board Harley as she trained. Claire, Harley's mother, pointed out more than once that Camille had two sons near the same age as Harley. Camille took offense to that and clearly voiced that her sons were southern gentlemen, not brood stallions.

Nevertheless, Camille built a two-bedroom apartment over the main barn. Everyone assumed it was for Harley simply because it was no ordinary barn apartment, but built to perfection, built with southern luxury, but in the end the boys took over the apartment and Harley stayed in the main house when she was there. Wyatt and his brother, Truman, didn't mind, in fact, they loved it. It was their independence, their freedom. Their mother had warned them more than once that it came with responsibility, and daily she walked the apartment, twice, not only to make sure it was clean, but also safely kept.

This side of the farm, this side of the business, was not where Wyatt's interest lay. More times than not, he was on the other side of the farm, the one his father managed. That side had the bulls, the broncs, was the wild side as his mother called it, but Wyatt managed to find a reason to be in his mother's world, in the mix of her endless riding lessons more often than not when Harley was around. That should have made them obvious, but it didn't.

Clandestine was green when he first came to Willowhaven Farms, scarcely broken to ride much less jump, which was where Wyatt and Truman came in. They had grown up breaking horses, training them. Wyatt's long, strong legs and build were assets in that heart-racing addiction, not to mention that the ability to bond with horses was instilled in him from birth. He had a raw respect for the ride, knew the limits, when to push, when not to, a notion he used in more than one area of his life, meaning when it came to Harley.

Girls were just girls before Harley. Wyatt may have had a wayward crush here or there at school, gone to a few middle school dances or hangouts with a girl now and again, but most times he was too into when his next ride would be, into the boy toys the farm was stocked with. Four wheeling, the tractors, fishing, the trucks, all of it; Wyatt's world was his family's farm.

Then out of nowhere, Heaven descended on his family's farm when he was just shy of sixteen and life hadn't been the same for him since. Every thought, she haunted, more so when she was not at the farm, when she was away at school or home, when they couldn't even dare to call one another. That was hell on Earth, Wyatt was sure of it.

Wyatt could still remember how uptight his mother was about the 'Tatum girl' coming to the farm. Camille had met Harley's mother and found it offensive the way she looked at their farm as if it were some backwoods redneck playground. The woman seemed disgusted with nature in general. Even the plantation home that had been in Wyatt's family for near a hundred years failed to impress that woman. Insulting, considering it had hosted several presidents in its lifetime.

The only reason Wyatt's mother even dared to put up with the notion of the proposition of training Harley was that she knew Clandestine's bloodline. She had heard of Harley, too, seen clips of her riding.

Camille had pulled out all the stops weeks before Harley arrived. Twice the number of farm hands were hired, and she brought on board a full-time housekeeper and cook.

Wyatt hated Harley before he met her. He was sure they all did, simply because instead of riding his four wheeler or even breaking horses, along with everyone else he was making sure that water buckets were scrubbed, if not replaced, cobwebs were swept away, the rings were dragged, the tack was cleaned, and anything and everything that could be was cleaned or restored.

But when she stepped out of the rig that had brought Clandestine, when the wind brushed her long, strawberry blonde hair over her shoulder, when the sun hit her eyes, which were a mix of green and blue, when he saw her shy smile—he felt the wind sucked completely out of him.

He was expecting some holier than thou girl, uptight, rude. What he found instead was that she was timid, somewhat at least.

Harley was the one that let down the ramp to get her horse off the rig, a horse he was sure was too big for her. She was barely five-three, a hundred pounds soaking wet, and Clandestine was well over seventeen hands, a warmblood, nothing but power. It would be up to Wyatt to harness that power and his mother to finesse that grace, to bring that out in the horse and the rider.

At first, they assumed Harley was just with the transport driver, his daughter or something. Truman even made the wry comment, "Well, look-a-there, boys, money *can* buy happiness." He glanced at Harley. "Did you meet the owner, or was the butler there when you picked him up? If his rider is anything like the mother, ya'll might want to hang close. Apparently, they don't like dirt."

Harley looked him dead in the eye. "I have more of my father in me than my mother. And yes, Donald, the butler, was there when we loaded. He likes to give Clandestine carrots and wanted to make sure he had plenty for the long ride."

Truman's eyes went wide, and his mouth gaped in mortification. Wyatt burst out laughing at that point. Camille had rounded the trailer just in time to hear her youngest son humiliate her, and she let her hard glare say as much.

"You rode all the way down with him?" Wyatt asked once he had backed out Clandestine.

"Why would I not?" she said as she ran her hand across Clandestine's neck. Under her breath, she said, "Everything that I own is on this trailer."

And that was true. She may have had a top-notch education, any clothes and what have you to her name, but all of that was handpicked by her mother, a suffocating mold she was forced to fit into. This gelding. She found him. She was the one that carefully laid out all the reasons she wanted him to her father.

At the time, there wasn't even a stable at her New York home, but there were ones at the school, and that was a point she used with him. She told him that because her grades were flawless and she already rode at the school that without a doubt the school would board him. Harley ensured she had the history of Clandestine's bloodline, the name of the finest trainer in New York, every detail in place, literally months of planning before she approached her father.

She had to wait for a moment alone with him. She wanted to look him in the eye when she asked, wanted him to see that this was not some whim, but a well thought out request. Even though Garrison spoke to Harley every day while she was away, when Harley was home her mother rarely left her alone with her father and was obvious about that point. Harley could not figure out how any mother could be jealous of her own daughter, but she was almost positive her mother was.

One day at a charity event, her mother rose to give her speech to the crowd. That was when Harley spoke to her father. She even handed him the file that she had strategically hidden under her place setting. As she made her plea, she caught the glare of her mother from the podium.

Garrison Tatum was well aware of the tension in his family. Though he knew what kind of woman his wife was, Garrison was the type to use every adversity as an advantage, which was why he was so revered, why his wealth had more than tripled in his lifetime.

"Why is your voice shaking, Harley?" he asked her, leaning before her, blocking Harley's view of her mother. Even though Harley knew she would catch hell for that later, she gave all of her attention to her father.

"Daddy, I've never wanted anything this badly before. It feels perfect to me."

He smiled. It was a warm smile he only gave to her. "Then demand it with reverence, passion, and determination. That makes it yours. Never beg for what already belongs to you."

At that moment, he clapped just like the rest of the crowd. Harley had no idea if that was a yes or a no. Colleagues pulled her father away before she could reshape her plea in the form he had asked her for.

Not long after that, once the charity party's entertainment was in place, Harley felt a sharp pinch on the back of her arm. She didn't bother to make a face or pull away. Instead, she walked with her mother into the house and down the hall to the library.

"How *dare* you," Claire Tatum said after she pulled the doors closed. She only barely glanced over her shoulder as the words spilled from her like ice.

Claire Tatum was a stunning woman. She was fit (should be, she had two personal trainers), her deep red hair was pulled into a complicated twist, and her royal blue cocktail dress was fitted and accentuated the diamonds around her neck, as well as the ones on her wrists.

Harley made no point to comment; it would only have made this worse.

Claire turned around dramatically, anger dwarfing her green eyes. "You have humiliated me, your father, and this *entire* charity event." She stepped forward, even angrier that Harley had not looked down or even flushed.

In her mind, Harley was hearing her father, him telling her to demand what she wanted. There was always a lesson when she spoke to her father, some hidden message. He was always trying to make her stronger.

Claire was well aware that Harley wanted a horse. Harley's riding instructor at the school had mentioned it more than once to Claire, and each time Claire would use her fake smile and say something along the lines that she and Garrison would take it into consideration. First and foremost, Harley was at that school to learn, not meddle in the dirt.

"Is that what the finest girls' school in New York teaches you? That it's fitting to throw temper tantrums during charities? Maybe I should look into schools abroad."

Claire Tatum was the second generation of her family to live in the U.S. and often threatened to send Harley overseas for refinement, among other things. Basically, she threatened to take Harley away from her father, but thus far her father had never allowed that to occur.

"I was discussing an investment with my father."

"An investment? How so? Are you really that naïve? This little whim of yours will do nothing but cost money. You are already spoiled beyond measure. "

That statement was ludicrous. Harley never asked for anything, mainly because at a very young age a response like this would come. Somehow, she had taught herself never to show how much she wanted something, loved something—she knew if she did, whatever it was could or would be taken away in some form.

"It's an investment in my future."

"The *nerve*," Claire said with a furious gasp.

Harley never spoke back to her mother. She took what she was given, seen but never heard.

"This sport teaches me respect, patience, diligence, mannerism, pride. I could go on," Harley said as evenly as she could, she could hear her heart thundering, feel the heat in her cheeks. She felt the danger in this plea.

Before Claire could say a word, they both heard Garrison's voice from the second level of the library. "Character. An investment in character, no doubt."

Claire let out a tense smile. "Darling, why on earth are you in here? The governor was asking for you."

Garrison moved down the stairs gracefully. For an older man, he was fit, too. He was fifty-eight when Harley was born. His greatest accomplishment, as he said in the statement he gave to the press when they sought a comment, as well as any other time he introduced Harley to someone new.

"I was rudely interrupted when speaking to Harley before. I wanted to finish our conversation."

"It's nonsense, dear. Just a whim, some girlish daydream that she will be over before the next week is out."

Garrison had reached the bottom stair now. Under his arm was a file, but it wasn't the one Harley had given him. She assumed she had just lucked out, that he was in his study on the second floor getting that file and happened to overhear them. It was rare that Claire had been caught speaking to Harley in this tone. In front of Garrison, she treated Harley the same as he did, basically doted on her.

"Girlish daydream," he grunted. "Strong imagination you have there. Harley, how long has this fantasy played out now? Six months?"

"At least," Harley said, a bit shocked that he knew that—but then again, not much got past Garrison.

"Garrison, the horse her trainer brought to my attention is an infant, only four, and will cost a fortune, and I'm not even speaking of all the training he will need, everything he will need. Harley needs to focus on school now. This horse, that bloodline, is intended for professionals. It would be a travesty for him to have an inexperienced rider."

Garrison smirked, glanced at his wife. "This horse is worth less than what you are wearing tonight, my dear."

Harley glanced over at her mother, not sure how her outfit added up to two hundred and fifty thousand dollars, but she was positive the jewels, if not her wedding band alone, helped meet that mark.

"I do, however, agree that a horse such as this needs a skilled rider." Before Harley could even dare to think that her dreams had just ended, he went on. "So I had my assistant contact the best trainer for Harley. Willowhaven Farms has agreed to meet with us."

Harley's gaze was shifting between her parents. She knew her father was efficient, so was his staff, but researching farms in under an hour was a push. Harley knew exactly where Willowhaven Farms was. She had ridden in competitions against Camille Doran's students. She knew it was at least a thousand miles away, deep in the south. In her mind, her father was going to buy this horse, but she would never ride it, at least not for years down the road.

Garrison laid out a file on the center table of the library and pulled out a pen from his breast pocket. His glance motioned for Harley to come closer. When she reached his side, she saw the four-year-old gelding she had been dreaming about endlessly, his coggins, all of his papers.

"You sign here, and he's yours."

Harley was speechless. She wanted to ask how he knew or when she could ride him, everything.

Her father let out a deep laugh at her expression. "In order for the Dorans to train you, your horse, you will need to board there. Does that bother you? Are you willing to give up your summer holiday for this?"

"Yes."

She heard her mother gasp, but she didn't care. Harley had no desire to go abroad for the summer or on whatever lavish vacation her mother had booked.

"Exactly where is she boarding? In a stall? Garrison, we should discuss this."

"You are correct. We should have discussed it when the trainer brought this matter to your attention, how advanced Harley was. Instead, I heard of it from one of my colleagues that had seen her ride. You can imagine how shocked I was when I called the school and spoke with her trainer to see what we could do to help Harley aid this passion, only to discover options were already laid out."

Garrison nodded for his daughter to sign, then looked back at his wife. "Tomorrow, you will fly to Willowhaven Farms. If you find any reason that I would not want Harley to stay there, you will tell me, and then I will fly there myself to see your reasons. If the place is not found lacking, when the semester is over Harley and her horse will be traveling to and staying in Willowhaven for the summer."

Claire didn't bother to argue. Instead, she turned cold, almost pouted, the way she always did when she felt that Harley had gotten away with murder.

"She could get hurt, Garrison. She's your legacy, and you're placing her in danger."

"No. I'm teaching her to face danger, for she *is* my legacy, and any Tatum knows that we do not ask for what we want—we claim it."

The next day, after Harley's mother left, her father took her to a stable not far from her home, took her to her horse. They spent that weekend buying everything that Clandestine needed.

When her mother returned, the only complaint she had was the fact that Harley would be staying with two boys that were her age. Garrison did travel to Willowhaven, but not until Harley had been there for three weeks, and he found no fault in Wyatt or Truman, the cousins, or the other farm hands' kids that were also on the property. In fact, when he wasn't watching Harley's lessons, he spent his time with Beckett, Wyatt's father, watching the bulls, watching Wyatt ride. He even made the comment that Wyatt was him made over when he was a boy.

When Harley came home after her first summer at Willowhaven, she found a new stable in her own backyard. It was her sanctuary, where she spent all day when she was at home.

It took Wyatt half of that first summer to understand that first statement that Harley made, the one about how everything she owned was on that trailer. When he did figure out the life Harley came from, the stiff line she had to walk between her parents, who seemed to be worlds apart, in some way that broke his heart. Harley seemed so lost, so alone.

"His barn name is Dan," she said to the crowd around her that first day at Willowhaven as she led her horse from the trailer.

"Come on, Danny Boy," Wyatt had said as he led him inside the barn. When he looked over his shoulder, he was surprised to meet Harley's gaze, even told himself she was watching her horse, not him, but when his brother Truman elbowed him and said, "Mom got enough hell about us being on the property, you want to stop drooling?" he had a spark of hope that she felt the same odd pull he did when he saw her for the first time.

Before that day, Wyatt was his father's son, always had a dare in his veins, a wild streak that pushed every button his mother had, or anyone that had to oversee him, to the limits. Most times, what damage was done was undone. If he was ever grounded, or limited, his father Beckett would come to his defense and say that, "Boys will be boys, they only push you when hold 'em back. Let 'em run, Momma, let 'em run." Camille would dare to smile at her husband, and then whatever heat Wyatt was under faded.

After that day, all bets were off. Wyatt walked a tight line. He kept his nose clean, for more than one reason. One, he didn't want there to be any chance that he'd be sequestered from Harley. The other, Harley drew something out of him, some kind of respect, maturity, balance—she made him want to be a better person just by breathing. Of course, his mother assumed that Wyatt had just grown out of his rebellious ways, just the way her husband had promised.

During the day, there were only brief moments Wyatt and Harley had alone, sometimes seconds. The time they cherished was just after dawn, when they would both be at the main barn alone, and then just after the farm went to bed. Sometimes, at least a few times a week, they would sneak out, find some nook or hiding place on the property, secret lovers that had never crossed that one sacred point of no return.

They didn't always use that stolen time to steal a kiss, to push that physical barrier. There were also a lot of long conversations, deep ones. Ones where they saw the inside of each other, where they discovered a part of the other that no one else knew.

Wyatt's hand brushed across Harley's as he pulled Danny Boy's halter off. Harley's breath caught when she knew it wasn't an accident, when she glanced up to see his bright blue eyes raining down on her. "Is he still pulling too hard?" he asked in a ghost of a whisper. Remembering the night before, when his calloused hands had moved across her shoulders easing the tension there, she replied in a whisper of her own.

"Not so bad."

"Anything else hurt?" he quipped as his stare moved down her body.

He had watched Harley evolve into a woman. Even though she was only seventeen, her body indicated otherwise. Every day, Harley was in riding pants and a tight tank, a walking fantasy to him.

She elbowed him, daring to laugh before moving to take off Dan's girth.

Wyatt moved behind her; she barely reached his shoulder. His long arms were over her, reaching for the saddle. Once again, they both hesitated, feeling the sensation of their bodies so near to each other. Harley had no idea how Wyatt had the power to stop time, but he did, at least in her mind; the world would stop when they were this close.

"There you are," Ava, Wyatt's fifteen-year-old sister, said causing both Wyatt and Harley to step away from each other a bit quickly. It was masked, though. He pulled away with the saddle in hand while Harley was whisking away the saddle pad.

"We're ready to go to the creek," Ava said.

"I already told you this morning I had chores. I still have to ride Boss Man," Wyatt protested.

Ava and her friends were not allowed to swim in the back creek without Wyatt there. He hated that babysitting gig. It took him away from the barn, from the seconds he stole throughout the day.

"Boss Man pulled a shoe, and we unloaded the hay, dropped flakes in the pasture. Everything is done. Mom said so," Ava countered.

Her two friends from school had come to her side, both repeating the same plea. All of them were drenched in the summer heat and looked exhausted, like they had earned some kind of escape.

"Is Easton here?" Wyatt asked one of the girls, Kate. Easton was one of Wyatt's best friends, and Kate was his younger sister.

"Him and Truman are getting the four-wheelers. Come on. Memphis is here, too," Ava said.

Memphis, Easton, and Wyatt were all around the same age. Memphis was a little older, but nevertheless the two of them were Wyatt's boys. Most times, Harley rarely saw Memphis because he was always on the road with his father, a fairly famous racecar driver, Lucas Armstrong.

What she did see of him, she liked. He always made sure everyone was happy around him, he had a way to calm an already mellow world. Easton, he was downright stoic. Quiet for the most part, he turned as many, if not more heads than Wyatt and Memphis, but the boy was too blunt for many girls to stick around. Wyatt's personality was a little of both of theirs, a fun loving guy unless circumstance caused his dark or wild side to come out, a side he'd yet to show Harley and doubted he ever would.

Harley softened the edges around Wyatt, and somehow he brought out the sharp edges in her, at least for brief moments.

"Help untack the last lessons first," Wyatt said. It was the best delay he could come up with.

In the peak of July, the heat was so heavy that you felt like you were wearing it, which was why Camille had back-to-back lessons in the A.M. Harley went first each morning, had her own private lesson, then would walk through the other lessons. Oftentimes she learned just as much by watching as she did doing. Harley always came in first, though. Danny Boy was territorial, so she wanted him untacked and bathed before the others came in.

During the back and forth between Wyatt and his sister, Harley had attached her lead and was guiding Danny Boy to the back wash bay. She had barely rinsed him when she felt Wyatt's hands slide around her waist. She looked up, a bit apprehensive—that was when he caught her lips with his, when she lost all of her senses, when it would not have mattered if the world itself came crashing down. She turned in his arms, only barely breaking their contact, and when the flesh of their lips met again, with a gentle force his lips urged hers open, his warm tongue slid across hers, and those long, strong arms of his pulled her against him.

She had never kissed another boy besides Wyatt, but she could not imagine a sensation that could be any more heart-racing. They had figured out this maneuver together, summers ago, made it through the awkward stages and somehow had managed to find sensuality, a burning passion that only grew hotter with each day.

Wyatt urged her against the wall. "Wyatt," she whispered in protest, scared they would be caught.

"You're safe," he promised as his lips met hers again, as his hands slid down her sides, his thumbs grazing her chest.

She knew then that they were safe. They were each other's safety net. Sometimes when she cautioned him, he would pull away, knowing he had been swept away in the moment, in the touch; others, he would just say, "You're safe," which meant he had made sure they were alone.

Her hands rushed up his chest as his fell past her waist, squeezing and pulling. There was not a sound beyond their elevating breaths.

Just as his lips moved from hers, reached her jaw, they both heard, "It might rain tonight," from a deep, baritone voice. Easton's.

Wyatt pulled away, gave Harley a sly grin, and mouthed, 'Safe,' as he picked up the hose that Harley had dropped and sprayed it out in the aisle. He then turned and held the stream of the hose up to Danny Boy's mouth, who lifted his lip, then swayed back and forth across the stream. It was Danny Boy's trick, and in truth, unless you let him do that as you hosed him, he would protest any water on him.

Easton rounded the corner a second later and leaned against the wall as if he had been there the entire time. Thirty seconds after that, Ava and her friends ran down the aisle, yelling all the while for Wyatt.

Easton had that same build as Wyatt—tall and stoic with a strong frame and haunting green eyes and dark hair. He was the only one outside of Memphis that knew for sure about Wyatt and Harley, and that was simply because outside of Harley, no one knew the real Wyatt like Easton and Memphis.

Wyatt knew how to be his father's son, how to be his mother's son, how to be a rider, how to be whatever, and he knew that manners and respect were expected, demanded—but under that there was a boy, a boy that was still figuring out who he was. Harley knew that boy.

Harley knew without a doubt that Wyatt had asked Easton to be the lookout for that stolen moment.

Knowing that, it was hard for her to look at Easton, but she gave him a shy smile anyway. He responded with one straight face nod and a wayward wink.

"Come on, Wyatt," Ava said again. "No more excuses. I'll tell Mom."

"You got this?" Wyatt asked Harley, hoping she had come up with another excuse to keep him there.

"Have fun," she answered.

The girls squealed, then took off running. Both Easton and Wyatt shook their heads. Easton walked on, but Wyatt brushed his lips across Harley's forehead and breathed, "I love you," before he vanished from her side, leaving her breathless as always.

www.ingramcontent.com/pod-product-compliance
Lightning Source LLC
Chambersburg PA
CBHW071300300325
24313CB00016B/177